Praise for T[...]

"This is a fascinati[...] [...] and God's pursuit of lost chi[...]"

Library Journal

"Politano's latest is an absolute gem of a novel about the power of stories in the pursuit of truth, understanding, and meaning. The novel sparkles with creativity, and its elegant layers balance the weight of the philosophical with the levity of a literary wonderland."

Booklist starred review

"Rich with biblical allusions, the layered plot accrues tension and texture by alternating perspectives between Lily and Peter as the mystery intensifies. Readers will be kept guessing through the many twists and turns."

Publishers Weekly

"This rollicking romantic mystery novel sweeps readers through the streets of London in the early 1900s. Using a real setting as inspiration for this fanciful novel gives the plot a unique depth and intrigue."

The Historical Novels Review

"Joanna Davidson Politano brings Edwardian England to life as she matches silent film star Lily Temple with handsome underground investigator Peter Driscoll. Readers will be captivated as they follow Lily and Peter's journey to solve the mystery of the Briarwood Teardrop. Romance, mystery, and clever twists and turns will keep readers turning pages until they reach the very satisfying ending. Well-written and highly recommended!"

Carrie Turansky, bestselling author of *The Legacy of Longdale Manor*

Praise for *The Lost Melody*

"*The Lost Melody* serves a pitch-perfect blend of history, romance, mystery, and faith."

Booklist starred review

"Joanna Davidson Politano perfectly balances faith amongst the very dark backdrop of an asylum to write a beautiful tale full of struggle and triumph."

Fresh Fiction

"Joanna has masterfully given life to those who had no voice and has captured the essentials of the human soul. You will be inspired, encouraged, and moved to remember that God always has a plan, even when you are in the darkest of places."

Interviews & Reviews

the
CURIOUS
INHERITANCE
of
BLAKELY
HOUSE

Books by Joanna Davidson Politano

Lady Jayne Disappears

A Rumored Fortune

Finding Lady Enderly

The Love Note

A Midnight Dance

The Lost Melody

The Elusive Truth of Lily Temple

The Curious Inheritance of Blakely House

the
CURIOUS
INHERITANCE
of
BLAKELY
HOUSE

JOANNA DAVIDSON POLITANO

Revell

a division of Baker Publishing Group
Grand Rapids, Michigan

Published by Revell
a division of Baker Publishing Group
Grand Rapids, Michigan
RevellBooks.com

Printed in the United States of America

Library of Congress Cataloging-in-Publication Data
Names: Politano, Joanna Davidson, 1982- author.
Title: The curious inheritance of Blakely House / Joanna Davidson Politano.
Description: Grand Rapids, Michigan : Revell, a division of Baker Publishing Group, 2025.
Identifiers: LCCN 2024044648 | ISBN 9780800742980 (paperback) | ISBN 9780800746810 (casebound) | ISBN 9781493448708 (ebook)
Subjects: LCGFT: Christian fiction. | Detective and mystery fiction. | Novels.
Classification: LCC PS3616.O56753 C87 2025 | DDC 813/.6—dc23/eng/20240920
LC record available at https://lccn.loc.gov/2024044648

Scripture used in this book, whether quoted or paraphrased by the characters, is taken from the King James Version of the Bible.

Francis James Child, comp., "The Unquiet Grave," Child Ballad #78, *The English and Scottish Popular Ballads* (1882–1898), public domain.

Cover image © Yolande de Kort / Trevillion Images

Baker Publishing Group publications use paper produced from sustainable forestry practices and postconsumer waste whenever possible.

25 26 27 28 29 30 31   7 6 5 4 3 2 1

To the two sweet friends
who have been my cheerleaders
for eight books and counting,
and who asked to be in a book.
Rachel and Angie, you're now
officially written into a story.

chapter
ONE

They call you odd, and perhaps you are. Or perhaps
. . . perhaps the scope of normal is wider than any of
us believed.

~*Sophie's letters to Emmett*

GRAFTON, SHROPSHIRE, ENGLAND, 1901

It was a strangely calm morning in March, with no wind off the dales, when the woman I assumed to be my mother slipped into the shop. She hovered in the back like a wraith, peering at me through the dangling pendulums, gears, and clock springs, her veiled face wide-eyed and lovely.

She pretended to peruse the merchandise, gaze slipping my direction from time to time, observing me. Appraising. Looking for the maker's mark she'd left on my soul.

I steeled myself. *Yes, I received your letters.*

No, I haven't money to lend you.

Her requests over the years had come with different forwarding addresses, from Australia to the United States, and now after nearly two years without a letter, she'd come in person.

I was of a mind to begin the conversation with a refusal, but then I spotted the little wooden box tucked beneath her arm, and I couldn't get my mind off what it might contain. My imagination fixated on it. And once fixed, my foolish mind would not be moved.

The bell above the door jingled, and a man in cheap gray serge glanced quickly around before approaching the counter and doffing his derby hat. I pressed my lips together in polite welcome, still eyeing the woman in black. And her box.

I forced my attention to the only paying customer in the shop.

"Is Mr. Lane available?" He slid a midsized clock loosely wrapped in soft linen onto the countertop.

"What a beautiful clock. A Vienna Regulator with the most lovely enamel dials." I peeled back the linen, turning the clock over and springing open the back. "Looks to be a standard two-train movement with—"

He pulled it back and smoothed it shut. "Mr. Lane. He's in, I hope? The sign on the door. It says Mr. Daniel Lane, proprietor."

"So it does." I offered a warm smile. He must have traveled from another hamlet to see us. This was a curiosity shop, filled with all manner of trinkets and wonders, but word had spread of our repair work too. In this part of the country, there were few skilled in clock repair. "I can assist you, though."

"I'd rather see Mr. Lane."

I pressed my lips together. People take one glance at a book's cover, half a glance at the title, and decide in that instant if the words inside are worth reading. I was a book whose library card stood nearly empty. "Of course you would."

If the man had been a local, he'd realize I was far better equipped to repair his Vienna Regulator than Daniel Lane. Mostly because Daniel Lane was dead. Had been for many years.

I held out my hands. "I'll take it right back for assessment. Mr. . . . ?"

"Morgan. Henry Morgan." He hesitated but passed the swaddled clock to me. It had a surprising weight to it—the clock's movement must be solid metal, in the way of older pieces. I carried it behind the curtain, into the back room filled with the scent of lathe oil and lavender. "Mr. Lane, are you in?"

Aunt Lottie crossed the space in three quick pecks of her boot heels, fists on her pert little waist, and flashed that dimpled smile. "Another one?"

"He insisted. *Mr.* Lane only."

She rolled her eyes as she retrieved a metal file and turned back to the lever escapement she had taken apart. Her file and polisher whipped over the tiny teeth with precision. "Well then, shall you be Mr. Lane today, or shall I?"

Mr. Lane, Aunt Lottie's late husband, had owned the curiosity shop for a mere two years before succumbing to apoplexy. It had been in Lottie's capable hands for twenty-three years and our joined hands for nearly ten.

"You have a project already. I'll take this one." Popping off the back again, my fingers immediately searched for the maker's mark, and found no less than four. Each were carved subtly into the movement, three outside and one within, a quiet claim to this exquisite workmanship and all its modifications.

I tightened the coil spring and felt about for anything loose. I gently urged a few bolts and pinions off the movement and felt the problem immediately—oil coated every inch of the verge escapement as if someone had drenched the poor thing every time the mechanics slowed. Now it had thickened and nothing moved.

Foolish people.

Fine flakes of rust had gathered along the pins, and the delicate fusee chain had snapped. I worked out the rust and glanced through the slit in the curtain.

Speaking of foolish people. What did that woman want? Why not simply write again? Her letters had always been sent along from my address in Compton because she'd believed I still resided there with Father—that's how little she knew of my life. Yet now she'd gone to the trouble of connecting the post office box from that foolish ad with our shop, and she'd come to see me directly.

But why?

Clocks made sense. People seldom did. Perhaps if I could pry off the backs of them—people, that is—and peer into their gears, everything would become clear.

I reassembled the movement, secured the back, and threw a passing wink at Aunt Lottie as I carried it back out to the waiting customer. "A simple repair, Mr. Morgan. You'll need to leave it with us for the night."

"Did Mr. Lane say that?"

"Just a bit of oil stopping up the pinions, and a broken chain."

He frowned. "My clock doesn't have pinions."

A tight smile. "It'll be ready for you tomorrow morning, if that is acceptable."

He eyed me suspiciously but took his leave after placing his card on the glass countertop. Exhaling, I peered below the hanging pendulums and weights. My heart thrummed a rapid beat. Had she gone?

There—a swish of fabric, and a veil. And that box. She was still here. "Might I help you, ma'am?"

She lifted her gaze, clutching that box.

But then the door banged open again, bell whipping against the wood frame, my heart hitting my ribs. In strode a bull of a man in a finely tailored suit. A bull who had the right of way on whatever path he trod. He charged up to the counter and planted both palms on the glass, gaze roving over my face. "You're the one." Low and quiet, his voice set off warning bells. "The chit who placed the advert in the personals."

I watched him, eyebrows raised, gaze roving to the rear of the store. The guest had turned her back on the new customer, veil down, blending expertly into the shadows.

Not so very missing, this woman. Not just now.

"Answer me, girl. You're the one looking for Lady Gwendolyn Forrester of Manchester, are you not?"

I looked him up and down. "Sorry. You couldn't pass for her." I slid an open clock toward me—the two-hundred-year-old, gilt-metal-mounted Joseph Antram table clock in ebony veneer that I actually wasn't meant to touch—and threaded out the tiny screws.

Two other men marched in and took up posts behind him, arms folded over their chests.

I couldn't have known that Aunt Lottie's reasons for forbidding me to find my mother were decent ones. My mother, the shooting starlet, as we called her, was actually quite famous—or infamous, rather, posing as a lady and driving up debts, blackmailing married lovers, and leaving a wake of destruction in her path. I had learned all that from placing that advert during a moment of weakness less than a fortnight ago.

The letters that had trickled into my hired post office box

offered a rather sorry picture of the woman who was not here to tell the story herself. And now she had brought that infamous life directly to our shop. Along with a passel of wronged men, it would seem.

Aunt Lottie would be hopping mad. If this man didn't strike me dead with his glare first.

His eyes narrowed. "I have a certain interest in her whereabouts, as it happens."

"So you've come to me, the one who *advertised* she doesn't know where she is." I jammed the pliers into my finger and winced, putting the injury to my mouth to keep the blood from the fine ebony veneer.

He leaned over the counter. "Lady Gwendolyn. Has she been here?"

My gaze flicked to the back of the shop . . . which now lay dark and still.

Cowardly woman.

"If she has, she has not announced herself." I picked up my tools, feeling an odd sense of loss. Over the mysterious box and the woman.

He dug about in his pocket. "When she happens to show her face," he said, striking a match and watching me through the flame, "you'll kindly notify me. You won't *forget*, will you?" He dropped the burning match into the open clock.

With a cry I slapped a cloth over it, smothering the flame with shaking hands and fanning away wisps of smoke. I grasped the counter with shaking hands. "Leave now, before I take this clock over your head!"

He struck another match, held it close to my face. "I'd be careful who I threaten, girl. Especially in such a nice little shop." He dropped it into a pile of buffing cloths.

I sprang to smother it as the men behind him laughed.

"*Out!*" I lifted an empty clock case over my head, but the gent merely tipped his hat and departed with all the gravity of a bull who feared no one.

They left, sucking all the tension out of the room . . . and the steel from my spine. I wilted onto the counter and trembled. How many men had she angered? *How many?* Three long, deep breaths, then a shuffle stirred my attention. I popped my eyes open and there she was—that veiled woman, staring at me through the gears and springs hanging from the ceiling.

And the box. The unopened box was tucked beneath her arm. She approached, weaving through the cluttered aisle, and pushed the box toward me on the glass counter as if offering treasure. "For you." Those lovely violet eyes tried to warm through my defenses.

Still shaky, I dropped my gaze to the catch on the box. Longed to spring it and peer inside.

But the aroma of singed veneer gave me pause. The image of that man's face, the barely controlled anger . . . and the letters I'd received from her other men hidden in the back of my bureau. If they couldn't find her, wring their vengeance from her, they'd wring it out of me. Out of Aunt Lottie. Dear Aunt Lottie, who had once swept me up as a throwaway and tucked me neatly into her life at the shop.

I had become like a viper she held close. Her ruin.

After a moment with my hands on the box, I shoved it back. "I don't want it." Dynamite is what it was.

She perched her black-gloved fingertips on the box, blinking at me. "You do repair clocks, do you not?"

Regret rained down upon my pent-up bitterness, dissolving it instantly. "Yes. Yes, of course. My apologies, I thought—

that is—it doesn't matter." A puff of breath. Probably not my mother. "Yes. Yes, I repair clocks. Anything with gears, actually. Here now, let us have a look." I triggered the mechanism, and the lid sprang open. Tucked in a soft cloth lay a mahogany clock whose maker I did not recognize, gold hands from the last century but a newer glass faceplate, clear of the fog that ordinarily encroached with time.

"You'll notice, Miss Forrester, that it isn't like other clocks."

My hackles rose again. I stole a glance at the woman and lifted the clock, turning it over, running a finger over its polished surface.

"You *are* Sydney Forrester, are you not?"

"I am. And you are . . . ?"

"Quite glad to speak with you." A soft smile.

"How long since it has kept time?"

She shrugged. "Five, maybe ten years."

I pulled the little piece toward me, sliding the back off and exposing a wealth of tiny gears, springs, and delicate pulleys. I gasped. It was a marvel. Hundreds of tiny pieces were all neatly packed together—more than I'd ever seen before. I dared to touch a tiny gear, its teeth barely thicker than my fingernail. "What . . . what is this?"

She merely smiled.

On the finely polished surface, an extraordinarily long-winged, graceful bird had been etched into the wood. Something about it drew me. *"My little bird,"* Father had always said of Mother. Even years after she'd flitted away from us.

I touched the etching and ran my fingertips over the fine casing, then I wound the little key in the side. Gears sprang into motion. The mechanism whirred and spun, harder and louder until the thing grew warm.

What in heaven's name . . . ?

I dropped it on the counter, expecting an explosion, but a beam of light shot from it. An exact likeness of the clock's face shone out beside me but magnified and hazy, a large ghost clock dancing on the air, haunting the wall it lay against.

Mouth hanging open, I reached out and sliced my hand through the beam of light, the shop's grime dancing like fairy dust in it. "Magic," I whispered, touching the wall where the clock face was projected, but I felt only plaster.

"*Fifty-three degrees two*," said the clock, in a gravelly voice. I jumped back. "How—?"

The woman's solemn gaze studied me through the veil. Evaluated.

Then she touched a trigger on the back and the light vanished, the ghost clock on the wall disappearing. It shrank back into a regular mahogany clock that clicked innocently through the seconds, then died out again. My heart pounded twice that speed.

"I thought you might like to see what you're turning down . . . before you make your decision. That is, if you *are* still deciding." She clung to the counter. "You are, aren't you? I received no reply to my letter."

I gripped the clock. Secured the back in place. "Who are you? What is—"

The letter. That *letter*! It came back in a rush, an odd feeling settling over me just as it had when I'd opened the missive from the unknown "Mrs. Holligan." Me, inheriting a property. What a lark! It had seemed a silly prank, coming into the post office box with all those letters from my mother's jilted lovers. A trap, perhaps.

But now it inflamed my imagination, stark and real and

full of untold possibilities. "You're the one who wrote to me. About that . . . that place. With the clocks." No, this woman was *definitely* not my mother.

"There's far more to Blakely House than clocks." She smiled behind the veil. "And now you've had a taste of it. Here's another." She slipped a metal object from deep within the folds of her gown and set it on the counter. It was a key. A long, elaborate one that shone with fresh polish. Birds encircled its stem and formed the handle, hinting at the marvels and beauty awaiting me.

I took that key, turning it over. Surprised at its weight. I used to believe I wanted adventure, as does every girl who buries her nose in books. Except for the part about leaving home. That was what novels were for—having adventures without any of the discomfort. I clutched the counter, the same one I'd once grasped as a small, terrified orphan, and stared at that key. And all I could think about is what it might unlock.

"The master said you were to have this when he was gone." She pressed it toward me. "That you'd know exactly what to do with it. And . . . I hope you do. I hope you'll come."

"I'm not certain I can get away." Or that I wanted to. But I desperately needed to know what the key unlocked—and why the late master thought I would know. My mother's family had always been shrouded in mystery, as had the woman herself, and I hadn't any idea who any of them were.

She laid her black-gloved hand on my bare one. "We need you, Sydney Forrester. Please come."

I looked at her face behind the thin veil—so lovely with rounded contours and bright eyes, inviting me into something extraordinary. Yet for one accustomed to fighting uphill battles, striving hard to eke the bare minimum out of life, I hardly knew what to do with good fortune simply being held out to me.

She turned to go.

"Wait! Your clock."

She smiled. "See if you can work it out. Then bring it back."

That notice. That rotten advert in the personals that had put my insignificant name in print. Who would have thought anyone would be hunting for a throwaway orphan with no connections?

But they had come, all those letters . . . and her too. This Mrs. Holligan, who had startled me with the information she'd given in the letter, and troubled me with what she'd left out. This wasn't a typical inheritance, this Blakely House. But she didn't explain what that meant.

I perched on my stool, curling over the clock she'd brought and opening its back, laying bare its intricacies. No nameplate advertised the designer, but each metal surface had been black polished to perfection until the gears, which few ever saw, shone like ebony. The corners had been neatly rounded, and tucked inside the inner frame was a tiny little hummingbird, carved in relief. The finish was its own sort of maker's mark.

Why on earth would someone decorate the inside of a clock?

I peered deeper. There was something jammed into the topmost gears. I loosened a few screws, shifted things, until orange fluff suddenly obscured my view.

"What do you think, my Micah Bear?" I whispered into my orange kitty's fur as he shoved his face before mine with a rumbling purr, and my troubled heart calmed. I could not remain unsettled when Micah came and found me, tugging at my attention.

My heart melted as I met my cat's dignified gaze. He was one of a kind. His crooked little stub tail. His terrible howl from across the house when he decided he was lonely. The large, pitiable eyes, and the way he hovered. My annoying guardian angel. A castoff like me . . . who had found love and a home. Also like me.

I didn't need more than what I had right here in this shop. I didn't.

He paused with a look of expectation on his face, ears perked. "I suppose you'd rather I stay, selfish thing that you are." Another affectionate rub with my free hand, and he leaned in harder, tucking his head beneath my chin and vibrating with contentment. How I'd miss this boy if I left. Miss the life that had formed around me here.

Leaving had never occurred to me. Not once. Not until today.

I stared at that brilliantly complex clock and again caught a whiff, wild and windblown, of Blakely House.

A taste. An invitation.

A leap off a cliff.

I threaded a pair of tweezers deep within the clock to retrieve that cloth and nudged the tiny bird etching by accident. It activated like a small button, and when I stood the clock up, a tiny compartment on the bottom opened and something fell out and hit the glass counter.

Tink.

I lifted the tiny golden circle to the light. An engagement ring! A stunning opal that shone like the moon was settled neatly inside a love knot on a band of gold. I turned it over in my hand, holding my breath. Inside, an inscription—*For my Sophie. Deepest love, Emmett.*

Emmett. Emmett Sinclair, the great-uncle who had supposedly left me his fortune. And the ring was here, in this clock. Not on this Sophie's finger.

The deceased had no immediate family to inherit his holdings . . . That part of the letter sprang back with the pang of loneliness I'd felt upon skimming it days ago. No family. No one to inherit, except a relation he'd never met.

Laid out before me, the clock, the key, and the ring gave a tiny glimpse of Blakely House, like three pieces to an intriguing puzzle. Even when I tried to focus on Mr. Morgan's Regulator, taking apart the pieces and laying them in perfect order on the counter, my gaze drifted to those three objects.

They called to me in a way nothing in this stale little hamlet did.

Finally, with a quick glance about, I slid open the money drawer and poked inside. Blakely House should be only a train ride away. Might as well keep the coins on me, just in case. Then I could flee in a moment, if that door opened to another of Mum's bitter lovers. But inside I found only worn felt lining the drawer.

Nothing. Truly, *nothing*? I pulled the drawer open, and it was true. The tax payment and the month's notes had taken everything.

Except . . .

I shoved a stool over to the shelves on the back wall and climbed up, reaching for a jar on the very top, just out of view. Mad money, Aunt Lottie had called it, and this was a moment of madness. A mere handful of coins jingled as I brought it down, which meant she'd dipped into these too. Quite a bit, actually. A breathless shock filled me with dread. Punctured my security.

I dumped out the meager stores. Sixpence for third-class

train travel to Northumberland, a few shillings for a hackney from the station . . . nothing for food.

And absolutely nothing to leave Aunt Lottie.

When I arrived, if the letter was true, there would be money to repay her, and extra besides. If nothing else, I could sell the seaside cottage called Blakely for a tidy sum, and the profits would more than replace the mad money.

Yet if I didn't take the risk, nothing more was likely to appear in the drawer. At least, not for quite some time. The notes we owed piled up beside the ones still owed to us.

It was only practical that I go. Wise and forward-thinking, just as Aunt Lottie always pushed me to be.

But it meant leaving. And it meant not changing my mind. There would be no scurrying back if anything was amiss. And wiring Aunt Lottie to rescue me wouldn't work, for I'd leave her with nothing with which to come fetch me.

Stay or go.

Stay . . . or go.

I must have stood there many moments, staring at that door, for when Aunt Lottie flicked aside the curtain and her little boot heels clicked out into the shop, she sighed and offered a gentle reproach. "You're drifting again, Syd." Her quick smile showed her dimples, her sparkling eyes. "Where oh where has your lovely mind gone?"

I turned back to the two clocks on the counter. "Oh, the usual places."

I'd been called a daydreamer, called lazy, people assuming I stared off into nothing, thoughts like white puffy meaningless clouds of emptiness. I missed what's happening around me at times, forgot so much and said very little, so they'd assume I was thinking nothing.

When in fact, I'd be thinking of a great many things, deeply and richly, and hadn't yet surfaced to keep up with everyday goings-on around me. My current flurry of thoughts circled around two very distinct words.

Stay or go.

Stay.

Or go.

chapter
TWO

Your brilliant mind enriches the world, dear Emmett—
but also keeps you from being part of it.

~*Sophie's letters to Emmett*

What happened next was the fault of a scruffy, very pitiful-looking boy who was thrust down on the ground at my feet just inside the snuff shop by one flurried-looking mother as she shoved three older children through the interior shop door.

I'd slipped into this tiny smoking porch in search of a broken bell tacked to the wall. No one had been able to fix it, Aunt Lottie had said, and the owner wouldn't hire anyone. My brain had hung on the word *broken*.

Broken things drew me, especially those others had given up on, because there was always *something* to be done about it. Yet before I could investigate, the broken heart of the scruffy boy had caught my attention, and all other repairs seemed far less important.

Tears streaked erratic paths over his dirty skin, but I busied myself with the bell so as not to call attention to his sorry state. Men had pride, after all, even when they topped out at three feet in height.

I worked my fingers behind the bell's plate and felt about for what might be jammed in it. "Out on your ear, are you? Me too." I found the pull chain and followed the path of action to the clapper and release mechanism, but both moved freely. "Filched a bite of pasty from my aunt's basket, and she sent me off on an errand to keep me out of the way. What about yourself?"

His frown puckered into a duck bill, and he whipped his face away from me. He couldn't be more than five or six.

Ah! A severed wire. It must have worn down and frayed apart. I dislodged the bell from its plate and sat cross-legged before the boy. "I don't suppose you have time for a story." I twisted the split ends of the wire together, wrapping them around the post and pressing them tight.

He shrugged, trying not to look at me.

Leaning forward, part child myself, I set into the story of the frog I'd found in my bed—but only *after* I'd slept with him the entire night. The more animated my story became, the more he forgot himself. His smile crept out. His chin lifted, signaling courage.

"What did you do?" he asked.

"Well, it leaped onto my face like this." I dropped a leaf from a potted plant onto my forehead. "And I shrieked!" I fell backward, catching myself with my hands behind me.

The boy laughed and my heart swelled to ten times its normal size.

"Then I fell out of my bed, and I screamed some more, and—"

Thunk. The door hit my shoulder and I jumped, rolling to the side, suddenly and acutely aware of the inconvenient place I'd settled. And I looked up.

A very sharply dressed, handsome man of marriageable age stepped out of the shop and looked about for whom he'd bumped. Warm brown eyes traveled down to me sitting cross-legged on the ground—and blinked in surprise. And I realized Aunt Lottie's scheme in sending me to this shop.

He recovered quite nicely, I'll give him that. I scrambled. Two shakes and he was extending his hand to me in one smooth, quietly confident gesture. "I beg your pardon, miss. May I help you up?" Of *course* he was perfect.

Before I could respond, the owner of the snuff shop, Mr. Barley, came blustering out, broom in hand as if to shoo pickpockets from his shop. "What are you doing out here?" he growled.

I sprang up and spun, bumping the gentleman's offered hand, then settled the bell back onto the wall, securing it with trembling fingers. Turning around, I bumped the owner, stumbled back, and fumbled for the button to the newly repaired bell. It gave a satisfying *ding-dong, ding-dong* . . . which faded into awkward silence as the two men stared at me. "It's fixed, sir. Your bell. It's . . . yes—*ahem*—fixed."

He frowned. Raised one eyebrow. Handsome Man simply looked at me. No lingering smile of mutual interest, as in novels. No immediate connection, no meeting of gazes. Just staring.

The leaf. It was still on my head, wasn't it?

I plucked it off.

Marvelous.

The world was waltzing, and I couldn't catch the rhythm.

Singing, and I couldn't carry the tune. I felt my oddness through their eyes, and suddenly I couldn't think of a clever thing to say. "Good day, then." I pulled out my emergency book and buried my burning face in it as I pushed my way out the door.

This was precisely why I would never marry. Not unless I met some man while blindfolded and proceeded to entertain a comfortable friendship with him for years before I ever actually spoke to him face to face. Men to whom I was drawn were like the sun—one could not stare directly at them for too long before becoming acutely aware of . . . well, everything.

And suddenly, with their looks on my back, I felt my oddness. My otherness. Everyone in town looked at me that way. The roots that held me to this place loosened, and I felt myself floating up and away like the hot-air balloons in Regent's Park. Why *did* I refuse to leave this little hamlet?

I couldn't put Blakely House from my mind either.

The key. It had to be the key. Like bait dangling before my electrified mind, the riddle of it left me unsettled. Hungry for resolution.

Now I'd be fixated.

My brain always did this, tossing pros and cons about for days, agonizing over every detail. Making decisions impossible.

I marched through the square, sure to keep my smile in place. "Hello, Mr. Marks. Good day, Mr. Simms."

Polite smiles in return. "Good day, Miss Forrester."

But after the snuff shop experience I was absolutely exhausted with the routine. Smiling like my face would break, hoping I didn't appear too eager or not eager enough. Hoping I blended in, while still being a little bit memorable, so I could capture that fleeting sense of belonging. But usually not succeeding.

And really, it was not a bother. Most days, anyway. There was the odd, lingering day when I wished to just walk into the circle of laughter and take part. But in the end, I always came home to Aunt Lottie, and—

Lottie!

I scanned the streets until I spotted her, then ran up and bumped her shoulder, igniting her dimpled smile.

"Well, there. How was the snuff shop?"

"No snuff to show for it . . . nor a handsome gent." I shot the schemer a pointed look. "You saw him walk in, didn't you? Just before you sent me off on that little errand."

She puffed out a breath, hands out. "Did you even try, Syd? You didn't try, did you?" She pulled me close with one arm as we walked. "One of these days you'll find a man that fits you like a left boot to your right. Then you'll fall in love with love, just as I did a long time ago. It'd be good for you to have something besides the shop to love."

"There's always you. And of course Micah."

She threw back her head and laughed, crushing me to her. "You're a delight, dear girl. A true delight."

Her arms, I noticed with a jarring sense of panic, were empty, save a wicker market basket with only an old towel inside . . . and a pile of our shop notes not yet paid.

"Now if only we could get you to stand still around a man long enough for *him* to discover your desirable attributes." She said nothing about the missing mad money as we ambled home without the items she'd meant to fetch from the green-grocer and the butcher. Perhaps I should simply slip the coins back in the jar. Or perhaps, I thought with flighty impulsiveness, I should make the trip to Blakely Cottage and return with a pile more.

We still had a bit of bone broth in the larder, and some leeks that would soon go bad. No sense wasting those.

"The man, Sydney. What did you say? Can we recover?"

I frowned. "What was special about this one? Aside from being unattached."

"Well, his eyes are symmetrical and his teeth all seem to be there. His hair—did you see his hair? He had some!"

I shot her a look.

"Very well. He's intelligent and good-natured and he was reading a riddle from the paper aloud to the greengrocer yesterday. In addition to possessing a reputation for enjoying the more unique things in life." A jostle and a wink.

Unique. Not strange or addled or "a little odd." Simply one of a kind. That's how she saw me.

"He's been the talk of Grafton since he arrived, and I just knew he'd be perfect for my Sydney. He's from Bristol, I believe. Oh, how you'd adore living there!"

Or in Northumberland. In my own little cottage. My heart pounded at the very idea of leaving home. Leaving Aunt Lottie. Inheritance be hanged. What did I want with running to some out-of-the-way cottage in Northumberland when I had a wealth of home right here?

Sometimes I felt brave. This was not one of those times. Safe felt far too wonderful at the moment, walking beside the woman who was my dearest friend and stand-in mother and father, all in one.

"You know, Syd, sometimes you just have to step up and grab the bull by the horns." She made a yanking motion, her empty basket swinging. "Just . . . *grab it*. Face that fear and wrestle it to the ground!" She pretended to throw down a bull. "You'll never know what you'll get if you don't try."

I frowned. "Bulls are dreadful creatures. I'd rather not grab any part of one, thank you."

"Certainly, there are risks. But you might come away victorious too, having everything you ever wanted. I did, twenty-eight years ago. I proposed marriage to *him*, you know, and look where I am." She held her arm wide, empty basket swinging off one wrist. "A beautiful life, a shop all my own . . . and the memories of love."

A shop going bankrupt, a life headed for the poorhouse, and an odd duck of a niece saddled to her.

But there was another bull I might grab. I fingered the key in my apron pocket.

"Come now, Syd." She caught me by the shoulders and spun me around. "There must be some man somewhere in County Shropshire who catches your fancy."

I cringed. "Is it truly important to you?" It wasn't *my* fancy we had trouble catching, but she always seemed to forget that.

"Well, I rather like the notion of you settling down, finding your place in the world, even if it takes you away from me. And more than that, it'll give somewhere for all that bottled-up love to go. I want that for you, dear one."

I did too. But . . .

Take the bull by the horns. Just grab it. I looked at her bright, pretty face. I just needed to go there and accept the inheritance, settle things, and return with far more than we needed. A lavish blessing for the one who had lavished everything upon me. How many years had she eaten the bare minimum so we both had enough? Worn the same tired frocks? At least since I'd known her, which was ten years. It wasn't fair that such a—

"Syd. Syd, are you listening?"

"Hm?" I blinked, thoughts slamming into one another as I yanked on the brake and made a sharp turn back into the conversation from the wilds of my mind. Aunt Lottie had asked something. "Right," I said. "Marrying, finding my place. So you're saying you *could* do without me? Perhaps just for a time?"

She stopped in the street, turning with a swish of her skirt and a stricken look to stand before me. "I know what you're thinking and I'll just state it plainly—looking for your mother will be futile. You'll simply have to trust me."

"You *knew* her?" Betrayal tightened in me.

"Only what your father told me. My poor brother was enamored of her and I couldn't dissuade him. But I hope to dissuade you."

"You don't think I could find her?"

"I didn't say that." The gentle affection in her eyes nearly undid me. "Oh, Sydney."

"Very well. I promise from this day on *not* to look for her."

She smiled as if that was settled.

But as the breeze stilled on the edge of town, an awareness whispered through my bound-up soul: *Let go. Release. And grab on to something new.* I caught my breath, bundling my arms and my familiar life in close.

Worry had been my constant companion, perhaps because Mum was the opposite. She feared nothing . . . and that had ruined everything. My fear had not been a healthy companion either. Rather than protecting the future, as I'd meant for it to do, it had done little but smother the present.

31

My heart thrummed as we reached the shop, leading to a pickax headache behind my eyes. In a glance, Aunt Lottie sized me up and reached for my temples, massaging small circles into the pain that had been building on the walk back. The edges of my panic warmed under her gentle touch. How could I leave this woman? *How?* There wasn't another like her in all of England.

A pitiful *rawr* from the corner snapped me out of my thoughts.

And then there was Micah. My Micah Bear, to whom I was the first and best creature in all the world. How could I walk away from him?

I scooped him up, lavishing upon him the overflow of my affection, and climbed the stairs to my attic bedroom where all was quiet. Until I kicked a small metal square and it skittered and spun across the floor.

I set Micah down on the bed and bent to search for it. It was a gentleman's lighter. I dropped it with a cry. The initials *LMD* meant nothing to me, and that was the problem. My safe little life had been punctured, our very home invaded by the men who sought my mother. All because of my foolish, utterly childish desire to seek her out.

The little box I'd rented at the post office now seemed futile. I was shielding us from exactly nothing.

Micah gave a low, rumbling meow in my arms, as if warning me not to leave him in this room that had been penetrated so easily. It wasn't safe, his pleading eyes seemed to say, and I had to agree.

Yes, that decided it. I definitely couldn't abandon Micah.

I'd take him with me.

chapter
THREE

I knew from the moment I first met you that I wasn't supposed to love you, but I rarely do what I'm supposed to.

~Emmett's letters to Sophie

ONE DAY LATER
NORTHUMBERLAND COAST

I carried the storm into the pub with me in one big sopping-wet *whoosh* through the door, rain pouring from my cape, my hair, my gown onto the rough wood floor.

The flushed innkeeper leaned on his elbow and glared his question my way. *What do you want?*

"Blakely Cottage," I said firmly above the raucous laughter, forcing the shiver from my voice. "I want to find Blakely Cottage, in Farneham Heald."

"No, you don't." He turned his back on me.

I shoved through the crowd. "Why? What's the matter with it?"

"Aye, chaps. The lass wants to know what's the matter with Blakely Cottage."

Glass thunked onto wood, and the chaos liquefied into silence, all eyes in that crowded pub riveted on the stranger dripping in their doorway. Lightning flashed jagged behind me and thunder rolled over the stillness.

"First of all, luv, it's not a cottage."

I spun to face him. "Then what is it?"

"The master's a beast of a man," grumbled the innkeeper. "A deranged madman not fit for human contact. You'd do best to turn away now, for you won't be coming out of that place."

"Whatever do you mean?" Fear curled in my belly.

"The house, it swallows up pirates. Grown men in their prime. Warriors. Adventurers. Cutthroats and criminals. And no one ever hears from them again."

Then in the hush, in the dim pub with the low ceiling, they offered pieces of the legend of this seaside cottage and its terrible master.

"He were a prison guard in the Boer wars," said one. "He'd beat men senseless if they made off in the middle of the night. Then he sequestered himself in that old house after the war and shot at anyone who attempted to come ashore."

Like a medieval captain of the guard, old Emmett Sinclair had positioned himself on the defensive and protected his fortress from anyone who dared come near.

Other guests at the inn looked on, throwing back a mug now and again, but never making fun nor disagreeing. A heaviness hung in the air.

I clutched the few remaining coins in my apron pocket. "I don't suppose anyone would be willing to escort me to Blakely Cottage."

The men exchanged glances, looked down into their mugs. "I can pay six shillings." Then I'd be penniless. I'd have nothing, and I'd be stuck there. But it was better than where I was now, which was stranded.

"Ain't so easy as that, luv," said one, squeezing through the crowds and guiding me toward the window. He jabbed a finger toward a sloping stretch of land positioned in the middle of the water some distance out. An island. "That's Farneham Heald across the way. And that," he said, pointing toward a giant rock formation held aloft on the hill, "is Blakely House."

I shivered at the dark gray water thick with unseen dangers between me and the house. "It seems I shall require a boat, then. I don't suppose any of you will rent me one?"

"If you wait till low tide—"

"It must be now." I had nowhere to stay, and no more coins to obtain a room. Besides, any longer of a wait and I'd change my mind and *walk* home.

At last, the sorriest excuse for a fishing vessel was rented to me for the remainder of my coins, but no escort. Blakely House had thoroughly terrified these grown men, and perhaps that was for the best. Once I reached the place, I'd never have to navigate society again. It would be a perfect haven.

But as I shoved off the shore with the cracked oar, bracing Micah between my wet boots, the storm magnified and the waves punched the boat around. Clutching the side until each wave receded, I paddled farther out, aiming for the rocky island, until a giant wave lifted the boat, tipped me out. I grabbed desperately for Micah. Gasping, slapping the water with one hand, I forced my face out of the water, over and over again, and sucked in breath as the waves sloshed me here and there . . . then eventually, mercifully, dropped me onto a muddy shore some distance from Northumberland's coast.

How long I'd lain there was lost to me as I coughed and pushed myself to my feet, trembling and blinking at the sight of a rain-drenched paradise. Rain pelted down while I scanned the cliffs, the encroaching sea, the rocky beach, and then . . . movement.

The first time I saw him, it was clear that I, Sydney Forrester, a logical and practical human being, had ruined my brain with literature. A chill shook me. Cold. *Freezing.* I could catch my death here, dripping wet, having nearly died getting to this wild island. My senses buzzed. Yet as I stood watching a man in a long black cloak leap from cliff to cliff in the distance, all I could think was, *A pirate!*

I shivered. Convulsed. I was dead, wasn't I? Or I'd fallen into the pages of one of my clothbound novels. Reality was muffled here, except for a wet moaning and the call of seals echoing across the beach. The vibrant land, lush and bursting with waterfalls and wildlife . . . and its pirate guard—none of it felt quite real.

That must make this heaven. I was dead, and this was eternity.

But were there pirates in heaven?

Because there was one here. I stared at the man leaping from jutted rock to cliff with the ease of a buck. Black garbed, leather booted, hunched against the lashing rain as he scaled the rocks above . . . he could hardly be anything else.

I collapsed again on the gritty beach and coughed out half the ocean, trembling against the weight of my body. I sniffed, and coughed again, shaking.

Definitely *not* dead.

Which meant I had made it after all. The wretched little dinghy I'd rented had gone down in the storm, but I had washed ashore and found the fabled Blakely House, the giant castle nestled on its own island. I stood and looked up into the clouds. Atop the cliffs sat an enormous manor that must have been forged from some seismic shift on the rugged island, driving the stones up to form the towers that loomed above me.

Seaside cottage, indeed.

That should have been my first clue that this little adventure wasn't what it seemed, but I had only my whimsical, book-filled instinct to go on. I grabbed up my soggy carpetbag and felt a sudden sense of loss. Of forgetting something. Water swirled around my ankles, and the soles of my boots sank into the sand as the tide pulled at them. What had I—

Micah! I twisted about, sloshing in the mudflats, but the encroaching darkness blotted out much of the island. "Micah! Micah, where are you?" A thunder of heartbeats, but no cat. I cried out again, my breath suddenly wispy and thin. A leak in my lungs, and all the air was leaving.

I climbed up and into the overgrowth, the wide, wet leaves slapping me as I shoved through them, screaming for Micah. Again and again. Loss snaked through me and tightened.

Then . . . a howl. Long, angry, and familiar, as if he were yelling *Owwww!*

"Micah! Where are you? Kitty, kitty!"

The howl came again, and I spun, scanning the moss-laced ledges above me. "Micah!"

A desperate howl, then a branch snapped.

I stumbled back, and there, clinging to a dead tree halfway up a steep rock face, was a very soaked ball of orange and white fur. Eyes wide and terrified, Micah clung to the dead tree jutting out of a rocky cliff, howling pitifully. He scrambled back and the tree cracked. My chest seized. "Micah, stay. Stay there!" I bolted toward him, sloshing through the water, grabbing the rocks to pull myself toward the tree. But he scrambled farther up and clung. Again it creaked, leaning over the water. He gave a long, low howl.

"Micah, I said *stay there!*" I jumped, but the wind pushed me back. A sturdy arm grabbed me from behind and spun me around with a spray of rainwater.

Electrified, I swung and kicked, heels striking my captor's side, his thigh. He hoisted me over his shoulder, anchoring me with one arm, thick stubble on his chin scratching my skin.

Pirate, pirate, oh stars, pirate, pirate, pirate!

He bolted up the cliffs with superhuman strength, arm clamping me firmly to him. I screamed in the darkness, pounding his back. But he climbed higher, sure-footed and strong. My voice carried uselessly over the vast island, swallowed up by the storm like my boat. Another boom of thunder.

My heart pounded against his shoulder as it shifted and tightened, working to propel us both up the rock face. His boots thumped over a creaky bridge, leaving solid ground. I squeezed my eyes shut, clinging to his tunic as we charged, swinging, over the rushing water that had tried to kill me already. I whimpered, then hated myself for it.

Another bolt of lightning, and I cried out. He plunged us into a cave—wet, dark, and quiet—that chilled me through.

He stumbled with a grunt and dropped me. I hit the rocks with a dull, flat pain in my side and scrambled. I sprinted toward the faint glow of light at the opening, but he caught me, rolling us both onto the ground. I reared back and screamed, then sunk my fist into his jaw—a crack like a shell hitting stone.

He grunted, falling back.

I stumbled forward, clutching my throbbing hand, but all was black. I'd gone blind. Or the darkness in this cave was so complete that sight was not possible.

The man spoke a rapid silkiness of foreign words under his breath that echoed in the cave. Then he righted himself and grabbed me by the arm. Heaved out a breath. "You are well?"

My heart hammered. *Well?* I lifted sopping hair off my face and my heart shuddered as he shifted into the moonlight, and I had my first look at a true pirate.

He was enormous. Not his body, but his presence. Without even speaking he filled the cave with bottled-up energy. Even if I turned away, I'd feel his presence. A fierceness radiated from the shadowed figure, his craggy face bearing the scars of a turbulent history beneath a thick, erratic beard. Dark hair whipped around his shoulders and hid most of his face, torn white tunic flapping against his chest as he stood firm against the howling wind, with an air of wildness to match the island.

And an empty shirt cuff whipping about in the breeze where his left hand should be.

Captain of a pirate ship, I quickly surmised. Until he'd taken on a storm too fierce even for him. He'd run aground, where a fish—no, a sea creature—had eaten the hand he'd used to steal his loot. Now he no longer stole. He couldn't.

But I had two good arms. He wanted *me* to do the stealing. That's why he'd captured me. I would be his trained monkey. His thief.

Micah. I have to get Micah. Is he alive?

Wind howled just over the man's shoulder, and he pulled his

hood further over his face, providing a moment of distraction. I flew up and crashed into him, that solid mass of adventuring sea captain, and he grabbed for my arm.

And missed.

I bolted into the rain, scrambling over rocks, through crevices, looking for that old bent tree. Then I grabbed a mossy wet rock and slipped, tumbling onto a boulder. I leaped up and winced, grabbing my arm that felt like one giant bruise, and tucked myself under a small rock overhang. "Micah! *Micah!*"

I paused with pounding heart to listen for his *rawr*. For the footfall of my would-be captor.

Two deep breaths, then a *whoosh* of fabric. It was him, the one-handed pirate, coming for me again. Leaping, climbing, swinging with the ease of a circus performer until he shadowed my little alcove, and I could smell the rain and wildness on him.

"You should have stayed in the cave." A foreign roundness to his words magnified that otherworldly feeling. This was a book, and I had stumbled into the pages of an adventure story. Me, of all people, in a novel with pirates. But then his cloak fell open and a little orange-furred treasure was tucked safely in the crook of his mangled arm. "It is still good for something, it would seem," he said wryly from within his hood.

I gathered the poor, sopping creature in my arms and hugged him hard, despite his pitiful complaints. With his little, wet body against my chest, life was anchored once again. I kissed his wet head. "Micah. Oh, Micah."

Raaaawr.

And now, I owed the man. This pirate. What would he ask of me? How much would he make me steal? Perhaps he wanted me to sneak him past the constable. Out of the country. Sail with him on the high seas. "Thank you. I'm deeply grateful."

A request of some sort flickered in his eyes. He leaned close, leather boots creaking, rain pouring down his high, jutted cheekbones, and I braced myself. It was two clear words. "Go away."

I blinked. "What?"

"Go. Away." His gaze locked on mine and his eyes were just as intense as the rest of him. "This is not the place for a holiday, yes?"

French. He was French. Slight hints of his accent remained.

"I'll make do," I said through chattering teeth, raising my voice to be heard above the winds.

He looked at the sky. "The storm will pass. Then you will leave."

"I'd rather you direct me toward the house. Please."

He looked my way, then out at the storm, as if he had something pressing to do. Some treasure to secure, a ship to wrestle to shore, and I was keeping him from it. But he sighed. "As you like."

With that, he shielded me with his good arm, and guided me back out into the cold rain as I clutched my cat.

A steady climb, a rocky path high up into the cliffside, then we were at the mansion, crossing under a domed archway that shielded us from the rain. He hunched under the eave, fingering his darkly whiskered jaw with a wince.

I'd hurt him.

My face flamed, even in the moist air. I turned, looking down at the stones. "Well, I'm sorry, but what did you expect? When a strange man flings a woman over his shoulder, he can expect at least a mild expostulation, no?"

He stared.

"You know, a protest. Opposition." Sometimes I forgot not everyone read books.

He turned and looked out over the wild island, the water pouring down rocks, the distant waves smashing upon the cliffs below. "Farneham Heald, it is the name of this island," he said. "It means 'foreign traveler's refuge.' But it is not that anymore." He turned a heavy look my way.

What was he saying?

"How did you come here?"

"Boat." Peering over his shoulder, I looked for the beach where I'd been standing, but it had been consumed by the angry rising tide. Swallowed by water, as I would have been if I'd stayed to save Micah by myself. Yes, he had indeed rescued me *and* my cat—two large points in the pirate's favor.

"You will leave in the morning then, no?"

I turned and faced the house, the great, mysterious Blakely House that was somehow to be mine, and I shivered. "No. No, I don't believe so." I hadn't a choice. I'd run away from Shropshire, from dear Aunt Lottie and all the beautiful clocks and the porridge in the morning, the opening of shutters every dawn and the long stretch of morning quiet before anyone came into the shop. I had left my home and my life . . . for this.

I *would* make a go of it.

Another bolt of lightning, a crack of thunder, and he leaned near with a hard grimace. "You will leave. You must." The empty sleeve of his left arm flapped in the sudden gust of wind, and I almost asked. Almost put it to him if he'd lost that hand on this island. Or *because* of it. Was it true, what they'd said of this place in Northumberland? That it swallowed up pirates and adventurers and never let them leave?

The cold made me convulse, and he stepped back. "You should go," he said simply, his voice clipped. "Blakely House is a strange place. And the madman master . . . It is not safe for a woman."

I stiffened. If only he hadn't added that last bit. "I shall brave it." I set Micah down and gathered my skirt to wring it out. "As it happens, *I* am the madman."

His brows lowered, his look dark.

"That's right. The master of Blakely House . . . is me." I shook out my wet skirt and held up the key, which flashed in the dying storm. "And you, as it happens, are the trespasser upon *my property*."

Bold. Brash. Technically untrue. For now, at least, as the papers had yet to be signed. Part of me still wondered if the supposed inheritance was all a farce too. But he had pushed me.

He stared down at the key. "Who are you?"

"I'm Sydney—"

"Forrester." His voice was soft. "No. It cannot be. You are . . . *you* are . . ." A different storm darkened his face that was shadowed by the cloak. "You should not stay the night. Not even the night, Sydney Forrester. Now, *go!*" He dropped my carpetbag in the puddle and lunged away, the darkness of the wild island swallowing him up.

"Wait!" I grabbed Micah and charged after him, into the driving rain, tripping over my skirts.

He looked at me over his shoulder, then sprinted over the swinging bridge. I stared with eyes wide as he charged directly into the stone cliff . . . and vanished.

I looked down at my lonely carpetbag, the same one that had been dropped before another door ten years earlier. I had been heavily aware then, for the most unsteady moment of my young life, that I was not wanted by anyone. Those same panicked feelings washed over me, like the rain that pelted from the heavens.

It was only then that my scattered mind funneled toward fear. I hugged my cat close and looked up toward the great stone mansion towering above me, wondering as I had years ago what sort of welcome awaited me on the other side.

One thing I knew. As fearful as I'd been around the pirate, being without him was worse.

chapter
FOUR

Perhaps, dear one, instead of shaping yourself to fit the world, you should search for a little corner of it where your strengths flourish, like exotic wildflowers that would wither anywhere but the rainforest.

~Sophie's letters to Emmett

Rain burst sideways from the skies as I huddled beneath the arched doorway. I glanced over my shoulder, hoping to see the man's outline coming toward me, but he was gone. I ducked beneath hanging ivy and yanked on two brass handles. Blakely House was as unwilling to welcome the new master as its pirate guard had been.

That was the precise moment I wished I hadn't come. But I was driven forward by thoughts of that empty drawer at the shop, and of one haunting phrase that had played through my mind as I'd clung to the sides of that careening dinghy. *We need you, Sydney Forrester.*

I'd never been needed before. Tolerated, yes. Sometimes

even admired for what I could do. But needed? That had awoken something instinctive in me. Something irrepressible.

Setting poor Micah on the step, I put my shoulder into the stubborn doors and forced them apart inch by inch. I stood back. With a few breaths, I searched the ivy and found one tiny hummingbird that matched the one on the broken clock and pushed it. Pushed it again, harder. And the doors swung open to their new mistress.

Lightning shot through the sky and Micah bolted inside. I stumbled into inky blackness, boots echoing on tile. I blinked, steadying myself, straining to make sense of the shapes around me. Tall and wooden, long and glinting metal. "Hello, there." My voice rang through the emptiness. "Hello? Micah!"

When my eyes adjusted, I saw a house asleep. Abandoned, but not long ago. A cuckoo clock with the bird hanging out at an angle. A marionette of some sort, wilted and still. Somewhere outside, a cacophony of birds called out and flapped, and inside the house . . . a voice. Distant and muffled, but clearly a voice.

". . . the projection of air must be equal to . . . and the velocity of displaced air . . ."

It was the same crackling sound I'd heard from the clock. Broken and garbled, interrupted by a strange hiss, it carried on a conversation with itself. Heart hammering, I strode through the forgotten Blakely House. Dust covered the surfaces, illuminated at intervals by lightning slicing through the sky.

I shivered, dripping rainwater on the wood floor of a narrow hall. "Hello?" How long had this mysterious great-uncle of mine been dead? Surely the servants would not simply vacate the premises. Perhaps there were no servants. That'd be a lark—me, alone on this island with only my fear of the sea and the vast unknown to accompany me.

Well, and the pirate. Mustn't forget him.

Air moaned through rafters, and the walls shook, as if the house were complaining. Regret stirred, nearly making me turn back. But . . . to what? The storm? The high tides, and no boat? The cross pirate?

A *boom* echoed through the house. Footsteps. The warnings came rushing back then, in a swarm of hissing voices in my too-sharp memory. *"The master's a beast of a man. A deranged madman not fit for human contact."*

I'd thought them a superstitious lot at the time, but now their warnings seemed eerily accurate.

"The house, it swallows up pirates . . . And no one ever hears from them again."

I shivered in the dank emptiness. What had become of them? Had the house sucked them in like a vortex? Or had they merely become stranded and then succumbed to the island's wildness?

In the distance, that odd voice crackled again and I moved toward it, palms against the peeling paper on the walls. "Prometheus Kelley noted . . . effect of gravitational pull against a machine . . ."

"Hello?" My voice once again echoed through nothingness.

But the people of this house needed me. Somewhere, they were here waiting. Hoping. And I was *right here.*

Where were they?

Then outside, a *thunk.* It shook the house. Vibrated in the air. Water gushed somewhere in the distance as if released from some dam. Wood groaned deep within the house—or maybe without—and large gears clicked and clacked. An odd metallic buzzing, then the faintest glow warmed the room. I whipped around. "Who's there?"

It was the room itself, coming to life. The anticipation of fully seeing my new home was like the breath one takes just before making a vital announcement. It was important, this first meeting. Lamps and chandeliers gave a faint light, and it gradually grew brighter—all on its own. It dimly illuminated brass knickknacks, a great carved cavern of a hearth, and piles upon piles of parts and pieces, odd trinkets galore that inflamed my imagination. And books. An entire wall covered in books.

Then the lights snapped out. I stood rooted to the spot. Blinked in the darkness.

A rumbling sounded in the distance like a steam engine powering through the upstairs. I gripped the doorframe. The house was caving in. My heart exploded. This was it, I'd come here to die.

A low hum. A groan. A gurgling of water through pipes. Then the lights glowed again, stronger and stronger, until they swelled to blinding brightness, and Blakely House awoke, a spell lifting. Organ music poured through the hollowness, seizing me with fear . . . and then with *wonder*.

I stepped deeper into the room. Clanking and chugging erupted from every direction. Electric mechanisms and clock-gear machines whirred into motion. Dancing figures projected on the wall. A sagging cuckoo sprang up and smacked into the side of my face. Color and motion and bright, blinding light came from every angle as the organ music in the distance swelled louder. I hardly knew where to look.

A tiny dog—a live one—ran yapping by on two legs, dragging squeaky wheels that held up his back end. Fire blazed from the hearth, lights buzzed, and the heavy doors just behind me shuddered and closed with an echoing boom. Warm air whooshed and music came faintly from everywhere and nowhere. A large glass ball began to glow, an orb on a clawlike stand. A music box was playing a familiar folk melody that I could hum from memory.

When will we meet again, sweetheart?
When will we meet again?
When the autumn leaves that fall from the trees
Are green and spring up again.

I turned, taking in the beautiful, chaotic madness. The house . . . it was alive. So very *alive*. I'd stumbled upon a dream world, movement and color at every angle and a touch of the fantastical woven through the air. And it was *my home*.

Shivering, shaken, I laughed and spun with the dancers projected on the wall, spraying rain droplets over the rug. I spun and spun right over to those massive bookshelves and laid my face against the book spines. Drank in the scent of ink and paper and leather. Touching them, just their spines, grounded me. I exhaled and backed up to look at them, so I might get a sense of the worlds into which I could bury myself, but they were not books I was used to seeing.

Steele's Series of the Natural Sciences
A Gentleman's Guide to Horse Racing in Modern Times
The Political Hierarchy of Great Britain and Beyond

I crinkled my nose. "Where are the *stories*?" I said under my breath. And despite the presence of hundreds of books, I felt the chill of strangeness—of being away from home.

No matter. I would *make* these books intoxicate me. With a quick breath, I grabbed a thick one. Behind it was a man's face. Crooked nose, bright green eyes, and a gold-toothed smile. "'Ello, luv."

I screamed and dropped the book, hurtling backward, tripping and sprawling on the floor. With a creaking groan, a narrow section of shelves swung out like a door. My gaze met with a pair of very dull, scuffed-up boots. I breathed hard, shaking, and followed those boots up to a man in livery. A servant.

But not quite.

I sat up and a line of them poured in from a dark room beyond the bookshelf door. They stood like an army, a well-groomed collection of broken men missing a leg, an ear, a handful of teeth. Together the dozen of them must've formed maybe three whole men. Yet every last one looked poised to kill. Me, specifically.

A skinny, weathered man spoke up with a wicked grin. "Look here, gents. We have us an intruder."

Well, then. I knew what had become of the pirates.

"Good day." I struggled to stand in my waterlogged traveling clothes, my heavy cloak pulling at my throat. I unclasped it and let it fall in a pool around my feet. "I've come to see to the estate." As the shock wore away, a sureness surged through me. A swelling of confidence. "I'm the heir of Emmett Sinclair."

The shortest one gave a short bark of a laugh. "Get in line, luv."

My blood froze in my veins. There were others? No.

No, no, no.

Suddenly the memory of that empty money drawer blinded me.

But . . . the key. I had that key, and they did not. That must mean something. And I wouldn't tell anyone else about it until I knew exactly what it unlocked.

And who it was that needed me here.

They broke their line of defense and scattered about the room, turning off a dancing monkey here, an extra light there, bringing the room into order again.

I shivered. "I'm not a fraud." I stepped to the hearth and wrung my cloak onto the tile. "I truly am the heir. My name is Sydney Forrester."

They all stilled. Instantly, as if my name had cast a spell.

They turned, exchanging looks, sizing me up with new interest. Deep frowns.

"I'm not going to sack you, if that's the worry. I've nothing against pirates."

Another glance back and forth between them.

"As it happens, I'm rather glad to see all of you. Truly. Relieved, in fact."

They were statues. Angry ones.

"There are all sorts of rumors, you know." I shook out my skirt and looked for something to busy myself with as my nervous thoughts spilled forth. "I don't believe them, of course, as one shouldn't, but I admit to hesitating a little before I arrived. The island is said to be dangerous, and I nearly died coming here. Although that speaks more to the sea than the estate. And there did seem to be wrecks on the island, and no survivors in evidence, just as the legends said, so you can imagine my relief when I find the house and the first people I see are . . ." I stepped back toward the wall, my voice fading away. "I'm sorry. Have I . . . have I said something? Wrong, that is. I know I've said a great many—"

"Those rumors," said a raspy voice from the shadows. "Who says they ain't true?" A line of mostly gold teeth glinted in the light.

I stilled, blinking. A thousand responses twirled through my overwrought mind.

"We might be specters. Every last one of us."

I forced myself straighter. "I don't believe in ghosts, gentlemen."

Another exchange of looks. "Should we tell her?"

One tall and bent-over shook his head. "Let 'er find out for herself."

"Have a seat, Miss Forrester. Let us tell you a story or two." The lanky man shoved a rickety chair my way and towered over me, compelling me to sit. What he told me about his first nights at Blakely House had me recoiling, clinging to the chair, then feeling as though I was reading a novel.

"If Blakely House doesn't like you," offered one man who moved toward me with a crooked gait, "it'll let you know. Sure enough, it'll let you know."

The gold-toothed man grinned, eyes narrowed upon me as I shrank back from his advance. "Just keep your room double-locked at night."

"And during the storms," added another.

"Sleep with a dagger beneath your pillow." Gold Tooth leaned close, his voice a whisper. I strained back even farther. "And never, ever, under any circumstances, leave the windows open at night!"

I gripped a wooden surface behind me, not giving in to the chill that wanted to send me into convulsions.

"Blakely House *eats* grown men, Sydney Forrester. Eats them and spits them out!" The man's crooked limb hung limp. "It has battered and broken us." He leaned into my face, his eyes wide with a sort of madness. "What do you think it'll do to you?"

I straightened under his gaze. "If you'll excuse me, I could do with a little tea." I busied myself with the pot on the sideboard and glanced back at the men over my shoulder. The tension melted as they turned away, busied with their tasks.

I spilled the tea.

Cleaned it up.

Did I *look* as unsettled as I felt? While I stood trembling, a shadow fell over me and I spun to face a different sort of man. Comfortably suited, in possession of all his teeth and limbs, he stepped close with a disarming smile. "Begging your pardon. Didn't mean to frighten you."

My voice snapped a little. "Who are you?"

He approached, hand extended. "So this is Sydney Forrester."

Another neatly pressed man sailed in behind him, this one a little younger.

"Such a pleasure to make your acquaintance, my dear. I've heard a great deal about you, and I'm eager to know more."

I hesitated, then took his hand. My arm was covered in gooseflesh, and I had only now ceased to tremble with cold. I must smell like a lake. Certainly, the pleasure must be all his.

He tipped his head to the side. "There isn't much of a re-semblance. You must be quite a distant cousin." They both had similar shades of reddish hair—the first man had gone gray, but auburn streaks at the temple gave him away. My hair was exceedingly plain brown. Rather dark and erratically curly to the point of frizz. Not a hint of red.

"Niece, I believe. Great-niece, actually."

"I say, she does have something of his essence," said the rather jovial, red-cheeked second man, casting the first a significant look. "You'll know what I mean, Dane. It's that . . ." A flick of his fingers.

"Right, right." The first man, that Dane, squinted at me. "Not the beast he was, but she has that . . ."

"Quite," said the other man, evaluating me. "Almost as if she's his . . ."

By all that is holy, *finish a sentence!* "And you are?" I crossed my arms.

"Dane Hutchcraft." The man who'd first welcomed me took my hand and laid his other one over my fingers. "Emmett Sinclair's nephew. We've been keeping the estate from dereliction, readying it for its next chapter. And now, fortunately, we're here to help you settle in and keep you safe."

Cousin. No, second cousin. First cousin, once removed? "Safe from what, exactly?" I tried to feel kinship to the man. To see us as a family.

"Oh, you'll find out." Dane smiled sympathetically.

I looked back at the line of militant servants, their dark looks boring into my back. Then to Dane Hutchcraft, whose look was warm and inviting.

But eerily so.

Again, with the literature ruining everything.

"Of course, we are the other heirs. Two of them, anyway." He indicated himself and the other man. "The solicitor has no doubt told you all about us."

I swallowed. And felt quite small.

He indicated the man with reddened cheeks and nose, and flame-red hair. "Mr. Tom Jolly, a well-connected landowner from Leeds who has turned several estates into holiday stays for nobility."

"Nobility. Brilliant." I pressed my lips into a smile that I hope looked polite.

The dapper man bowed with a dramatic flair and a look of barely concealed irritation. "At your service, *Miss Forrester*."

Dane continued. "And I, Miss Forrester, have spent my

life in an alchemy shop. I'm humbly known as the Wizard of Sheldon Downs." A deep bow from the waist.

A wizard. A *wizard*.

"There's also another cousin, but he's at university."

"University."

"Professor. Very well respected, I hear."

So these were the other heirs.

And then there was me.

Don't ask. Don't ask about my suitability. It would be a painfully short conversation.

Because I was a watchmaker, my world had always been minuscule—able to fit in the palm of one's hand. I knew everything there was to know about intricate pinions and precision mechanics, springs and torque, but the scope of the universe outside of those things now seemed quite vast. And something I had missed entirely.

A sudden pain in my chest had my thoughts racing. What were we meant to do, divide up the house and hand out a piece to each? Attempt to rule the estate together?

I jumped as something bumped my ankle.

Micah. I let out a breath as I stooped to scoop up my kitty, whose every muscle was tensed, ears back.

I turned. "When will we have a reading of the will?"

"Why, that's been done ages ago." Mr. Hutchcraft the wizard frowned. "The solicitor did not tell you when he wrote? He'll likely explain the details, but someone should have warned you before you traveled all this way. The terms of the will are a bit unconventional. It's something of a contest. The fittest and best of us inherits the estate."

And three losers returned home empty-handed.

chapter
FIVE

Distractibility is not always a flaw, dear one. If we all kept our heads in the real world, nothing new would ever be added to it.

~Sophie's letters to Emmett

Nightmares plagued me. The sort that constantly pricked you from restful sleep, drawing you too often to the surface, then plunging you back into colorful imaginings. Giant mechanical animals screeched from behind dungeon bars, and clockfaces turned to human ones, dials spinning about their noses with desperate pleas.

Then a bang.

I jarred awake, mind still thick with sleep, but the voices continued in the real world. I lay weighted to the mattress, the gentle pressure of my loyal Micah against my leg, and dark legends of my great-uncle and his Blakely House still fizzling in my subconscious. I had been dreaming of him. Of Emmett

Sinclair's ominous, slightly mad presence hovering over his house, unwilling to fully relinquish it.

A bang echoed below. A door slamming in the great hall.

I forced myself upright and looked around at the room into which I'd been deposited for the night—the owl suite, they'd called it. The bird's image had been carved into each of the bed's four posters and papered over the wall. Little figures graced every dusty surface, giving the room the feel of an owl sanctuary, though none actually lived in the room.

Yet as my blurry vision centered on the inquisitive little faces, the plaintive voice called again.

An owl. It was definitely an owl.

Or a human.

Heaving out a breath, I swung my legs around and looked about for a distraction, and my gaze landed on the mysterious broken clock that had drawn me here. The clock that refused, no matter what I tweaked, to keep time. I fingered the clock gears, saw how they fit together. But there were so many pieces I didn't even recognize too. Like a small version of Blakely House—of its master—a puzzle I wasn't equipped to figure out.

I triggered the secret mechanism again and poked about for the ring, but it wasn't there. Somewhere between the shop and that wretched boat trip, I had lost it.

I pulled on the stiff clothing I'd hung on the back of the chair to dry, wrapped myself in my oversized shop apron, and dropped the key into the pocket just in case. Then I moved into the hallway. "I'll be back, Micah. Stay here."

Trees and large-leafed ferns were painted on the walls of the narrow corridor, simulating a garden walkway. Real plants bowed from stands at intervals, and small stone and marble waterfall structures were tucked within little alcoves that normally contained marble busts. Everywhere I turned in the upper floors, nature greeted me.

Another wooden groan, then the bang. And . . . a voice. Gravelly and distant, it was the same odd voice I'd heard when I arrived, fading in and out as if the speaker paced up and down.

". . . More than the displacement of air . . ." *crackle.* "Propulsion in the form of . . ." *hiss.* "Against the weight of a human body . . ." *crackle-crack.*

I jumped out of the way as a tiny creature crab-crawled past my feet. A spider, with metal bow compasses for legs and a little candle snuffer for a body. I knelt and watched it move like a little windup toy. "Well hello there. What is it you do?"

He did not pause to answer.

But then a light shone ahead—a lovely glow in an otherwise dismal hallway. I rose and walked toward it, but it faded and went out as I reached it. Another came on farther ahead, so I followed it. But that one, too, went out when I reached it, and another took its place.

Up one corridor, down another, from open-raftered areas to long halls with curved ceilings, I followed lights that glowed then faded. It was like an invitation, as if the house had something to show me. Every fantastical book I'd ever read had danced through my memory since I'd arrived at this odd island.

I reached a dead end and slowed in a long hallway of framed sketches. A series of shipwrecks. Splintered wood rising up out of wild, frothy, blue-green waves that had smashed the ship into the rocky shore. Brokenness and dark, bleak colors. The artist had scattered tiny men all over the beaches like broken twigs. They were so lifelike that the scene made me ill.

A handful of dark figures had come to attack the fallen men, weapons raised overhead.

So this was my uncle, the great Emmett Sinclair. How wretched to be related to such a man, but I would make something good of his estate. I'd remake it, cast out all the stale memories that lingered like mildew and dust in the corners and bring light.

And yet . . . I ran my fingertips over the paint strokes. Somehow, even these renderings of wreckage and violence were richly detailed, lifelike and textured. Almost delicate. It had taken a gentle, patient hand to create these. In the corner in tiny print arced the name Emmett Sinclair, along with the year.

Then my gaze fell upon something lilac-colored in the topmost corner—a woman, flying down like an avenging angel, a sword in her hand ready to strike the attackers. The glow emanating from her person made it clear she was the rescuer.

A noise, and I jumped. Down the corridor, a heavy wooden door banged open against a floral-papered wall over and over. Heart pounding, I hurried toward it and stepped into the dark old room. It had been plush and red at one time but was now thick with dust and disuse. "Hello?" I stood in the center, spinning a slow circle to take it all in, and the door creaked behind me, then slammed shut. A lamp came on.

"I say!" I ran to the door, flinging it open. "Who's there?"

But the knob jerked itself from my grasp and the door slammed shut again. With a huff, I pivoted in the forgotten room thick with stale memories. Worn, well-used furniture was crammed against floor-to-ceiling bookcases that brimmed with cloth spines and gold lettering.

At last, the stories! Novels lined the walls like old friends.

A lamp glowed in the window bay, dimly at first, then

brightening, illuminating an overstuffed chaise lounge with a tasseled afghan thrown over its back and a book, open upon its cushion with notes in the margins. I turned to go, but the room had embraced me. Enchanted and warmed me, subtly inviting me to remain. It was an understanding, rather accepting sort of space, and I didn't wish to leave.

I crossed to the window bay, reclining across the lounge and paging through the novel, holding the reader's place with my finger. Although my uncle wouldn't be returning to read it.

The scrawled notes in the margins seemed a form of shorthand, which I could not decipher, except for one. It said, *I am a clock that's missing pieces; I am a clock that is broken.*

I traced those words with my fingertip, absorbing the pain they represented. Feeling them within my own soul. That clock from Blakely House—how like both of us it was. Odd and slightly broken, with no obvious way to repair it.

At the end of the third chapter, a yellowed paper was stuck between the pages. It was fiction. A continuation of the chapter, actually. No . . . a *rewrite*. I pulled more little notes out of the pages and read someone's reimagining of the classic tale, and the adaptions were quite clever. The reader's sense of humor was wry and intelligent, and his ideas creative enough that the author herself might have been taken with them. Toward the end a lovely postcard covered with neat, feminine handwriting was tucked within the pages:

Dear one,
  No one has the right to tell you who you are. They call you odd, and perhaps you are. Or perhaps the scope of normal is much wider than any of us ever imagined . . .

I caught my breath. Touched the effusive, spidery handwriting that had been penned with such affection to the madman of Blakely House, and signed simply, *S*.

Sophie. The Sophie from the ring. It had to be! I stared at the postcard, desperate for the other half of the conversation. What had he written to her? Had he been as boorish to her as he had been to everyone else? If he'd been gentler natured, more approachable, might she have accepted the ring and remained here?

Dear one. She'd called him that. Perhaps . . . perhaps he *had* been gentle once, but Sophie had broken his heart and he'd rejected the world.

Suddenly quite awake, I needed to know more. I hurried to leave, to explore the quiet house, but when I reached the door it was stuck—not the difficulty of warped wood or aged fixtures, but rock-solid *stuck*. I stiffened, heart racing.

It was just a house. A *house*. One I could leave any time I wanted.

I turned back to the room swirling with dust I'd stirred up, glimmering in the glow of a single lamp. There beyond the tall four-poster bed was an opening in the paneled wall, cracked open just a hair. Had it been there before? It had been hidden by the bed perhaps, but there it was—an escape.

Crossing the room, I slipped through the door and into the narrowest, most cobwebbed corridor I'd ever seen. I hunched in the darkness, eyes wide, curving then climbing a few steps to who knew where, then coming to stand at the very top of a rickety set of wooden steps that plummeted straight down into the bowels of darkness.

As I descended, an arched wooden doorway appeared on the lowest level, the dim light beyond illuminating a dark, fluttery curtain hanging over it. But then the curtain seemed to float away, leaving the doorway below fully open. Eyes wide, I continued down the creaking steps to the bottom. I caught my toe on the doorjamb and stumbled into a corridor.

A round metal pie pan on three squeaky wheels rolled by, sucking up dust from the carpet with a gentle whirring. I rose, brushing off my still-stiff garment, and made my way down the hall, half-eager to see more, half-afraid.

Muted colors of early dawn glowed through stained-glass windows, falling upon dusty chairs against the walls and rows upon rows of clocks. Rafters framed a rounded ceiling, softening the austere edges of the place, but nothing moved. No one appeared.

I was not alone, though. A gallery of portraits watched me from the papered walls. Their eyes seemed to track me down the corridor, shifting to watch me go.

But that couldn't be. For all the places a body might feel seen and acknowledged, a portrait gallery was not one of them. Yet I paused, backed up, and noted that the eyes did indeed shift together to the left, then back to the right as I moved before them.

Then one portrait, a noble-looking man of middling age with a solemn brow, arrested my attention, peering out at me as if he desperately longed to speak with me.

That voice—the one coming at odd times from odd places in the house—it belonged to *this face*. The settled nature, the intelligence, it fit this man and no one else. I paused and looked into those dark, serious eyes under gently knit brows. The generous mouth that looked sad, tired, but eager to smile if given the opportunity. Perhaps playful, in the right circumstances.

"Hello there," I whispered, smiling at him. "I'm Sydney,

and I'm new here." Those steady eyes beseeched me to say more. Shoving aside minor feelings of foolishness, I obliged. "I'm rather fond of this place, you know. There's nothing to be afraid of, is there?" I sighed. "No, I didn't think so. It's rather odd, but . . . in a good way. Did you think so too, when you lived here? Or did you wish to escape it? I suppose living on an island can be a boon or a trap, depending on how you look at it."

"A boon."

I jumped at the voice that echoed in the arched corridor. Dane Hutchcraft strode toward me, hands in his pockets.

"At least, it was for them." He gave a nod toward the portraits.

"So this is . . ."

"Yes." He smiled, pointing at the portrait beside the one I had been speaking to. "This one is your great-uncle. He never left the island."

"How terrible." I looked at the portrait Dane indicated—Emmett Sinclair looked like a wild boar without the tusks, brutish and perpetually angry. "You can't mean that he never left the island. As in, *never* never." His part in the Boer War, I now realized with a sense of foolishness, must have been mere legend.

"I do, actually. Not once. Excepting, of course, the trip that killed him." His lips pressed into an odd little smile and he rocked back on his heels. "It gave me no little pleasure to bury him at the family crypt . . . on the mainland. He will forever be parted from his precious island in death."

But perhaps . . . perhaps there was only so much about a person one could remove from this house. I closed my eyes and saw that "curtain" fluttering down the hall. A shiver shook my shoulders. "Why didn't he leave, Mr. Hutchcraft? Mr. . . . Dane, that is. I suppose I should call you Cousin Dane."

He stiffened. "I suppose you could."

"So why didn't he leave?"

He was silent for a moment. "Blakely House has a way of holding on to a person. Like quicksand that anchors your feet until you cannot move. It seems it's doing the same to you." Down the hall, a groaning sounded, then cabinet doors popped open and a bell dinged. Dane crossed to what looked like a dumbwaiter with thick pulley cords. He lifted two teacups, handing me one. He pressed a button and the doors closed, the little thing rumbling away. "A singular house, is it not? One could spend a lifetime exploring it."

I ran to it and peered into the cavity, watching steel cords lift the metal container. Down below, a mass of levers and gears worked seamlessly to operate it. Brilliant. Absolutely brilliant. No matter how brutish he was, one could not deny his ingenuity. I turned back to this man who was something of a cousin. "Were you afraid of him?"

He shrugged. "Afraid? No. Most angry people are simply attempting to wrestle their way out of a web of insecurities and failing. He wasn't pleasant, but neither was he terrifying—to me, at least. My mother adored him, but she was rather a glutton for punishment. She couldn't wait to be off the island when she was young, but she forgets that part. They all left quick as they could—or were banished by him—and he eventually had his little kingdom all to himself."

"What became of him? How did he die?"

Dane's gaze shifted away. His easy flow of words ceased.

"It's just that . . . it seems as though he's still here, in a way."

Was it possible for a house to simply absorb the master who

had spent his entire life inside it? To hold on to his presence, even beyond his lifetime?

He looked at me, head tipped a fraction. "You're not afraid, are you, Miss Forrester? Of the house? The stories?"

I chose my words carefully. "There are quite a few odd things about Blakely House, I suppose, that give me pause." I took a few steps down the hall, touching the gilt frames. "For one, lights that dance along the corridor in the dark hours. They flicker and blink like fairies, and they led me—"

"Power surges, Miss Forrester."

Ah, of course. A flaw in the mechanics. And me, with my mind stuck in the fantastical.

"When the wind is strong, the waterwheel speeds up. There's excess power and no one manning the battery station that collects . . . well, all that to say, it's merely a quirk of the electrical system. Uneven power creates uneven brightening and dulling of lights. I've learned not to pay them any mind."

I fought the sinking sensation. Of *course* it wasn't the house. Stone buildings did not live and breathe. "What about doors that open and close on their own?"

"A button, Miss Forrester. Everything in the house is operated with buttons and levers. There's no magic. Many of the doors are rigged to open and close mechanically."

"And that darkness last night? Inside, I mean. When I first arrived. What caused it?"

He smiled. "You'll grow used to all these little malfunctions. You must understand that Blakely House is the first in all of Northumberland to be powered completely by water pressure. Hydroelectricity, they call it, but it's an unrefined process. The weather affects the power supply at times—as it did last night. Then the system was repaired, and as the power built back up . . . Well, I won't bore you with the details." He flicked his hand dismissively.

"Oh please. Bore me." I was inches away from grasping the magic of this wonderland.

He raised his eyebrows. Impressed or offended? "I suppose you bury yourself in books as well."

I smiled. "Only when I'm awake." I left off mentioning that most of those books were novels—rather fantastical ones at that.

"A bluestocking, are we? You'd best keep that to yourself. You'll find Northumberland rather unaccepting of forward-thinking women. Of anything unusual, really."

I was used to being unusual. But in this house, I felt merely as unexpected as everything else. Which was to say . . . I fit right in.

"But you'll change their minds, I expect, if you stay."

If? *If* I stayed?

"You *do* plan to stay, don't you, Miss Forrester? The house isn't so terrible, once you grow accustomed to it."

I faced him in the shadows, his oddly narrow face with a prominent nose and well-arched eyebrows. It was an expressive face—an interesting one. But a carefully guarded one too. He said much, but kept back even more—such as, why he wanted me to stay. Me, who was competing against him to inherit Blakely House. "Won't you tell me about this contest? I shall stay for that much, at least."

"Of course." His smile was tight.

Again, a sense of vertigo swept over me—something was off. Something.

He rocked forward and backward on his feet. Cleared his throat. "I suppose I should show you his workshop." He led

me round through a tower staircase and down a long, win-
dowed breezeway. He batted palm ferns out of his way as they
slapped him in the face. "These confounded plants."

"There are a lot of them."

"Hundreds. And they all require watering and pruning. He
had a few obsessions, our uncle. Plants was one."

Then in the very center of the house we stopped in the
drawing room at an elegant six-paneled door.

"The contest—it involves something in here?"

A thin smile. "You could say that."

I slipped my hand into my pocket and fingered the key, but
my guide simply pushed the door open.

Then I exhaled, looked about, and came utterly alive with
wonder.

chapter SIX

You are a book whose pages others have only skimmed.
Whose cover they can appreciate without ever realizing
the depth of the content that far surpasses the lovely
image presented to the world.

~*Emmett's letters to Sophie*

Here we are." Dane gave a generous sweep of his arm, encompassing the entire room and all its magnificent oddities. "The workshop. Home of the scattered chaos of Emmett Sinclair's madness."

"What a wonder," I breathed. An enthralling, high-ceilinged cavern with gadgets and metal winking, light bulbs and chandeliers hanging from every beam. A banked fire in the hearth and woolen blankets draped here and there made me wish to spend all day cocooned here.

I touched a gilded birdcage as I passed beneath it, setting it swinging. Several half-built creations lay open on the table in the center. I ran my fingers between gears where they met in one complex cluster, complete with pumps and rods that were meant to move.

"What is the contest, creating something new from all these parts?"

"Not exactly."

I lifted a half-sleeve wrap featuring a tiny compass, a timepiece, and several other unknown little gadgets and secured it on my arm with laced-up corset ties. The trinkets clicked and buzzed as I tipped them back and forth, giving direction and time and perhaps the weather, all in a neatly portable package.

From the descriptions of Emmett Sinclair, one might expect crudely assembled machinery bent on destruction or shock. But there was a delicacy about Sinclair's work—a genius sort of complexity that spoke of a gentle touch and immense patience. I tried to imagine an angry, uptight industrialist stiffening to thread a pinion gear onto a cam shaft and couldn't. But perhaps he had a special affinity for machines and not humans.

Then a crackle. A nearby voice. "... Western seaboard ... with a sizable ... across the wingspan ..."

I spun, heart thrumming. It was that voice again. But it was here, in this room.

Crackle-fizz. "... never enough ... in the world ... the beauty you ..."

There. Up on the heavily laden shelf. It was a squarish box of no consequence with a grate screwed on front. And it was speaking.

Dane followed my stare. "Ah yes, that. He has captured his voice in that box, and sometimes it plays when it isn't meant to. It never did work correctly, although it was a credible feat."

I lifted it down, turning it about in my hands, mentally

absorbing how he'd managed to bottle up his voice for later. "Fascinating."

But when I turned after replacing it, a bright light caught my eye. A single beam of sunlight shot down from a high window onto an elaborate metallic man lounging on a stool with head thrown back. I could scarcely breathe. "Impossible!" I whispered.

An automaton. A real machine man. I closed the distance and knelt before him, reaching out to touch his arm. His carefully jointed fingers. "And who are you?" His body was a brilliant array of cords and gears tucked within a birdcage for a torso.

"It's his most far-fetched invention, and the crux of his mad genius." Dane Hutchcraft crouched beside me, lifting the man's limp arm. "A pile of metal is all it is now. Uncle Emmett had a bevy of investors with a sizable stake in it. He worked endlessly on the contraption, and all to no avail. He never discovered how to make the automaton functional. And now there isn't any money to finish."

"No money?" I frowned, looking over the machine man. "He must have a hundred completed inventions. He should be sitting on the largest fortune this side of the channel."

"Uncle Emmett wasn't the cleverest of businessmen. In all his brilliance, he was a fool about paperwork and finances. As you can imagine," he said, waving his hand about the crowded room, "he has managed to misplace nearly every single patent he's filed. They *might* be in here someplace, but they're quite lost. Thus, the revenue from them is too."

But my brain was fixated on the *never able to complete it* part. My heart pounded. A riddle that hadn't been solved. A puzzle with no solution. "I see." I stared at Dane. When would he leave? How desperately I wished to tangle my fingers in the mess of circuitry and wires and begin to make sense of this mechanical being.

I began to imagine then. Imagined what it would be like to wake with the sun streaming through the stained glass, to rise and pace through the ghostly corridors and odd gadgetry with the freedom to lose myself in the minutiae of them, limited only by the breadth of my imagination, because it all belonged to me.

The Mr. Henry Morgans of the world, the Mr. Barleys in all their snuff shops rolling their eyes at me wouldn't ever matter. I wouldn't have to face anyone, answer to anyone. I didn't have to leave the island if I didn't wish it.

Uncle Emmett suddenly made a great deal of sense. How odd and wonderful to find one's relative and realize you are made up of the same stuff.

Except this Dane creature. His glare registered on the fringes of my mind, and I remembered the contest for a moment. The one that made him my opponent. Why had he pretended to welcome me at all? My brain filed it into the "later" box to sort through. A nagging feeling tainted my enjoyment, but only for a moment.

I peered around the back of the automaton and sucked in a breath at the wonder of tiny gold weights, the polished clockwork gears and pinions. And a curious stack of discs like vertebrae up his back. "What are these?" Cut and polished like large coins with a rod driven up the center of them, they looked rather like the notched rollers in a little music box.

His lips pressed together. "They are camshafts on a hydraulic roller."

"Yes." I ran my finger along the stack. "Yes, this is the crux of the piece, isn't it? Somehow they tell this little man what to do." I lifted the jointed fingers again. What purpose could all this delicate mobility possibly have? "Had Mr. Sinclair worked on him for very long?"

He blinked. "This automaton has been a constant topic in our families for years. It's all we ever speak of when Blakely House comes up. How curious that you've not even heard it mentioned before." A thin layer of accusation was tucked between his words, and again I wondered at everyone's reaction to my name.

I tugged a dangling spring, and ducked as it leaped out at me. "I'm rather an outcast, actually. Or, my mother was. She ran away to elope when she was sixteen or seventeen and never spoke to her family again."

"Ah. So that's why the solicitor couldn't locate her—he wouldn't have known her married name."

"She never wed, actually. The man she meant to elope with did not meet her in Gretna Green, and she struck out on her own." I forced two interlocked clock gears to turn, but they were too tight.

"So your father is . . ."

"One of many men she fell in with for a time, then abandoned. She met him when she was already expecting me, then she disappeared when I was quite young."

"And she was Sinclair's . . ."

"Niece. His sister's daughter, I believe, from the letter I received."

"You had a letter from the solicitor?" His frown was deep. Doubtful.

"It was from a woman, actually. She wrote me about the inheritance. Then she called on me and persuaded me to come." I stopped short of telling him about the key.

"Did she, indeed?" He frowned. "A woman, you say? What woman?"

Ah! There, a pair of pliers. I could at least pry the thing apart. I snatched them up, but Dane's hand stopped me. "Perhaps we shouldn't disassemble the gadgets. Especially before probate is complete." He eased them from my hand and set the tool aside.

"Right. We mustn't ruin him."

"And really, nothing's to be gained by disassembling the thing. One can clearly see the use of pneumatics here," he said, lifting the delicate finger joints, "and of course the simple hydraulics and . . ." He rocked back on his heels, casting a glance at me. "Ah. I've overwhelmed you. How thoughtless of me. It's terribly a lot to take in, if one isn't involved already in the little underground world of power and industry. You shouldn't feel badly, my dear. Why, not even the inventor himself understood it well enough to complete it."

"It does sound terribly complex." I rose, crossing the room with barely restrained energy. Would the man ever go away? Then I paused. "This automaton. He's the contest, yes? Whoever unlocks the secret that makes him function becomes the heir."

"I wouldn't count on winning *that* way, Miss Forrester."

"Sydney. Please. And what other way might there be? Perhaps you should show me the will."

"We've already made progress, Miss Forrester. Quite a bit, actually. If you destroy what—"

"I'll destroy nothing. Believe me, I'm enamored of him, and I want exactly what you do—to see him completed. Hand me a turnscrew, would you? Or a wrench, please. I promise I won't force anything apart." There'd be no getting to the mechanics of this man without loosening a few things. "I don't suppose he left notes about."

A forced smile, even as his eyes narrowed. "I'm afraid Uncle Emmett's tools are antiquated and he wasn't organized enough to keep notes."

"The tools, then. Antiquated or not, I shall need *something* to work with if I'm not to use the pliers."

"Of course." His smile turned soft. Patronizing. As if he thought me *adorable* for wishing to tinker with the machine. He rocked back on his heels. "Should you decide to work on the project after you've settled in, the servants will supply more appropriate tools."

That. *That* was the dark cloud hovering over my little fantasy. The servants. "I doubt they'd purposefully give me anything useful. I believe they resent my presence here."

"They're very protective of Blakely House, Miss Forrester. They've all crashed upon its shores, mind you, and been rescued and restored here. They belong to it, much as the Sinclairs did."

"He rescued them?" I pictured those elaborate paintings of the wrecks along the shoreline. The legends of a madman. "I thought Emmett Sinclair didn't like people."

Dane laughed, clasping his hands behind his back, walking toward the far side of the workroom. "Have you seen those men? Not so much *people* as . . . well, they're an odd lot, to be sure."

I frowned. "Maybe." Or perhaps the scope of "normal" is simply much wider than any of us ever imagined.

"He made use of them, to be sure, and I doubt he even paid them. Yet they owe him their lives and they know it. So that's all it is, my dear. You are a stranger here, swooping in and threatening to take over their safe haven."

But it was more than my being a stranger. It was. The reader in me sensed a great undercurrent to this story, something wider and deeper. They had reacted to my name specifically, tried to scare me off with their absurd ghost tales . . . It was *me* they disliked.

I stole a glance at the man, who was still watching me. How I wished to pry open the back of him and peek into the mechanism and see his truth. See what he actually thought. What he truly knew about Blakely House and my late uncle.

The pirate! That's who I needed to ask. Where had he gone? Unlike Dane, there had been an openness, a trueness, to him that wouldn't have allowed him to tell me anything less than the facts. If I was to learn anything about the estate, it would come from him. "Cousin Dane, are there pirates about the island who have not been domesticated?" I cringed. "That is, who have not entered into domestic service. For the estate. Men who roam about the caves and live elsewhere on the island."

His mouth twitched at the corner. I clenched my jaw, wishing for the millionth time that I'd kept quiet.

But how else was I to know things?

"In a word, no. There are none. Not outside the house."

My heart sank.

"Buccaneers and adventurers who wreck along this shore are nursed back to health and released to their fate on the mainland . . . or given the option to remain here on staff."

"So there are no pirates wandering about, say . . . missing a hand? With scars and long wild hair and—"

His eyebrow shot up. "I take it you've met such a one."

Last night seemed surreal. A tumble down a rabbit hole from which I hadn't yet found escape. I realized now I couldn't

75

even picture his face—jutted cheekbones, stormy eyes, dark beard. It had been so dark, and his hood had shadowed everything, leaving much to the imagination.

Perhaps I had dreamed him up. Conjured him from my mind filled with fables and stories and . . . well, seawater.

I shrugged. "It's hard to tell what a person sees in the dark on this island."

"Quite right." His unruffled, benign smile returned. "Now, I've spoken to the servants on your behalf, Miss Forrester, not knowing of course that you were . . ." He twirled his hand overhead to indicate whatever he meant that I was. "I have encouraged them to treat you with respect. I hope you find them more agreeable."

"Thank you," I said with a nod. I bent to pick up Micah and the heavy old key fell from my pocket.

His eyes widened, suddenly focused on the floor where my key lay on the worn rug.

I snatched it up, slipping it back into my apron pocket. Heat radiated up from my chest.

"Where did you get that?" His voice was taut.

My chin edged up. "Uncle meant for me to have it when he died. So I have it."

His stare drilled into the pocket where the key lay, but he made no move to take it.

As we were leaving the room, a face on a brochure snagged my attention. It was in a tiny oval tacked to the wall at an angle, her smile brilliant and self-assured as she looked directly at the artist. Her name was what made me pause—Sophie Holland. I crossed the room and squinted at the black-and-white sketch. She posed with gloved hands crossed in her lap, a hat perched atop that artwork of thick, chestnut-colored hair.

I felt someone watching me and I turned—Dane Hutch-craft had returned. "What are you doing?" His frown was accusatory.

"Who is this?" I snatched the brochure off the wall and brought it to him. "Who is she?"

He blinked. "You do not know? That is Sophie Holland. Rather a well-known woman." He eyed me, taking the brochure and turning it over, pointing to a heading listing her as a speaker at a symposium in Portugal.

Dame Sophie Holland, horticultural artist

"Yes, but . . . who is she to Blakely House? Why is this in Uncle's workshop?"

"She was one of Uncle Emmett's many investments. All the money he refused to give his sisters when he inherited was thrown away on frivolities like this." He sighed. "We believe from the accounting books that he aided in sending her to university some years ago, in exchange for designing the gardens at Blakely House."

"She designed the grounds?"

One eyebrow arched. "I'm not certain why it matters. She was one of Uncle's obsessions—he had rather a lot of them."

But only one had a ring hidden in a clock with her name carved into it. "What became of her?" I couldn't take my eyes from her smiling miniature on the brochure. Nor could I force myself to tell this cousin of the ring. Casting pearls before— well. Anyway.

"She vanished from the public eye years ago, when she married and abandoned her work."

"She married." My heart sank.

"There was some speculation she'd been murdered, or some such romantic rot. Quite a to-do about it some months back, perhaps a year, but most of the world has forgotten about the matter."

Most. But not all. Hers was the only picture tacked to the workshop wall.

Dane's look asked why *I* should care. I did not give an answer, but slipped around him. "Perhaps a little refreshment."

We rounded the corner into the morning room, and I did find the servants more agreeable. At first.

Sunlight shone down upon their shoulders, casting long shadows over the rose-colored rug and settee. There were twice as many as the night before—at least a dozen. To a man, they were polished and shined, standing tall and ready for orders. I scanned them, but none had the look of a wild pirate, and none were missing a hand.

"Miss Forrester, I present to you the staff of Blakely House. Gentleman, Miss Forrester. See to her needs, please." Then he moved across the room to pour tea.

I stepped toward them. "I'd like to find the kitchen, if you please. I will fetch my own breakfast. And then tools. I'll need wrenches and turnscrews and perhaps a spring winder and . . ."

They only stared.

"I believe I've forgotten where the *spring winder* is," said one of the servants, watching me. "Haven't you, Petey?"

"Indeed."

"Afraid you'll have to wait until you inherit it all proper, miss."

Hutchcraft was still across the room, wiping spilled tea off his sleeve. The other heirs had use of the tools, I was quite certain. I straightened, huffing a quick breath. "Then I'd like a tour, if you please." If I was to try my hand at this contest, I'd at least need the benefit of a rudimentary education on the place. I held my breath, waiting for another snide remark . . . or outright refusal.

Their gazes flicked back and forth to one another.

"André will help you," said Mr. Hutchcraft, returning to our little gathering. "André Montagne is the butler of Blakely House, head of staff. He knows more about this place than anyone else here."

One man, tall and elegant, stepped forward and bowed. When he straightened, he surveyed me with a cool gaze—and by heaven, he was *striking*. Not handsome in the way of well-scrubbed nobles or lords, nor thick with muscles, but he was spirited with banked passion that shone from the masculine, clean-cut planes of his face.

My mouth went dry. "On second thought, breakfast can wait," I said quietly. "I'd like a tour, if you please."

A slight nod, then the butler lifted his hand, palm up, to indicate I should lead the way. My, how his eyes sparked—from hidden amusement at my expense or from pure animosity, I couldn't tell.

The moment I stepped out of that morning room, out of the subtly hostile atmosphere, an unexpected rush of calm blanketed me. My eyes fluttered closed and I exhaled, steadying myself. "Now." I faced the man in the shadows of the wide stairway. "I'd like to see everything. And explain it all to me, if you please."

He gave a small bow of assent.

"And I should like to know about my great-uncle. I have so many questions, and I just know you are the man to answer them."

This place had cast a spell upon me, loosening my words and allowing me to speak easily with him. Maybe it was merely the darkened room. Or perhaps knowing there was nothing I could foil, for the man already despised me. And clearly, he did.

But the *why* did niggle at me.

chapter
SEVEN

"S he won't be staying," Dane announced when Sydney had left with the butler. He backed away from the crack in the door where he watched the would-be heiress, the most unsuitable person he could imagine taking over Emmett Sinclair's holdings.

He spun to face his cousin as he stepped out of the little doorway hidden in the paneling.

"Well, you're doing a first-rate job of convincing her to leave." Tom Jolly stood before Dane, nearly empty drink in hand.

"I'm merely making myself agreeable to her, and it wouldn't hurt you to do the same."

"We really should bring poor Purcy up to date before this goes any farther."

A second cousin and the other possible heir, Irving Purcell, served as a professor at King's College in London. Stuffy old Purcell was keen enough and boring enough to step into their reclusive uncle's shoes quite well—while also leaving each of them what they needed most from the holdings.

Tom Jolly, on the other hand, would liquidate absolutely everything of value and make some sort of business of the place. At least Blakely House would be lucrative, and far less gloomy.

Dane glanced at Jolly, who was impatiently tapping his fingers against one arm, clearly anxious to be back on the hunt for the updated will he was certain existed. The man had far more faith in their late uncle's foresight and organizational abilities than Dane did. "What'd you get out of her? Anything useful?"

He stared at the wood grain of the desk. "She's likely Aunt Genevieve's granddaughter. She only had one child, didn't she? A girl?"

"Indeed! And a sorry one at that. Ran off without a word and we haven't heard from any of their lot since."

"Which is why the solicitor couldn't locate Miss Forrester. Her mother had run away years ago."

"And how is it that this Sydney Forrester just *happened* to appear at Blakely House," asked Jolly, scrunching his face, draining the last drops, "when no one could even *find* the fool woman?"

"Something of an heir hunter, from the sounds of it," said Dane. "Someone who wrote her of the details and encouraged her to come."

"For a fee, you mean."

Dane shrugged. "She did not say. But she did seem eager to take over the automaton, and by extension, the whole of this estate. She had quite a gleam in her pretty eyes." He squared his shoulders and stared at Jolly's empty glass.

"She certainly doesn't *seem* like an heiress," Jolly said. "Any one of us would be better suited to run this place than her. Even you, Dane."

Even Dane. Jolly the clever businessman, Purcell the brilliant professor, and then there was himself. Though he hadn't any experience in mechanical gadgetry, Dane Hutchcraft had mastered the art of making something out of nothing. Of squeezing gold out of worthless rocks. From the almshouse to the church house to the alchemy shop where he had made his mark in Liverpool, Dane had been pressed and battered into a powerful machine that could produce its own sort of magic. In his little shop, one look at a customer, and he could determine a person's deepest need . . . and he had a tonic—like a potion—for every one of them.

And just like a wizard was not quite subject to the laws of nature, Dane had once considered himself exempt from certain man-made laws. Not all, but the ones that were pointless to begin with.

The sign on his door marked him a common chemist, mixing up hair tonics and powders for stomach pain and gout, but those who knew came for what they truly needed. Remedies for abusive husbands were his specialty. There wasn't any limit to his capabilities. No difficulty he couldn't solve.

Like the automaton. If anyone could have the thing working, it would be him. He'd done the impossible before, and this time his name would be tied to it. His name, attached to something *good* and *useful*. Something perfectly legal, and acceptable to everyone.

Even his *oh-so-perfect* son.

He was so close. So close to outright owning a piece of history. A marvel of the modern world. A different life was within his grasp. Failing was not an option. He wouldn't even think on it.

Another two swigs, and the tiny teacup was empty. "What'll you do if you inherit?" Dane asked, forcing a casual air.

"I have my plans for the place."

"Nothing that involves the automata, I hope."

"Not a bit of it. Eerie little buggers, if you ask me." Jolly poured a little more into his cup. "I never go back on my word. Every scrap of those machines are yours, for better or worse. No matter who inherits."

"For better." His mind raced. "I will do what no one else has been able to with it—not even crazy Emmett Sinclair himself."

Jolly dropped into a chair, dangling one leg over the other and inspecting his glass. "So you'll finish it. Then what?"

"Oh, you know." He poured more tea, his back to Jolly. "Tinker here and there. Keep busy." A quick swig that burned his throat.

"You'll get your son involved, I suppose. He'll be quite stirred up over it, won't he? Perhaps he'll even speak to you again."

That tightness. Dane turned, clutching the shirt over his chest.

"Arthur *is* still interested in such things, isn't he, Dane?"

Silence. Dane's long fingers smoothed the wooden chair arm. "Let's hope so."

"You might even work on the thing together. Rather a bonding experience, aye?" Jolly's half-cocked grin was irritating.

He forced a smile. "Yes. Yes, I suppose." Was he truly so transparent? "But first we must cast out the interloper. And we must do it right, so she cannot come back to lay claim."

Jolly poured more from the decanter into his cup, then swirled it. "She'll go to prison, then, will she?"

"I should think so, long as we can prove we're right about what happened. That'll be the most difficult part."

"You're still convinced after speaking with her, then? Truly, she *is* guilty?"

"More than ever." Dane turned the bulky ring on his fourth finger. "You'll never believe what I found in her possession."

He jolted forward. "What?"

"A certain key. One that his sisters claim he never parted with, and that hasn't been seen in this house since he left on that final trip. The servants have been in an uproar searching for it. The only person who'd have it now is . . ."

Jolly collapsed into a chair, looking as though he suddenly needed to punch something. "If she thinks she's getting away with it, she has another think coming."

Dane studied the younger man's face, his unusually uptight demeanor. "I don't see why it matters so much to you. Emmett Sinclair did nothing to deserve our loyalty. Rather a cold fish, if you ask me."

Jolly shrugged, not looking at Dane. "Even a cold fish deserves justice."

Dane gave a thin smile. "He'll have it. No matter what we must do, he'll have it."

Jolly eyed him, suspicion lining his brow. Then Jolly rose and resumed his ongoing hunt for the other will he was confident existed. Dane had ceased arguing with him over it, because his cousin was infuriatingly stubborn.

No matter. Soon he'd be opening the door to Arthur, bright-eyed Arthur who had been obsessed with stories of the automata as a child. He would come and they'd patent and sell the machines in every corner of the Orient, where machine men were a rabid obsession just now. Arthur could spend his life using the model to build hundreds of them, and Dane would be here, beside him.

He rubbed his aching chest again, as memories surfaced like a delightful lantern show. The boy had adored him once, following him about and asking questions. *Begging* to spend time with him. Dane had delighted in the boy, but he hadn't fully appreciated the sweetness of that bond . . . or the delicacy of it.

He tried to remember him with that youthful look of adoration, but whenever he thought of Arthur now, all he saw was that black expression he'd worn on the day he had stormed into the shop, full knowledge of his father's most important work brimming in his expression.

Hatred. That's what it had been.

Dane had been proud to be the Wizard of Sheldon Downs, being of real service to people, but in that moment he'd seen himself through Arthur's pure eyes. He knew immediate and immense shame. He was, in some ways, a murderer. A *monster*.

Had been. *Had* been those things. This was a new chapter, in which Dane the wizard would again accomplish amazing feats . . . but everything would ring with truth and goodness. And his son couldn't fail to notice.

Nothing was as big, as legendary, as the rumored automaton of Blakely House. Stirrings had even reached Liverpool and London papers, and the world had begun to talk. The only other man in all of England to successfully produce such a curiosity—jeweler James Cox—had been dead for one hundred years, and this one was finer. Better. Once completed, Dane would have the most complex, lifelike automaton the world had seen. And his son would witness his rise to fame— proper, legitimate fame—as his business partner. Unless . . .

His gut twisted. Jolly toppled a pile of papers, and Dane shot out of his seat. "Stop! Stop with this will. There *is* no other will. No, we must focus on ousting this woman."

"We will. Without question. The truth has a way of working itself toward the surface."

When Tom left, Dane slid into the little secretary at the rear of the room and dipped the pen in the ink. There wasn't time to wait for the particulars to iron themselves out to begin his business ventures. Not when his letters must travel oceans and stir wealthy hearts. And then, when the time was right, it would open the door to the most unreachable heart—Arthur's. But it began with these business letters.

> Dear Mr. Misho,
>
> I'm writing to you from Blakely House, where a very interesting development has occurred. I would like to offer you an exclusive contract for one of the most anticipated innovations of the century . . .

chapter
EIGHT

The only reason machines ever break down, the one element keeping them from eternally perfect function . . . is friction.

~Emmett's letters to Sophie

I pressed my shoulders back, forcing myself not to stare openly at André Montagne. "Perhaps we can start with the front rooms."

"Of course." He bowed his head, briefly shrouding the storm snapping in his eyes.

Blakely House's butler did not like me.

"I'm rather confused on the particulars of this contest between the heirs. Perhaps you can explain it."

He paused in the dark corridor, eyeing me as if I'd asked him to undress. "I am not privy to the particulars of the master's will."

Of course. He was in service and not a member of this

house. And I, in all my wild brilliance, had just pointed that fact out. *Lovely work, Syd.*

Mouth shut. Eyes open. And for all that was holy, keep the brain awake to avoid such blunders.

The first rooms were small and darkly paneled, with curtains drawn as if an invalid suffered from megrims within. I touched a torn scrap of paper, one of many about the little office. It read, *No talking until the other person has finished.*

Curious. A touch of insecurity. A chink in the armor. I touched another tucked into the rim of a lampshade. *Eyes left, history. Eyes right, imagination.* This was a cue to spot a liar. "All these notes," I said. "What did he do with them?"

Mr. Montagne hesitated. "He would come here before a meeting. He'd walk around and touch each one and then he'd be calm."

"Meetings? I thought he didn't—"

"Investors, on occasion. Sometimes it was officials from Northumberland concerning his installed mechanics."

I lifted my gaze to the stained-glass windows up high, and the delicate prisms hanging from chandeliers. Then down to another note folded onto a lampshade. *Any man bearing enormous flaws also possesses enormous strengths in equal measure.* Something in me softened at this intimate look at my uncle. With each pivot in understanding, like viewing pictures painted from different angles, I knew more but understood less. He didn't scare me, as it turned out. He fascinated me.

Which made me feel odd. As odd as my uncle.

One need not attempt to be a duck, said another, *even if he is the only swan.*

"He hardly seems a beast," I whispered.

"He wasn't." The answer was quick. Confident. "That was simply how people saw him. *Some* people."

I watched his shadowed face. This was the first I'd heard another soul speak kindly about my uncle. "What *was* he like, then?"

"I cannot say, miss. You would have to have known him for yourself."

I watched the butler carefully—the tension and the withdrawing as if he wrestled within. "Surely, a few words come to mind."

He stood for a moment, polished boots planted on the rich blue rug. "Practical. Sensible. In possession of a wealth of secrets from his men, without the slightest urge to betray them. Extremely clever regarding all mechanical things—less so about relating to people."

"I see." I felt another stirring of kinship with this man.

He turned away, hands clasped behind his back. "Shall we move on, miss?"

As we left, I saw one last note tacked unceremoniously to the dark, paneled wall: *Make time to leave the train tracks now and again. The station isn't going anywhere, and there's much to see in the fields along the way.* I smiled, feeling as though he'd spoken directly to me.

If only I'd stopped searching for my mother and simply looked for the rest of my family! I could have come to Blakely House. Visited in this study. Heard these thoughts in his own voice.

Mr. Montagne's face appeared in the doorway. "You are lost, miss?"

"I . . . no. I'm coming."

He led me with long, confident strides through the darkened lower floor—the bountiful morning room, the dining room with a hearth so large there were benches inside, the magnificent drawing room with a mural over the ceiling. White plaster angel faces looked down upon us.

He paused just inside. "This was the room intended for receiving guests."

"Of which there were few, it seems."

"Very few." His dark look held subtle accusation.

I brushed it off. "How I would love to carry home this lovely mantel." I ran my hand along its detailed etchings.

"That would be quite a task. It weighs nearly ten tons." He rocked on his heels. "And you do not own anything in Blakely House. Yet."

Like the sting of a very polite, mild-mannered bee. He turned and swept his arm toward the door before I could speak. Then he took me to a rather dim library.

I blinked. "How does one bring more light into this place?"

Mr. Montagne motioned toward a long table. "Place the lamps on these stands." He demonstrated, placing a lamp onto its copper base, then lifting it again to turn it off. He set it on the stand and the bulb stayed lit.

I hurried over to him. "Fascinating!" I turned it on and off, then lifted the lamp to inspect the copper plate beneath. "How . . . ?"

"Mercury." Terse, as if he were leaking national secrets to the enemy by force. "A conductor that carries electricity to the bulb."

I crossed to another table and availed myself of an overstuffed chair.

"I wouldn't sit there, miss."

"Just for a moment." I sank into its velvety cushions. "What a welcoming—" *Thwunk.* My legs flew up, straight out before me. I scrambled for decency, shoving petticoats and skirts down over my stockinged legs, which suddenly caught a draft.

What was this *creature*, this—ugh—what sort of chair was this?!

Dash it all. I jerked forward, and it launched up to its upright position, locking in place with a click as I clutched the arms. "What in heaven's name was that?" I jumped up, smoothing my hair, my skirts, my pride. I side-eyed the bothersome contrivance as I caught my breath.

"As I said—I wouldn't sit there, miss." There it was again, those snapping eyes, almost playful behind his practiced demeanor. He tried hard not to smile, bless him.

"You did say it. Almost." If I had let him, that is.

"The chair was a work in progress, I'm afraid." He cleared his throat, busying himself with the cuffs of his livery. "He meant for it to prop the legs and recline back without any effort from the person using it. The springs were . . . how do you say . . . a bit too eager."

"I'll say." I crossed the room as far from that fool man-eating chair as I could, to a little secretary where something caught my eye.

"How clever!" I picked up a modified set of opera glasses and held them to my eyes. "But why create such a thing if he never visited the theater?" I blinked, but as I held it to my face, my eyes met not with some distant sight in the room, but a lovely floral scene. "Oh." The Orient, perhaps, with winding rivers and short, flowered, umbrella-like trees. "Oh my!" A woman wrapped in a long pink Oriental gown stood on the banks.

How lovely. How utterly lovely.

I lowered the glasses and turned them over, looking for the

mechanism. Instead, what I spotted was another small hummingbird etched into the metal case on the bottom. I pressed it.

"Perhaps you should set those down."

With considerable effort, the image shifted and another clicked into its place. Pyramids, tall and shadowed. A pair of camels in the foreground, with the same woman holding the reins. A familiar woman. Another click, and the mountains loomed before me, stretching up into the clouds.

"What are you doing?" His voice was low, but not entirely accusatory.

"It's a button. Spring-loaded to shift through stills. There are several."

The next click brought before me a field of antelope grazing, one with its head up, watching the photographer. Another showed a lighthouse, red and white but with a distinctively purple front door with flowers painted on it.

And *her*, with one hand resting on the stair rail outside.

"These are beautiful," I said, a bit breathless. He *did* travel. Much the way I always had—at home. I lowered the glasses and was met with the butler's glare.

"You've truly never met the master? Never spoken with him?" He glanced up and down the length of me. "No one but Mr. Sinclair would have known how that operated."

I shrugged and turned my back on him, repositioning the glasses on my face. Rude, but suddenly it felt quite necessary. "It isn't hard to understand, because it's so very . . . *him*. The birds—they often mean something. A lever, a button . . ." Anxiousness bunched my shoulders. I could feel his stare burning holes in my back. I did not lower the glasses, though. This little gadget was proving as handy as an emergency book.

I clicked a few more times. "Emmett Sinclair's signature was in his finishing. Everything the man created had a polish and a precision. Even in the parts no one would see. And birds. Always birds. This type, in particular."

The next picture showed a large stallion and a woman, the same that had appeared in the other pictures, astride him and clinging to his mane. She threw a vivacious look of challenge toward whoever had snapped the still.

Sophie.

The birds—they must have been for her. Everything about her said flowers and gardens . . . and so, I now realized, did Blakely House. "He was so in love," I said, almost to myself.

A short laugh. "No. Emmett Sinclair was many things, but never in love."

"Just look at her. She's in every single one." I held the glasses out to him.

He lifted them to his face, clicking through. "He had women in his life—his mother, his sisters, even a few cousins. This could be any one of them."

"A ring! There was a ring in an old clock with her name carved on it."

"You're certain it's from him?"

"Quite sure. I—" I paused, voice catching. His name *had* been on it, hadn't it? If only I hadn't misplaced the fool thing . . .

He set the contraption back on the desk and surveyed me with a frown. "You seem to think you know all about the man, Sydney Forrester, but I worked beside him. And I am certain that if the most beautiful woman in England waltzed into his front room and stood before him, he would not have said two words to her."

"You cannot know for *certain*."

"Once his cook merely mentioned that he might meet a

young lady she knew from Northumberland, and he nearly sacked her. Didn't speak for the rest of the day. And when a woman *was* brought over here, a most charming and clever lady, he could hardly bear it until she left. No, he wasn't the sort to fall in love. He simply wasn't interested—or able."

"You're telling me he wasn't *capable* of feeling affection?" The gentle sweeps of brush on the paintings. The little notes. The blossom of creativity and artistry across every inch of his home. Yes, he was a boar . . . but he was more besides that too.

He quietly replaced everything I'd disturbed in the room. "I do not wish to ruin whatever idealistic image you have of your great-uncle, Miss Forrester, but he simply did not possess a romantic nature. He was an inventor and a very brilliant one. But hadn't the desire for entanglements."

My roving gaze spotted a plain wooden box. Exactly like the one the veiled woman had brought to my curiosity shop. I dropped to my knees before it, running a hand over its lid. "What is this?" I lifted it, playing with the catch.

"A box. For holding things." His words could cut stone.

But the box had weight to it. I lifted it and turned it on my fingertips. On the back was an old metal key, its prongs buried deep inside the box. I turned it, and nothing happened. I flipped the box over, searching for another bird and found one—a hummingbird, nestled down in the corner. I pressed it and the lid sprang open, and a small pair of dancers spun to the music.

But it wasn't a human couple. A slender purple flower danced with what looked to be a mechanical man. His metal arm curved around her stem as he guided her in their circular waltz. "He loved her," I whispered. "I know he did."

"I can only tell you what I saw with my own eyes."

I touched the little replica man. "Perhaps you looked but did not see."

His expression stiffened. "I believe the tour is complete. I'll return you to the morning room." He turned in one fluid movement toward the corridor, expecting me to follow.

I stood and held my stance in the center of that white and gold room. "I haven't seen the power room yet."

He hesitated. "Perhaps you should speak with the solicitor first. Make certain everything is in order with the inheritance."

"Because you believe I'm a fraud." I crossed my arms. That's what all this tension was.

A tic in his jaw. "You are merely not what was expected."

"And exactly who *did* you expect?"

He hesitated. "A man. We expected Sydney Forrester the heir to be a man."

"Ah." Slowly, all the gears slid together, teeth sinking into place. "That's why the servants seemed so hostile. They don't believe a woman can head this ship. Don't think a woman can possibly be clever enough to understand the gadgetry and mechanisms."

The lights around us dimmed several times, then surged to full strength.

"No." His voice was soft. Controlled. "They do not resent you because you are a woman."

"But you just *said*—"

"Mr. Montagne." A lanky servant with thinning blond hair slipped into the corridor and addressed the butler, holding out a wire. "Mr. Penvense sent this 'round. The crane is fully broken now, and the whole Northumberland coast is complaining. Everyone what works on the docks."

The butler's eyes closed. "Very well. I'll see to it presently."

And he left. Without a word, a glance, or even a farewell. Well, it wasn't as if we'd passed a pleasant morning together. I was a professional matter for him. No . . . an inconvenience.

A threat.

And he was probably my only true source of information. I moved in the direction the men had gone, but when I recalled his steely looks, a wave of weakness softened my knees. *Good gracious, I need Aunt Lottie. I need her.* Only she would know how to win the servants over. Only she would be able to charm her enemies. *Dear God* . . . I fell back into the practice she had gently pressed upon me. *Please send her.* It had been so long since I'd done such a thing. So long since I'd needed to.

They were once flowery and earnest, these prayers, but reality had blunted my hope following what always seemed a one-way conversation. Still, desperation caused me to press this request into the atmosphere with hope that it didn't disappear into the black hole of Sydney Forrester's prayers.

It thudded against the same dull emptiness as I moved through the silent corridors. I took a breath. I came upon the men talking, heads bowed and voices earnest.

The butler's voice rumbled down to me. "Have they looked over the rods, checked for leaks?"

"They've done all the things the master told them to do. No one can fix it."

My ears perked. No one?

"They give us to the end of today to have it working or they'll shut it down. And they won't pay."

He smoothed his hair back with one hand, exhaling loudly.

I approached, stiffening my muscles. Not too eager. Not too— "I can help. Let me come. Oh please, let me come!"

Mr. Montagne turned. A frown, as if I'd offended him. But what had I said that might offend? If only someone would *tell* me what I was doing wrong. Saying wrong. To men in particular. Life would be a whole lot simpler.

"Why ever would you wish to come?"

"I want to learn. And to be of help. Perhaps if no one has managed to figure it out . . ."

He let out a breath. "You needn't feel you must. Giles, send word that I'm on my way." Another bow toward me that showed the thick, dark hair smoothed over the top of his head. "If you'll excuse me, my lady."

He turned and strode down the hall, but I followed him. "Thank you for the tour, Mr. Montagne. I know the house is a private matter for all of you, and I can see why you hold it so dear. Why you wouldn't wish to escort a stranger through it."

He softened, just at the edges. "You expected me to refuse?"

"I expected at least a . . . well—"

"A mild expostulation?" He ran his fingertips along his jaw, one eyebrow raised.

I froze. In the flickering shadows, I saw it. Snapping eyes. Scars muted by soft light. A roughened past etched into his expression—now clean-shaven. That wildness barely restrained below the surface, just as his wild hair was now smoothed back into a leather strip tied at the nape of his neck.

But it shone out through his eyes. A stormy gray-green, hooded by the darkest lashes. One had the impression of a volatility that must not be tested, a lurking danger—and my troublesome brain skipped ahead to the same conclusion as that first night.

Pirate!

His words did curve at the end with a light accent. Softer

in this environment, more controlled, but still there. And his left hand hung with an odd limpness I hadn't noticed before.

Wooden. Finely painted and carved with detail, but it was wooden.

I grabbed the polished stair railing. "You! You are . . . *you*."

He held a hand to his chest, offering a slight bow. "All day, mon amie." A glint of humor lit his eyes. Then he was gone.

When I'd fully caught my breath, I turned back to explore —no one had told me I couldn't. Warmth and steam rolled down the hall as I passed the butler's pantry, and the lovely aroma of rising bread. Pie too, perhaps.

The kitchen, as it turned out, would be more a haven than the library, provide more answers than any book, because of one single aspect.

One I would soon come to call the kitchen angel.

chapter
NINE

A man's legacy is the flavor he leaves behind in the mouths of those close enough to taste his character.

~Emmett's letters to Sophie

I thought of her that way because when I first saw her, the light shone down upon her from high windows, lighting her filmy white gown and projecting a halo of light around her gold-highlighted hair. Humming a sweet tune with a nature as delicate as her dress, she seemed positively celestial.

Most astonishingly, when she turned to face me . . . *I recognized her.*

I caught my breath. "You're here." I entered her light-filled kingdom, and she looked up from kneading, rays of smile emanating from her face, drawing me irresistibly. Her dark veil must have covered a great deal when she'd come into my shop, for here in Blakely House she looked entirely different. Brighter. Her instant welcome, like an invisible red carpet rolled out to me, warmed the exact same places in my heart that Aunt Lottie always had.

"No," she said with a grand twirl of her skirts. "*You* are here! And that is an immensely wonderful thing." She grabbed my arms. "So what do you think of our Blakely House? Don't you adore it?" Where Aunt Lottie was bright and efficient, this woman was whimsical and joyous—but they both had a way of folding me into their presence with warmth and sincerity.

"It is everything you said, but more—more unexpected, more interesting, and more . . ." Hostile? Eerie?

"More splendid than you ever dreamed!" She lifted a flaky delicacy up between us. "Have a scone. It's blueberry."

She floated away and the thing was in my hands. I nibbled it and fell completely under the spell of the woman's cooking, which exuded as much warmth and flavor as she did.

The kitchen itself was a modern wonder. Machines and gadgetry clanked and steamed throughout the room, rising to the high ceiling. Three great hunks of meat hung from above, turning slowly with a mechanical whir and pump of power. She caught me looking at them. "A hydraulic rotisserie. Quite brilliant, is it not? I shall make pheasant for dinner."

"You are the cook?"

"Head cook, housekeeper, and only female on the island, until now," she said with a flourish and a bow, flour puffing around her. "Mrs. Holligan, my lady. But you needn't call me that. No sense in playing favorites with Mr. Holligan simply because he was my *last* husband."

"You've had more than one?"

"Six, actually." As if she was describing the loaves of bread rising on the windowsill. She held out a hand. "My full name is

Angeline Connely Treadway Bengali Smith Watson Holligan. But you, my dear lady, may call me Angel."

I took her hand. *Angel.* Yes! And this was her haven, because she seemed infinitely more at home here than she had in my little shop, behind the dark veil.

She mounded her bread dough into loaves and came around to take my hands in her warm, floury ones. "You *are* glad you've come, aren't you? Here, have a little cheese." She bent and whipped a tray out of a low metal icebox, sliding it before me.

"Blakely House isn't at all what I thought it would be."

"Come now, it isn't that bad, is it?"

"It isn't that I don't like it here. I do—more than I thought I would. It's just . . . well, the staff . . . and the other heirs. Why didn't you tell me about them?" A quick rush of ire. "Why didn't you mention it was a *contest*? You might have saved me a lot of trouble, you know."

"Saved you a trip here, you mean."

"Why didn't you tell me?"

She leaned onto the worktable. "Because it *isn't* a contest. Except to that overgrown, pompous—well, never mind." Her hand fluttered above her head as she turned back to her work. "Whatever he said about a *contest*, he's completely fabricating."

"But why?"

"There are those who believe that they have an exclusive claim on the estate, and they are doing all they can to overturn the master's will. But they're no more owed Blakely House than I am." She scooped up her baking dishes, carrying them in her apron to a tall metal automatic dishwasher built into the wall at eye level and fitting them neatly into the racks within.

I crossed my arms. "What sort of claims?"

She sighed, pausing with a plate in her hands. "Nothing worth considering, if you ask me. But no judge is doing that. The master had three sisters, you know—Gertrude, Geraldine, and Genevieve—and it is mostly their offspring trying to claim the place.

"Dane Hutchcraft, the wizard as he calls himself, is Gertrude's son. He is the oldest of Emmett's nephews, so he is the most direct blood relation and the legal heir if the original will is found to be invalid. He claims the master wasn't in his right mind when he drew up the will.

"Your mother and Tom's mother are the children of the other two sisters, although I can't be certain which is which. I don't know the family history very well, I'm afraid."

"My mother's name is Gwendolyn, I suppose named to fit with the family, but I haven't any idea which one her mother was."

"You've never met your mother's family."

I shook my head. I'd barely met *her*. "So it's only the three of us who might inherit?"

"Well, there's Mr. Purcell, a professor over at King's College, but he's only a second cousin. He claims he had a letter from Mr. Sinclair stating that he was to consider Blakely House his home for the duration of his life, although *whose* life he meant remains to be seen. The wording *might* be interpreted as a bequest, and he is convinced that's what the master meant."

"Those claims seem unsubstantiated. Have they any proof?"

"Oh, some rough wills." She waved her hand over her head.

"They all have *wills*?"

"Oh yes, but it's all very . . . you know." Another twirl of her hand.

"But wills. Signed, official ones."

"None of the wills were dated except the one naming you, so there's a bit of a to-do with the solicitor about which one is *most* valid. That'll have to be decided soon."

"So it *is* a competition." I clung to the table's edge. "Who is it—that is, who decides . . ."

"That fool solicitor says that unless we can prove which will is valid, it's up to the investors to name an heir. Something about a codicil in their contract."

"Investors? The *investors*? The ones who have a stake in the automaton?"

"None other," she said with a snap. "Thousands of pounds they sank into that tin man, and since it sits unfinished, and since they own a partial stake in Blakely House, they get a say in Emmett Sinclair's successor."

"And of course they'll choose whoever can deliver on their investment."

"That's what your cousins are saying. Like pulling Excalibur from the stone, finishing that metal man will prove one the rightful heir of Blakely House."

I groaned, hand to my face. "Hutchcraft. He has been working on the automaton, hasn't he? And I haven't even begun."

"He's not been at it for terribly long, Miss Sydney. Only been three or four—"

"Days?" I squeaked out.

"Weeks."

I puffed out a breath. "And has he made much progress?"

She shook her head. "I hear some terrible noises coming from that workshop when I bring 'round the tea. He's certainly making *something* happen. But I've not seen it do anything truly remarkable yet."

I closed my eyes. Steadied myself. "It's all right. It's still all right. I have the same chance he does." But I hadn't even been able to make that clock work.

"It's not merely about finishing the thing but understanding it. They want blueprints for future machines. So everyone has a fair shake, far as I can tell. It's every man for—*person*, that is—every person for him—*her*—self!"

I paused my pacing. "Yet they seem to be on the same team. And they're both against me, almost as if I'd caused offense even before I'd come. What is it I've done?"

"Yes sir—ma'am—it's any man's game just now." She glossed easily over my question, her work of sweeping all the flour into her cupped hand suddenly all-consuming. Very much like Aunt Lottie, who always hid big secrets by busying her hands but accomplishing very little.

There was more. I could smell it folded into the yeasty dough rising beside her. Like a tiny linchpin, this unspoken bit would prove vital, wouldn't it? I folded my arms. "I'd never even heard of Blakely House until my great-uncle died. I have no history here, no education, and I know nothing about running an estate. Any of them would be a more logical choice for heir than me. *And* they don't want me here. So why *did* you fetch me?"

She swept flour into her cupped hand with swift, efficient movements, her soft red-tinged curls catching the sunlight. "You will come to understand in time, dear one." A wink.

"So I could bring the estate down around our ears?" I grumbled.

She threw back her head and laughed, a lovely ringing sound, and her amusement was contagious.

"I don't care to compete for something, especially when I'm not certain I should have it." Even though I desperately wanted to. "I feel as though I've entered a match and I'm the only one who hasn't seen the rule book. You need to tell me whatever it is you aren't saying."

She brushed the swept flour off her hands, then proceeded to sweep it up again. "My third husband was like that, I do recall. A kind and gentle man, not given to being competitive. But do you know what I told him? I said, you don't gain freedom from your hardships by clinging to certainty but by releasing it. Every finger released from the grasp of control is an inch of freedom gained. Yes, I told him that."

"So a risk means . . . freedom?" I could feel my brow furrowing.

She smiled. "It means clinging to the boat rather than the shore. Let go of that white-knuckled grip on certainty so your hands are free to grab on to your adventure. Can't you feel the beauty of it? Just grab on! *Seize* it!"

A tingling in my chest. An awareness. An echo.

Her smile twinkled at me. "Come, now. You'll do it, and you'll do well, and it'll be *amazing*. Have you toured the house yet? I should think that'd be enough to tempt you to stay." Then she once again dusted the swept-up flour off her hands.

"The butler gave me a brief tour. Mr. . . . something." Warmth seeped up from my chest to my neck, staining my cheeks, most certainly. I could not even speak of the man without becoming overly aware of his distaste for me . . . and feeling his weighty presence as if he were standing behind me, watching. Judging. *Mis*judging. "He showed me the front rooms, but it seemed— well, that he couldn't wait to be rid of me."

"Ah! That's André Montagne." She shook her head. "He's grieving in his own way. He was the master's right-hand man, you know, doing everything with him. Rigging up the generators, shoring up the water, tinkering away on those infernal projects of his."

Right-hand man. The sort who might expect to inherit the master's work, if not his entire estate.

Angel was back to kneading, pounding that lump of dough and flipping it to punch it down again. "Oh, he's a surly sort, of course. They all are. But he's reasonable. He won't hate you forever, once you've proven yourself."

Except he acted as though I was forever stepping on his toes.

"They've all had a rough go of it, remember."

"*Had* he been a pirate, then?"

"Those are his secrets." Another flip of dough. "So don't go telling him I told you, Miss Sydney." A puff of flour. "He was the most piratey pirate that ever pirated! Except he didn't steal anything, exactly." She shook her head. "You'll have to ask him for the details. Oh, but don't *ask* him, because he's sure to know I told you!"

"What else can you tell me about him, then? How did he— that is, what happened . . ." My voice trailed off weakly.

"You're wondering about his hand, is that it? He won't talk about how he lost it, but it happened when he wrecked here off the island. Oh, he's sour grapes now, but you'd have thought he was a walking thundercloud back then." She paused kneading for a moment. Her voice softened. "Nearly lost him, simply because he didn't want to get better. He's a terrible patient, you know. And far too strong for his own good."

My chest squeezed, absorbing the pirate butler's pain.

"'Twas the house that saved him. All the metal, the power, the immensity of Mr. Sinclair's brilliant inventions sparked a little life back into him. Leave it to a shiny object to catch a person's eye when nothing else will." A wink. "He always said he'd leave if the house had another master. He couldn't bear these gadgets going to rot around him. Unless . . ." She glanced up at me through a wisp of escaped hair.

"I don't know where to begin." I held out my hands. "His inventions . . . he was so brilliant. But I'm no industrialist. I cannot even repair any of them so far." The automaton was entirely out of my abilities. And the clock she'd brought to my shop, which should be a simple repair . . .

She continued working as if she hadn't heard me. "I heard you sunk your dinghy on the way over to Farneham Heald." She plopped the dough in a pan, set it with the others on the sill, and slapped her hands against her apron, erupting little clouds of flour. "Went right down in the storm, no?"

"No. Well, yes. The wind was quite impossible."

She shook her head, loosened curls swaying. "All of us living on the island know the first rule of the sea. If you're fortunate enough to have a boat, grab that oar and just keep pulling it through the water." She came to stand beside me, catching my gaze. "It's the only way you'll get anywhere. But you've got to grab on. *Grab on.*"

I caught my breath. Lottie's words echoed again, reverberating through my heart.

I blinked away tears and looked at the woman who had, in a roundabout way, offered me what I'd needed most—advice from Aunt Lottie. "Grab on." I looked about the tall, sunny kitchen pulsing with mechanical life. Thrumming with brilliance and power at every turn. "All right then, I'll grab on."

Yet what I grabbed tossed me into unexpected waters. I'd set out to find that room with the door that closed me in, to verify what I'd seen there. To learn more. What I found instead was a tiny study with a secretive air about it.

How dark and gloomy the room was! The heavy drapes muffled some sort of color, though. I yanked them back, revealing full-length stained-glass windows with sun pouring through. I breathed in the light and unlatched the windows, pushing the center one open. A light breeze ruffled the papers scattered on every surface, then a gust swept off the entire desk.

Ah, mahogany. Inlaid leather covered the little secretary that was actually quite lovely beneath the chaos. I swept up the papers and, with a thudding heart, began to leaf through them. To focus on words and phrases meant for other eyes, and steal a peek at the secrets of Blakely House.

My name stood out on one. I pulled the letter from the stack. It was from Blakely House's solicitor concerning the heir, Sydney Forrester, and the assertion that *he*—which must be why they expected me to be a man—must not have control of Blakely House. All the feminine ire of Aunt Lottie boiled up in me. What a bold assumption, that the heir would be a male.

> *If the heir-presumptive is, in fact, responsible for this crime, the inheritance would of course be voided and the perpetrator imprisoned. It is unlawful that any man should benefit from the commission of a crime, especially in probate matters.*

Crime?

> *The circumstances supporting this Sydney Forrester's guilt are sufficient to convince me. Therefore, I will continue looking for him as you dig up the solid proof we*

need to invalidate his claim to Blakely House. You have
my word of honor that this Sydney Forrester, whoever he
is, will not profit off of the murder of his uncle.

"Something catch your fancy, miss?"

I spun with a cry, dropping the letter. A lanky servant in dark livery leaned against the doorway as if he'd been observing me for several minutes. Hand to my head, I breathed deeply. "I didn't see you there." I set to work tidying papers. Neat stacks, sorted by size.

"Evidently not."

I summoned a polite smile. "Have you need of something?"

"Was about to ask you the same." He looked at the desk, then back to me with dark, unblinking eyes.

I gripped the papers remaining in my hand and gave a dismissive nod. "Thank you, I believe I have what I need. Mr. Montagne was just showing me about."

"The same Mr. Montagne what's packing up for the mainland now?"

I set aside the papers. "Packing?" An odd sense of loss. He *wasn't* taking me. That riddle, the crane no one could figure out, would keep me awake all night. A few nights.

"'E's got to have his tools, now don't 'e?"

That tingle again. An unsolved riddle. "What exactly is he fixing?"

"Mr. Sinclair's giraffe machine—the one what loads the ships in Northumberland. No one but the master can make 'er work. Like so many things at Blakely House." His eyes were accusing, and at last, thanks to the letter behind me, I had an inkling of why.

chapter
TEN

André Montagne couldn't shake the tightness from his chest, even with a hearty walk from the corridor to the butler's pantry. A chorus of voices greeted him from inside the little space. In the years he'd served as Blakely House's butler, this pantry was seldom quiet. The servants' hall was adequate and the kitchen enormous, but this cramped office, lined with mismatched tables and shelves of canned goods, had become the place where the shipwrecked adventurers felt at ease and the truest words were aired.

He gently kicked the door shut behind him and folded his arms. "A fine holiday, I see."

"Aye, it's our tea hour, Captain," Jinedath said, perched on the table with his feet planted on a low chair. "We're just discussin' the interloper." The man had blown from coast to coast, picking up habits and dialect from each place, but never quite erasing the Australian outback of his nature. As unpolished as the bush country that had birthed him, he was a firecracker of opinions and facts, with a brain that snapped along faster than most trains. "Like a fine puff of cotton—with nettles. She has a tongue in her, she does." Jinedath swung back to face James standing in the corner. "Not much substance, though."

André frowned, setting aside his heaviest wrench and rivet setter.

"Pretty enough to catch a husband, but scatterbrained enough to drive 'em all away too," James crowed.

"That's why she needs the fortune so bad, aye?" Jinedath laughed and tipped back his mug, downing the last of his cider.

"You've spoken with her?"

"Spied on her, more like," Jinedath said. "You're the one what speaks to 'er. What did you get out of our Miss Forrester, Montagne?"

"Very little, actually." He couldn't recall anything she'd even said just then, but there had been an urgency to her questions. A pointed curiosity in pursuit of some very specific thing. "She wants to know why you haven't taken to her."

Guffaws echoed in the small space.

"Of course she do. You told her, didn't you?"

André cleared his throat. "We don't know for certain yet if she's guilty."

"Oh!" Jinedath jutted out a finger at André, leaning back. "Oh, she has you convinced, does she?"

André's jaw tightened.

"She won't last," James said. "Blakely House won't coddle her the way she's used to, and she'll hightail it out on her own."

"We'll all watch her blow away like a linen scarf in a sea gale," said Jinedath. "End over end." The men laughed uproariously. "With all her scattered thoughts tumbling after her."

More laughter.

André lifted the box of gathered tools, tucking it beneath

one arm, and gave a salute to the men as he exited. Still his chest did not ease, even in the master's workroom, where the muffled quiet usually calmed him. He shuffled through the contracts, his heart pounding again at the chaos. The reckless disorder was an accurate picture of the estate's condition in general, especially in finances. Patent applications never sent in, invoices halfway filled out, and dozens and dozens of unopened letters covered the surface.

"You cannot expect my desk to be tidier than my mind, André," the master had said once, smoothing one giant hand across a polished clock movement. "It is brimming with so many—oh, where's that caster? Here, here." He'd flicked his fingers over his shoulder, requesting a fresh sheet of drafting paper. "What if we did parallel braces on that repeater rather than perpendicular?" He'd turned in that squeaky chair, his blinking eyes magnified by the ridiculous gold spectacles. André had remained at his side, ready to offer any tool or word of advice he needed.

Now all that remained of their partnership, all those hours spent working side by side, was one small envelope, still sealed. André sifted through the chaos until he found it again. *André Montagne* was printed across it, in that familiar handwriting. He thumbed the intact seal on the back, wondering if he should open it. He'd put it off until they'd found his body. Then until the burial. But now, he had no excuse for not opening the very last word he'd ever receive from the great industrialist.

Except it meant the end. If he left it sealed, he still had a letter to read from him one day.

No one else could possibly understand what the world had lost. Emmett Sinclair had brought power, a flood of light, to the entire Northumberland coast. His hydraulic cranes, which could lift several tons of cargo onto waiting steam liners, had turned Northumberland into one of the most effective shipping centers this side of the channel. In short, he'd waved his magic wand and left Northumberland teeming with light and life.

But now with Emmett dead, the spell was wearing off. Two of the three hydraulic cranes had broken down, and the generator converting power from the waterwheels had lost function several times. And the only person with enough knowledge to fix them . . . was the late master himself.

Emmett Sinclair had had a certain magical effect on everything he touched. From lawless pirates to piles of steel and wire, he had effortlessly set things and people into useful motion. Suffused the idle and inert with purpose.

André ran his hand over the leather-backed chair on castors, easily recalling the man's shoulders hunched against the brass studs. The leather had molded to its master so that no one else could possibly belong in that chair. Sometimes he'd pause, squeaking back in it, staring at nothing, but seeing a great deal with his mind.

André's parents had been fickle, changing locations, changing positions. Changing where he lived, and usually it was not with them. When they had died, his father first and then his mother, they simply vanished as if they'd never been. No family home, no real belongings, few ties to any community save the theater world, and their names on playbills were the only evidence they'd ever lived.

And him, of course.

But Emmett Sinclair had left his mark upon Blakely House as clearly as the indent on his chair. This office, the cluttered desk, had been so very *him*, and André had left it brimming with gadgets, just as it was. He hadn't even been able to bring himself to sit in Sinclair's chair. Though the staff looked to André as the natural head of their late master's affairs, there was something sacred about this little space. When Emmett Sinclair sat in this chair, all was right in the world. The anchor was down, the storm would blow past.

His absence was felt so keenly in this house.

André had experienced very few personal losses over the years after his parents' deaths, since he'd attached himself to almost nothing. He supposed this was what grief felt like, and he made room for it in his soul. Invited it to stay and drink its fill for a time, unwelcome as it was. A thick, uncomfortable quiet that made him feel nearly human again.

Click-click-click. He cringed as he heard Miss Forrester's quick little footsteps—for no ex-adventurer walked about that way—then he stiffened as she burst into his quiet with rose-cheeked energy and a mission of some sort, wraps draped over her arm. "Splendid, you've not left yet."

He turned as she entered. "Miss Forrester." She hardly looked like a violent woman, but there was something guarded about her—something disguised or duplicitous. She talked in circles as if avoiding the truth, and she never looked him in the eye.

"I've brought my cloak and extra boots as well. A few small watchmaker tools, but I don't suppose those will do any good. Shall I find a scarf too?" She shoved a delicate old hurricane lamp around—one he'd spent hours piecing back together after it had shattered.

He clasped his wooden hand behind his back to keep from yanking the lamp away. He forced a polite smile. "You are leaving for home then, m'lady?" She'd want a transport to Northumberland, of course. But at least she'd be gone.

She plopped into the master's chair and spun it about,

squeaking it as she bounced and fingered the desk pulls, the engravings, every blessed thing. "Oh no," she breathed. "I thought I might accompany you."

His stomach fell to his boots. "Accompany me?"

"Yes. See to the repairs. If I'm to have any grasp of this estate and all its inventions, I must begin to understand them firsthand."

"No, I think not. But you are kind to offer." His smile was tight. If she went, it'd turn into a nursemaid position for him. But . . . it would also give him ample time to catch her in a slipup. To uncover important information.

"I've heard no one has been able to repair it yet." She twirled the feather of a quill pen on the desk, then poked an automatic wax seal applicator. "What is this?"

"No one understands his machines as well as I do. It would be best if I work on them by myself."

"It can't hurt to have another person look it over."

He pursed his lips. "I work best alone."

"You haven't had the right sort of help." Leaning back, she set the chair spinning.

"Until now, of course." He schooled his emotions.

"Right! So you'll let me come?"

A breath. "I don't believe you'd enjoy it."

"But I *may* come, if I choose to." She spun about in the chair to face him. "Yes?"

His jaw tightened. "I suppose I cannot stop you."

With a small squeal of glee, she spun again.

Thunk. Ink poured everywhere. He leaped to the desk and righted the inkpot, then applied a handkerchief, blotting frantically at the sticky blackness dripping over the papers, the feather pens, the tiny palm-sized gadgets.

"Oh! Oh, I'm so sorry." She froze, hands framing her pale cheeks.

A sickness. A tight pit in his stomach. He snatched the envelope—the precious unopened envelope addressed to him—and held it by the corner as thick ink dripped off it. His name was obscured. The soaked edges curled. With a long, low sigh, he dropped the thing—just paper, after all—on the blotter and turned away. One big breath, then two. Paper. Just paper.

She merely sat dumbfounded, staring down at the ruinous mess she'd left behind, waiting for him to clean up after her. He tried to scrape off the ink with his hand, sorting through and rescuing other papers where he could.

Her voice was unsteady. Delicate. "I didn't see it. That jar was buried, and I—I only bumped it a little. It's such an untidy desk. One cannot possibly be expected to—"

"It isn't *your* desk." His words tasted like shards. He wouldn't let his eyes land on that unopened letter—the one that had caught most of the ink.

"I'm so very sorry. Let me make it up to you by helping with the repair. Please."

chapter
ELEVEN

S he didn't chatter endlessly, at least. In fact, she went
through bouts of silence that made him feel as if he were
journeying in the boat alone. And she still wouldn't meet
his eyes—almost as if she couldn't. Each time she averted her
gaze, or glanced quickly down at the floor of the boat, he could
feel her duplicity. His seaman's instincts had dulled, but they
were sparking to life again.

They took the estate's fishing vessel to Northumberland,
then a hackney to the quayside operations. When the bustling
city captured her attention out the window, André allowed
himself a surveying glance of this woman who had supposedly
murdered his master.

There were no sharp edges to her. She was all warmth and
gentle curves, a radiant eagerness and curiosity usually re-
served for the young. She had her hair done up in that wispy
Gibson Girl style, and somehow it fit her. "You're a relation
through your father, then?"

"My mother." She kept her gaze glued to the window. "I was

given her surname at birth since the man who raised me . . . well, he wasn't actually my father. Other than sharing a name, I know very little about the Forresters or the rest of her family, so this came as a surprise."

"What has she told you about Emmett Sinclair?"

"Nothing, actually."

"She did not care much for her uncle."

"It was me she did not care for." She stared out the window. "She left when I was barely walking."

A slight tug at his chest, but he shook it away.

Actress. She was an actress, even if this detail was true. "'Tis a pity. If she was anything like her uncle, she'd be worth knowing." He cringed at the unintentional insult, but the woman didn't seem to notice.

She glanced his way and tipped her head. "You cared for him immensely."

"I've not met his equal." He straightened his back against the buttoned leather. "If the man caught wind of a problem, anyone's problem, he'd fix it. He must have created hundreds of gadgets, all quite brilliant. I regret deeply that his life was ended—what might he have accomplished with a few more years' time? Had he been allowed to live . . ." His voice drifted off, allowing her to ruminate, to regret perhaps, and she seemed to. A flicker of discomfort flitted across her features.

Then they were nearing the quay and his chest swelled at the sight of Sinclair's machines—behemoths that towered above the ships they loaded. Only now, those tall, slender giants stood still, swaying slightly in the sea breeze.

When they disembarked, five men emerged from the noisy chaos of the docks, faces edged with grim politeness. "Mr. Montagne." Mr. Guthrie, if he recalled correctly, gave a quick nod and did not extend his hand. He looked more than a little vexed. "I had hoped Mr. Sinclair himself would be around to repair it. A shame about his passing."

André swallowed the fizzle of resentment at the man's insulted demeanor. As if he blamed Emmett Sinclair for having the audacity to die and leave the man without his quayside magician. "I am acting in his stead, and I hope the replacement is satisfactory."

The man eyed him, running a thumb over the top of his cane. "He never mentioned this was a possibility."

"It's enormous," breathed a feminine voice behind him, and he turned to see Miss Forrester staring up at the crane that towered nearly three stories over them. "Simply enormous. What does it do?"

André shoved his hands into his pockets, vacillating between annoyance at her intrusive presence and pride at her awe. "It's a hydraulic crane. It loads cargo onto the ships."

"It's meant to, anyhow." Guthrie turned, arms folded, and stalked toward the edge of the dock where the crane was bolted to metal plates on the pier's frame. André followed him. "Two weeks now, this monstrosity has been inoperable. Barely lifts the cargo above my head, and it has dropped several costly crates of goods. I won't be paying on the contract until it's fully operational again, which I hope will be today."

Worry tightened across André's shoulders. "I shall do my best, sir."

"What's wrong with it, then?" she asked, squinting at the inert giant.

André shored up his frustration. "It has lost power."

He turned, but her voice drew him back with a jerk. "But *why* has it lost power?"

A deep breath. "Likely there's a leak in the hydraulics or . . . something. Stay here. I'll return for you." Gritting his teeth, André sprinted over the pier and leaped up the ladder, using the crook of his bad arm to anchor himself to each rung until he reached the base where the crane was anchored onto its metal platform.

Standing beneath the tons of metal, he stared at the massive cylinder and pulleys that normally surged with power, suddenly struck with his own smallness. A helplessness that he, a former ship captain and lauded adventurer, would never grow used to feeling. He let his damaged left arm hang uselessly at his side and ran his other hand up and down the cylinder, feeling for broken pieces or missing valves.

Nothing.

No liquid on the docks either, which meant no leak in the hydraulics.

Two men climbed into the control booth below, eyes on him expectantly, ready to test out the machine when—no, *if*— he managed to locate and repair the problem. He felt around again, then he ran and leaped, hooked his broken limb on the crane's scaffolding, and climbed the metal arm toward the topmost joint where the pulleys arched and traveled downward along the second and third cylinders.

With his good hand he pulled himself up, feeling strength and power surge through his underused muscles, remembering as he gazed out at the ships in the wet, blustery sea air, what it was like to scale the masts. To climb with two hands instead of one, and to be master of a hulking wooden beast.

But more than that, he remembered what it was to explore new worlds from the deck of his ship. For his eyes to fall on new and exotic sights every day. A vibrant array of voices, clothing, aromas, and lush, leafy foliage covered the world, but now he lived and worked in one small speck of it. Any corner of the world grew stale if one remained in it for too long, banging about the same walls, hearing the same voices speaking the same thoughts.

Taking in a gulp of wet air, he lashed himself to the metal crane near the top with his bad arm and felt around with the other, tugging at the pulleys that seemed taut still, feeling about the cylinder for any explanation.

He sighed. Emmett Sinclair would have already had it fixed. He'd have poked about, mumbling odd little phrases and scrunching his nose, then eventually there would be a surge of life under his magical hands, and the machine would stir and rise in full power to its task.

No such magic occurred at André's touch. After a few more moments of wonderful breeze cooling his skin, André climbed down and faced Mr. Guthrie. "The problem isn't in the hydraulic arms."

"Well, then." The man rocked back on his heels. "I'd like you to see to its removal within the week."

Removal. Of a one-hundred-fifty-ton machine? The stub of his left arm throbbed from the climb. "That won't be necessary." Or possible, really. Dismantling the thing would take more men than Blakely House had just then, and the loss of that royalty payment—it might break the estate completely.

He tried not to picture the house and its delicate gadgetry being scattered to the waves the way his ship once was, debris washing up on the beach. "I'll need a little more time for—"

Hisssss. Clunk!

A flood of water gurgled through pipes, through cylinders. The valves clunked as water hit them with force.

". . . for that. A little more time for that."

Men yelled from the control box. A deep metal groaning. Everyone spun and Mr. Guthrie's face tipped back, back, back until he was staring up at the crane's long arm now stretching awake with all cylinders firing and the base rotating smoothly from shipside to dock.

André braced himself on the shuddering pier, again feeling the immensity of Emmett Sinclair and the magic he must be working, even from the grave.

"So you managed to fix it." Guthrie folded his arms. A little tic jerked his jaw. "I suppose you'll want your royalties now."

André blinked, looking at the crane hovering above them. He wasn't even certain what to check over before he left. What to verify. The machine might stop working again eight seconds after he turned his back. "Not for the last two weeks, of course. Going forward, yes—I suppose so." He swallowed. By some miracle, if the mysterious repair did hold, the pay would be very welcome in Blakely House's ledgers.

Burying his shock, André turned and caught sight of the guest who had invited herself on this errand. She was hurrying, face eager, from where he'd left her. "It's working!" she cried.

He'd forgotten all about her.

"What's she doing here?" Guthrie waved toward Miss Forrester, who now joined them, staring up at the groaning, hissing crane. "The docks aren't a fit place for your wife, Mr. Montagne."

"This is Miss Forrester, a guest at Blakely House." He clenched his teeth, neck suddenly hot. "She insisted . . . that is, we shall be leaving presently." How would it go if he had to introduce her as the new master of Blakely House?

André hurried to the carriage after some gruff parting words to Mr. Guthrie, bundling his charge into the seat and heaving a giant exhale. "Well, now you've seen it." He banged his forearm against the roof of the carriage and the vehicle lurched into motion. "Was it worth troubling yourself?"

"Indeed." Her bright face looked out at the crane, watching it work.

Only then did he realize what had actually happened back there—it was the wet gloves she was peeling off that gave her away, but even then, he couldn't believe what he was seeing. He frowned at the subtle dark smears on her apron and her skin. He hadn't noticed with such coarse material, but her frock was quite wet.

She paused and blinked at him.

It wasn't possible . . . was it? "You—you repaired it."

She shrugged. "Mere conjecture. Not exactly an anagnorisis, just a fortunate guess."

"Anag . . ." Those words fit her like the oversized apron always doubled around her waist.

Her eyes flicked upward with a sigh of long-suffering. "You know, the realization. When the heroine discovers something that helps her solve the story problem. Truly, it was mere luck."

"And you fixed it." He blinked. Swallowed. The magic touch. She had Emmett Sinclair's magic touch. In André's experience that only came from one source. "No luck about it. God has blessed you with great skill, Miss Forrester."

At this, she bristled. "Is it so impossible that I used my own faculties to arrive at the solution? Why must everything be attributed to some unseen divinity—or a *man*?"

"Your intellect came from somewhere."

"Yes. My own *head*."

He paused a beat, stepping hesitantly into uncharted territory. "Surely you believe in God, Miss Forrester."

She pressed her lips and ducked her gaze.

He stiffened. "You do *not* believe."

"I don't understand him, I suppose. Not the way one understands a clock's motion by taking it apart and looking at it. I'm simply too practical to stand on a ledge I cannot see." She sighed. "Give me anything with gears and pinions and I shall tell you all about it."

He leaned back, looking over her rumpled garments, that ridiculously oversized apron. "What exactly was your 'lucky' guess?"

"It was that tower on the other side of the dock. Up at the top a little lever was stuck."

The float switch. He hadn't even bothered to look at the accumulator. He'd looked over every inch of the machine and forgotten the giant tower of water that supplied the water pressure, and thus every inch of the machine's power. And it was only a tiny sensor mechanism with a cork floating on the surface, regulating the water level and power, which had set off all this trouble.

He gritted his teeth. Perhaps it was for the best he wasn't captaining a ship anymore. Yet this plainly garbed slip of a woman . . . "You climbed up four flights of steps? To make a guess?"

She shrugged. "The tower door was open. I only meant to peek."

He breathed in and let it out, attempting to meet her flitting gaze. "Why?"

"You said it was broken." She clung to the window, seemingly unimpressed with her "lucky guess." "There is always a reason. I wanted to find it. I'll sleep better now."

"So, it's a riddle to you?"

"Much as I enjoy a corner you can't quite see around, or a suspenseful chapter ending, or—a door. A door that *must* be opened. Like the one in Blakely House. There's a door that opens on its own and I couldn't resist seeing why."

"Many of the doors at Blakely House are rigged to open and close automatically. With a trigger switch, actually, but perhaps one malfunctioned."

"Cousin Dane said as much, but I'm not certain. I looked at it this morning and I couldn't find anything the matter with it. Which is even more intriguing. But then again, there's a clock in my suite that I cannot repair either, so perhaps it's simply the inventions I do not understand."

He steered her quickly back to the subject at hand, like yanking a ship's rudder back in the right direction. "The accumulator, Miss Forrester. Tell me exactly what made you think to climb those tower steps." Especially when he'd told her quite clearly to stay put.

"It's . . . well, the path of power." She faced him again, face alight with what he'd mistakenly deemed flightiness before. "Energy always follows a path—in a motor, inside a clock, or in this crane. You must find . . . well, wherever the path is broken. Where the power stops. You were following it forward to the tip of the machine, so I went backward and found the tower. It truly wasn't complicated."

Indeed.

"You let the men assume I'd been the one to repair it." He frowned. "Why?"

She reddened. "It wasn't my intention to deceive anyone. It's only that . . . people find anything unusual—such as a woman repairing machines—to be remarkable." A quick sigh. "And I'm rather weary of being remarked upon."

He stared at her profile. She was used to deflecting credit, almost like a reflex. That much, at least, was not an act. The way she'd stumbled to explain herself, it was clear she wasn't asked to do it often.

Yet she'd risen to defend her intellect when he'd tried to attribute it to God. What a curious mix of pride and humility.

"You're staring."

He smiled. "Perhaps I enjoy riddles too."

"I'm no riddle."

He shrugged. "At times you say many words. Other times you are quiet."

"Only on the outside." She sighed. "Inside, it's like the streets of London at coronation time. Utter chaos, all moving in different directions at the same time. Lots of yelling and flashes of color everywhere."

"What sort of celebration is going on in your head, Miss Forrester?"

"There's an awful lot of thoughts packed in there, and they simply shoot around, bouncing around in my skull and building up like pressure in a pot. Sometimes they spill out. You know, I'm glad I haven't a hinge on my head because opening it might prove explosive."

He laughed, and she shrugged. He knew one thing—she was clever. Dangerously so, perhaps. He couldn't decide if that made her a terrible heiress for Blakely House . . . or the perfect fit.

He couldn't release her from his mind for the remainder of that day. Still, he didn't *mean* to spy upon her, but the situation forced itself upon him. Much like Sydney Forrester herself.

He'd been back at Blakely House for several quiet hours when a backward step ignited an unnatural squeak and howl. He had spun to see an orange and white ball of fluff dart off—with a limp, pausing to shake its leg. And its tail was a crooked stub curling in quick jerks to the left.

Had he broken her cat?

With a groan he reached for the little creature, but it shot away.

Rotten little overstuffed rodent.

A glance out the tall drawing room window told him Miss Forrester still walked outside, circling the grounds for fresh air. She disappeared beyond the hedgerow—too far to call out to her.

The kitty darted, its limp more pronounced. With a loud exhale, André followed the creature with long strides that only made it dart faster, all the way up the stairs to the safety of the owl suite. "Here, kitty. Here!" André wasn't well-versed in animal care. What could he possibly do if he caught the thing, anyway? Mend a ripped sail or pound in a new nail?

A loud, plaintive howl drove him on. "Come here, won't you?" Under the night table. In the wardrobe. Where was the little blighter? Another howl had André scurrying into the adjoining sitting room where two marble-green eyes watched him from beneath the overstuffed chair by the window.

"There you are." Approaching at an angle to block his escape, André knelt and scooped up the kitty—a rather large, pillowy creature who couldn't have worked a day in his life.

To his surprise, the animal didn't claw his way to freedom or even struggle. He merely looked up at him with big, pitiful eyes, as if trying to manipulate André into something . . . and purred. "You're a scoundrel, aren't you?"

A mournful *rowr* was his answer. More purring.

André felt the fuzzy tail first, then the hurt leg. The tail, it seemed, had already been a short, crooked stub. His leg seemed merely sensitive to the touch. All was intact.

The diagnosis—feline dramatics.

He exhaled in relief just as voices floated in from the corridor. Ladies' voices. André was stricken at once with the significance of his presence in their guest's personal bedchambers, and how mortifyingly invasive that was. How very inappropriate.

All for a rotten cat.

The door to the connecting bedchamber flew open and two women entered, talking excitedly. Urgency drained his logic, and André twisted around toward the window. Filmy curtains, glass china hutch . . . *window seat.* Lifting the lid, he folded himself easily into the empty space and crouched there, waiting—still holding the cat, he then realized.

Hopefully they wouldn't have much to say.

"I'm so relieved we can speak freely now," Miss Forrester was saying. "Come, Aunt Lottie. They call this the owl suite."

"How lovely, Syd. Why, it's like a sunny forest. Now, come and tell me everything. Absolutely everything."

André gulped and braced to hear everything he wasn't meant to.

chapter
TWELVE

What wandering hearts like yours do not realize, dearest, is that the "somewhere else" you seek is not to be found on this earth—especially since restlessness fits neatly into one's steamer trunk and goes along on every journey we take in life.

~*Emmett's letters to Sophie*

I was shaking to look at her, that familiar face in unfamiliar surroundings. Nerves. Excitement. Homesickness. All of it in excess. "Oh Aunt Lottie, I'm so glad you've come. How did you manage the expense?"

"I have some things of value, don't I?"

I grabbed her arm. "What did you sell?"

"I merely gave Daniel's pocket watch to the grocer for safekeeping. In exchange for the cost of a train ticket."

I groaned.

A box sprang open at Aunt Lottie's elbow. She cried out and batted the spring-loaded jack-in-the-box away.

I slammed the lid shut and guided her to a settee. "I could not live here alone. There are so many odd noises and—well, at least I have Micah."

"You've brought your cat—here? That would explain where he's been these past days."

"Of course I did. I couldn't bear to leave him behind."

Hurt instantly crossed her features.

My brain scrambled to pinpoint the reason. "I suppose I should have asked you before absconding with Micah. He *is* your cat, after all."

She straightened, forcing a smile. "He most certainly is *not*. I may have chosen him, my dear, but he has quite clearly chosen you. Besides, every girl needs a little comfort in a new place. He is adjusting well, I hope?"

"Oh yes." My heart lightened. "Yes, quite well." I glanced about the room. "Micah? Micah, where are you, little bear?"

A *thump*. An odd noise from near the window. I ran to it and looked, but no orange cat appeared, inside or out. I returned to the settee. "That's odd. He's always about. It's still a strange place to him, of course, but—"

A warm hand slid over mine. "Sydney."

My chatter disintegrated.

"We must speak plainly. Tell me what's happened. Why have you left home and come all the way out here?"

I explained the letters and the visit, the promised inheritance and how it could save the shop. I felt a fresh surge of determination to rescue her the way she once had me. "I know you don't wish me to know about the debts, but I do, and I want to help. I *will* help. This could be the exact way providence means to hand us out of this mess, Aunt Lottie. Truly."

"You know I don't believe in providence, Syd." That pained look stretched over her features.

Again, with the talk of God. I shifted on the settee. "God, then. If that's what you choose to believe." She had her whimsies and flights of fancy, perhaps more than I did. Whereas I enjoyed fantastical novels and the like, Aunt Lottie outright put her real-life trust in a being that had, it seemed, little bearing on daily life. "You know how I am, Aunt Lottie. My mind simply doesn't function that way."

That set look came over her face and I knew. Knew I'd be on the receiving end of a lecture. Three . . . two . . . one . . .

She merely pressed her lips together, dimples blooming on each cheek. "And?"

I raised my eyebrows.

"I know you, Sydney Forrester. You're a mathematician, but there's something deeper to this doubt. So what is it?"

I dropped my gaze. My skin warmed. Blazes! This was worse than a lecture.

"You used to believe." She said it quietly.

"Yes, well." I pulled my knees up to my chest. "I was a child. I did what I was told." I sighed. "But when my father died, I pleaded with God for my mother. *Pleaded.*" My hand shook. "Ten years later, I'm still waiting."

With a little sob, she threw her arms around me. "You deserve so much better, dear one. So much. If only she knew what she's missed all these years. I don't understand it either."

Her warmth wrapped around me, around my anger, though it tried to surface. But in the familiar embrace the internal war melted away. I simply sank into the lilac scent of her, the softness of her hair on my cheek, exactly as it had been the day I'd arrived on her doorstep, clinging to the hand of a former neighbor I barely knew. I'd been barely twelve years old. I remember how I'd jumped when the man had dropped my bag with a thud, and I felt as if I, too, had been dropped.

And I had. For no one, after Father died, had wanted me.

When Aunt Lottie answered the door, my neighbor, who had taken temporary responsibility for this now-homeless waif, laid it out in painfully blunt terms. Father dead. Mother ran away years ago. She was the only relative he could locate from the letters about the house, so now, he guessed, I was *her* responsibility. Even though her brother hadn't even set eyes on her since he'd taken up with my mother.

Aunt Lottie had stood there, cross as a provoked rooster, looking from me to the bag, then the man, horrified. I had cringed, wishing I could climb into myself and disappear. She didn't want me either. But I later discovered this petite, sharp, rather opinionated woman was put out with the adults in my life. Not with the little girl dropped on her stoop.

We'd gone inside that cluttered shop with its ticking clocks and I was brave. Dull. Impervious to pain. But then, before a crackling warm fire, she embraced me and my tears broke loose. Hot, thick, wet. Unstoppable. She had let them come.

She did now too. Her nearness loosened something in me and any pretense of boldness leaked away. "Oh how I've missed you, Aunt Lottie. I'm no good at life without you." I hugged her hard.

"I could hardly stand it, trying to figure out where you'd gone. Now for the answer to the question that's plagued me for days—why on *earth* didn't you tell me?" She held me away, and tears sparkled in her eyes, leaking down her cheeks.

This winded me. Gears and mechanics I could understand. But emotions?

I sat back and closed my eyes, letting out a breath. "I was

afraid you'd talk me out of it. I had to talk myself *into* it as it was, and my will on the matter was precarious at best. Easily reversed. But then where would we be? How desperately we need this inheritance." I steadied my breath and opened my eyes. "I've never done this before—had an adventure. I'm afraid I'm not very good at it. But I needed to do it. I want to help." I looked at her so she couldn't lie. "It's quite a desperate situation, isn't it? The debt. The notes."

"It isn't *your* job to save it, Syd. It's my shop—"

I frowned. "*Our* shop." Her words bruised my heart.

"Our shop, but my debts. You won't be saddled with it. I've made certain of it."

"It's not being saddled to, but anchored by. And it's not the shop." I looked at her face, the familiar dimples that appeared when she licked her lips. "It's you."

Her angry expression melted, and I thought she'd wrap me in her arms again, but she merely swept her hand tenderly along my cheek. "You can come back with me right now, Syd. We'll make do. We always—"

A *thud.* She spun.

"Mercy, did that window seat *move*?" Aunt Lottie rose, eyes glued to the cushioned seat before the large window. "Why in heaven's name would you stay in this place, Syd?"

"I know, it's all very Alice through the Looking Glass. Things move that shouldn't, surprises around every bend . . ."

She threw me a look that restated her question. *Why?*

I steadied my gaze on her. *Please understand.* "I needed to leave Grafton, Aunt. I needed to come here."

"You're overlooking one important fact, dearest." She squeezed my hands. "When you run away from your problems, you take yourself with you. It won't be the fix you hope."

"It's more than that. There is something magical about this place, Aunt Lottie. All my life I've been peculiar. I'm used to standing out. I shall always be scatterbrained, disorganized, odd, and awkward. A clock missing pieces. But here, where everything is odd . . ."

She pressed her lips together, eyebrows lifting.

"Walking into Blakely House for the first time . . . it felt as if I'd stepped inside my own brain. Scattered. Disorganized. Brimming with wild and unusual things. It didn't simply feel like home, but like *me*." I glanced about. "Odd as I am, Aunt Lottie, Blakely House is more so. And I find that rather perfect."

"I see." Her smile was quick and genuine. Glistening with tears. "Then you shall have it."

"Well." I fidgeted. "It may not be that simple."

"Is there a dispute over the will?"

"A bit."

Her eyebrows rose again.

"Just a problem with probate matters."

"Sydney."

I explained about my new cousins, and how clever and educated they were. How easily they could run me out of the inheritance, and that they believed it to be theirs.

"That's nothing. You're brilliant, Syd. They don't stand a chance against you."

"There is one other small complication." I took a breath. "They seem to believe that maybe, perhaps . . . well, that I've sort of killed our uncle."

"You've *what*?" She shot up, cheeks pink.

"Yes, something to do with the inheritance." My pulse was racing. I couldn't look at her. "But you know, it's all rather silly.

They'll soon find they have no proof. It's a matter of time, of course. Micah!" I rose, hustling about the room. "Micah, where *are* you?" He had a built-in sensor, always knowing intuitively when I needed him. Clearly, it was broken. "Micah Bear!"

A *thunk*, once again by the window.

"He must be over here somewhere." I perched on the window seat, peering at the ledges just outside.

Aunt Lottie strode over with a smile and sat beside me. The window seat squeaked beneath her added weight. "Now tell me something, Sydney. You've come to a house full of men. Unattached and—"

"No. No, don't even think it, Aunt. You are only allowed to play matchmaker in Grafton."

"So I have your blessing when you return, then?"

"Now, listen here. I didn't—"

"The butler. Tell me about the butler, Syd. Isn't he smashing?"

I huffed, cheeks burning. "Please, Aunt. Not him."

"I couldn't decide about him. I liked him straightaway when he admitted me into the house, but he has the look of the devil about him too. Rather intense and perhaps too handsome for his own good." She brought her lips to my ear and whispered, "Which is exactly why you're smitten with him, isn't it?" She winked.

My skin warmed, head to toe. "Don't you dare say such things around him. He'll think I have ideas."

"Oh, but you have!"

I huffed, fanning my warm face with a blank paper. "You cannot possibly know a person from a glance. You've not been here around him as I have. Wait until I tell you how it has been."

"I'm all ears." She leaned forward, hands perched on her knees. "He vanished the moment he brought me into the drawing room, and I cannot imagine why. Does he do that often? So mysterious of him," she said with a twinkle in her eyes.

"He's not mysterious, he's . . . he's rancorous and enervating and as supercilious as he is perspicacious."

"Rancorous, now?" Her eyes twinkled, and my face warmed.

Perhaps I'd gone a bit far, but ordinary words wouldn't sufficiently describe a pirate.

I handled her scheming the way I always did. "Come." I sprang up from the window seat, nearly knocking off the lid. "Let me show you the real reason I wish to stay." Then I simply strode out the door, hoping she'd follow.

And she did. Thankfully. Across the landing and through the portrait gallery, I slowed and pointed out Blakely House's late master. "That's him, by the way. Rather a bulldog of a man. He doesn't *seem* mad, but perhaps a little grouchy. Anyway, that's what the legendary recluse looks like."

She squinted. Crouched to inspect. "No, it isn't."

"What do you mean?"

She ran her fingertip over a fine engraving along the bottom of the frame, tucked beneath the curve—a name. "It says here this is Sir Charles Magnus Sinclair." She paused before several of the others, then stopped before the face that had first drawn me. The hopeful, inviting countenance. "*This* is Emmett Sinclair."

I stood before it, looked him in the eyes, and ran my own finger over the name tucked into the bottom curve of the frame. "So it *is* you." Something in me had recognized him immediately, on that first day, which I found wonderfully fascinating.

Also interesting was the realization that Dane Hutchcraft had lied to me about which one he was. I couldn't think why, though.

We continued down the stairs. "I can have tea sent in, if you'd like." I bit the inside of my cheek. "I *think* the servants will bring some."

We stepped onto the plush rug of the armory, and instantly, a dozen suits of armor snapped to attention along the wall. Each saluted as we passed by, metal glove clinking against helmet.

Aunt Lottie ducked, eyeing the metal men suspiciously. "Oddities do abound in this place." Then we entered the drawing room, and she tipped her head back to look up at the domed ceiling with angels carved into plaster.

With a pounding pulse, I reached the workshop door and pushed it open, revealing the very heart and soul of Blakely House—Emmett Sinclair's workshop.

Mouth open, eyes wide, she was sufficiently awed. "Oh Syd, what a marvel. Simply astounding."

"It's perfect, isn't it? Aren't you surprised?"

"Perhaps a mite jealous too." She wandered through, touching a long gold telescope, marveling with a half smile at a metal forearm and hand wrapped in half a dozen timepieces around the wrist and fingers. She bumped against a bellows and it inflated and exhaled, spinning loose gears that worked a half-broken marionette. "Who in their right mind would dream up some of these things? And to not finish them!" She shook her head.

I clutched my hands before me, my face heating considerably. "Quite a mess, I suppose."

Much like my mind at times. Most times, actually.

No, all the time.

Like now. Thoughts skittered like scared rabbits, bounding off in all directions, down holes and into the woods.

Aunt Lottie paused, gaze wandering the room. "All of this tucked away on its own little island I never would have guessed existed."

I crossed my arms over my chest. "How *did* you know where to find me?"

"The letter from Mrs. Holligan. You left it out on your bed table. You're rather a rotten runaway, as it turns out." She smiled at me, then looked about the room.

"Oh! Oh my!" I turned and Aunt Lottie was kneeling before the automaton, stroking his cheek. "Will you look at this!"

"He's a wonder, isn't he?"

"It's . . . it's an automaton, yes?"

I beamed, nerves untangling. "It is."

"What is he meant to do?" She lifted his hand, running one fingertip down the length of his arm and fingers. "Never in my life . . ."

"That's the mystery. No one knows, and they've all tried working on him."

"And my Sydney will untangle it and make him work again."

"There's no *again*, Aunt. He was never completed."

She rose and turned to take my hands, eyes sparkling. "Until now."

"Come, let's see about a guest suite for the night." I looped my arm in hers. "You'll need to rest after rowing yourself here."

She laughed, a familiar almost floral sound. "Why ever would I row myself here? I simply waited for low tide and walked across the causeway. Why it's . . ." She blinked at me. "You *did* know about the causeway, didn't you?"

Of course not. Because it was me. And I seemed to naturally do everything the hard way. I bit my lip.

"Well, then." Her smile was bright. "There you are, we learn something new every day."

I laughed, a glorious release of tension. Oh how I needed Aunt Lottie's visit. And how desperately I wished it would last forever.

But peace still eluded me. Especially at night. I'd always had a fickle relationship with sleep, my brain having no circuit breaker by which to switch off the power. Any little thing wound it like a clock, and the moment Aunt Lottie closed our adjoining door, it went to work.

"It's an automaton, yes?"

"What is he meant to do?"

"My Sydney will make him work again."

The mechanical man had a striking beauty all his own. Smoothly polished, complex . . . and bearing a presence like a kindly human being, hoping someone might recognize his untapped potential and coax him to life. I'd dubbed him Fitzhugh, because somehow a name made him seem more human. More in need of a rescue.

I lay in that lonely owl chamber, nerves buzzing as if wired for electricity, until I felt a calm steal over me. Something . . . some sound . . .

Music. Deep within the house someone played a pianoforte. A languid tranquility swept over my body, stilling my thoughts. Restoring my mind. Then pulling me sharply awake. Music didn't belong in this house—who would be playing it, a pirate?

The automaton, that's who. Yes! That's what the mechanical man had been designed for, with those jointed fingers and that delicate precision.

So it was that at nearly four of the morning, before dawn warmed the windowsills, I gave up on sleep, dressed, and crept down to revisit the remarkable Sir Fitzhugh.

chapter
THIRTEEN

Men have opinions on how things "ought" to work, but only a machine's creator understands the full breadth of the potential he placed within his creation, and only he can wake it.

~Sophie's letters to Emmett

B ut the house had other plans. I had gathered a filmy robe about me, for the chill stole through my thin shirtwaist and camisole. The garment that had been laid at the foot of my bed floated about me like flower petals sewn together. I felt rather like a fairy in a book as I made my way downstairs and through the drawing room.

The door to the workroom held fast. Locked.

I hurried back to the stairs to fetch my key, but two steps up, the stairs collapsed with a *thunk*, flattening beneath my feet. I slid down with a small cry and fumbled for the banister, scrambling to keep my footing. I breathed and looked around the shadows for an explanation.

But this was Blakely House. There wasn't one.

I took a deep breath and put a hand to my pounding heart. *If the house doesn't like you, it'll let you know.* It was trying to eject me. To kick me out and lock the doors behind me.

The distinctive *pop-pop-pop* of footsteps on marble sounded . . . somewhere. They quickened into a sprint. And the question billowed up around me like a sparkle of dust on the breeze—*who?* I squinted into the darkness for a moment, expecting to see a chase. I edged forward. Even in my robe, I wasn't missing this.

But the sound faded, all fell silent.

I wandered the labyrinth of halls and doors and oddly placed narrow staircases. I poked into rooms and gaped at shiny contraptions until a faraway plunking sound caught my ear. It was the box—that lovely music box from the front room. But unless I'd completely lost my way, it was coming from a different place.

I tiptoed through the halls, scanning for the box. One door stood ajar, a small lamp glowing in the far corner, and the music box was opened and playing on a table.

An invitation.

I approached the room carefully. I half expected to see the master bent over a machine, eagerly waiting for me to come speak with him at last. But the room lay still and empty, draped in shadows. It was, of all things, an art studio. A cramped little office with easels set up at every angle.

I entered with my breath held, feeling invasive and meddlesome in so messy and intimate a room. But also wildly curious. Large papers lay spread over every surface—quick, unfinished sketches but with careful strokes. Clear pencil hashes that lent elaborate shading and dimension, giving each the appearance of a photograph rather than a rendering. A very deliberate, artistic mind had created these—Emmett, the madman?

The first sketch was a duck. A puff of feathers was blowing off the creature's body, revealing a steel clockwork design beneath. Hydraulic rods extended through the length of the wing where bone might have been, and a tiny pinion gear was nestled in its shoulder blades as a steering mechanism for the wings.

The next was a giraffe with the long neck of a crane, and a pulley system running along the neck to raise and lower its head. Clock gears hinged every joint.

Running my fingertips over the giraffe sketch, an idea formed about Fitzhugh, the automaton. I traced the path of power along the giraffe's body and up the neck and—

Click.

A lamp flicked on, its stained-glass shade glowing colors. I shivered in the cool night air, a draft seeping like specters through old windows. "Who's there?"

The lamp's table was littered with sketches and jotted notes that I did not stop to inspect. A shiver ran up my arms. I turned to go, but hesitated, taking a second glance at the far wall with darker papering that seemed odd. How different the paper was in this room. How very—

Words. The wall was papered in words. Thick vellum notes, long letters, picture postcards from exotic places around the world were plastered smoothly to the wall. I drew near and dared to invade the recipient's privacy.

I have seen so much evil, dear one. The more I see of new places, the more the taste of new things sours in my mouth, and home seems the most pleasant of all. Yet the longer I am away, the more I realize home is not a place, but a series of memories, familiar scents and sounds, deep comfort and rest—and sometimes, it is just a person. You are "home" for this wandering soul.

I stared at those lines lacquered onto the wall and let the sender's thoughts soak into my soul. Who had penned these words? And who had papered the wall with them?

I've hardly known life without you in it, dear friend. Your face is one of my earliest and dearest memories, and you have been my companion through every season since that summer we met when I was merely seven or eight. The breadth and depth of me is known only to you. When I close my eyes and think of Blakely House, I hear the lovely music that pours from your very being. You are a sort of alchemist of the soul, dear Emmett, able to pull out exactly the sort of tune I need for any occasion. For you always know the condition of my heart, what will repair it.

Dear Emmett. *Emmett.* I read the last one over again, then glanced across to the complex renderings, grasping to understand the legendary former master, the picture shifting as the jewels in the kaleidoscope fell into place again and again.

How can I possibly express my gratitude for your kindness? It should not surprise me, for you always have been gracious, but how could you possibly have known? I write of my need, but before my words had reached England's shores, you'd already sent help. How dearly I love that about you.

This beautiful, nearly life-long friendship, and his nephews hadn't any idea she'd even meant anything to him. I ran my fingers over the lovely postcards spread over the wall. He must have come here to saturate himself in her words. In her absent presence. The entire room was full of her. Yet he likely never spoke of her.

I walked along the length of that wall, reading postcards at random. Most closed with the dashed-off signature, *Your Sophie.*

Click-click-click.

A little carousel stirred on another tabletop and began rotating, but a smaller table in the far corner drew me. A box lay on top of it. A writing slope, to be exact, tooled with intricate vines and the same birds that seemed to unlock every important thing of Emmett Sinclair's.

More. I wanted more puzzle pieces, more letters, *more love story.* I sat on a little chair, running my hands over the box. I couldn't help myself. Scientific minds had a tendency toward nosiness. As well as minds saturated in fiction. I was both things.

I lifted the lid and found a thick ream of blank stationery. But there were always layers to Blakely House. Feeling about the box, I located one of the etched birds on the inside and pressed it. Found another and pressed it too. Nothing. Then a third proved to be a catch. It released a thin velvet bottom under which was tucked a neat packet of letters, all flat and without crease, as if never folded into an envelope. Never sent.

At the top, the name that made me catch my breath.

My dearest Sophie,
   Time has weakened the careful sieve of my mind,
wearing many holes in it, and I find truth leaking out more

often than not. Perhaps that's a fruitful turn, for truth is always of value.

Here's the truth that has pressurized in my soul these many years—I love you quite desperately, Sophie. I love you from the inside out and back again. Every curl, every quirk, every glorious curve is beautiful to me. Yes, I love you, I love you, I love you. Now that I've penned it, I cannot stop bleeding this truth onto the page.

It has been so long, but my affection for you is a flame, pure and bright. Years ago it was a spark, but over time your nature, your beauty of face and soul, has only inflamed it. Like heated coals that glow long after the fire is gone, I'm afraid it will never be put out. You are a rare treasure in this world, and I would give up everything to have you for my own. To keep you close, to both guard and empower you, to love you infinitely as my wife.

So now, Sophie my dearest, these are the raw and unfiltered contents of my heart. I find, when I empty it upon the page, my heart is not full of ambition or striving or even discontent. It is only full of deep and abiding affection for the one my soul has always loved.

If you should ever happen upon these shores again, this Farneham Heald, a home to foreign travelers, Blakely House shall open its doors to you no matter how long you've wandered—and I shall open my arms. There shall be no one for me but you.

Forever yours,
Emmett

I paused, hand to my chest. The great madman of Blakely House *did* have a love story. An epic one, spanning decades.

They were wrong about him. I knew it in my soul now, standing amidst their letters. No human had ever been created without a capacity to love. Some merely kept their affection bottled up for one reason or another, but even with the recluse, the brilliant madman Emmett Sinclair, affection brimmed over and spilled out, though no one was here to witness or receive it.

No one but me.

My dearest Sophie,

We have both constructed our stories with a series of choices—threads woven together to create our own tapestries. Perhaps it seems we've woven such different patterns, you and I, but in the end I find that God has chosen to weave our tapestries together at many points, to create a more dynamic design for us each. Your threads have tangled with mine and knitted a unique pattern that would not have been if you had not run away to my little island all those years ago.

Your loving me, nearly right away, opened my eyes to the truth about humanity. Everyone has beauty and evil in them, everyone a piece of the divine from which he was cast, as well as the sin that tarnished him, and it is a holy practice to recognize traces of God in other people. You saw it in everyone, dear Sophie, including me. I believe that's what made me love you. There is no greater beauty than one who recognizes it in others, and takes the time to draw it out.

I remember kissing you in the old ballroom, dearest Sophie. It was years ago, but sometimes I feel I am still kissing you, lingering over your scent, the feel of you, waiting eagerly to dance with you. I was so afraid that day, and we never danced. But I desperately wanted to. Perhaps that surprises you. Forgive me my fears.

*Should you come back to kiss me again, you'll find
a wealth of affection behind it this time, waiting to be
unleashed. In fact, the ballroom itself has been made
new—for you.*

*If you recall, you asked me for a garden that would last
through every season, and thrill your senses even in the dead
of winter. My dearest, my love for you may be measured by
the number of blooms that now fill that ballroom, for I am
not a man of floral painting. Every petal and leaf is placed
only for you. I hope your garden delights you.*

*How I wish you'd come back to me. Let me love you
and delight in you and build up your wings so you can fly.
So we can fly together.*

I read through stacks of letters, dozens of them all from
Emmett Sinclair but never sent, then settled them back inside their hidden compartment. Was this what the house had
wanted to show me?

Perhaps it needed me to send these letters. Fear had kept
Emmett Sinclair silent, hadn't it? Kept him from offering her
that ring and his love. Yes, they should be sent. Words as lovely
as these deserved more than a coating of dust. Now that Emmett Sinclair was not here to be embarrassed by them, or to
risk rejection, the house of course wished me to—

Oof. What a fantastical creature I was becoming.

When I left the room, the pianoforte sounded in the distance again, dulcet tones lacing the darkness with a certain
magic. I crept out of the studio and down the hall toward the
sound. I had half a mind to peek in and see who played. And
the only thought pounding through my head was, *Emmett*. He
was here, playing for his Sophie.

chapter FOURTEEN

I write to you only at night, dear one, because daytime
is for productivity and night for the sublime.

~Emmett's letters to Sophie

It was a simple melody line, like a thin stream of water falling
through the rocks, but with smoothness that came from experience, one note connected to the last. The music stopped,
and a deep voice caught my ear. It was that butler, André
Montagne, speaking in low, private tones. I stiffened and tried
to assess which direction I needed to avoid on my way back
up to my bedchamber.

But when he spoke again, the voice that answered Mr. Montagne's shocked me.

Rawr-rawr.

Little turncoat.

I tiptoed around the corner into the long, dark corridor
and brazenly eavesdropped.

"Rather a shame, you being shut up in this big house all day. Have you found much to do?"

Mwrrrr.

"So." He shuffled. "How did you come to lose your tail? A heroic tale, I take it? Story. That is, a heroic *story*."

Humor tickled my chest.

Mmmmrwawr. Wrawr. He said it with such authority, confident of his answer. I could picture him tossing his lion-like head back as he said it too, the way he often did when he had something important to express.

"Ahh, I see. And did it hurt?"

Mrw.

A long sigh from the butler. "Rather difficult going about life without a piece of yourself, no?" His languid French accent grew animated. "Other cats probably do not even think about having a tail. They simply have it. No one realizes how necessary it is until . . . well, until they don't have it, and life is suddenly quite limited."

A low grumble. Micah's very manly form of agreement.

"I don't suppose you've learned any workarounds, have you? Using your ears to balance or something of that nature. Swatting the flies away with a—no, it is the *horse* who does that." A pause. Another shuffle, followed by a low, throaty rumble which meant Micah was walking back and forth before the butler, nub tail cocked to the right as he rubbed against his leg.

Double turncoat!

"You still have adventures, though, don't you? Quite a few, I'd imagine. That missing tail would not hold you back. Although I suppose you grow a little self-conscious around other cats. Always aware of your lack."

Rawr-rawr.

Another sigh. "You're right, I should consider that. You are quite a good listener."

I smiled. "So are people."

He spun where he crouched, his vivid sealike eyes standing out in the shadows as he slowly rose. He stared at me, that tall, impossibly handsome butler with his hair still restrained by a leather tie, and in that quiet moment I felt every inch of his pirate-ness pulsing in the darkness. He was trapped, run aground. But still wild inside.

"I couldn't sleep."

"Nor I." He considered me from his higher vantage point. "They have frightened you with their stories? The men?"

"I'm not afraid of Blakely House. On the contrary, I'm awake because I'm too excited to sleep. But that's often the case."

He frowned. "Excited by what?"

I opened my arms and turned in the vast openness of the odd manor home. "By everything. All of this. I cannot stop thinking about the legendary Emmett Sinclair. Of poor Fitzhugh."

"Who is Fitzhugh?"

I turned to him, ignoring the question. "There's something we're missing—all of us. The puzzle pieces are all there, only we have to arrange them the right way. I thought I'd best let my hands be busy since my mind was already working out the problem. Only . . . the workshop is locked, and I haven't a key."

"I do," he said. "Come. I'll show you in." He strode through the shadows.

I followed. "Why are *you* awake?"

"The opposite reason, I suppose. Because I am intensely *not* excited by this place." He turned into the drawing room, shifting a light to turn it on, and I suddenly realized he was in his shirtsleeves. "I grow restless." He turned to me with a somber smile.

"Do you?" Avoiding his gaze to save my own sanity, I knelt to scoop up Micah. The creature purred and went contentedly limp in my arms.

After fitting a key from his chatelaine, André let us in, and I paused to inhale the palpable magic of the place. Then he pointed out various gadgets. "A duster. Meant to ease the work of a maid. And this . . . a book binder, so that people may compile all their notes in one place. A tarnish remover, a push-button fishing reel, and a retractable fetching hook."

Most, it seemed, were meant to replace common household tasks or to ease everyday burdens. Others, like projected butterflies floating over a lamp and a tiny fish that swam in one's tea, were purely whimsical. I scrambled to grasp the essence of the absent master, his clever mind and humor and whimsy all rolled into one. He was odd.

I was odd.

But on him, oddness equated to brilliance. I laid my hand on a glowing blue ball and all the bright blueness centered on where I touched it. "I believe we might have gotten on well," I said quietly.

"And neither of you would have ever left the island again."

I removed my hand and the ball dimmed. "The lack of adventures would be criminal to you, I suppose."

And to Sophie. That was why he hadn't sent the letters. Why he'd buried the ring in that old clock. Because she was an adventurer and he was not. "Adventures are everything to some people, I suppose."

"Which you do not understand. The kitty, he tells me you do not care for such things unless they are in a book."

"You two have spoken about me?"

"At length." A crooked smile. And suddenly we were back to skimming the sun-dappled surface. "I find him rather perspicacious."

A belt of sudden panic tightened around my chest.

"But then again, apparently I am too, no?"

I grasped my apron in both hands. How could he have possibly—?

"And supercilious and rancorous and a few other things."

Noooo! Oh how the heat bloomed up my torso, through my neck and across my face. But . . . it was dark. "Well, Mr. Montagne, if that's what the cat believes you are . . ." Somehow in the night, in this otherworldly quiet, it was easier to talk to him. Perhaps because it was too dark for him to stare me down, but still. This was a journal-worthy development.

Once again Aunt Lottie was right. Absolutely right. Every inch of this shadowed pirate with the twinkle in his eye enticed me. A true novel hero standing before me, but very real. Interestingly imperfect. And able to magically hear through walls, apparently.

Which made it even more impossible to look directly at him.

I gave my kitty a squeeze. "For what it's worth, Micah isn't the least offended about my lack of adventures. He's quite lazy himself."

"So who is this . . . Fitzhugh you mention?"

Setting Micah on the settee, I crossed the workroom and knelt before the automaton, laying a hand on his birdcage chest. "This . . . this is Fitzhugh. At least to me."

"The automaton. You've named him."

I tangled my fingers up in the wires anchored to the board

and set the movement going, just to give him a heartbeat for a moment. *Tick-tick, tick-tick.* But it stopped. "Everyone deserves to be called something. So he is Fitzhugh. It means the son of brilliance."

"Hm." He considered the metallic man. "Fitting. Sinclair would have liked that. So what do you intend to do with him, now that I have let you in here?"

I took a deep breath. "Bring him to life." I turned my back on André, feeling slightly sacrilegious. "Of course, it would be far easier if I had tools from my shop. The servants will lend me nothing, and I'm afraid my cousins aren't inclined to help their competition." I angled my finger into the cavity and adjusted the treadle with a delicate pressure, then tilted the movement to the right and eyed its levelness. I tapped the counterbalance and set the thing into motion again. "This is his beat." The balance tick-ticked, this time in perfect, endless rhythm.

"His beat. Like a heartbeat?"

I turned in surprise to study his face. "Yes, exactly."

He pressed his lips together doubtfully, but he'd understood. And that gave me goosebumps. "Now, he has to breathe."

André knelt beside me, his presence suddenly enormous and nerve-racking and all-consuming, and . . . what was this power he had? Pulling my senses this way and that, consuming and enticing, eliciting a spiraling delight. Had he cast a spell?

No, that was wizards and such. Pirates did not cast spells—they stole and broke in.

He'd done some of that too, for I certainly hadn't *meant* to let anyone in.

"Perhaps . . . try this." He pointed at my hand holding the narrow pliers. "Twist and hold it. Then let it go. It'll go in and out. In the clock world, it's called—"

"Breathing." I blinked at him, but he only smiled, as if he *hadn't* just caught on to a rather obscure connection.

I tightened the spring inside Fitzhugh as my own breath came in short, desperate gasps. I held it with one finger while he watched over my shoulder, then I let go as I thought, *Breathe. Breathe, Fitzhugh.*

And he did. That spring snapped out, then recoiled back in and out again, dancing with the beat of the movement. "Look," I whispered.

He leaned in, his shoulder bumping mine. My pulse took off at a panicked rate. The butler moved his good hand into the birdcage torso. "May I?"

I nodded, he turned something within, and life surged through the automaton. The mechanical man sat forward, joints creaking, insides whirring and pumping. I caught my breath. Clutched the pliers. Nearly stabbed myself with them.

The butler grabbed my hand and pulled us both up as the automaton pulsed, whirred faster. I could barely breathe. I gripped his hand so tight I was surprised not to feel bones cracking.

Then something popped in the automaton and the gears slowed, their teeth clacking harder and harder until the machine man slumped back against the wall, the light dimming in his expression.

But my own heartbeat had escalated. Doubled. There we stood, the pirate butler's hand clutching mine, hearts pumping in rhythm as we stared at the machine that had, for a moment, come alive. "You saw that, right?" I whispered.

"I think so." He stared. "We brought him to life."

I smiled. "Him?"

He dropped my hand as if suddenly realizing he still grasped it. "For your sake, miss." He dipped his head, hiding a smile.

Which made my heart pound.

I cleared my throat. Felt the flush of hot and cold through my body. "Is it true what they say about my great-uncle, that he never left this island?"

André looked me over. "We shall say . . . you remind me of him. I could not imagine him adventuring either. For such a brilliant man, his life was rather dull."

I looked away, unsure how to take his comment. "I don't find life dull. The life of the mind . . ." My voice trailed off. "Perhaps he—and I—simply like to understand things. To keep to a small piece of the world so we may learn every part of it. Know it thoroughly and completely."

"And to protect yourself, no? You are afraid."

I had been called boring and cowardly. Perhaps it was true, some of the time. Well, most of the time. "I simply haven't had a reason to be courageous. Being wet and cold and seasick, floating on a vast ocean just waiting to swallow me up . . . I simply don't see the point." I didn't admit how terrified I was of water. "There are buildings and people and trees and flowers at home, just as anywhere else. Why change my location simply for the sake of changing it?" I grasped a loose wire and sighed. What I wouldn't pay to have a simple screwdriver to open up dear Fitzhugh.

"Yet you came here."

"Yes." My hand stilled. How did I explain the decision over which I'd agonized? Fought against, even?

"Come," he said. "I'll see you back to the stairs."

He did. When we stood at the bottom, he faced me. "What you did . . . no one's ever been able to do that before."

"What *we* did." I fidgeted, running my thumb along the smooth mahogany railing. "I enjoy challenges. *Those* are my adventures." How alive it made me feel, being here. "And Blakely House is one large bundle of riddles." There was, of course, the initial draw of the inheritance, which seemed petty to mention just now.

But *he* did. "The very large sum of money must have been some encouragement, no?"

"The news came at a very opportune time, I will admit." My voice was tight. Too high. I trailed my fingertips over the wood. "It seems you don't care for me." As soon as the words were out, and his face went stony, I felt their wrongness. *My* wrongness. I was always doing that. It was too direct, almost confrontational.

And now he was uncomfortable.

But in the dark, my new ability to speak to men—this one, at least—persisted. "Well, then. We'll have to put our differences aside. We have a cat between us now."

"We do?"

"He's chosen us both, it would seem. We're both as nocturnal as he is, so he has chosen us for his companions."

"I suppose we must be civil, then. At least in the middle of the night."

"Truce, then. At night." I held out my hand.

A glimmer of a smile as he enfolded it with his own. "Very well, Miss Forrester, truce. For now."

"It's nighttime, André. Call me Sydney."

He bowed at the waist, and rose with a twinkle in his eyes. "Good night, then. Miss Sydney." And released my hand.

chapter
FIFTEEN

Man allows emotion to become his control panel; a machine hasn't that level of capability. It can only rely upon logic.

~*Emmett's letters to Sophie*

The small envelope appeared in my room on a tray the following morning at the same time that Aunt Lottie did. She burst into my room. "What a lovely day to be at the seashore, is it not?"

I looked from her to the sealed envelope propped between the empty cup and the kettle of hot chocolate, intuitively sensing I should keep the two apart. Then I noticed she'd pinned on her hat. "You're leaving." I rose.

She placed her gloved hands on my shoulders. "You'll get on well here, Syd. I know it."

My gaze flicked to the tray. The envelope was bad news, wasn't it? "You're forgetting—I haven't inherited the place quite yet." Bad, *terrible* news.

"But you *will*. Remember, a woman can pave her own path. She can do anything—especially what men tell her she cannot."

I attempted a smile at this woman so full of passion and talent. In some ways her little speeches were empowering, but at times they had the opposite effect. As if pointing out that I *should* be strong, but often I was not. Not the way she was. In many ways I must be a disappointment to this strong, vivacious woman who knew who she was and what she was about. Who *could* go toe-to-toe with men rather than simply tripping over them.

Her mind did not trouble her as mine did, teeming with so many wild and windblown thoughts that she walked into a door or missed entire conversations going on *outside* her head. She was the sort that had one train of thought, and it drove through like a steam engine, parting the chaos and accomplishing goals. Me, I had several trains all zigzagging madly about at once. I'm not certain any of them actually reached a destination, and often they collided. Or sailed off the tracks entirely.

"Sydney . . ."

She was looking at the envelope. Or was she? Her mind was sharp and keen while mine wandered all the livelong day.

Like now. I was doing it again. She was watching me, waiting for an answer to . . . something. I shook my head, forcing my thoughts into line. "I'm sorry, Aunt. What were you asking?"

"Only if you'll be all right." She stepped close, cupping my cheek. "I do love you so."

I smiled and brought my hand up to hers.

When she stepped back, she spun to gather her bag and

hat. "You will astound them all and they'll see what I've always seen." She smiled. "Your sheer genius." She turned to pin on her hat before the looking glass.

"And that little obstacle we talked about?" I snatched the little envelope on the tray and tucked it in my pocket while her back was to me.

"That can be solved easily enough. Why, *you* know you didn't kill the man," she said with a flourish of her gloved hand. "So find out who did, and you'll be right as rain."

I forced another grin toward her bright, dimpled smile. That's that, as if it were but a flick of the fingers. I didn't even know how he died, or when or where, and no one seemed inclined to tell me much of anything. Which meant I couldn't even provide an alibi. "There's every chance I may return to the shop in utter defeat, you know." That envelope had felt rather thin.

"Which is why I forbid you from returning. You must dig in your heels. Earn that inheritance and prove to them who you are." She angled her hat and stabbed it with a pin. "Finish that mechanical man and step into your uncle's shoes. Become Blakely House's next master!"

I looked at her, and my attention narrowed onto her face. "What is it, Aunt? What aren't you telling me?"

"You are *not* to worry about a thing, Syd. Just do as—"

"You've done something. I can tell by the way your face is." She laughed. "I do a great many things every day."

"Aunt." I touched her shoulder.

She turned. "I must be—"

"Tell me." I snatched her bag, swinging it behind me.

Her shoulders drooped, and she looked me in the eye. "I've sold the shop." She huffed out a breath. "There, are you quite content? I've sold the curiosity shop and I'll be taking rooms above the printer's."

I stared, mouth agape. "The *printer's*?" As if it was a rodent-infested rookery.

It wasn't. Really, it wasn't. But it wasn't home. Nothing but the shop ever would be. "So when you came to fetch me—asked me to come back with you . . . ?"

"I would have *told* you, Sydney! Before we'd reached Grafton, I'd have told you everything. We'd have shared a flat, found work . . ."

I blinked, hand on my forehead, trying to breathe. She'd truly done it. She'd actually given up the shop.

"I've left you my new address, up on your bed table." Her voice faltered. "Do write when you can, Sydney dear."

"How could you *do* such a thing? I've been gone for mere *days*."

"I had an offer from a man in Bristol well over a year ago." Her tight, pale face looked vulnerable. Suddenly I felt vulnerable too. "It wasn't a good offer, but it was either that or give it over to the tax collector when he came 'round next." She was shaking.

"And how will you live?"

She smiled, smoothing the fabric on my arm. "I always land on my feet, don't I? Although it shall be much less fun without . . ." She blinked back moisture. "Without . . . well."

I threw my arms about her. Held her close as she'd done for me so many times before. "You're right, Aunt. You *will* land on your feet—right here." This was a terrible idea. But a perfect one. "You're going to stay here, with me."

"You needn't be my savior, Sydney Forrester." She clung hard for a moment, then held me at arm's length, tears filling her eyes. "Promise me one thing, my dear." She gave me a gentle shake. "When you inherit Blakely House, don't become like him. Don't bottle yourself up in this house until you're mad. Go out and have a normal life. And make it a *good* one. For both our sakes."

Panic swirled through my chest. This felt like a good-bye. "Then you'd best come right back here after the sale." I clung to her hands, desperate at the thought of her selling the shop alone. Of moving her canning jars, her smartly polished shoes, her carefully made-over gowns to some obscure little flat above the printer's. "Please, Aunt Lottie. Please say you'll come. Your company shall keep me from becoming a hermit."

A smile brightened her face. "I suppose I should, at least for a while. Oh Sydney, I've missed you so!"

Another tight embrace, then I forced myself to walk her to the door and bid farewell.

The footman, who had taken a liking to her, stood at the door with his boots hanging from his neck by the laces. He had offered to escort her across the causeway to keep her from tripping and soiling her traveling garment. So as quickly as she had bustled into life at Blakely House, Lottie Lane swept out, leaving a great deal of quiet and gnawing dread in her wake.

I watched from halfway up the steeply angled path as they squished far below through what looked like endless chocolate cake batter, the beach popping and whistling as birds yanked worms from the mud. Then, the water closed over the mud-flats, erasing Aunt Lottie's footprints, and I realized what I'd done. What was now at stake.

I stood, forlorn and feeling quite young as I shoved my

hands into my apron pockets . . . and my hand crunched the note. The bad news.

As I sprinted back to the house, I retrieved the envelope and whipped out a small card with neat script on it.

> *With an open mind,*
> *perhaps you'll find*
> *Half or whole,*
> *A key that unlocks nothing,*
> *except one's soul.*

Frowning at it, I ambled into the breakfast room, thoughts firing in a dozen different directions.

Key.

Soul.

I took a croissant from the platter and scooped clotted cream onto it, then balanced a cup of tea on the edge of my plate. One of the servants took his time arranging the teacups, eyeing me out of his peripheral vision.

Half or whole.

Unlocks nothing. *Nothing?* Then why have it?

A dollop of honey into my tea, and I gave it a stir.

It was metaphorical. Or perhaps a clever play on words. It had to be.

The creaking door jarred my thoughts. Dane Hutchcraft swept in, neatly pressed and freshly groomed, and my mind drifted to the larger riddle that had been lingering in my mind since Aunt Lottie had brought it to the surface: *Who killed Emmett Sinclair?* Tom Jolly came in after, dressed as the dandy he was but with a strained smile. He was putting on a show, and he didn't want to be here.

I began to look at everyone as suspects, which was rather dreadful of me. But my innocence only meant someone else's guilt and it had me endlessly wondering . . . *who?*

Micah jumped into my lap and I stroked him absently as my gaze landed upon a pianoforte at an angle in the corner of the room. I pictured André hunched over the keys, his tall frame drawing music from the instrument, and a delightful chill passed through me. It must have been him playing the other night. I must thank him for calming my sleepless mind. With only one hand to play the—

Keys. A *key*. It unlocked nothing . . . *but my soul.*

Yes! I perched on the edge of the settee, eyeing the enormous instrument as Dane and Jolly eyed me. "Keen to take on your new role, are you?" said Jolly, not bothering to disguise his feelings.

"Keen about everything at Blakely House." Especially riddles that appeared in my bedchamber.

The moment the men left, I ran to the instrument and peeked beneath the lid over the keys . . . and there lay several long, gleaming metal tools. A cry escaped my lips. I touched them, running my fingertips over them with a smile. A key to Fitzhugh. That's what they were.

Was he a soul?

No. That had been about the pianoforte.

But Fitzhugh had mysteries to be explored. And now I could unlock them. I gathered the instruments and hurried to the cluttered workroom so full of possibilities. I dropped my tools before the automaton and touched his face. "Good morning, Sir Fitzhugh." I laid out my tools, inspecting each. "A fine day to crack a riddle, is it not?" But I could barely see the small gears.

I rose and shifted lights on their tabletops, turning on every one until the room was sunny as a meadow. The lights flickered and faded, but then they came on full strength. I knelt before the complex gears and springs and threaded one of my new tools into the heart of the man.

It was the cams that interested me most, those gold discs stacked like vertebrae, each with notches meant to activate . . . something.

If I could only loosen the movement and see what lay behind—

Snap. A spring struck my cheek. No, no, no, no! I put pressure on the gears around it, as if shoring up a bleed, and tried madly to fit it back into place.

Then there were footsteps. They stopped in the doorway, and a man's voice came. "What do you think you're doing?"

chapter
SIXTEEN

I am a clock that's missing pieces; I am a clock that is broken.

~*Emmett's letters to Sophie*

Tom Jolly leaned on the doorframe, sleeves rolled up. "You don't own the place yet, you know."

I exhaled the sudden shock. "It's a shame, him sitting here this way. Someone ought to finish him."

I pivoted again to the automaton, but I felt Jolly's glare upon my corseted back. Out of the corner of my eye, I saw Dane Hutchcraft the wizard join him.

"She's only interested in the gadgets, Jolly. Let her have a look." He took down a notebook and flipped it open. "It isn't as if she's made any real progress now, has she?" He smiled, but his eyes narrowed.

I had the immediate sense that the wrong answer would prove dangerous. "What do you consider progress?"

They were both watching me now.

No emergency book in sight this time. My neck tightened.

I straightened to turn my back on them, but their suspicion ran taut like a cord around the room. When I stole a glance in my peripheral vision, Tom Jolly was leafing through papers, skimming their contents with a frown. Dane Hutchcraft, on the other hand, was staring at me.

Trying to brush it off, I lay on my side and at last had the right angle to peer into the birdcage torso from the side. More power. It needed more power, from somewhere. He'd lost power too quickly the other night.

There, on the table—an electric lamp sitting on its copper base. Not daring to look at the men, I untwisted a section of slender cords, cut them with shears, and spliced them onto the cords leading up to the copper and mercury base, twisting the cut ends together.

Come on now, Fitzhugh. Show them—show them what you can do.

As I held them together, the automaton surged with life. He vibrated. Pulsed. Lights flickered and low, garbled sounds emerged as if he had something to say. My pulse exploded.

Breathe. Keep breathing.

Somewhere on the fringes of my mind were the voices of my cousins. Bickering, something about lights . . .

Yes, light. More light. As I held the wires still with my right hand, my left felt about for a closer lamp to shine upon the underside of these gears. I lit it. But it flickered and hissed. A pop of brightness, then all went dark and machines sputtered as if breathing a deep sigh. The sleeping spell once again blanketed Blakely House.

I blinked. Silence prickled. I rose, feeling my way toward a window. There weren't many of those in the workroom, since the house had been built into the side of a hill, so it was quite dark. Except . . . except for a candle glow in the mirror. Not reflected by it, but *inside* it.

And a figure. A clear outline, standing still.

Impossible.

My heart fluttered against my rib cage. I blinked, staring at the looking glass again, but suddenly there was no light. No supposed figure. I spun and stumbled toward the others. Or at least, where I thought they should be.

"Now she's done it," said a voice. Jolly, maybe? "Letting her in this room was your idea."

"She has as much right to be here as we do. She's family, after all."

Dane at least pretended to accept me, but Tom Jolly . . .

"But look what she's done."

Realization tightened my chest. The lights. They'd said something—too many lights. The warning shifted up in the mental queue from where I'd stored it, now coming front and center. Too many lights would overload the system, he'd said. Be careful. Nine at most at one time.

I had done this. I'd cut the power to the entire estate. Was it permanent? Had I broken Blakely House?

Pulse thrumming, I felt my way out into the corridor. Several other figures moved about in the dimness. Oddly quiet. The usual whir of electricity, the rush of water through pipes, the clink of movement and industry—one hardly noticed them until they all ceased. The silence felt terribly wrong.

"I'll see what can be done," said Dane somewhere within the hallway. "Stay here."

See all you want, Mr. Dane Hutchcraft. I wouldn't do any staying. I could repair my own messes.

chapter
SEVENTEEN

As a general rule, Tom Jolly hated his late uncle. Leaning back in Emmett Sinclair's stiff armchair in the pitch-dark parlor, he indulged in a long sip from his glass. It wasn't lost on him that he should have grown up in Blakely House, his mother's childhood home. Yet because of some imagined slight in their youth, Emmett Sinclair had ousted his sister and they had nearly starved in a rookery instead. Perhaps the famed industrialist was actually a machine like the things he created, with a water pump for a heart.

Oh, he'd tried to buy Tom off years ago and assuage his guilt when he got word that they were in the poorhouse, but Tom couldn't abide being beholden to anyone. Especially Emmett Sinclair.

When Tom had grown up and made good in the shipping industry, capitalizing on the decline of the East India Trading Company, he'd become obsessed with restoring everything that had been taken from his mother. The first purchase he'd made was a respectable flat for her, then a few trinkets and baubles.

Tom's ships had done uncommonly well, and his success garnered Uncle Emmett's attention. They'd exchanged letters over the years, Tom stirred by familial guilt and then a niggling hope for something to come of the tenuous relationship. Then when Tom's mother died, the childless industrialist began mentioning his pressing need for an heir. He hinted he was considering Tom, and being master of Blakely House seemed the frosting on Tom's life. A full-circle moment he couldn't resist.

It became his new fixation.

Then just before news of Emmett's death, a curious letter had come—the last he'd ever received from the man:

I'd like you to know that after meeting my chosen heir, I intend to change my will just as soon as I can. I warn you, in case circumstances prevent me, that my previously named heir Sydney Forrester is never to be trusted. Not with so much as a fig. Please ensure Sydney never lays hold of Blakely House or anything in it. My life is in a precarious state at the moment, and I'm not certain I shall return home to make my final arrangements, but I know I can trust your cleverness, Tom Jolly, to make certain Blakely House doesn't fall into the wrong hands.

It had come from the Continent. Some unknown place.

Soon after Dane had written with news of the old man's death, an odd righteous indignation had come over Tom Jolly. Perhaps it was the complicated relationship he'd had with his uncle. Or the infuriating knowledge that the estate and all its genius, everything in it, would wrongly fall into the hands of this Sydney Forrester.

The jewels. His precious mother's jewels, which symbolized the lost essence of the true woman she'd been. Would they be clasped around someone else's neck? Tossed aside as interesting little baubles with no real meaning?

He had traveled immediately to Blakely House and shown Dane the letter. They had both agreed on what should happen next.

He rose when Dane came into the room with a whale oil lamp. "What did you find?"

"She cannot stay." Shadows lengthened his solemn face. "She is a hazard. She would bring an eight-hundred-year-old house down around our ears, and all the inventions besides. And . . . she will have won. She'll have caused a death, and gotten away with it." He lowered himself into a chair. "There is one little thing I cannot get around. *How* she is related."

"Explain."

"We know how Purcell ties in. And we know Uncle Emmett's three sisters—your mother, my mother, and Aunt Genevieve, who died giving birth."

"To Sydney Forrester's mother, supposedly."

"No." He drummed his fingers on the arm of the chair. "That's the part I've just remembered. It was a boy. A son. But she claims her *mother* is the Sinclair relation."

"So Sydney's a fraud. Well, that certainly changes things."

Dane's frown darkened. "Or there are family secrets of which we aren't yet aware."

"So if she isn't related, why would Uncle—"

"I don't know that yet. But this makes it even more likely she's guilty. With no familial tie, all he is to her is a future inheritance. One that he didn't want to give after meeting her."

"So she made certain he couldn't change his mind." He

clutched the chair arm, blood pressure rising. "Then she jolly well covered her tracks so she'll escape justice and inherit everything. What if we find no proof?"

Dane drummed his fingers. "Then we shall have to create some."

chapter
EIGHTEEN

There is no mechanism so delicate, so easily put off balance, none so hard to repair, as one human's relationship to another.

~Emmett's letters to Sophie

Slipping out the garden entrance, I breathed in fresh, chilly air and blinked in the daylight as I clutched my wrap. The path of power—that's what I needed to find. I'd follow it to the source, reignite it, and all would be well.

I looked back at the enormous house, rendered still and cold. I had broken it. I had done that, wrapped up again in the cotton of my own thoughts.

Water glistened at the peak of the hill far above the house, which must be the lake. The source of the water pressure and power. Sparkling waterfalls tripped down through the rocks and crevices, running alongside the house, and straight down past it. There—the path of power.

I plunged down a rocky path, breathing in the aroma of pine

and a dusting of floral scents. Sand popped and hissed below as birds yanked worms from the mudflats. Halfway down, that long iron bridge stretched across a ravine. I neared the edge, heart shooting up to my throat as I foolishly looked down.

It wasn't so bad. Not truly. No rushing water—just a creek. A ravine. Way down there. I wouldn't drown, at least.

Do it. Just do it. You're not a child.

I closed my eyes and edged forward, then forced myself to open them and look down. My stomach seized and tingled. I glanced back, and two servants had stepped out of a lean-to up the hill, observing me.

It had become a whole event, apparently. How wonderful. *Breathe.*

No rushing water, no murky depths. Just a creek. I wouldn't fall.

I *could* fall. Painful electricity in my midsection. I forced my feet to carry me across. At the end I scrambled onto land and fell on all fours as the prickle of panic receded over my skin.

I'm alive. I'm here. And I did it.

After a moment I rose, still shaky, and walked into a wooded fairyland. As my heart thudding in my ears quieted, I heard a waterwheel, creaking and groaning beside a modest stone cottage. Purple flowers spilled over every inch of the ground and dripped off the thatched roof.

The cottage—had that been for Sophie? I stepped closer, and a figure moved in the window. My pulse exploded. I climbed through overgrown vines and edged the door open—a man was inside, back to me, overcoat discarded, one shirtsleeve rolled up.

He turned with a frown. "Miss Forrester. What are you doing here?"

"Mr. Montagne." My already-tight shoulders cinched tighter. "You're here."

My gaze flicked over the little cottage, which obviously housed the power. Large glass boxes were stacked on top of one another in the center of the room, wires extending out like spider legs from each one. "I came to see about the power."

But I couldn't tell a thing about it from looking at all these controls and levers. Not a thing. Like a foreign language—I spoke in physical gears and connections, and this was something else entirely. Something strange.

"That isn't necessary. I am seeing to it, my lady."

"How did you—"

"Mrs. Holligan. She rang down about it, and I was in the stables. Came straightaway."

I blinked, glancing about the cramped space. "She rang what?"

"What I do not know is *where* it's broken. Quite peculiar." The words rolled from his mouth, the velvety soft vowels marking his melodic French accent. "I've seen wires chewed by mice, slipped gears on the cylinder, broken accumulators, but this I do not understand." He sighed, resting his handless arm on the black cylinder. "Nothing is the matter. I cannot understand it."

I looked down, clasping my hands behind me. I didn't want to say it.

Don't look at me.

"What might happen if the system became . . . overloaded?" Heat spidered up my face, just as it had when I'd toppled the ink on those papers. Why did I make so many mistakes? Why did it seem I was the mistake? My every step. Every word. My brain, which skittered off in a million directions and missed the fire blazing right in front of me.

What was *wrong* with me?

Do you see, Aunt Lottie? Do you see? This is why I cannot accept God. A perfect, all-knowing, all-powerful being.

Because a perfect God could not have created a broken clock.

I looked up—the butler had disappeared. There was a heavy *thunk*, a gurgle and a low mechanical hum, and power vibrated in the little cottage. Buzzed on my skin.

When he emerged again, eyeing me, I dropped my gaze before he could give the lecture I sensed in the air and thrust out the first thought that came. "Thank you, by the way."

"For what?"

"The gift. Those tools."

He watched me for a moment more, his restless frown full of the admonishment, then turned back to the wires, feeling along each string with his good hand. "Have you made progress, then? On your Fitzhugh?"

"A little, perhaps." It was difficult to repair a machine I didn't understand. "Have you any idea what he does?"

"Very little, it would seem."

"Yes, well. What was he *meant* to do?"

"You'd have to ask the man who created him."

I huffed. What a dodgy answer. "You worked beside my great-uncle every day. What was he passionate about? What vision did he have?"

He gave a short laugh. "You might as well ask me what color flowers are." He paused, leaning for a moment against the hydropower cylinders bolted to the worktable. "Come, I will show you something, Miss Forrester. Perhaps it will begin to explain Emmett Sinclair to you."

chapter
NINETEEN

The best I can hope for as a creator is actually a mechanical re-creation of what God has already thought up.

~*Emmett's letters to Sophie*

I followed him out the door he held open for me, darting a look up into his face. I hadn't won a smile, and his thoughts simmered just behind the mask of his expression—whatever he was about to reveal to me.

But then the wild island beyond captured my attention. The *whoosh* of sea breeze, the squeal of birds, the rush of water over rocks swept me up in their spell. He led me up the path and around an outcropping to a stone outbuilding that looked like stables. Through a canvas-draped doorway he guided me, and when it opened into a large domed room, I caught my breath. "A bird sanctuary." Wings flapped, feathers fluttered down to us, and soft coos echoed in the dimness.

My guide lifted his buttoned-up arm, wooden hand now discarded, and a white bird sailed down to perch on it. André drew the bird close and stroked its head. "This is a kittiwake. Thousands of them nest on this island." He pointed with his right hand toward a distinctive black-and-white bird watching us from the ground. "That is a razorbill. Very penguin-like, but it has the ability to fly, which is why it's here. It's why all of them are here, actually."

"My great-uncle brought them here?"

"For years he rescued the injured ones, then kept them a while to study them in flight." André gently spread the wing of the little bird on his arm. "Wingspan, wind resistance, bone structure."

"He was trying to fly!" I crossed to a set of wings made of bundled willow cane.

"Trying, but mostly not succeeding. Especially at the end."

I desperately wanted to ask, but I waited.

André released the little bird and waved me on to another section around a beamed corner.

"There's a German man attempting the same. Otto something, I believe. Everyone says it isn't meant to be, this method of travel, if humans haven't figured it out by now."

He paused, holding up an oilcloth draped over the doorway. "Is that what you think, Miss Forrester?"

"I believe . . ." I breathed in the scent of straw and earth as my mind loosened its grip on what it knew, in favor of what it saw. "I believe it proves the brilliance of the bird's creator. He designed on a whim what we are still unable to replicate, even after thousands of years." I marveled for a moment at the effortless swoop and soar of these creatures. Nothing with so intricate a function would come together by accident. Not a chance. That realization unwound the cramp of doubts just a little and brought surprising relief.

Then he pushed back a tattered curtain, and sunlight shocked my senses. In a large, open space, dust hovered in beams of light shooting down through holes in the thatched roof, highlighting great, winged birds with hollow bodies, poised and ready to fly.

I gasped. Ran to them and touched their wings. Smaller models lay about with catgut stretched over metal frames. The three giant creations were not merely gliders but the entire bodies of birds, hollowed out with leather seats fitted inside, big enough to hold a man.

I crossed to a second one, then a third. "Absolutely incredible." The metal was smooth, the rivets nearly flush with the frame. Standing on tiptoe, I peered into the opened nose fitted neatly with mechanics. "Who made these last two?"

The first shone with Uncle Emmett's usual black-polished gears and minute precision. The second and third machines were a collection of odds and ends, gears and thin metal belts, all ingeniously repurposed from other projects and fitted together with a clever rightness to them, but a distinctly different finish. I paused in an empty space with scattered straw and oil stains on the floor, where another machine had clearly rested.

Again, I couldn't bring myself to ask.

I returned to the first machine. "This one was his. Yes, I think so. And these others . . . they must be yours."

His face was stoic. "Is it so plain to you, the difference?"

"I mean no slight—the intelligence behind all of them is obvious. It's only . . ." I ran my hand over the metal casing. "This is so very *him*." And the prominently missing fourth machine—had it been his or Uncle Emmett's?

He frowned. "You're quite certain you've never met the man?"

"I don't need to have met him to recognize his work. There are patterns. Trademark elements to each of his creations."

He looked dubious.

"Oh—a map! There's a map on the wall, with a route charted out." Which only solidified my suspicions. He'd at least meant to fly.

But where? Where had the man who never left the island planned to take a great metal bird? The thick line arced from Northumberland to somewhere on the Continent, with tiny numbers and straight lines, likely calculating in intricate detail how far this innovation had to carry him.

I hadn't ever paid attention to geography. Now I wished I had. The place he'd indicated jutted out like one of three fingers. It wasn't a long trip, wherever it was—not Africa or anything. Just on the opposite shore, and a little north. A holiday, perhaps?

No. It would take more than a holiday to shake Emmett Sinclair loose from his island. "Might I see the map?"

André the butler had gone very still. His face twitched. "I suppose he has no use for it now." He tugged it off the wall and handed it to me, his fingers loathe to release it.

I squinted at it, straining to read the tiny scrolling print of the place marked. "Have you any idea where he meant to go?"

"He told me he had a special project for us to take on together. A mission."

"He never mentioned what it was?"

He frowned, stretching his shoulders. Something had made him uncomfortable. "He seldom gave me information before I needed it. There was some element of danger, I believe. He was quite fearful. He did not wish to take this trip."

I folded the map, watching André the pirate-turned-butler run a hand absently over the sleek curve of the machine's belly.

I petted Micah that way. He'd come lie on my lap while I read a book, belly-up, and I'd stroke him with this same gentleness. "You came to work on this in your spare time because *you* wish to fly. This is your project. Your dream. Isn't it?"

"Not a dream, exactly." He shoved his hand in his pocket. "Something to do, I suppose."

"But you have a ship. What would you need with a flying machine?"

His jaw firmed, clefted chin outlined in sharp relief. "What makes you think I have a ship?"

"All pirates have a ship." *Drat.* "That is, you seem like one . . . a man, that is . . . who might have sailed. You know, in a boat. A ship. On the water. Before you . . . well, you gave up. Apparently. Broke your—uh, ship. I heard you wrecked on the . . ."

The deep pain splayed over his face finally registered. He turned his back to me.

"So . . . flying." I curled my fingers into my palm. "That was my uncle's passion, I suppose." No, it wasn't. We'd just established that. "*Great*-uncle, that is. You know." *Why* was I so broken? Like a machine put together wrong. Like many inventions here that did not quite work. That clock, which, pretty as it was, did not keep time at all.

He ran his fingers over the stubble of his face. "You've seen his other gadgets, no? A dishwashing machine. A lift. Binoculars. Music. Projections. What I meant to show you is, Emmett Sinclair had no one driving passion. He liked many things. Began many projects. There is no connection between them, except that he created them."

"So he made these because he knew they were important to you." I stole a glance at him. *Why* though? Why would a pirate wish to fly?

"Because," he answered my unspoken question, "I love to sail—*need* to—but can no longer do it on the water."

My gaze shot to his buttoned-up sleeve, his brokenness that I sometimes forgot about. We were both a little broken, it seemed. "A shame they don't work."

His look was grim.

"Nor the automaton, or so many of his gadgets. You'd never expect a man of such brilliance to turn out so many failed projects."

"He did not make mistakes, Miss Forrester. Every one of these inventions of his . . . they simply were not finished yet."

I glanced at my reflection in the dirty window. A little hope. *Not finished . . . yet.*

I gripped the gate before me, inhaling the powdery scent of birds. The depth of creation's aroma. My voice was quiet. "How I wish he were actually here to speak with."

He let my words sit for a moment before answering. "Yes."

I turned to look at his face, to see the source of that roughness in his voice. But he refused to meet my gaze.

"Come. I shall escort you back to the house." He strode away but paused to hand me up over the stones onto the path.

I worked up courage and cleared my throat. "I'm sorry. I don't always say the right words."

A smile flickered. "No, but they're interesting ones."

I smiled back. My bravery thickened. "I did appreciate the gift, Mr. Montagne. It *was* from you, wasn't it? The tools. The riddle."

"Of what do you accuse me, Miss Forrester?" A wry smile inched up his lips. "It is the daytime."

Up near Blakely House, the sound of rushing water jarred me. Rushing water and the creak and groan of that terrible swaying bridge. He looked back at me with a frown. "You are coming, yes?"

My feet were rooted. Wonderfully rooted on solid, dry ground. "Is there perhaps a different way back? I don't . . . care for bridges."

He tipped his head. "How did you come here?"

"Over the bridge." And I'd barely lived through it.

I felt the questions in his gaze—but he asked none of them. "Well then, this time will be far easier." He came back and took my hand, a smile warming his face. "There are two of us now."

And with those simple words, which I would never forget, relief bloomed and a warm sense of security took root. A small miracle occurred. My hand in his grasp, my feet loosened their leaden hold and followed him onto the bridge. And all the way across I felt the immense treasure of this singular idea—*there are two of us now.*

The bridge creaked. It shifted under our weight.

I shuddered.

Keep moving, just keep moving so I can walk across in one— don't look down—one piece and get to firm ground on the other side and then I'll be safe and it will be perfectly fine and I will be good and probably alive with no falling and no drowning and—

The bridge wobbled. I wobbled.

"Look at me," he commanded gently.

Back up to his face. And there, in those darkly intense eyes, the firm cut of his jaw, his gentle fierceness grounded me. The edges of panic smoothed.

I scrambled onto firm ground and he caught me, wrapping his mangled arm around my back to hold me up, and I stiffened, trembling, to keep from sobbing into his shirt as I caught my breath.

Closing my eyes, I breathed. I willed away the painful tingling heat that climbed my body. The sight of that water so far below, the twist and spin of my dizzy mind. Now that I was safe, I felt as though I was about to drown. But not in water, in panic. As it receded like the tide, I straightened and looked toward my guide.

But he merely smiled, as if I hadn't been the biggest fool over a bridge. "Ready for a climb?" Just like that, he folded my childish fear neatly into the moment and let life carry on around it. I looked up into his steady face as we climbed toward the house and couldn't help but smile back, just a little.

When we reached the level part of the path near the house, he released me. "You are well now?"

I nodded. Somehow my soul had settled more deeply into my body and I truly was well.

"I must cross the causeway while the tide is down and see to the cranes in Northumberland. You should be able to see yourself the rest of the way."

"Thank you," I said feebly, for those two words were meant to cover a great deal of things that day.

A flicker of a smile, then he was gone, white shirt billowing against his solid back.

I turned to the house and another set of fears. But when I looked up again, a lovely vision in blue came floating down the path, arms spread like wings as she sailed down to meet me. "Miss Forrester, Miss Forrester. Up at the house—there is a *happening*!" She reached me breathless and flushed, grabbing my arms. "It's men. They're hurt. And the others—oh, they'll perish! We can't have more souls on our hands. Please, you must stop them! They won't let them—oh, but they *must*! They won't save them. It's wretched of them. Wretched! Come, no time to waste!"

With a quick exhale, I allowed myself to be propelled up the stone walk and toward whatever catastrophe had occurred at Blakely House.

chapter
TWENTY

Interesting that when a ship wrecks, men bypass the waning human lives to rescue the cargo. Perhaps I am a backward man, for I do exactly the opposite.

~Emmett's letters to Sophie

There's been an accident," Dane said when I joined my cousins in the drawing room. Angel Holligan had shoved me into their little meeting then vanished, leaving me to inquire after the details. Reluctantly, they allowed me into the conversation.

"What sort of accident?"

"It's an island," snapped Tom Jolly. "What sort do you *think* it is?"

I gasped. "A wreck. But I was just out there—I saw nothing."

"It's on the ocean side of the island, not the land side," Dane said. "You'd have to go behind the house, up and over the hill to see it."

"A great big, splintery mess," Jolly said. "Several men injured. Many severe."

"What?! We must get to them. Can we rig up any stretchers? Some bandages, perhaps. And have the staff fetch blankets and hot-water bottles and . . ." My voice died off. "What? What is it?"

"Didn't you hear me? Severe injuries." Jolly's eyes snapped.

"Yes," I breathed. "So they'll need care immediately."

"Certainly." Dane rocked back on his heels. "But not from us. We are not equipped."

"What?" I sank into the chair behind me.

The men exchanged glances. "We've already voted to send them ashore. There are innkeepers and surgeons in Northumberland. The sailors can be *their* burden."

I stiffened. "But they're *sailors*. Penniless ones now. No one will help them on shore. You know that as well as I do."

"If they're good, honest men, there'll be someone to help them."

And if they were pirates, a little "broken," they were not worth the mangled clothing on their backs. Anger stiffened up my spine. "We have tools. Plenty of space and loads of servants. Why *wouldn't* we help them?"

"Because we're not *fools*, Miss Forrester." Jolly sloshed liquid into his glass and drank it down.

"What he means is, there's simply too much at risk. Look about you." Dane Hutchcraft waved his arms to indicate the great expanse of Blakely House, alive with machinery and power. "News of Uncle Emmett's death has traveled. People have heard. They've come sniffing about, hoping for a peek. A gem to carry off. And we aren't armed to stop them. Think of it—all his hard work and ingenuity . . ."

"Was to serve others. Always! Don't you see that?"

Jolly snorted.

"Besides, he *always* helped the men who wrecked here. Yet no one would consider Emmett Sinclair foolish."

Another look exchanged.

They would.

They *did.*

I stiffened. Steadied my breath. I closed my eyes and all I saw were those beautiful, carefully detailed paintings. The wrecks, little stick men scattered on the beach, with pillagers approaching . . . and that lovely avenging angel descending upon them all.

Like Aunt Lottie, staring down that neighbor man who had so neatly dropped me at her door and fled. I knew what it was to be cast out. And I knew what it was to be swept up and rescued.

"Tell her about the thefts, Dane. Seven different times— *seven*—some shipwrecked men left with all the valuables they could carry. With ingenious, one-of-a-kind inventions representing *years* of work. Years! Do you think they'll appreciate Emmett's innovations? His raw brilliance? Think of what Blakely House *is.* Just look around."

But I didn't need to. I closed my eyes.

Farneham Heald. It means a home for the weary traveler. But it is not that anymore . . .

I felt it melting away—the house's very identity. In the hands of these men, it would be like a machine switched off. All shiny metal and intrigue . . . and utterly lifeless. "We *must* help them. How can we not?"

"No," Jolly said. "I won't be opening Blakely House's door to thieves."

I shot out of the chair. "They aren't thieves! They're *injured people.*"

"Who have no place in my house!" His red face came near mine.

"It's. Not. Your. House." *It should be mine. It should be.* I felt it to my marrow.

Dane inserted himself like a knife blade, speaking quickly. Tersely. "I'll tell you a little secret about the men who work here, Miss Forrester. Not a single one of them is paid. Yet they remain—for years. Why? Because they're evading the law. They're brigands and criminals, every one. Those are the people who crash on these shores." He was close enough that I could smell cedar and sandalwood on his person. "Emmett Sinclair may have seen the value in using them, but I, for one, have no interest in welcoming vagabonds into our midst *or* in taking advantage of them. And *that* is the final word. Are we clear?"

We stood there, face to face to face. The three heirs, in the center of the great manor house.

This time next year, which of us would be master?

A shocking stillness came over me. Goose-down softness protected by the oil of outer feathers that suddenly wrapped around me, and his words slicked off me. I unclenched my fists but held my position. "If you won't bring those men up here, I will. It's *my* name on the will, whether or not you like it, and my name that should be on the deed to this place."

Dane's eyes narrowed, every wrinkle under them accentuated. "Do you *honestly* fancy yourself a fitting heir? Mark my words, Sydney Forrester. You will *ruin* Blakely House if you're given so much as a *crumb* of ownership. There's something damaged in that head of yours. Something quite wrong and I *will not* let you bungle this estate."

I stared at this man, this compact and overcharged clock, and saw with sudden clarity the way he was put together—

how all his gears functioned behind the clockface. He called me broken because he himself was; his desire to be impressive was simply because he knew he was not. "What has made you so bitter, I wonder? Whose approval are you so desperate to have?"

His lip flicked up in a snarl for a flash. Then he banged the tabletop with a fist and stalked off. "Keep her out of this. And get those strangers off our beach."

I was a coil of anger. Red-hot and glowing. "You *beastly* man!" I lurched at him. Jolly grabbed me, pinned me against him.

Dane paused. Met my gaze with a look of pure hatred that normally would have made me shrink into myself. Yet liquid calm washed over me again, and I felt rooted firmly to Blakely House. A sense of belonging and rightness. Of Dane's wrongness, despite all his education. "You're sentencing those men to death."

His eyes flashed. The blaze of rivalry passed between us without a word. "Ring the servants. Let's have these men off our shores."

"No one'll come if I do. It's the first of the month and they've gone to Northumberland for supplies. You round them up when they return," Jolly said, his chin digging into my shoulder. "I'll see to her."

Moments later I paced through the upper corridors, rubbing my upper arm where Jolly had gripped it. Up the stairs he had marched me, tossing me into my suite which had no lock. "I'll set the men to watch every stairway," he had snapped, then he vanished.

I'd paced nervously at first, then set to work feverishly on the clock, simply to keep busy. To have something I could see and touch and take control of. I laid the clock pieces out on the floor as an archaeologist lays out bones and tried to make sense of how it all worked together. Why it was still not functional. If I could solve this clock, its brokenness, perhaps I could solve myself.

Restless. I was restless. I leaped up and paced, then darted out into the hallway, guards be hanged.

Which is the moment I remembered they were all in Northumberland for supplies. There was no one to guard me.

I went in search of the stairs, which seemed to have a very fickle location. They never seemed to be where I remembered leaving them.

Jolly. What did he think of this? Of the injured men suffering on Farneham Heald's shores? For all his irritability, there was something more authentic about the man than Dane. Emotions nearer the surface. A raw sense of justice.

I came to the end of a hallway, but when I reached what seemed to be a dead end, it opened into a sharp left instead. I sped up and seethed. *We need you at Blakely House*, Angel had said. And she had been right. She'd been *right*!

I slowed at last, and let my forehead fall with a *thump* against a papered wall. As it struck, a cuckoo clock sounded the hour. Fourteen times. Then, in the distance a light metal *clink*, over and over. As if someone walked with a metal cane.

Or metal feet.

"Hello?" I looked down the hallway, right then left. "Who's there?"

Nothing. It was nothing. I was fine and this was nothing.

But . . . it was *something*.

Water gushed in some distant part of the house. Electricity buzzed as the power surged. I paced down the hallway and a single sconce warmed the wall ahead, casting long shadows over the paintings of wreckage. I stepped closer, peering over every one of them again. I stared at the lilac-clad angel descending on the shipwrecked men, my heart in my throat.

Sophie. That had to be Sophie Holland.

The only spot of color besides her dress was the purple door set in a thick, gray lighthouse. I touched that door, wishing I could walk through it. Ask Sophie what she'd have done. The painting rested crooked against its mount, and I straightened it.

A paper crinkled behind it. I took it out and found a printed image of that very lighthouse with a woman, that avenging angel, perched on the front steps, head tipped to the left. I slipped it back behind the painting, but it didn't go. Reaching up to see what was catching, my fingers touched the paper backing of the frame, and there was more, tucked inside against the canvas.

I braced myself and lifted it down, setting the rather heavy piece on the ground and turning it over. A whole satchel of papers had been jammed inside, between the canvas and backing. I tugged them out and smiled at more images of the woman, the lighthouse with the purple door, and the familiar handwriting of Sophie Holland.

My Dearest Emmett, how I wish I could fly home to you. The birds are migrating from the coast, headed toward Northumberland on their way to new territory and I'd give anything to climb on their backs and be carried along. My gardens are no sanctuary anymore, for I hear the waves whenever I step outdoors. I see the ships coming and know what will befall them in the night. Armand has been

gone these five years, but his voice reaches me even now,
demanding that I come inside so I do not witness their evil.
Screaming at anyone who dares stop him.

I cry far too often, Emmett dear. I cannot bear to think
of the human lives on board who will be lost. I will go mad
thinking about it. What can one woman do?

Wrecker. Sophie's husband had been a wrecker. That's what
Emmett had painted here. Not the wrecks on Farneham Heald,
but the wrecks on Sophie's coastline.

Then, another Sophie note.

I did it. I warned them, dear one, just as you said I should.
I found an old lantern and I broke my looking glass to put
the biggest shards into it. The light shone so brightly! So
warm and alive. Like those people. They are now rescued
and protected by the Norwegian authorities, because of
your idea. Because of you, dear Emmett.

And now I shall rest. The ship saw the light, but so did
Armand's men. He isn't here to protect me anymore. They
turned on me and all my fears came to pass, but it wasn't
so terrible. I only felt it a little, because I felt strong. I knew
that I'd saved so many of them. They're alive, Emmett. The
entire ship of people. And now, so am I.

So am I!

I was dizzy. I forced a deep breath and realized I'd been
taking quick, shallow sips of air. A few faded news clippings
were next in the jumble, which mostly retold the facts Sophie
had relayed. The wrecks, the rescue . . . and a suspected band
of pillagers who had stripped the ships of cargo.

For all his scattered messes, Emmett Sinclair *had* been organized. Where else would all the details of wrecks belong than with the paintings they had inspired? As if he had kept them there to draw detail from as he painted.

Another letter, in Sophie's recognizable hand. This one begged Emmett to fetch her. Pleaded with him.

You'll know where to find me. Past the lighthouse, tucked in the most perfect circle that ever was. Please come for me, Emmett. I cannot bear to witness death and greed any longer.

But beware of the snare. Wrecks happen in the fog, because of the lights on each side, like an inlet welcoming boats to ride out the storm. Yet it's rocks, jagged and treacherous. You'll know it when you see three lights on one side and four on the other. Many a ship have attempted to moor in during a storm, only to be caught unawares . . . and crash into the coastline. Families are dying out there, Emmett. Women and children too. I cannot bear it!

With a cry I dropped the letters and ran through the halls until I found a little oval window that overlooked the beach, down the hill and beyond the cliffs. Women and children? Figures lay like discarded linens along the wet beach far below me, struggling to rise, hunched over injuries. Some figures were quite small. It was the frizzy-headed child who did it for me, face in her hands as the wind tumbled her curls about.

My pain arced from Blakely House to the beach.

Backing away from the window, I ran down the corridor and found a larger window, threw up the sash, and after a quick glance down the hall, I climbed out.

chapter
TWENTY-ONE

Why hydroelectricity, you ask? Why water? My dearest
Sophie, I simply sought out the most inane, undervalued
element in all of nature and harnessed its great power.

~*Emmett's letters to Sophie*

A slender young man lifted his head as I reached the
beach, pulse pounding against my temples, and he
locked pleading eyes onto my face. A gash on the
side of his head had begun to dry, but his skin was alarmingly
pale. He looked so like my father as a young man—thoughtful
and quiet, studious and earnest—and it jolted me. Yet death
seemed to hover like a shadow over the man, ready to yank
the last bit of soul from his body.

I ran to him, cradling his head in my lap as if to hold his
soul earth-side and brushed sand off the wound with my skirt.
Blood gushed onto my hand from somewhere—his neck. No,
his shoulder. I shifted him. He grimaced with pain.

Bunching up the edge of my apron, I clamped it to his wound. He jerked, and the wound gushed again. "Don't move, don't move. You're safe here. You're on Farneham Heald, and those who wash ashore here are taken care of. We'll have you fixed up soon."

He met my eyes. Blinked. Then felt about beside him with weak movements, fingers spidering over the sand. Just out of reach were a pair of spectacles, one stem bent. I blew sand off them and placed them into the well-worn grooves on the sides of his head.

With metal spectacles askew on his face and a high white collar, he looked more academic than seafarer. A most inappropriate giggle bubbled up in my throat, borne of so many things cluttering up my heart. The utter ridiculousness of the argument I'd just had with my cousins. "They think . . ." I laughed even more. "They think you're pirates. They thought you might steal . . ." The bubble of laughter overtook my sentence.

He blinked, his blue eyes suddenly quite large behind the spectacles, pressed his dry lips together and licked them, then a measure of calm stilled his body.

I giggled some more and a deep sigh escaped his chest. The barest smile tipped the corners of his lips.

I sobered. How could they deem this man unworthy of help? Claim his life had less value than the metal and wood curiosities in the house? How could they not see it? He jerked, and I laid a hand on him. "You'll be restored to health. I shall see to it myself." His eyes rolled. Color drained from his face. "Stay with me, mister. Stay here." I gently smacked his cheek and he shook his head, color returning to his cheeks.

Another whimper sounded nearby. A small child—a boy— lay stunned on the sand, staring directly up at the sun. Still cradling the man with spectacles in my lap, I passed my fingers over the child's mouth and felt wet breath. From a cursory glance, the lad didn't appear hurt—only stunned.

The man on my lap gasped, arching his back. I fought to regain pressure on the injury, clamping on to another gush. His eyes flew open. "Must . . . help . . ."

"Shh." I laid a hand on his narrow chest. "Tell me who you are. Where were you going?" Anything to keep him talking. To keep those eyes focused on me.

He blinked rapidly, eyes wide. He opened his mouth, and croaked out a sound.

"What? What did you say?" I bent near, careful not to jostle him.

He opened his mouth wide once again. "Please. Have . . . wife. Baby. Get . . . home."

Pain squeezed my heart.

But then a shadow loomed over me. I turned, dreading the sight of the servants come to toss the survivors onto stretchers and haul them away. But it was a glowing, feminine figure wreathed in smiles and linen skirts. *Sophie*, my heart whispered, but a familiar voice came. "I knew you'd find a way, Miss Sydney."

"Angel!" I waved her closer. "He needs help. They all do."

She knelt beside me on the sand and swung a large, burlap bag from her back. "I can help." Jars and bags tumbled out of the sack's mouth. "I have a knack for herbs, be it in pastry or poultice."

I exhaled a ragged breath, then glanced toward the causeway where the men would cross, but the rocky cliffs blocked it from my view. "We must move them off the beach. Are the others coming?"

"The servants?" She tapped a stoppered jar, holding it up to the light. "The men were gathering tarps and poles when I left. Took some doing since there hasn't been a wreck here in some time, but help should be along."

I shook my head. "They're not coming to help. They're removing them from the island."

Her head snapped up. "What?"

"Dane's orders."

The man's hand gripped mine like a vice, nearly breaking me. His eyes pleaded. He wouldn't survive a trip anywhere right now, and we both knew it.

I held his gaze. A vow. I'd do my level best.

Angel's mouth hung open. "We can't—they'll—"

"I know." I shifted the man on my lap and grabbed him under his armpits. "I was outvoted. Now, help me get them off the beach. Here, put pressure on his wound." I yanked off my apron and put her hand over it.

Doors banged far in the distance and I threw myself over him, bridging his broken body with mine. Soon they'd be making their way down the path. "We need to move them *now*." I yanked the man's dead weight. *God . . . help him. Help me to help him.* I cried out and yanked again, falling back into the sand. Pain shot up my arm and into my shoulder in streaks of red-hot lightning. *I cannot do this! Cannot run Blakely House!* I crouched, braced myself, and heaved again. A great, guttural cry and I fell back again, hot tears blinding me.

A gentle touch on my shoulder. "Your strength," Angel said into my ear over the wind. "Use your strength."

I did! rose in my mind, but not *that* strength. That's not what she meant.

"*Your* strength."

I froze for an endless moment, staring over the bodies of injured and dead. The torn humanity. Then my gaze flicked about for resources. Tools. What *was* my strength?

"We'll have to hoist them. Make a lever."

I laid hold of the ship's broken hand truck used for transporting the cargo and fetched a board from the wreckage to form a flat surface. We slid the injured man onto the board, lifted him onto the hand truck's frame, and with his feet against the toe plate, levered him gently upward. Suddenly his weight felt like nothing to move. Together we rolled him around the rocks to an inlet where the open mouths of caves greeted us. We deposited him just inside and straightened.

"We cannot move them all, mistress," said Angel, wringing her hands, panting. "There's only one of these contraptions and the servants have reached the bridge. What'll we do?"

A stout, mud-splattered man appeared at the cave. "I'll lend a hand. A few of us aren't too bad off." He touched the gash on his forehead. "Just a flesh wound."

"Very well." I turned to Angel. "Are you quite certain you can help him?"

A firm nod.

"Then let's rescue the ones who need it most. Leave the strongest to be brought ashore by the servants. They won't know there are more."

I rose to go, but something grabbed my hand. The rescued man, his blue eyes iridescent behind thick spectacles in the dim hiding place. "Thank . . . you . . ."

A nod, then we all went to rescue more of the injured.

chapter
TWENTY-TWO

For every gigantic flaw, I possess an enormous strength in equal intensity, so that if I plot the extremes of my personality on a graph, they look rather like a star—the only thing that shines in the night sky.

~Emmett's letters to Sophie

W hen I stumbled into the owl suite hours later, winded and smelling of salt air, Angel's dough-scented warmth filled my bedchamber—along with the aroma of tart cherries.

We had both vanished when the servants swarmed the beach, and I hadn't any idea where she had gone as I had crouched for an eternity behind the rocks. I'd snuck up the path and hidden in the stables until I could return undetected. I needed to remain at Blakely House now. More than ever.

Angel twirled to face me, fresh and dapper as if she'd never left the house. "I've something to show you." She presented me with a plate. "But first, cherry tarts to liven the senses. I do so love what a cherry does to my mouth, don't you?"

"I love cherries." Were we going to speak of the rescue?

"My dear husband—God rest 'im—asked me nearly every time I made a crust if I'd fill it with cherries. Anything else was a perfect waste of baking material."

We were *not* going to address it. "Mr. Holligan had superb taste." Almost as if the house had ears and eyes, and we both knew it.

"Oh no, dear. That was Mr. Bengali, my third husband."

I eased into a chair and blinked, warmth tingling over my body. Had she fussed over Emmett Sinclair when he'd returned from a rescue too? "The master. My uncle. What sort of pie did he like?"

Her lips twitched in a smile. "What a strange question. He didn't, actually. He preferred cured pork with a sweet relish sauce. He always had the meat dried and salted with a special hickory flavoring, and he ate it night and day—especially when he worked. I delighted in making it exactly the way he liked it. Oh!" She stiffened, a look of shock on her face. "What have you done to it?"

I looked past her to the few remaining clock pieces on the floor. "I wanted to look it over—fix the problem."

"Fix?"

"Yes, I'm determined to repair it." To repair me. All the scattered pieces. I put the clock back together quickly, turned it over. Still it did not click through the seconds. "There's never been a clock I could not repair."

"But it isn't broken."

I blinked, pausing to look over the reassembled clock. "It doesn't keep time!"

She crouched beside me and took my hands. "Darling, it was never meant to."

She took it, flipping switches and winding the clock hands backward. *"Fifty-five degrees, ten,"* it said. It whirred, and the clockface cast itself upon the wall, dim now in the daylight. She handed it to me. "Around this place, some clocks are put together differently." A wink.

I stared at that clock. There were plenty that *did* keep time, but this one was odd . . . remarkably so.

"And now, what I have to show you." She disappeared into the hall and returned with an armful of thick, dust-laden leather books. "In case you've nothing to do when you can't sleep at night."

"How did you know—"

"You're a woman with a brain—one that I imagine cannot be switched off as easily as the lights. These should keep you occupied on nights you lie awake. Now, eat up so I can bring down an empty tray and feel I've done my duty."

I looked at Angel Holligan, who I'd once thought whimsical—simple, perhaps. She didn't miss a blamed thing, though.

I ate the tart, suddenly ravenous, and licked my fingers, then turned to the stack of books. At first it looked like the inner workings of madness on the page. But as I studied the columns, the tiny notes in code, I realized it was a financial ledger.

"He liked to rewrite the endings of stories. This is how he rewrote real life. I thought you might find these an amusing way to learn about your uncle."

"My cousins should see these. They could help us understand so much about Uncle Emmett."

She wrinkled her nose. "These ledgers have been lying about for weeks, and they've glossed through and cast them aside when they couldn't understand them."

"You do not care for them, do you? My cousins, that is."

"Well, do you?"

I cringed.

"See? You've good sense too." Generous hunks of cheese followed, laid out on the tray beside the remaining tarts. Then she lowered her voice. "Now you see why I came to fetch you from Grafton. This place needs a decent heir."

"Which would be nearly anyone besides the other two."

She considered me, setting down the tray. "You do remind me of him, you know. He was a singular man, that Emmett Sinclair. Many called him odd."

I licked the cherry off my lips, trying not to appear as intensely interested as I actually was. "Did they?" I knew that label all too well. Wore it like a garment most days.

"Indeed, and thank heavens he was." She poured me tea and slid it over.

I raised my eyebrows.

"He had rather large, noticeable flaws, but also more brilliance in his little toe than the whole of Northumberland on a good day."

I gathered her words up in my heart and held them close. Calling a person *odd* or *quiet* was incredibly limiting. Because there was always more to them—*much more*—than those labels.

"Rather an uneven distribution of traits, if you ask me," Angel went on. "But 'even' is overrated."

"I've yet to hear of any flaws he possessed. I cannot imagine him having any."

"He was simply *terrible* at courting a woman or hosting lavish parties. Anything to do with people, really. He never could negotiate a deal or keep his records organized. Why, I once found a holiday card from Her Majesty—the Queen of England—jammed between the pages of a novel."

"Perhaps he was keen to keep it safe."

"It was holding his place. As a *bookmark*!"

I snorted my tea. Coughed.

She pressed her lips together and eyed me. "How lovely one of us finds it amusing."

"Relatable, perhaps."

"Aha!" She poked one flour-dusted finger my way. "You see? The perfect heir. You carry his blood in your veins, Miss Sydney." She sat on the stool before me, our knees touching. "One is never given enormous flaws without also having some equally enormous strength to counterbalance it. You, for example, are terribly sensitive."

"Indeed." My face heated.

"And thank goodness for that." She laid a hand on my knee and smiled, seeming to finally acknowledge the rescue effort. A pat to my knee, then she rose, balancing on one foot, then the other. "He did have one project I never understood. You didn't have a special affinity for hyacinths, did you, Miss Forrester?"

"Not me, no."

"It was the ballroom. He had it done over with very specific instructions. Prisms and tulle and wild amounts of little mirrors—it must look like stardust, he said. And hyacinths. Everywhere, he painted purple hyacinths until the whole place looked like . . . well, his gardens. I thought perhaps he had it done up for someone in particular."

I slowly shook my head. "It wasn't me he had in mind." But I didn't mention Sophie. I couldn't say why. Perhaps because I was tired of hearing their love story brushed off as make-believe. "How have I never seen this ballroom?"

Her brow furrowed. "He had it shut up so we wouldn't have to keep it up."

Because she had refused him. She'd refused, and he had hidden the ring and the ballroom.

"There are a great many rooms about this old place that most of the staff have never set foot in. Much less a guest like yourself."

After Angel left, I turned over the words of a certain letter in my mind. It had been in the writing slope, the stack of unsent letters he'd written. A sketch of a splendid room had been attached.

To give you hope—a glimpse of what you have waiting for you. One day we will dance together in this room, as you asked of me so long ago. My dearest Sophie, I would be honored to dance with you.

chapter
TWENTY-THREE

André let his fingers trip over the piano keys, picking out a familiar melody. It merely took the edge off his restlessness. He stared down at the limp arm in his lap.

But then . . . music sounded in the distance. Gentle and plinking, echoing through the largeness of Blakely House. It was that music box. The one that had convinced Miss Forrester that Emmett Sinclair had once been in love.

Rising, he moved down the hall, following the sound into the old, unused ballroom. Edging the door open, he looked upon a lone figure spinning over the wide-open floor, prisms casting rainbows over her white dress that for once was not wrapped in that oversized apron. She was quite poised—tall and slender. Bare toes peeked out under the hem and it made her look . . . not girlish, but authentic. Honest. Off in the shadows, a little orange mountain of fur observed with grave dignity.

"Oh I'd be delighted!" she was saying in her lilting voice. "Perhaps we could walk in the gardens. Blakely House has a most splendid one, and have you seen the flowers by the bridge? A veritable wreath of color!"

A smile curved André's lips as he watched her, loose chestnut waves flowing over a straight back, dainty chin tipped up as she embraced her imaginary partner and let him spin her around the room with the rhythm of an old worn-out music box open on the table.

"And oh—*you* have a Steinhoffen?" Her hand went to her chest. "How on earth do you keep it wound?" On and on she chattered, laughing and spinning and answering herself.

The world overlooked those who were unusual. Who did unexpected things. *What a loss.*

Sliding into the room, he caught his breath. It glowed with natural beauty. A canopy of flowers arched overhead. Rainbows danced on every wall with hundreds of tiny crystals reflecting slices of light from every angle. And the tile shimmered like polished geodes.

But it was the spinning woman in the center who had his attention, and her rapid, one-sided conversation. "Do tell me you've read Chaucer. Because I couldn't dream of marrying anyone who hadn't. But let's not fall into circumlocution over Chaucer before we've even discussed Wilkie Collins!"

Careful not to let his boots click on tile, he approached and bowed at the waist. "Might I cut in?"

She spun, a look of horror on her face just as her toes caught on her opposite heel and she stumbled.

Instinctively his mangled arm shot out, catching her in its crook, and he stared down at her wide eyes, the lips parted, and he felt it. Felt the tingles in his chest. He only ever felt this way as his ship drew up at a new port.

She awoke something in him—that pull toward discovery.

Toward something original and fresh. Every blink of her eyes, every tip of her pure face, every unexpected word that fell from her mouth intrigued and charmed and surprised him. And he enjoyed that immensely. She was a quiet burst of intelligence in the place one least expected to find it. And somehow, every encounter with her left him feeling outwitted.

Which he found irresistible.

He allowed himself to stare at her as he slowly stood her back up. Then he swept her into the rest of the waltz, as if the fall had merely been a dip. "You are dancing alone. In the ballroom. In the middle of the night."

"Yes, well." She glanced away, cheeks flushing deeper. "The rooftop wasn't available."

A smile flickered. She was close enough that he could see the light smattering of freckles bridging her nose. "Also. Circumlocution?"

A quick blush. "You know. Wordy. Overly talkative. Using far too many . . ."

He cocked an eyebrow.

"Oh come now, it wasn't *that* ostentatious!"

He raised both eyebrows.

With a huff, she lowered her gaze, long hair curtaining her face, which was sure to be even more flushed as she muttered something about dragging him back to the schoolroom.

He turned her gently in a waltz, looking over the ballroom. "Do you know, I've never been in this room."

She relaxed a little in his arms. "Never?"

"He's kept it closed."

"Because he designed it for her. She never came back."

Sophie again. "You are an incurable romantic, Miss Forrester. I never would have guessed."

Her gaze wandered the room. "The winters must have been incredibly difficult for her. So stifling! Being indoors crushed her spirit."

His shoulders tightened. André could identify with that.

"So he created a garden to make Blakely House tolerable for her, even in winter."

"It would seem it was not successful. She is not here."

"No." They slowed and worry puckered her brow. "And it's a terrible shame."

He stiffened. "Some are not satisfied with less than what is real."

"But this *is* real." She walked to the center of the blue marble floors that shimmered like a lake, and spun slowly. Overhead, solar-powered prisms turned in the candlelight, giving the effect of rain falling. "You're missing the point. *She* missed the point." Her voice was soft, as if she weren't speaking to him. "And now he shall never have the chance to waltz her about her garden."

He took a deep breath and let out the frustration. She was rewriting the master's ending. Taking the story, as Emmett himself used to do, and casting a more palatable one with her glittering imagination. But his supposed love story, like this splendid room, was not real.

He sighed and approached her. "At least someone was able to dance about this room. With *and* without a real partner."

She turned and blushed again. "You'll forgive my quirks, I hope. I do try to tame them. I am rather odd, I know."

"Rare." He brushed a tender thumb over her cheek as if to brush away her insecurities, then tucked wayward curls behind her ear.

Her eyes fluttered closed, and she leaned into his hand just a little. "Hm?"

He drank in the scent of her, almost undone by her subtle reaction to his touch. "If you were a gem among rocks in a cave, you would not be considered odd." The music plinked slower, nearing the end of its windup. "You would be called rare." He leaned near and gently kissed her forehead, sealing his words.

Then her eyes flew open and she jerked back, as if just realizing how close she'd let him. How dangerous that might be. "Who would call me that?"

I would. But he did not voice the words while she was already frightened. She didn't move back, but she crossed her arms, putting up a clear barrier between them. He fought a slight sense of rejection, but then read the situation and bolstered himself—she was exactly like the late master. "You are afraid of new things, yes? Of whatever you don't know." Few men paid her compliments, he sensed, and even fewer had dared kiss her face.

"No, I'm not." She leaned on her right foot. Then left. "But I do like knowing. And it's so much nicer to experience new things in *books*."

"You settle for someone else's adventures."

"I simply don't see a reason to face what I don't have to. I love my life as it is. I've always been . . ."

"Bored?"

"Content."

He stood before her, longing to sweep her into a spin and draw her close. He could almost feel her warmth in his arms. Smell the closeness of her skin. His voice was suddenly lower. Raspy. "What if there's far more than content?"

"Boring is highly underrated. And many exciting things end tragically." Her face angled away from him, toward the window sash. Her cheeks, which had flamed in the brief tenderness they'd shared, grew even rosier now. Her arms tightened around her middle. "If you want adventures so badly, Mr. Montagne, you should have them. But don't go telling me how to overcome fear when you've never faced it yourself."

"Perhaps I have."

She scrunched her nose. "You are not afraid. I don't believe it."

"Come." He crooked a finger.

She looked at him, at last. "Now?"

He shrugged. "Sleep eludes us both. What else have we to do?" He swept his arms behind himself, grabbing his broken limb with the good one. "I promise not to lay an untoward finger on you, Miss Forrester."

She backed away. "Bed. I should . . . sleep. Someone might—"

"What do you throw out when you need it, and bring back when you don't?"

She blinked, frozen midrejection. "Words?"

He shook his head, grinning and rocking back on his heels.

She fluttered her hand and turned away. "I cannot think of the answer in the middle of the night. I'm certain I'll think of it in the morning. Good night, Mr. Montagne."

"Good night, Miss Forrester."

He ambled out to the servant's hall and lounged on a stool against the wall, made himself some tea . . . and eyed the door.

Not ten minutes passed before she burst through the doorway. "A bullet. It's a bullet! Or an arrow."

He took a casual sip, then sat forward. "I would never retrieve a fired bullet. Nor an arrow, for that matter. Would you?"

"It cannot be anything else!" She raked her fingers through her hair. "Just *tell me* so I can sleep!"

He smiled and shook his head. "I will show you."

She bit her lip. Looked about. "I suppose no one will miss us at this hour." So she gathered up a lantern, fetched her heavy cloak, and allowed him to lead her out into the chilly night. He felt as though he'd won something important.

For once, André was grateful for the lights Emmett Sinclair had installed at intervals along the path and scattered over parts of the beach. Darkness still ruled, but light interrupted now and then.

"Do you enjoy making me look foolish, Mr. Montagne?"

He smiled, then dipped his gaze. "Actually, I delight in the nearly impossible challenge of outwitting you."

She only stared at him, as if trying to determine if he was serious.

Rather than continuing toward the bridge, he led her between two rock outcroppings and down a narrow, unpaved footpath.

"Where are you taking me?"

He smiled. "That would spoil the fun."

She frowned.

"*My* fun." He reached for her hand, and together they stepped over the path that was barely a path. Down they crept, grasping boulders and tree branches, heading to the northernmost side of the island.

At last the rocks parted just above the shoreline to reveal a great ship, blue and gold panels winking in the moonlight, four crisp sails snapping in the breeze. His heart swelled to three times its normal size at the sight of the vessel that had once been his home. His fortress.

She didn't speak, but she trembled, her breath coming in quick puffs as she looked down upon the distant reflection of his past life. Then the water hissed and foamed upon the rocks below, and she backed into him, sending pebbles skittering down to the shore.

He held her against him for a moment, surprised at the warmth inside him at the mere closeness of another human. Her tension loosened perceptibly as he held her firmly against him, and he drank in the moment, but craved more.

He took the lantern from her and placed it on the rocks. "Close your eyes," he said with a tinge of mercy, and led her the rest of the way.

He slowed at the shore, feeling the salt on his skin, hearing the *thwap* of mainsail and topsail that he knew so well. He seldom came within view of the thing anymore, if he could help it. But now he crossed the rocky beach, strode up the ramp, and slowed on the ship's deck.

Positioning her toward the main mast, he placed her hands on the helm and curled her fingers around the wood. He closed his eyes for a moment too, inhaling and feeling the familiar sway of the ship, the creak of thick boards under his feet. "Now. Open your eyes, Miss Forrester." This was his world. His home. What an odd delight, inviting her into it. Seeing what she'd make of it.

chapter
TWENTY-FOUR

She stiffened, gripping the helm as it cranked and turned against her hold.

"Do you feel how much power you hold in your hands? Even with a docked ship, you can feel it, no?" He trembled. The wood under his feet swayed, the canvas sails whipping against the wood overhead. The smell of sea fed his senses.

"It's hard to manage something this large. I cannot fathom taking it out on the water."

"Imagine controlling it with one hand. It would be impossible."

"Especially when it's wrecked."

"It isn't wrecked . . . any longer."

"You've repaired it?"

He shrugged. "I haven't any idea why." He raked fingers through his hair, which was now loose of its constraint. "Perhaps just because there wasn't much damage—a hole in the hull from rocks. Easy enough to replace the splintered wood. Sinclair and I even fitted it with a furnace and a stern-side propeller from one of the flying machines."

"You've made it a steamship."

"It was merely something to do, I suppose, when I first came. I'll not be sailing it again, any more than I'll be taking the flying machine over the water." He'd worked on it fiendishly during his recovery, probably delaying his healing, but he'd slowly given up on ever escaping the island. The only thing still broken was now a part of him—or rather, a lack. And that wasn't going to change.

She turned and looked him full in the face, her eyes glistening. "There isn't anything wrong with the flying machines either, is there? It's you. You're afraid you'll wreck again. So you refused to fly him out in them."

Jaw clenched, he looked out across the placid waters. "If it had been only my life at stake, I could have done it. But not with another man on board. Especially Emmett Sinclair."

"So you turned him down. But he went anyway."

Pain lanced his chest. He gripped the helm's spoke harder. "He stood up and announced to the entire staff that he was to meet his heir, to make certain of suitability, then he would return. I assumed he planned to continue prodding me, to convince me to come along, and I'd have a chance to dissuade him, but he did not. I traveled to London for several days to handle legal matters for him and when I returned, I discovered he had taken the cursed flying machine and simply . . . vanished. Then he died. Alone."

"Oh." She was still looking up at him, reading his face.

"So you see, Miss Forrester, sometimes fear can cost one a great deal. And staying put isn't always neutral. I just wanted you to know that."

She was quiet for a moment. Then she said, "I should be saying that it wasn't your fault. Any more than it was mine, simply because he died on his way to see me. I suppose that's why they think I've killed him."

"That, and the tampering with his flying machine." He didn't even mention the odd letter he'd heard the nephews discussing—the one warning them of Sydney Forrester. "Someone caused it to crash, directly after he was to evaluate you as a potential heir. You can imagine how it looks." He watched her steadily, noticing every jerk and nuance in her face. A range of emotions.

"I never even met him."

He ran fingers over the stubble forming on his jaw. "He never reached you, then?"

Her lashes fluttered as she shook her head sadly.

He sighed. "Emmett Sinclair finally has the courage for an adventure, and he never even experienced half of it." *But he might have.* He placed his hand over hers on the helm. "Do not let fear cripple you, mon amie. Just grab hold. Grab hold of the helm and—"

"And pick up a novel instead." She jerked her hands off the handles, spinning her back to him, shoulders tight. "I wish everyone would leave me to my books and stop telling me to *grab hold.* I quite like my life."

He blinked at the sudden turn. He took hold of her hand, but she looked away, her features tense. He studied them anyway, and what he saw surprised him a little. Amused him a lot. "You are not angry—no, you're not. You are sensing a pull toward something. And you are fighting it, no?"

She blew out a breath and twirled her hand dismissively. "It's nothing, truly. Just a few odd coincidences . . . a turn of phrase that keeps coming up and . . . well . . . It hardly matters."

His grin stretched over his face. "Of course it does. Because coincidences do not exist."

"You're saying it's a *miracle*, these silly patterns and repeated phrases? That they mean something?"

He shrugged. "Does that frighten you? Or perhaps make you wish to *grab hold*?"

She huffed out a breath at the phrase she obviously did not wish to hear. "I don't care for being ordered about." She fidgeted. "But sometimes I want an instruction manual. There, now you see what an odd duck I am. I want it both ways."

"Mmm, I'd think of it less as an order and more of an invitation. A gentle prodding. God inviting you to look his way. Perhaps you should. Even if it means an adventure or two."

Her eyebrows, such expressive little slashes over eyes that glittered with thoughts, worked up and down and furrowed in turns. "Why does anyone care if I have real-life adventures, anyway?"

He walked around to stand in front of her, but she still didn't look at him. Not at his eyes, anyway. "Because everyone deserves to see God."

Surprise bloomed on her face.

"You cannot expect to see his greatness if you give him no cause to demonstrate it. That requires leaving the safety of the shore a time or two. Or ten."

Her look melted into longing as the wind toyed with her loose hair. "I wish I saw what you see."

He pondered her wistful face for a moment, then jerked his head toward the center mast, indicating she should go up. "Have a look."

She crossed her arms again. "So what *do* you throw away?"

He blinked. "Pardon?"

"The riddle. What do you throw away when you need it,

and . . ." Her gaze roved over the ship. "Ah! That." She crossed to the anchor lying on thick rope on the port side. "Am I right?"

"Congratulations, my lady," he said with a mock bow. "You are correct and have won a climb to a magnificent view." He pointed up at the crow's nest overhead.

She backed away, looking up with a frown. "I don't think I should care to see the water from that height. Or any height, really." A shiver.

"We won't look at the water, then." He swung onto the pole and climbed the spokes. "Simply close your eyes and climb." When he looked down, she was climbing, her skirt billowing in the breeze. Her eyes were squeezed shut. He handed her up onto the platform and lay on his back, inviting her to do the same. She did, looking directly up into the great starry mass above her. "Now." He settled against the wood, arms behind his head. "What do you think?"

Her breathing quickened, as if she was caught off guard, then slowed as she seemed to sink into the moment. The light of moon and stars glowed on her upturned face.

She did see it, didn't she? How could anyone not?

He cast his gaze up too. The great open sky overcame his senses, widening the awe in his chest. The out-of-doors did that—shifted one's gaze from the temporal to the eternal. He never grew tired of it. "How might one put that down on paper, Miss Forrester?"

"Sydney," she said quietly. "It is nighttime, and you must call me Sydney."

He shot a glance at her and smiled. "What is it you see, Sydney?"

The moon glowed on the rounded tip of her nose, lay against

the flush of her cheeks. "I see stars. Hundreds and hundreds of them. Like holes in the surface of the darkness."

They lay in silence, the beauty of nightfall resting heavily on his chest. He stole little glances at her, though. She was transfixed, swallowed up by an adventure novel that lived and breathed, full of wonder that muffled the chaos of everyday life.

Those men were entirely wrong about her killing the master. They must be. She would have enjoyed Emmett Sinclair—likely more than she would enjoy his fortune. It was merely coincidence that things fell the way they did.

He only wished he knew what it was she was hiding. There was something that made her hedge so, kept her from being able to meet his gaze, and perhaps it was also the reason for her hesitation around him. Her obvious nerves.

"I wonder how they stay up there. And why we cannot get closer."

He looked at her profile. "You remind me of him, you know. You'll grow weary of hearing it, but it's true."

She smiled up at the sky. "I shall never tire of such a compliment."

Then she turned her head to look at him and there she was, not three inches from him, a look of bright expectancy on her face. "Is it this way every night?"

It took him a moment to respond. "Except when there are clouds." He reached out and braved a touch to her face, brushing hair from her forehead.

Her eyes flew wide and he withdrew his hand. "I'm sorry, I should not presume so."

Her gaze remained on him. He could scarcely breathe.

"Have you a lady friend somewhere, Mr. Montagne? It's just . . . she might be put off. If she were to hear of this."

He smiled, lying back with his hand behind his head. "There is one young lady who has captured my interest, but there is no formal agreement. In fact, I have not approached her yet. She is no ordinary woman, so it is hard to tell if . . . how do you say it? How I might be received. Perhaps she would . . ."

"Reject you?"

"Become frightened." He turned his head against the wood to look at her. "And I wouldn't want that."

"A pirate, frightening someone?" Her smile was amused and content. The outdoors did wonders for her. Visibly opened up her soul.

Then she sobered. "This young lady. Perhaps she's rather inexperienced. It's a new journey for her, and she hasn't a good map handy. Compasses are out of the question."

He pressed back a smile. His dulled senses stirred, his thirst for adventure that had been muffled by Blakely House's stone walls now sparked to life. And when she looked at him directly, it was almost too much. Like twinkling starlight.

A burst of goodness inside.

He watched her. "Perhaps she needs an adventure guide." He tucked away his impression of her in this moment, stored for later use if he ever did travel again. He knew he'd always be looking, always comparing, and that he'd never find her like in all the world.

When she had been silent for some minutes, his gaze flicked back to her countenance. Her eyes were liquid and fathomless with thoughts, and the tension had melted from her brow. He dug in his pocket and held up a penny pinched between thumb and forefinger. "For your thoughts."

She smiled and reached for it, holding it up in the moonlight. "I used to think it was a punishment, not being able to draw men like other women, but it's a *calculated* flaw in my design, isn't it? To protect me from being wooed, tried on for size, then discarded several times before finding that perfect fit."

Instantly he saw the texture of her heart upon her face, in her voice. Her heart was the sort that shattered upon impact.

"I've read about pirates, Mr. Montagne. They don't do forever. I think that frightens me more than anything."

An unknown dullness settled in his chest, an unwanted pressure, and he rubbed the spot hard. He turned and pushed up with his good arm, then offered it to her. "The sun will be cresting the horizon soon. We should at least make a show of having slept in proper beds."

"You go along. I'd like to stay here and soak up the sunrise."

"And how will you be scaling the rocks?" He raised his eyebrows. "I'll not leave you here at such an hour. But now that I know you feel this way, perhaps we may find ourselves out here again, on some other night when sleep eludes us."

She smiled. "I should like that."

Together they climbed down. But when they reached the main deck, she froze, looking out across the beach.

"The water is shallow here. There's nothing to fear."

"No, look—out there." She grabbed his hand, pulled him toward the railing. "What is that?"

"A tarp, I suppose." He frowned. But what was a tarp doing way out here?

"A person. André, it's a person! Come, we must go down there!" Then she burst across the ship, and before he could think, she was flying across the beach. He ran after her, pounding down the gangplank, skidding through sand as she dropped to her knees over something just ahead of him. A form.

A man.

"He's alive!" She heaved the man onto his side and the stranger's body convulsed. He coughed, gasping in ragged breaths and coughing again. He'd only just come out of the water.

In the middle of the night.

André grabbed the man by his shirt and propped him upright, pounding him on the back. "He isn't from any wreck. No ship about. He's just nearly drowned from trying to cross the causeway." Wet and slick as a fish, the man came to himself, pawing the air and gasping for breath, then slumping against André, hacking and coughing. "Blake . . . Blake . . ."

"Shh. You can speak later." He turned to his companion. "Let's get him off the beach. He needs to be dry and warm. Can you bear some weight?"

She nodded, eyes wide.

He leveraged the man's torso against his own, anchoring him against his chest with his mangled arm and supporting his hips with the other.

Sydney gamely lifted the man's legs, shouldering them and rising. They stumbled across the rocky beach, winding through the night. Sydney fell once, crumpling to her knees with a small cry, then shot back up, scrambling to readjust her burden. "I'm all right. Keep going."

The sun was barely lighting the edge of the horizon when they made it up to the stables and laid him on the ground. Sydney threw an old horse blanket over him and André lit a lantern.

"Need . . . Blake . . . House. I must—*ugh*."

"Shh. Quiet now." She slid her fingers over his lips. "There'll be time for all that later."

But a cord went taut within André. He leaned near the man's

face, studying it. "What is your name? Who are you?" He had
come here on purpose. On foot.

"Manns. Herman Flatt Manns."

"We'll have to keep him indoors," she said quickly. Breath-
lessly. "But not at the house."

He lifted his eyebrows.

"My cousins are strongly opposed to admitting any strangers just now." She heaved a sigh, eyebrows knitted. "Well, we
cannot send him away. There'll be no one to tend a washed-
up nobody in Northumberland, and he'll die out here. He
needs good, strong bone broth and dry clothing." Her little
white hands flitted over the man's torso, his face, checking
for injury. Then, off came the horse blanket, off came the wet
outer clothing. She patted him dry with her skirt and tucked
the horse blanket around him, smoothing it over his chest as
if it were satin. "I shall see to him myself, and Angel will help,
I'm sure of it."

He laid a hand on her arm. "Be careful, Miss Forrester. We
don't know this man. Don't know why he's here."

She turned to him, that bright shining face alight. "But we
know he *is* here, which makes him our concern."

"I won't send him away, but your cousins may be right not
to allow strangers into Blakely House."

"Why, because no stranger has ever before crossed into
it?" She straightened, arms crossed. "I've figured out his passion, André. The connection between all Emmett Sinclair's
inventions. It's *serving people*. The dishwashing machine, the
dumbwaiter, the flying machine . . . He wished to ease the lives
of those he cared for—even his staff. What sort of man serves
his *servants*? The sort who also saved washed-up thieves and
vagabonds, healed the castoff, and loved every unlovely he

came across, that's who." She bent over the man again, who was far too unconscious to appreciate the wealth of compassion bestowed upon him by this dark-haired saint. "This stranger will have to prove himself unworthy before I shall treat him thus. For now, he is an injured person in need of help. And we will give it to him."

André clutched his chest. The encounter dragged him back in time, to a distinct memory. Back to a night of throbbing pain, great gasping breaths, and a sky that wouldn't cease spinning.

"He's a thief," a voice had said above him.

Then a crisp, steady voice billowed through the pain. "Who among you were not thieves and vagabonds when you washed ashore? He is one of us, and will be treated so. By the lot of you. I'll not hear another word about it."

He rubbed his chest, vainly attempting to alleviate the pain squeezing there. "Very well. I suppose we can set him up in some unused room. But for tonight, he should not be moved again. I'll check him over in the morn." He raked a hand through his hair. "That is . . . later this morn."

She was right. The master never would have turned him away, yet this new guest was up to something. He'd come to Blakely House on purpose, in the dark—and had given a false name. Not many would realize it, but Herman Flatt Manns had been an obscure theologian years ago. He recalled seeing the printed name on spines in the rectory when he was a child—and again at Blakely House.

When they'd made the climb back to the house, Sydney was leaning on André heavily. Her weariness was evident. He did his best to hold her up, one arm around her shoulders, but his heart was pounding. From the climb, and the assault upon his memories. He didn't wish to relive that night. Not at all.

Yet in the dark blackness of it . . . a light. A single star piercing the night.

They paused at the door, the pink glow of a barely cresting sun at their backs. He turned her toward him with one hand on her arm, but she spoke first.

"I've a secret to tell you." She looked at him, eyes wide. "I've rescued more of them."

"More of who?"

"Passengers from a wreck." She threw her hands over her face, then lowered them. "They're in the caves just inside the inlet."

"Without a surgeon?"

She chewed her lip. "Angel has been seeing to their injuries. She has a veritable apothecary of herbs. Which is far more treatment than they'd have as penniless strangers in Northumberland. And I've been checking in on them, bringing provisions. They're cared for well enough."

"But the men—they said they moved the survivors to town."

She stood on tiptoe and whispered, "Not all of them." Her smile was wide and proud.

Something hard shifted loose inside. "What I said about you reminding me of him . . . I meant it. You being here is like having him back at Blakely House."

Her weary smile glowed in the sun's lovely light. "You don't think I killed him, do you?"

He pressed his lips together, reserving judgment. But acknowledging he'd already decided.

She squeezed his hand and vanished into the dark corridors of the mansion.

André paused to look out at the stables down the hill. It hardly mattered if the man had lied about his name—most did, when they first washed up on Farneham Heald's shores. Likely he was some scoundrel evading arrest for petty thievery.

For now, he had been swept up by the woman of the house. The eccentric, charming, rather curious woman who had invaded the place with her warmth, affecting Blakely's atmosphere.

He stepped into the house with the same refreshing, wrung-out exhale he used to give when stepping down the ramp of his ship. As if he'd just come back, sea-soaked and happily weary for a good rest.

He was still stuck here at Blakely House. Anchor down. But he'd found a new adventure, and nothing was going to be the same again.

chapter
TWENTY-FIVE

Some men, like deep writing, are made complex to divide those who care to decipher them from those who
cannot be bothered—"he that hath eyes to see, ears to
hear." My dearest, have I remarked upon your lovely
ears?

~*Emmett's letters to Sophie*

There was an urgency to my days. More work than time.
More questions than answers. But a fresh excitement I
couldn't quite name too. I had tasted my own romance,
and it had made me feel feminine and lovely and . . . well,
normal. In the best way possible. I wouldn't let it progress an
inch further, of course, but I would cling to the memory of his
lips upon my forehead, hold it close for all my days. I often
replayed that moment . . . and in my most private thoughts, I
wished for a taste of more.

I found a sense of purpose in tending the shipwrecked men,
coming alongside Angel to help them heal, and they *were* heal-

ing. With every visit they appeared stronger. One of the servants had even helped a few cross the mudflats in low tide to get to Northumberland.

The books Angel had brought were, as it turned out, ledgers that accounted for Emmett Sinclair's anonymous gifts. The explanatory notes in the margins were written in code, but a simple one quickly broken. Once I'd mapped it out using the shapes of a tic-tac-toe board, I could nearly read the coded notes fluently. My cousins could have ciphered it out easily, intelligent as they were.

But that was just it—they didn't wish to. Perhaps if it had been a new will, or instructions on how to complete the automaton.

I poured over those ledgers, eager for details—keen for some clue as to who might have killed him. I mostly found a great deal of information on the family and their financial status.

Jolly, as it turned out, had quite a few holdings across England, but most were heavily mortgaged. His income seemed to ebb and flow—but was always shored up with anonymous capital from Emmett Sinclair, slipped into the margins of Jolly's ventures. Sinclair had made notes of explanation where he recorded check after check sent to Jolly over the years, starting nearly two decades ago. Tom Jolly had purchased an entire fleet of ships with money that "happened" to turn up in a legal matter, and as his business interests grew, his debt had "magically" disappeared several times.

Purcell, the professor from King's College, had had a falling-out with Uncle Emmett after Emmett had somehow offended him. From his notes, it was clear Emmett had no idea how he'd grieved his nephew, but he hadn't made any moves to rectify it either. Other than anonymous pound notes to ease some of his burdens as they came. They had not spoken again.

Dane Hutchcraft was not mentioned in the notes. I wasn't even entirely certain how he was related—one of his parents, presumably, was Emmett's sibling, but his life had not been notable to Emmett Sinclair.

Then came notes of shipwrecked men. He'd recorded every rescue, sometimes in batches—but always with individual names. Kindness oozed from the pages of these very factual entries.

Until I happened upon a loose page folded into the book. Vines and decorative flourishes bordered it, as if styled as a poem, or something significant—but still in his unique code. I pulled out a fresh page and, letter by letter, revealed its mysteries.

I cannot bear the thought of anyone else owning Blakely House. Who else would be able to finish every project as it was intended to be?

Who would care to?

Thus, I shall pen it here for posterity—I shall take drastic measures, as many as are necessary, to ensure that Blakely House and all its treasures do not fall into the wrong hands. I shall ensure the future of this place where saints have trod, where their bodies now rest. I will protect Blakely House and make certain, whatever the cost, that it remains what it always has been—Farneham Heald, a resting place for the foreign traveler.

And furthermore, to protect the most valuable gem that belongs to Blakely House, I shall go to the ends of the earth and I shall even kill, if need be. Yes, I shall break the

sixth commandment, and murder. I have no other choice.
Though I should not delight in it, and perhaps will not
even be brave enough, I must overcome my fears and do
this thing. I must protect the greatest gem Blakely House
has ever seen and restore it home.

I read it over several times, gleaning every drop of meaning. Murder? He'd wanted to *murder* someone? Perhaps he had set out on the mission only to have someone kill him instead. Or had he killed someone, then faked his own death to hide? Was he even now somewhere, concealed and waiting for the storm to pass? Perhaps there had been no murder, by or against Emmett Sinclair—he had simply sailed out into the world, unfit to survive it, and been killed by the elements.

What happened to you, Uncle?

Then I took the clock and headed to the workshop, but I paused and sat before Emmett Sinclair's portrait in the gallery. "You didn't have many enemies, did you? I suppose that's what a man gets, never venturing off his private island. Until the end, that is."

To find me.

Or was it?

The portrait smiled knowingly at me, revealing nothing.

I played idly with the mechanism until I felt a catch, and his voice sounded again. "*Fifty-five degrees, thirty-six.*" Terrible thing. It couldn't even tell the temperature accurately.

But it was Emmett's voice. I played it again and again, looking up into that welcoming countenance, and tried to piece together the puzzle of Emmett Sinclair. I touched the oil paint of his face. *What in heaven's name happened to you?*

Clutching the clock, I paced through the house until a

distant squawk startled me. A bird? Poor creature—he was trapped somewhere.

I wove through the corridors, but the sound echoed from everywhere and nowhere. In the dark stairwell, something soft and very human bumped my shoulder. I paused, flattening against the wall to let the person pass me. He stepped into the light, and it was Tom Jolly. "Cousin Tom."

But he said nothing. Nor did he hurry past me. He stood there, hand lightly on the opposite railing, an oddly contented smile on his features.

I tried again to move aside, but he did not pass. "A clock, is it?" he said.

He was waiting for something. "Seems so."

"You've given up on the automaton, then?"

"Just for the night." I squared my shoulders. "Well, then." I made as if to pass on the right, but he slid to the right too. I leaned left, and so did he. "Begging your pardon."

His eyebrows went up. "Not at all, Cousin Sydney. Not at all."

With a growing dread, I darted around him and down the hall. No one else had chambers in this little wing he'd come from—only me.

chapter
TWENTY-SIX

As it turns out, the flying machine I had once built to give you wings, to let you sail away from me, would be the very thing I would use to bring you home.

~*Emmett's letters to Sophie*

I veered toward the owl suite, but the bird squawked again— closer this time. Down the corridor, a light swelled and faded, swelled and faded like a fairy beckoning me. I followed, but the lights led to a dead end. As I turned to go, a flash of light on the dead-end wall caught my eye. I paced closer—*not* a wall, but a mirror wall reflecting the opposite wall. The illusion of a dead end.

So many illusions at Blakely House. So many false perceptions.

I turned left toward the squawk coming from a door slightly ajar. Inside I twisted and shifted a lamp until it gave a faint glow.

A mechanical bird flew in circles overhead, attached by twine to the plaster ceiling. "Fascinating," I breathed, watching the small creature whir in circles. With every pump of the wings, its body lifted and the twine went slack for a brief moment.

A second light clicked on over a small end table covered with papers, but it was the bird that had my attention. Reaching up, I grabbed hold and yanked it down with my free hand, severing its connection with the ceiling—but not its power. My heart pounded to watch those wings pump. Something inside the bird was making it move.

A functioning automaton in my hands. The key to Fitzhugh and Blakely House. The path to my future and a new home for Lottie and me.

I switched it off, turning it over to inspect the tiny body. A noise sounded nearby, but I couldn't take my eyes from the miracle of tiny gears and pinions. The lifelike movements and the compact brilliance. I set the clock down and inspected the bird further.

They'd forbidden me from taking Fitzhugh apart, but they'd said nothing about an automaton bird. Spreading the creature's wings, I inspected its gear pins, rods, and connectors. His body consisted of two half-circle gears parallel to each other, and its feathers, tiny spoon cups layered over the body. He jerked, and the feathers made a wave motion that was so lifelike I gentled my hold, as if I might hurt him.

I set him down and a metronome sounded inside, ticking like a tiny pendulum.

That's it—counterweights! Fitzhugh could stand erect, remain on his feet, and even walk with the proper counterweights.

The world had grown dark. But my brain sparked to life, turning over possibilities. More than that, I felt an immense sense of rightness. Of hope and belonging. A square peg finding a square hole in a sea of round ones. Blakely House was within reach, and so was Fitzhugh.

The lamp on the little table ticked on and off again.

I stiffened. "Who is it? Who's there?" I stood, shaking, turning about in that quiet space. Crossing the room, I bent over the table and switched off the light, but again it flicked on, shining down upon the scattered papers full of Uncle Emmett's handwriting. I glanced at the mess of pages but turned again to the marvelous bird.

The lamp on the table flicked off . . . and on again. Demanding my attention. With a huff, a nervous glance about, I perched on the edge of a little chair and paged through the clutter on the table.

A sketch caught my eye. "What is this?"

"It was his rescue plan," said a voice from the doorway. I spun, and there was Angel, pale and unusually solemn. Just as she'd been behind the veil in Shropshire. "He'd planned to fly in that machine of his, you know. To save her."

"Who?" Though I already knew.

"Sophie Holland." Her eyes widened, glistening with moisture. "I overheard the master fret over her. He said she's been missing since the spring."

"That's why he left, isn't it?" The trip hadn't only been about meeting his heir, preserving his legacy. That had only been one small part of the trip, and it wasn't what had motivated him to leave. It had to do with serving . . . and with *her*. He'd loved this woman from afar for so many years, filling his house with things that would please her. Making it a nest to which she might fly back one day. His love was made manifest in every little touch he'd added . . . for her.

Then at last, he'd gone to fetch her back. He'd left his island to rescue her.

I turned to Angel. "You knew."

"Suspected, at first. Then a letter came, just after he'd left. I opened it."

"Did you normally open Mr. Sinclair's mail?"

"Never! But I was concerned for the master. It wasn't like him to simply leave. *Ever*."

"And what was in the letter?"

"It was from a woman. Sophie Holland. The contents were veiled, but the meaning was clear—she was begging Emmett to come for her." She stepped forward, hands clasped before her. "You'll go, won't you?" As if she'd asked me to fetch her tea. "You'll find out what became of him?"

I bunched my hands up in my skirt. "That isn't why I'm here."

"But what if it is?"

A quick puff of breath, so much becoming clear. "I can't fly that machine. Not yet, anyway. Give me time, and I'll see what can be done. Now, if you'd be kind enough to direct me back to my chambers . . ."

She approached, laying her hand on my arm with a featherlight touch. "You should go to him—*now*."

Thoughts swirled like golden carousel horses, and I suddenly saw everything differently. The doors that opened and closed, lights dimming and going bright, secrets that seemed to unfurl themselves at my feet. I blinked at her, this fairylike woman with the bright eyes and keen wit. "You've been quite clever, haven't you? All this time . . . it was a scheme." She'd been the one controlling the doors and the lights, leading me to the letters and the pictures, hoping I'd grow attached to the man. So she could persuade me to search for him. The nephews certainly couldn't be convinced to do it. She must have been desperate when she'd shown up at the shop, looking for another heir.

"Something terrible happened to him, but it isn't like they say. The flying machine crashing—something isn't right about it." She was trembling as she wrung her hands, her lips quivering like tiny spoonfuls of current jam. "I can't sleep nights, thinking about it. He was always so good to me. So good."

I narrowed my gaze at her. "Why do you care so much?"

"I told you. He's special. A rare gem who deserves a far better ending than the one he got."

I crossed my arms. "If you want me to consider this, you'll have to tell me the truth."

"I did." Her voice was thin. Desperate.

I spun on my heel, grabbing the bird and the clock. "Very well then, it's off to bed—"

"He's alive! He is. I feel it in my marrow." She threw her hands over her flushed face and shook. "I cannot bear for him to simply disappear, with everyone believing he's dead."

I closed my eyes and exhaled, then wrapped an arm around the woman's shoulders. "Then we shall have to find out what became of him on that trip."

Her eyes flew open and she clenched my arms. "Truly? You'll go?"

"I shall try."

She flung her arms around me and once again came to life as the kitchen angel, bustling around me, cheeks pink. "Come. I have food prepared for you. And supplies. I'll show you the way, down the back stairs to the kitchen."

"Supplies will be helpful. And I'll go—just as soon as things are settled." I was so close to unlocking Fitzhugh's mysteries. So very close. He had power—sometimes. Movement. He was beginning to make sense. And now . . . the bird.

Her grip tightened, desperate. "Please. You must!" She pulled me again toward the back stairs.

"And I will go. Hopefully before another fortnight has passed." And as soon as I figured out a nonterrifying way of traveling. I would die of fear in that metal bird before I was three feet from the beach.

"Please. It must be now, Miss Sydney." She clutched my hands. "Before it's too late."

A small spike of worry. Was the woman actually mad? Did she not know Emmett had been buried? There was no mystery about his being dead—only *how*. "He . . . he has been found. And buried."

"Yes, yes, of course he has." She waved that away. "At least, that's what they say. But something isn't right about the whole mess. It isn't right. And someone needs to find the truth." She looked at me pointedly.

"I need to prepare. To figure out how I'll get there."

Her eyebrows pinched together. "You'll not reconsider, then? You are truly set on waiting?" Her face fell, as if she suspected I wouldn't go at all if I put it off.

I gave a slight smile. "Yes. For a few days, at least."

"Very well." She wilted. "Then we'll just take these front stairs to your bedchamber. Come, it's this way."

I followed her and soon became short of breath, my heart pounding against that useless clock. Down two short stairs, then around another bend and a hall that overlooked the main floor. I'd never been this way.

Then there were voices. Men's voices. "There! She's coming!"

Footsteps pounded. Lights went out, hands grabbed me, and I was propelled, stumbling, down a hall. "What is this? What are you doing?"

I looked at Angel, at her resigned face.

The back stairs. She had meant to help me escape—to get off the island. Perhaps she didn't think Emmett was alive at all. Perhaps she—

A shove. They tossed me onto a wooden floor. The door shut and locked as I reached for my smarting tailbone. I sat in stunned silence as the clock cast its face upon the ceiling, my heartbeat erratic in my ears. "Wait! Come back!"

She had allowed this. She'd known and let them lock me up. I screamed and beat on the doors, then sank to the floor and shook.

"You're certain?" asked a muffled voice. It rattled through a vent, vibrating into the room where I sat on a thin rug, hardly daring to breathe.

"Quite certain?" It was Dane Hutchcraft.

"I think so," came Tom's reply. "It's enough for an arrest, at least. Here, read it."

A paper was flipped out. "What is it?"

"A letter. In her own hand. She has a distinctive scrawl. I'm certain we'll be able to prove it's her writing, then it's up to the judge to read the contents of the letter as he will. It's clear enough, though, if you ask me. Here, look at this line."

"She's . . . she's threatening to murder him. Planning on it, from the sounds of it. Says here she's willing to murder."

Oh, for pity's sake. The translated page—that rotten manifesto on fancy paper. I'd left the translation, in my handwriting, on my desk. *Drat.* "Wait!" I banged both fists on the door. "Come back!" I was shaking. What a colossal mistake.

"It doesn't specifically say it's Uncle Emmett she plans to murder."

"HELLO!" I'd show them the coded page and explain . . . if I *had* the coded page.

Which I didn't. *Double drat!*

What had I done with it? It hadn't gone back in the notebook. Hadn't gone in the stack of papers. Had I dropped it in the rubbish bin? My mind skittered through the millions of possibilities. Once I'd translated it, the original hadn't seemed so important.

"Who else would she murder to inherit Blakely House? The constable should see this."

"Let's do it. If she's guilty, she's guilty. No matter how well she's cleaned up her tracks. Who else but her would understand how to tamper with the flying machine?"

A pause. "You're right. And with that letter Emmett sent you . . ."

I crouched against the wall, quick breaths making me dizzy. Frantic. Letter?

"I'll summon the constable."

"At this hour, Dane?"

"We'll claim she's a threat to us. Look at this letter—that could be us she's planning to murder."

"Horsefeathers. You know it isn't."

"Of course not," said Dane. "But then we'll have all the time we need to find solid proof."

My throat clenched.

"Or . . . to concoct it ourselves." That thin, reedy voice. "I'm not above helping the truth along, if we're certain it was her."

"The tide is high, dear cousin. And the constable will have nothing to do with this haunted island in the middle of the night."

A sigh from Dane. "Very well. Let's get some rest and fetch him first thing in the morning. She'll keep till then."

Footsteps sounded as the men walked away together.

"We'll go as soon as the tide is out. Perhaps by nine of the morning."

"Wonderful," I heard faintly as they left whatever room they were in. "We'll send someone . . ."

My heart pounded. Hot and cold patches bloomed across my skin. Panic took root.

But I had time. Until tomorrow, first light. But . . . to do what?

I stared at the projected clock that did not tell the time. How did I always find these scrapes? That's why I never took risks—my subconscious knew I'd fail.

I reached for the clock, and as I touched it, the face rotated one click. The ghost image shifted—a globe. What was this? I rotated it another click and out flashed the shape of a sector. "*Fifty-five degrees, thirty-seven, nineteen.*" I lifted the clock. "*Minus one degree, thirty-seven, forty-one.*" It wasn't the temperature—it was my location, in latitude and longitude. A navigational tool! Complex, unique, and multifaceted.

I flipped it over and opened the back again. It appeared to be a maritime chronometer and sextant in one—with directional positioning and a weighted compass to combat the movement of the waves.

He'd designed this for a trip—the only one he had ever meant to take.

Then the wardrobe door squeaked open and Angel's worried face appeared. "You see why it must be now? They're out for your head!"

"How did you—"

"There's a passage to all of these locked rooms behind the wardrobes. I checked each one, and now I've found you. So . . . you'll go now?"

"I can't simply *leave*, without any—"

A bang. "Grab on," came a muffled male voice in the distant rooms. "Come now, you must grab on!" Random words not even spoken to me, but they ricocheted through me. Echoing in Aunt Lottie's voice. The pirate's. Now Dane's.

Grab on. That ridiculous phrase that kept popping up, urging me on toward . . . something. Toward this.

Angel's eyes pleaded as they had at the shop. *We need you, Sydney Forrester.* I blinked as my eyes adjusted to the dark room, a junk shop of sorts. Despite everything, I did not want to leave. I was becoming a part of the house just as Emmett had, and it was becoming what it had been—a refuge for broken things and broken people.

But only with me at the helm.

The people. The ones from the shipwreck. Who would look after them if I were sent away? Who would look after everyone who washed up after? *You being here is like having him back at Blakely House.* I still felt the lift to my chest as I recalled the pirate's words.

But there was another, much brighter thread of his that I had not picked up. One task he had begun but left unfinished. I stood in the jumbled room, allowing him to silently beseech me. I knew what he'd want me to do, what I needed to do if I had any hope of proving my innocence. Of finding out what had actually happened to Emmett Sinclair. I *must* find Sophie and rescue her.

Grab on. Just grab on.

"Please, Miss Sydney."

At times decisions are difficult because we don't know what to do. Which path to trod. And then there are times God speaks our language—penetratingly, undeniably, relentlessly . . . like now. I *did* know the path. I simply didn't want to tread it.

I stood. "Show me the way out of here."

She brightened immediately and led me toward the wardrobe.

chapter TWENTY-SEVEN

André leaned back against the wall in the butler's pantry, sipping his nightly rooibos tea as the men talked around him. Ten years it had been since he'd seen the shores of the Ivory Coast, yet this habit he'd acquired there had persisted.

"Perhaps she hired someone to do it," said Jinedath, polishing a spoon and holding it up to the fading light. "Can't say's I blame 'er. A fortune, a future, and a whole house besides. I might have killed for less."

"I say she did it herself," James said.

"He met her, saw through the act, and threatened to write her outta the will. Even wrote home about it—*don't trust Sydney Forrester*, he says, because he knew she was about to kill 'im. Then . . . she did." Jinedath smacked the table.

André's jaw tensed. "That's a lot of speculation."

Jinedath's narrow monkey-like face snapped up. "Oh?" He narrowed his eyes upon his superior. "And he wrote that letter to Mr. Jolly on a hunch, I suppose."

André leveled a look at Jinedath. "There was no letter."

"There was a letter. Saw it meself. A clear warning—Sydney Forrester is not to be trusted nor let near Blakely House. That's what I saw, I did."

"She knows her way around the gadgets," added James. "Who else in this wide world would even know how to tamper with the flying machine?"

"Who else in this great world'd want to?" Jinedath bounced in his seat, spit upon the spoon, and polished it harder. "No one but she who is named in his will." The chair clunked down. "What do you say, Montagne? You've spent more time with her than anyone. How do you think she did it?"

Another sip, and the liquid warmed André's insides as he closed his eyes and remembered the African coast. The cresting waves with rare sheets of ice rolling along to the white sands. "Perhaps we ought to decide if she's guilty or not first."

"Bit late for that," said James. "They've got their proof. Got 'er locked up already, and they're calling the constable at first light. Alls that's left to speculate on is the details."

André's jaw clenched. "She's in prison?" A tingling sense of urgency danced around his midsection.

"Just one of them old pirate chambers."

The pirate chambers were a series of small rooms with the locks reversed to contain shipwrecked men who were caught thieving at Blakely until they understood the house rules—and proved themselves trustworthy enough to be a part of it.

André jammed his fingers into his hair and tensed. "What do any of those men want with the old place, anyway? They've all got lives and fortunes of their own."

"Aye, but Jolly's running out of money, I hear," Jinedath responded. "He wants to make a showplace of Blakely House. A regular holiday island for the ton."

"Can't say I'd mind serving the nobility," James said.

"That Dane wants his boy back, and he's using Blakely House as bait," continued Jinedath. "Spent years as a killer for hire, and his clever little son found him out and won't give him the time of day."

"And the professor?" André asked from his spot against the wall. "What could he possibly need from Blakely House? He has a fine position, nice home in London . . ."

"*Had* a position. Things is shiftin' in the world, and he hasn't kept up. No one wants his sort of smarts anymore, they says."

"Who says?" André responded. "Who has told you all these things?"

Jinedath's face creased into a most gratified smile. "Ehhhh, wouldn't you like to know, Mr. Montagne. I hears things, I does. And I sees the post."

"*Snoops* in the post," grumbled James. "You open every parcel and letter that comes through here, don't you?"

"And don't I know all about a lass who's been writing you for months. Had a surprise happen upon her," crowed the snoop. "A tiny surprise she expects'll look a terrible lot like yourself!"

James paled, then a blush swelled up his face. "Have a care."

"Perhaps we should take our drinks and call it a night." André raised his cup and slid off the table.

Once they'd gone, André blew out a breath and strode through the kitchen, pausing to pour hot tea and light a fire under a saucepan of bone broth, before venturing out to one of the many conservatories at Blakely House. With Miss Forrester locked up, caring for the newest guest fell to him. By morning, perhaps he'd have an idea about how to get her released. If nothing else, he'd break the door down himself. He wouldn't let the constable take her.

Parting large palm leaves, he came to the cot where he'd placed the fevered man, who turned into the pillow at the sound of André's entrance. A white linen shirt hung on his trembling back. André knelt and placed a hand on the man's shoulder.

He stiffened. "What do you want?" He shifted toward his rescuer, and he seemed so much more alive. Not a day after André had mistaken him for a washed-up tarp, he was moving and speaking.

"Exactly what I wanted when I carried you up here—to help you. Are you ready to eat?"

His face was gaunt. Desperate. Purple circles underlined tired eyes. "Food. I need food."

"We start with this." He helped the man sit and passed him a cup of weak tea.

He drank it, closing his eyes as the first gulp slid down. "That woman. The one . . . she looks like my wu-wu-wife." He shivered beneath the blanket, then took another sip.

André softened. "You'll return home to her soon, when you're well."

But he only sat still, breathing hard and staring into his tea. "Not going back."

"What of your wife, monsieur? She will worry, no?"

Another sip, and he exhaled. "I need to s-s-stay here. Just for a while." His stammer seemed accentuated by the recent trauma.

"I suppose that can be arranged. Shipwrecked men do have a habit of staying here for quite some time. Present company included." He offered a smile, but the man did not see it.

He set the tea on the floor and collapsed onto the cot, shivering. "Food. I need . . . I'm starving."

André pulled the blanket around the man's shoulders, tucking it around his shivering body. He went to fetch the bone broth, pouring it in a sturdy mug and returning to evaluate the stranger shivering hard enough to shake the cot. "I've brought you something to eat. I'm afraid you are trapped in here for a time. Just until we've made your presence known to the others. There are some unwelcoming individuals."

Again he shook his head, his gaze latching on to André's as he struggled to sit up. "Please . . . don't. Just let . . . me hide." Then his gaze slid to the bone broth with steam rising from its amber depths.

André frowned. "Who are you, exactly? Where do you come from?"

"S-s-s-stamford. And I . . . told you my name."

André frowned. "You are quite a ways from home, Mr. . . . Manns."

The visitor reached for the mug.

André pulled it back. "Your name, sir."

He whimpered.

"Your *real* name." He waved the mug of fragrant broth beneath the man's nose, then held it out of his grasp.

Agony stretched the man's countenance. Then he sighed. "Very well. My name . . . is Sydney Forrester."

The spoon André held clattered to the brick floor. He quickly retrieved it. With lead in his chest, André knelt beside the cot, looked the feverish man in the eyes, and said quickly, "Tell me everything."

chapter
TWENTY-EIGHT

ap-tap.

The noise jarred André from a painfully short sleep. He dragged his mind into reality and struggled to rise, planting bare feet on a cold floor to shock his senses.

It was her. Nose to glass she stood just outside, eager and flush-faced, wearing a smile the width of the Thames. No prison in sight. He struggled into clothing laid out on a chair, suddenly desperate for strong coffee.

She looked jittery with exhaustion, but her eyes shone when he went out to her. "May I beg a favor, Mr. Montagne, even in the daytime?"

He ruffled his hair and stretched. "You may ask. I won't promise a favorable reply."

"Come, I need to show you something."

He frowned, adjusting the buttons he'd gotten wrong on his shirt. Then the sleep fog lifted and he looked her over with new eyes. Fresh understanding. Even more questions, though. "Where exactly are you taking me, Miss Forrester?"

She smiled, the warm flush of dawn lighting her face. "You'll see."

The ship looked even more magnificent in the early morning light, with mainsails casting lovely shadows over its solid wood surface. His stomach pitched and tossed as he neared the thing—an instinctive combination of anxious longing and dread. His steps slowed. "Exactly what did you have in mind, Miss Forrester?"

"Merely a short trip, actually. Just to an adjoining coast."

"You wish to take the ship out? A person cannot reach very many places on the North Sea quickly."

"Not unless it's modified." She was dancing on the sand, only the toes of her slippers digging.

His eyes landed on a compass and a few small pulleys she'd added to the valves and cylinders he'd already installed. "Are these from the flying machine?"

"I didn't see the point of working on that contraption of aluminum and catgut. Especially after Uncle Emmett . . . So I brought a few small pieces to the ship instead and . . . well, I fixed it."

He ran his hand over the simple tweaks she'd added to his mechanics, loathe to admit how clever it actually was. "And if the engine seizes up under the load? I've never tested the power. It might explode, for all we know."

"Emmett has installed an automated shutoff valve here, but the mechanics are meant to work *with* the wind. Provided we have some. By my calculations, we can cover four to six miles in an hour with the wind, and three point four times more with the wind and mechanics combined."

"You've thought this all through."

"You are the genius—I've only finished it."

He folded his arms. "I suppose you've found a crew to operate the thing, have you? It's rather a lot for one woman and a pirate."

She pulled him up the gangplank, pointing at the cluster of gears and pulleys overhead. "A system." She yanked on the rope that controlled the sails. "So light that even I could operate it. Well, nearly. Here, look, I made this part." She gave the rope a yank and watched the sail billow out with a smart *thwap.* "One doesn't need more muscle power—only more wheels. You see? Levers. The more of them you have, the less the resistance. It'll be as if the sail weighs nothing at all."

"And navigation?"

"It's right here." She crossed to a mahogany clock mounted to the main mast.

He spun the useless dials. "A broken clock?"

"Not broken." She touched it and light shot out of its face, projecting out across the ship, over the water. It was a globe, rebalancing with each shift of the boat. "Put together differently. For a unique purpose."

Jaw going slack, he touched the thing, winding the little hands and seeing the scope of its abilities. Navigation, position, storm forecaster, and terrain sensor.

"The furnace belowdeck is already heating up. And look here." She danced backward toward the helm, like a small fairy who barely touched down. "Try it. Go on, give it a spin."

"It seems you've accounted for everything."

"That is my specialty."

"You forgot to figure in one small calculation—*I'm not going.*"

He might have considered the trip before, but after last night's conversation in the conservatory, he couldn't possibly.

This halted her immediately. She stood poised like a statue, head cocked to one side. "Not going?"

A gull cried and the wind whipped, blowing through his shirt and clanging a bell overhead in the crow's nest. He closed his eyes, savoring. Remembering. *Longing.*

He opened his eyes and the hurt on her face was genuine. Rather deep. Her tired, desperate eyes spoke of the work she'd put into it. "Well." He shoved his hands into his trouser pockets. "Not without trying it out first, no?"

Her face relaxed into happy relief, aglow with childlike anticipation, and he realized with a jolt what this actually was—a gift. It was a gift for him. She was traveling somewhere, yes, overcoming her own fears, perhaps trying to escape arrest. But she also wished to gift him with his deepest longing.

Which left him thoroughly muddled.

With a grim set to his jaw, he approached the helm as one stepping beside a horse that has thrown him, preparing to mount. He tested it and with the brush of his fingers, the helm shifted. He grabbed it with his good hand and it whirled easily. Too easily, as if a ghost were steering. He jerked back. "What have you done to my ship?"

"I told you—I've finished it. Mostly borrowed genius, I'm afraid." She stepped up beside him and the bell's clang sounded again, jittering his senses. "Good thing for us you have a rather small ship. Well, for a pirate ship, that is. And now, it will live to see another adventure, without the benefit of an entire crew. Why, it'll be crewed by machinery! And you, of course. I'd go alone, only I haven't any idea *how* to command a ship, or how to get where I'm going, or really, how to adventure at all. So I'll need a partner. One with experience." She paused and looked up at him, scrutinizing his expression, which he guarded carefully.

And every time he blinked, he saw the man's face. The one called Sydney Forrester lying ashen on the cot.

When she frowned, her face beginning to crumple a little, he cast his gaze away. Allowed the wind to blow his hair about.

"I can see a bevy of thoughts crowding just behind your eyes. So just say them. I want to know."

No, you don't. He studied her expression, her bearing. Trying to make sense of everything he knew . . . or thought he knew. The more information he had, the less he understood. The more confused he became.

"It isn't so very far, really," she pressed. "Just across the water to the next coast." She quickly spread a map on the ship's floor before he could protest. It was the map that had hung in the old stables with the aviation machines.

A jerk in his chest. He followed her finger along the line between Farneham Heald and Norway. "You . . . you wish to complete the master's journey."

"You've no objection, I assume."

She was either completely mad or wholly misinformed. "It isn't exactly a short trip, Miss Forrester. We'd be traveling to another coast."

She frowned, twirling one of those dark curls around her finger. "But my calculations. It's pure science, accounting for speed versus miles traveled and—"

"Tides. Storms. The whims of the great sea itself. You forget one thing, Miss Forrester. When you venture out on the sea, you are in God's domain. All the rules fluctuate at his whim."

"I thought the entire world was 'God's domain.'" There was a lightly mocking lilt to her words.

He leaned against the helm, felt the force of the waves tugging it about, and took in his fill of the crystalline-gray waves that stretched endlessly into the horizon. "It's more evident out here." The salty breeze called to him. Enchanted his senses. "Man may fool himself into believing he can control life within his own little house, but once he puts himself at the mercy of nature, he realizes who owns it all." A deep, heady breath that quickened his pulse. "It won't be predictable, no matter how much you calculate."

She jumped up, squaring her shoulders. "We shall do it. They can do without a butler for a time. And me . . . well, they'll be *glad* to see me gone. We'll leave now, before the house has risen. We have provisions. Dried meat and things from the larder. Angel prepared them. It's quite exciting, actually. Preparing and readying the ship, seeing to the details. I see why you want to do it."

His frown deepened. "Why are you so determined to make this journey?" She could escape to anywhere. Disappear quite easily. "No one even knows what he intended to do there."

"I do." She said it quietly. Unpretentiously. "He was going to rescue Sophie."

With a great sigh, he fell back against the mainsail post.

She crossed her arms. "You wish me to believe in a being no one alive has even seen, yet you won't entertain the possibility that a woman exists who Emmett loved?"

"You and your oversized words." He clutched the side of the ship. This was going badly. He glanced over the ship, out at the water.

"You did say it was repaired, did you not? The ship, that

is. You weren't even certain why you did it, but clearly, *this* is why. Because it was meant to have another adventure. This ship is seaworthy—and a bit extra."

Heat coiled through his midsection. Up through his torso and neck. He rubbed his shoulder. Ignored the sharp pain that shot through the stump of his arm whenever he thought about it. Captaining any vessel would take more than a few pulleys to lighten the resistance. "The ship may be seaworthy, Miss Forrester, but you forget—I am not."

She stepped perilously close, her inquisitive face tipped as she looked—truly looked—at him and the curtain of her daydreams parted, awareness dawning over her features.

She reached for his right hand and curled warm fingers around his palm, smiling up at him in a way that smoothed something old and brittle inside him. "Blakely House has taught me one thing—that nothing is truly broken. It's just . . . not finished. Now, stay here. And close your eyes." With a quick squeeze, she spun away.

With a twisting gut, he complied. He shut his eyes and pretended, for one precious moment, that he was actually going to say yes—to depart to the open sea again, command a vessel and steer it toward new places.

She approached with a swish of fabric and clicks of her boots, and he felt a leather strap laid gently across his back, spanning his shoulders. It settled there quite nicely, and then she fixed some contraption against his arm, running her hand down to the—

He jerked away. Something clattered to the ground. She bent to retrieve it. He opened his eyes and she placed a gentle hand on his wrecked arm, then slid the contraption easily over the place where his hand used to be, and buckled it in place with leather straps. "There you are. Just a spare automata part borrowed from my uncle's projects." She smiled up into his face. "There, now. I've finished you." She cocked her head. "Sort of."

He held up his arm, and there on the end of it shone a fully jointed and well-proportioned hand, with fingers made of metal rods and gears at the knuckles. A full extension of his arm, just as it used to be . . . almost. "What is this?" He cleared his throat and tried again. "Why . . . why have you done this?"

She ran her hand over the metal and leather, gentle expertise checking the fit and stability, adjusting the strap, then she pulled a pair of brown leather gloves from her belt and slid one over his good hand and one over the new. "Because I need a glimpse of God. And so do you." She came around to stand in front of him. "There. Finished."

Holding his breath, he held up his left hand, twisting his arm this way and that. It was surprisingly light and comfortable. He held out both arms, that pair of gloved hands with five fingers on each. How very normal he looked again. Whole. A jitter deep in his stomach. He could almost fool himself into believing it.

"It'll take some getting used to, but you can do nearly anything you wish. Whatever this hand does, the other will also do. Go on, try it."

Blinking, he held out both hands again. He flexed his right, and with a gentle squeak, the fingers of the left curled too. He released it, and the new hand followed suit. He turned the palms up. With a wiggle of his fingers, the glove-covered metal hand gave a ripple of smooth movement, so lifelike it jolted him. "You've spent much time on this."

She shrugged.

"All of this in one night?"

"Well, the arm has been in my mind for some time. I just haven't . . ." She looked away, blushing in the moonlight.

She hadn't known how to give it to him. How to offer such a gift.

Except that now she was asking for a favor which required the use of it.

He cast a glance over the ship at the rigged pulleys and levers, the combined genius of both Emmett and this woman. "Will you be terribly disappointed if we reach Norway and there is no lost love?"

"She's there, André. I know it. And no one else knows where to find her." She came near with her earnestness, and he felt himself melting. "Please—I have to try." She heaved a quick sigh. "And besides. If anyone will know who truly killed Emmett Sinclair, she will."

Ah, so that's what this was. He inhaled sea air, selfishly longing to say yes. Nobly realizing he must tell her what he'd discovered. But there was one thing he knew from years aboard ships—facing adventures, life-risking ones, brought truth to the surface like cream on fresh milk. And more than ever, he needed the truth about this woman. From her own lips.

"Just the one trip, no?" She couldn't possibly be genuine. Couldn't. And yet . . . her face. It was peaches and cream with hints of roses, everything good and simple and pure from his boyhood.

She lit. "Of course, just one trip." She planted her hands on her hips. "Ready for an adventure, Mr. Montagne?"

He looked her over from wild curls tossed by the wind to oversized apron bunched around a rather slender frame. "Are you?"

chapter
TWENTY-NINE

The longer I am away, the more I realize home is not a place, but a series of memories, familiar scents and sounds, deep comfort and rest—but sometimes, it is just a person.

~*Sophie's letters to Emmett*

Indeed, I was not. That became clear within moments of the sickening sway of that craft, lurching here and there over the waves. I threw my head back against the wall of the ship's underbelly, thankful for the ship's cabin belowdeck where I might hide the undignified emptying of my stomach.

It wasn't so much the rocking that bothered me, but the sheer power of the waves and the fact that I was now stranded out in the middle of them. I could control exactly nothing. And he was right—my calculations were rubbish.

Which made me even more eager to inherit Blakely House. I would hole myself up in that marvelous estate, just as my ancestors had done, and let my imagination run wild—*on dry land.* I was not made for sea travel and discomfort and facing the unexpected. No. Adventuring, from this time forward, would take place from the comfort of my window seat with my nose between the pages of someone else's escapade.

I rose and hugged my tender midsection, then I forced myself to climb the narrow ladder, pushing up the hatch that led onto the deck. I'd sat out most of the trip belowdeck, dozing and waking in fits, but perhaps it was time, before we reached shore, to make an appearance.

A wet, briny wind showered my face. How still it was down below—and how opposite up here. With a groan, I scrambled to grab on to the side and pull myself up onto the deck. I clutched it, enduring the continuous spray of waves and tasting their salt. Blocking the wind with one arm. I turned, still clinging to the railing, and I glimpsed my pirate.

My pirate. I'd subconsciously thought of him that way since his gentle forehead kiss in the ballroom, but he was never less *my* anything than he was right then.

I sucked in a breath and nearly cried at the sight of him manning his ship. *His* ship, for there was no question of it belonging to anyone else. He had been liberated, set totally free from what bound him to the world I knew, and he was master of this vessel. How very unsuited we were, I realized with a wave of clarity. The very thing that drained me of life filled him to the brim.

There he was, springing from mast to steering wheel, spinning the wheel and yanking on the rope that operated the sail, athletic and vibrant and glowing with life. "Good day, Miss Forrester!" Whatever had been bothering him when we'd first come aboard the ship, that careful fence he'd placed between us, had been blown away by the salty air.

He smiled and sprang to my side, wind blowing his damp black hair over his face that shone with vitality, and I almost thought he might kiss me again—a true kiss. That I'd be swept up in his arms on this windblown ship and he'd embrace me until I felt the way I had in the ballroom with his lips on my face.

My tender stomach fluttered, then coiled in regret. I watched him dancing about the ship, handling it with grace and power, as if he'd been born aboard such a vessel and he'd at last come home. The one consolation for my lonely heart was that I had been the one to give it back to him.

The ship lurched and I tumbled, but he caught me, slinging his good arm around my waist and holding me firmly against him until I thought I should cry from the closeness. The engulfing feel of being embraced. It only inflamed an appetite I never knew I'd had. I wanted both of his arms around me, pulling me into his strength and warmth, my head fitting perfectly against his chest.

I looked up into his rain-spattered face, so vibrant and alive, his lips so expressive, and suddenly my head was swirling. And then as his gaze lingered, I melted inside.

Lashes. He had such lovely, dark lashes. I'd seldom been close enough to see them before.

It struck me then that we were alone. Utterly isolated on a ship out at sea. "This . . . was a terrible idea."

"Quite possibly." His eyes sparkled. His lips, pressed together in a way that sharpened the jagged planes of his face, brought forth a cleft in his chin. "But I'm glad you had it."

Me too. Never before had I been so fascinated by a man—by the way he moved and spoke and thought—or so despairing at the differences between us.

I swallowed. Shifted back, and he released me, but his eyes did not. "You are well?"

"I will be," I said loudly over that awful wind. We'd been out here for so long already. "How many hours?"

"At least twenty or twenty-five."

I breathed out, whipping wet hair off my forehead. "No wonder I feel this way. At least we're almost there. How quickly time passes when you sleep."

He frowned down at me. "Twenty-five hours . . . left."

Left?! "I meant, how long have we been traveling? How many hours?"

A wry smile. "Nearly one."

I groaned, sinking down against the mast at my back. "I shan't be able to eat a thing until we're on dry land again." I laid a hand on my delicate midsection.

After a moment he hoisted me up, holding me gallantly to him, and captured my gaze with that sparkling look of his. "Go and sleep, mon étoile. Nights are for rest and you deprived yourself entirely last night. So now you must make up for it in the day."

"I don't think it'll help," I said miserably. When had I ever been a whiner? No, adventuring was not for Sydney Forrester.

But he helped me gently back down the stairs, tucked me into a surprisingly soft bedroll with a little peppermint tea, and soon my nausea melted away along with my wakefulness. I slept the sleep of the exhausted. I dreamed of Blakely House, and a flood of policemen and constables, all looking for me.

But in reality I was not at Blakely House. I was on the North Sea, stranded in the middle of an adventure.

chapter
THIRTY

BLAKELY HOUSE

A bang echoed through the great old house. The stranger sat up, feeling at once the relief of cooled, moist skin. His fever had broken. He blinked in the dark, reorienting himself as his head spun and the world narrowed and widened again. He blotted his face with the sheet. There were ferns everywhere and giant palm leaves like hands stretched over him. But beyond it, glass walls closed him in.

They'd put him in a conservatory. A vague memory of salty broth returned to him, and a low, masculine voice. But no one was here now.

With a furtive glance about, he slipped from the cot, blankets pooling on the ground, and moved toward the main house as his heart pounded, head spinning. He shouldn't be up yet, he sensed, as his body trembled. But he hadn't time to waste on that cot. They'd be on to him soon enough, and the house was large. He had a lot of ground to cover.

He tested the doors—unlocked—and slipped into an enormous white room heavy with marble and plush rugs. What decadence! It was a good job the man was dead, and all his wealth could be distributed to the rest of humanity now. No sense in bunching it all up in one house for one lonely person, no matter how brilliant.

As his body adjusted to being upright, blood draining, then trickling back to his head, his mind cleared and he collected the scattered memories of his arrival. The beach. A tedious climb. Darkness . . . and then a deep voice. A man, asking so many questions.

What had he revealed?

At least he'd made it. Foolish choice, crossing the causeway so close to the change of tides, but he was here now. And mostly undetected, which was imperative.

Emmett Sinclair's will had changed so many times over the years, and the man had threatened to change it one last time— leaving Sydney Forrester out of it. If the old man had been successful, Sydney needed collateral now, before he went to battle over the matter with the other relations.

He ran one trembling hand along some metal contraption, down to the lever with a little shiver. What a wonder this house was. A curiosity that should be opened to the public. For profit, of course.

He spun the crank on the little box, but it stuck. Lifting the lid, he fumbled with the mechanism, fitting a crooked gear neatly into the teeth of the opposing one. He tightened the screw holding it in place with his fingers and shut the lid, once again spinning the crank. It clicked and thunked, whirring to life and casting the image of a clockface on the wall.

This place was nothing like the periodicals had said—it was *better*. Yes, he could make a go of Blakely House. Fix it up and finish the creations that would stun the world.

Only one thing left to do.

Gaze fanning out across the elaborate room, he moved to the door and peeked down the hall. In a house of this size, one would normally find the gallery in the very heart of it, with great sweeping views looking up to a balcony. But he had the sense that this was not a typical house.

He'd begun to convince himself that he'd come all this way for nothing. That he'd have to go home to Amelia with empty hands. But now he knew, standing in the vast openness of the monstrosity, that everything he'd heard about Blakely House had been true and he would be very wealthy.

He turned down the corridor and moved carefully. Quietly. He was still weak. His breath came too quickly from the mere exertion of walking.

A door banged open behind him. "There!" Light exploded in the room and he spun. A cluster of men, including police officers, poured in through the double doors. His arms shot up, palms out as he backed, trembling, against the wall. "Don't . . . don't hurt me." He gasped, straining for several breaths. His pulse thrummed in his ears. "Please."

One rather sharp-looking man advanced. "Who in God's green earth are you?" He grabbed the front of his shirt. "And where is Sydney Forrester? What have you done with her?"

He shuddered, legs going weak. He lowered his hands. "I—" What had he said last night? *What had he said?*

A man. He'd spoken to a man. One of these men? Maybe. No, probably not. But maybe.

Think. He'd given a name. Which name—? "M-M-Manns. My name is Manns. And I haven't seen an-an-anyone." Had he said anything else? His brain chugged like a steam train, everything obscured by puffs of exhaust. He waited for it to clear.

"Where did you come from?"

"The cu-cu-conservatory." His teeth chattered and he suddenly realized how insufficient his clothing was. How damp and chilly the air. "Someone put me in there. On a cot. I was re-re-rescued." He trembled in earnest.

The man's brow furrowed, but he released his hold on his shirt. "You washed up on the island?"

"Last night. Or . . . the night before." He shrugged, looking away as the room tilted. Righted itself.

The man who spoke to him stepped forward, waving away the others as he narrowed his eyes. "Search the rest of the house. I'll find you in a moment." They filtered out with a few backward glances, all but two men. One of whom stood far too close. "There's no ship, no crew, which means you walked. You tried to cross the causeway and were stuck in the tide, weren't you?"

He swallowed. "Yes?"

"Which means you *meant* to come to Blakely House. Why?"

"I have business here." Another chill passed through him, from shoulders to knees.

"What could possibly bring you *here*?"

The room's tilt grew sharper. Whiteness framed his vision, closing in. "I didn't break in."

"Yet you sneak about the house. What exactly were you looking for, Mr. Manns?"

"I . . . I . . . nothing." He cleared his throat. "Just a peek around." His breathing came harder. He tried to smile over his obvious struggle, but he felt it falter. "Who . . . might you . . . be?"

"I'm seeing to the estate. Managing the legalities and such things."

Solicitors. They were merely solicitors.

The eager, bright-eyed one stepped forward, arms crossed. "Beastly time to visit, though. We're in a state just now, so perhaps it's best you come back another time. There's a fine little inn on the mainland, and it won't cost you but three shillings for the smallest room. Sixpence for a larger one."

No. No, he couldn't leave. There'd be no getting back in if he did.

"Oh, Tom," said the closer one, his voice suddenly liquid tones. "You're not sending him out, are you? In his condition?"

"He can't jolly well stay here now, can he?"

"Perhaps after a little rest, you can tell us all about the business you have here. Now, won't you tell us your full name?"

Name? His name. "I'm . . ." He blinked. Dizziness edged his vision. He had to lie again, but his brain had evaporated. "Not certain." He hadn't the capacity. He'd only muddle things.

The man's eyebrows rose. "Of your name?"

His ears rang. The sound intensified. With one harsh tilt of the world, darkness closed in and the floor came up to meet him.

chapter
THIRTY-ONE

When we haven't adequate language to explain God, the great expanse of his creation offers a wordless vocabulary to show us who he is.

~Sophie's letters to Emmett

THE NORTH SEA

I awoke to a calm, still world with coals still glowing in a nearby stove and someone lightly touching my face. I wasn't rocking anymore, and my stomach had settled. The ship—it had been a dream. A rather terrible, wonderful construct of my vivid imagination.

Thank heavens.

Another gentle *tap-tap* to my face.

Micah?

I shifted to the right, but no big marble eyes looked down at me. Only a folded bit of stiff wool blanket that had poked my face with my own twitching as I woke. I sighed and curled my body around my aching desire for my cat. My silly, demanding, no-good cat who always made the world stable. The ground beneath me lurched, and I sat up, blinking at the underbelly of the ship that was, unfortunately, all too real.

Groaning, I climbed out of the bedroll, stretching stiff muscles and smoothing my rumpled skirt and shirtwaist. The air was chilly, even with the warmth glowing from the stove. I grabbed a blanket and threw it around my shoulders. A little card tumbled out.

I can double absolutely anything
and my special gift is telling the truth.

Well, that was easy enough, as riddles went. I crossed the hold to a crooked little mirror hanging at a slight angle. Another note was tucked there, and a lovely marble-backed brush and comb hung from a hook beside it.

It's the beginning of eternity, an essential part of everyone,
and the absolute end of an adventure.

I stared about the room. I brushed out my hair and washed my face.

Beginning of eternity.

End of an adventure.

I chewed on some of the dried meat from our stores—there were several bags stowed in the cabinets already, and more from Angel—then studied every word, every beautifully formed letter. *Essential for everyone.*

Ah!

As I popped my head through the portal, blanket wrapped

tight, the sea breeze soothed my senses and felt oddly welcoming. The air was chilly, but it was no longer spitting in my face and the waves had calmed to a slow rolling motion. The distant hum of mechanics anchored me. The smaller propeller Mr. Montagne had borrowed from the flying machine was working rather well. If only I could have made the larger one functional before the trip too.

"Good morning, mon tête endormie." His smile was wide as he observed me from across the deck, pulling a thick rope taut and wrapping it around a metal spike on the mast. "Or rather, good evening." He knotted the rope and bowed at the waist.

"E," I said, striding toward him. "It's the letter *e*, isn't it? Your riddle."

His eyebrows lifted and a tiny smile curved one side of his lips. "Very good. I am impressed, Miss Forrester."

A bubble of delight popped pleasantly inside.

"And impressed to see you on the deck at last."

"I had to know the answer."

"The very thing I was counting on." He leaned back as he gripped the steering wheel, face to the breeze, allowing the wind full rein.

Never had I seen a man so at home. So unencumbered. I crouched before the oversized clock gears and connectors that operated the larger propeller—the one that didn't work yet—then glanced back at the ship's captain.

"Can I interest you in some dried meats? We have plenty."

"Only about two stones' worth." He laughed. "Whatever compelled you to pack so much of it?"

I shrugged, a smile tugging at my lips. "Thank Angel. She prepared it."

269

We shared some food and chatted amiably for a time. Then he sprang up and returned to his post.

As I looked over his countenance sparkling with good humor and wit, it was clear I'd only seen the strained, buttoned-up version of the man before. "You look rather at home."

He lifted his broad shoulders, unbuttoned oilskin duster flapping against him. "I suppose I am."

I turned back to the mechanics—something I understood—and knelt before the pressure gauge that was meant to operate the large propeller. I had all the time in the world to work on it now.

Everything appeared to be connected, every joint and gear moved smoothly, slick with white lithium grease, yet the propeller remained under the ship, curled up like a sleeping bird with its feathers tucked. I threw the lever that should have unfurled its blades, but nothing moved. There was no whir of an activating machine, no rumble of power.

It would take an age to move this thing without it.

I removed the glass and spun the needle. There was tension in the spring, but it didn't release. Almost as if it was waiting for some magical tweak from its creator to fully cooperate. I felt about the coiled spring, studying the action of the dial. I lost myself in the work for an unknown length of time, analyzing and testing. My eyes grew tired straining in the deepening darkness. If I could see it move just—

A touch. André placed his good hand on my shoulder and his automaton hand curled at his side, mirroring his human one. "There's something you should see."

"What, land?" I focused on that dial, willing it to move, even a fraction of a millimeter.

"No. Come."

I huffed out a breath and stood, my gaze lingering on the needle. André gently turned me toward the mast and pointed up.

I blinked. Blinked again, and frowned. An odd green glow had filled the sky, almost an electric color. A muffled light. "What is that?"

He led me toward the mast and indicated I should climb. I threw him a look, but he urged me on, squeezing his eyes shut to demonstrate what I should do. With a quick sigh, I complied and climbed the spokes, eyes closed, to the wide crow's nest near the top. He knelt beside me, good hand resting on the small of my back, and pointed through a thick veil of receding mist at a bright light shooting upward.

I squinted, leaning into the chilly wind as the ship's bow sliced through the waves, and as the clouds spread apart, the bright, iridescent green light speared through the clouds and spread graceful fingers across the expanse. Like a crack in the sky, and a portal opening to another world, bright green and blue streaked upward.

Awe swept over me in deepening swells, and I became humbly aware of a presence. A greatness I could not see, except for this glory left behind as evidence. It had always been there, waiting for me to notice it, even while my nose was buried in some riddle. Some broken clock. "Is it the heavens?"

"Not quite. Aurora borealis. We're fortunate to see it this far away. The season is right."

I clung to the rail of the crow's nest and drank in the exquisite show of color and light streaking across the night sky, then fading. "The northern lights. I've never seen them this way before."

He gave me an amused smile. "What way have you seen them?"

"Oh, just—"

"Between the pages of your books?"

I looked down at my little white hands gripping the rail. Those of us who worked on clocks and tiny gears, our world was often the size of our palms. I had become an expert at my own little handheld world, knew every Swiss lever escapement and mainspring, but in all these years I hadn't lifted my head. And the world had passed me by. *Look up*, I urged yesterday-Sydney. *Just look up!* I had never felt more like a timepiece that had lost its rhythm.

"You're not broken," he said, reading my thoughts. "You're still being modified." He steadied me with his automaton hand as the waves lifted and dropped the boat, operating his new limb with surprising ease. "Welcome to your first real-life adventure, Miss Forrester."

I smiled at him in the dimness, and as he looked at me, his rugged, roughly scarred face gentled. What a pirate. What a man! Just like the light show above, he was a unique blend of colors from the brush of a skilled artist.

"Perhaps now *you* will write books, Miss Forrester. Let other people live through your adventure."

But there was no capturing all of this in mere words. The texture, the vividness and intensity would never translate. I leaned back onto my heels. "Thank you. Thank you for showing me this." Every book I'd ever read contained sunsets and lights and natural beauty of every variety. But this moment of sailing into the great lights was experienced somewhere deep within my chest. Never could I make this lie flat on the page.

A quick nod and his smile deepened, seemingly glad that I appreciated it all the way he did. I laid down as the waves picked up, hands behind my head, and stared up at the great swirl of bright green, a sky alight with unexplainable magic. "How do they do that?"

He lay beside me, resting his automaton hand on his abdomen. The other supported his head. "There are explanations, I'm certain, but I don't have them. Creation is better appreciated than understood, in my opinion." He turned his head toward me with a smile. "Does that upset your scientific mind?"

"In this case, I rather like not understanding. I'd hate to be stuck in a world whose riddles were already solved."

"Yet you do not see God in all of this?"

God. Yes, that was the presence I felt out here thick in the air, delicate as mist yet pervasive as light. A weight, but a gentle one. "I think I do see it, actually." There existed in nature many patterns. Repeating nuances. Clear order by design that it was hard to deny.

It was in the murky, symmetrical waves. The way a tree sprouted from a seed and somehow managed to grow and produce more of its kind. From the human body fitted together with every gear and mechanical operation it would need, gently balanced in the only way possible for sustaining life. Everything blooming into life, working together so precisely. Behind it all, the pulsing presence of a most holy Creator. "We take it for granted, don't we?"

He turned to look at me again.

"Beauty is so readily available, in so many forms, that we almost . . . miss it." I closed my eyes. "I see what you mean about seeing God out here. His maker's mark is everywhere."

He sighed. "Perhaps it is possible, it would seem, to know an artist by his work."

I narrowed my eyes at him with a smile. "You do say brilliant things at times."

"I merely echo great thoughts." His smile toward me was warm. Quite close. And surprisingly *affectionate*. His expression always gentled toward me, every time our gazes caught for half a second. He stared at me, and quite often, I now realized. And this was why. This gentling—it was *affection*.

I looked away. My heart pounded. Too many times I'd come to this precipice and taken the wrong step. Found a crumbling ledge beneath my foot, and tumbled down to a familiar place— rejection. I sat up and looked down at my hands blurred by mist. He sat too, leaning against the mast.

I had been waiting for one of two things, I realized then. For André to wake up and see what everyone else did about me, to realize my oddity and gently separate himself from me. Or for him to kiss me again. For the affection in his glances to solidify into something tangible. Warm. *Delicious*. Maybe tonight . . . tonight he would kiss me.

But when I lifted my gaze, his face had shuttered. As if he'd suddenly remembered something. "Why do you look at me that way?"

"Which way?"

"Well, first you have this look of . . . well, that perhaps you don't despise me, *enjoy* me even, and then the next minute you look as though you suspect I'm plotting to rob you."

Indecision flitted through his features. "Sometimes I realize how little I truly know you. How much does not make sense . . . yet."

"I'll answer anything you ask. I always have. I haven't been blessed with an effective filter for my thoughts."

A tweak of a smile. Then it faded. "Who are you, really? The truth."

"I am Sydney Evelyn Grace Forrester of Grafton, County

Shropshire, twenty-three years of age with a deceased stepfather, unknown birth father, and a mother who has mastered the disappearing act. I have no siblings—that I know of—and reside with my only known relation, Lottie Lane. I fix clocks and solve riddles and say too much and . . . what? What is it, André? Please, just tell me."

"There's a puzzle. A riddle, I suppose. I must figure it out before I tell you about it."

I huffed out a breath and worried my lip. "Then I suppose you'll simply have to decide to trust me or not."

He cast his gaze out over the sea, away from me.

My stomach turned. Cramped. "I wouldn't be going on this trip if I had killed Emmett. I wouldn't be risking my life to find the truth if I already knew it."

He looked at me, gaze boring through the layers. "You are truly Sydney Forrester?"

I laughed, then leaned forward when I saw he was serious. "I'll bring you my certificate of birth if that would help. Only, you'll have to bring me safely back to shore for that."

He shook his head. "Then what *are* you hiding? Why . . . why are you so unsettled all the time? Why do you so often resist looking me in the eye? Only dishonest people cannot meet a gaze."

I took a breath. "You're used to assessing pirates, but you can't read me the same way, André." I worried the hem of my skirt. Picked at splinters of wood beneath me. How wet everything stayed out here. All the time, wet. "I have a thing."

"A thing. What thing?"

"A thing." He was actually going to make me say it. "With talking, mostly. Saying the wrong thing. I always manage to, and it's all I can think about. Especially around men. Some of them, anyway. The ordinary ones I can talk to all day long, but then there is the impossibly dashing sort, too handsome and fascinating and wonderful to look at directly, and I cannot—"

He kissed me. Kissed the end right off my sentence, cupping my jaw and drawing me close. I rose up on my knees, leaning into him, and savored the moment. The wild, unplanned moment there in the midst of the sea, clinging to his shirt as the waves rocked the boat, spraying over the deck below, and drank in his kiss. Warm and searching and eager . . . for *me*. So this was adventure.

The heavens above lit the night with a surreal wonder that exploded through my soul. My head lifted off my shoulders. Twirled a waltz. I was doing it, wasn't I? At last, I had become the heroine in a novel. I had found romance. Suddenly all the men who hadn't chosen me didn't matter.

But then he pulled away, resting his forehead on mine with a look of mild distress. Deeply longing, quite obviously hungry for more . . . but troubled. His fingers slid down my face and he turned away without a word. I dared not shatter the moment with bumbling words. In fact, I hadn't any to offer.

Instead I let the ship sway us back and forth, the waves growing choppier, the wind whistling through the sails and beating them against the masts as my skin tingled everywhere he'd touched it.

Until the moment melted away and the world continued on.

When we climbed down, he crossed to the ship's cabin and opened a storage door. He lifted out an ornate wooden instrument with a bow and blew the dust off its surface, polishing the reddish wood with his sleeve and settling the piece between chin and shoulder. He adjusted and readjusted, and finally sat and supported the piece with his knee.

I approached and pointed at the strip of leather tying back his hair. He undid it, releasing the strands to the wind, and I lashed his bow to his mangled arm with crisscrosses like a corset.

Positioning the instrument, he drew the bow across the strings, a little awkwardly at first, then in one long, low note. Back and forth he went across the strings, getting his bearings. Soon a graceful ascent of music followed that somehow matched the magnificent sky, magnifying its effect upon my soul. He closed his eyes and played by feel, putting sound to the glorious display.

I sank onto the ground beside him and let it wash over me as I leaned against his shoulder. He did not push me away.

Had I ever truly experienced beauty before? Or merely observed it from behind a glass? Here it surrounded me. Affected me. I had felt a great many things while buried in a novel, but never like this. The closeness, the surreal beauty, the music of his fiddle.

The way a kiss felt.

He played a sunset on that fiddle, long, silky draws of the bow that vibrated through his arm into mine. That was one of his signatures—music. It poured out of him onto the fiddle strings as easily as it had onto the pianoforte, and even when he hadn't an instrument within reach. He had a musical soul, that pirate, and it showed in the way he moved and spoke and thought.

Heavens, but I was falling for the man. Rather quickly. Then I let my imagination run wild into territory I might never visit in reality. A sweeping love story, a long and tender marriage, a sense of oneness. Waking up to his affectionate smile every morning. Wading through mistake after mistake only to be met with his patient look of amusement on the other side.

We spent the remaining hours deep in our own tasks. He managed the ship, running here and there to secure and steer and consult the gauges. I tinkered with the propeller and rationed out more food, still floating along in the moment.

Finally, when the night had stretched long and dawn was not far, we collapsed against the main mast together, and he said, "You hadn't plans to sleep, did you?"

"What do you think I've done all day?" I spoke louder as the wind picked up. "I've no intention of sleeping anytime soon."

"Good. Because . . . look." He turned me by the shoulders, pointing my gaze at something bobbing in the water. A dark, floating mass highlighted by a revolving flash of light.

No . . . land. It was *land*. A coastline.

"Have we turned around?" With sudden panic, I realized I hadn't any idea what I'd do when we returned to Blakely House. How I'd handle the accusations. I hadn't thought that far ahead.

He checked some contraption with a dial on the mast, then a map, before glancing up again with a grin. "That, Miss Forrester, is Lindesnes, Norway. The last place Emmett Sinclair went."

I sucked in a chilly breath. "The other coast. We made it." I shot up. "Really, we made it? We're here? We're here!" I shouted and whooped above the howling breeze.

"Very nearly. And you were right—the voyage was far shorter than anticipated. Perhaps half of the twenty-six hours I threatened you with earlier." He flashed a teasing smile.

I laughed and clapped. "We've done it. Oh, André. It seems we're destined to do our living at night, you and I." He rose and took my hand. I smiled up at him and it was radiant—I could feel it. "Thanks to you, I've done it. I've left dry land and gone on an adventure. And now, here we are. The hardest part is done."

But of course, it wasn't. Not even close.

chapter
THIRTY-TWO

Blakely House

He was a prisoner more than a guest, this new arrival. Dane Hutchcraft tapped a pen against his chin as he looked over the intruder, this Mr. Manns who still lay on the sofa. His legs dangled off the arm, his body too long for the petite little courting couch.

He wasn't chained to the cot, of course, but Dane had no plans to leave the man until he awoke and was thoroughly questioned. He'd been searching for something, of that Dane was certain. What it was, he hadn't any idea, nor how he knew to search for anything at all. He'd been so intentional, on the hunt for something specific.

What was his connection to Blakely House?

The police were coming back in a few hours to discuss the missing would-be heiress after searching Northumberland for her. Perhaps he'd add this intruder to his list of grievances. He'd let them take the man away—yes, that would be a fine solution.

He turned away and the muscles in his face relaxed—muscles

he hadn't even realized he'd been tensing. Claiming Blakely House had been more challenging than he'd imagined, but now it *must* happen. Because, for the first time in many years, Arthur had written. He had put pen to paper, written words to his father, and posted them.

It was easy to recall the last time he'd glimpsed Arthur's face—his eyes like two blades, eyebrows in one straight slash above them.

He forced the memory down, grasping for the pen and pulling his half-written letter toward him. He *would* get him here. He would. He'd find the exact words that would convince Arthur, soften his overzealous heart, and draw him back to his papa. Arthur had opened the door just a crack—now it was time to pry it open with news of his progress.

He had offers, he wrote. Offers from wealthy men in Japan who were eager to purchase tailor-made automata based on the prototype Emmett had designed. Mechanical men were the most sought-after item among the wealthy of Asia, and no one was better equipped to take on the task than Arthur. Even as a boy he'd been fascinated by the mechanical monkey in the store window, the little traveling automata instrument players. And the stories of Uncle Emmett's creations had nearly made him salivate.

Nine years and three months it had been since Arthur had spoken to his father, and now one letter about the automaton and Arthur had written back. He had to keep the momentum going.

Arthur would come, he would see those requests and the brilliant machine man. Then he'd dive into the work like a boy in a toy shop, and Dane would be at his side. *Teach me about the automaton,* Dane would say. *I'll handle the business end of things, finding clients and drafting contracts. You do what you love best—creating. Tinkering.*

He'd give Arthur large chunks of the money they made too.

He'd give him *all* the money, if Arthur wanted it. He wouldn't, though, because it was Arthur. Or if he kept any, he'd pour it into helping the unfortunates in his parish.

So be it. As long as he worked alongside Dane, as long as he spoke to him again, he could do anything he wanted. All Dane wanted was what he'd had in abundance so many years ago.

The man stirred on the sofa. Dane jerked from his thoughts and stared until the pen dripped ink on his hand. He quickly cleaned it off and went to him as the man shifted under the woolen blanket. He blinked, then focused on Dane.

A smile. "How do you feel, Mr. Manns?"

He blinked and rubbed his face. "Alive," he croaked.

"Good." He tented his fingers. "I suppose you'll want tea."

He exhaled. "That . . . that would be lovely."

"Very good. But first, Mr. Manns, a question." He perched on the chair beside him. "Why have you come to Blakely House?"

His gaze snapped to Dane's and held, as if judging how much he could trust him.

Dane curved his lips, draping his features in welcome and acceptance. "Not to worry. The others shan't hear a word of it."

"I've heard legends of this place. Since I was a lad."

Dane raised his eyebrows and smiled indulgently as if he were listening to a child's recitation of the day. "Have you, indeed? Well, I can tell you the tales of the castle monster are true." He gave a quick growl.

A weak smile. "But you're not Emmett Sinclair."

Dane stiffened. "And how do you know that?"

Color drained from the man's face until he nearly matched the pillow behind his head.

There was a knock at the door. "Mr. Hutchcraft." It was one of the servants—the tall, gold-toothed one. "The investors are here."

Drat. He fisted his hand. Wanted to punch something. Those rotten investors and their timing. "Show them to the drawing room. I'll be along presently." Jolly had insisted on notifying them of the recent events, eager to enlist their help in moving along probate matters in favor of a new heir.

But their presence meant the tide was low. And that the police would not be far behind, and he wasn't ready for them. He bit his lip. If only they'd held off another hour or so. Or this stranger had woken up an hour earlier.

They didn't even know where Sydney Forrester was, but they'd find her. They'd find her in some forgotten corner of this place and drag her into the light for an arrest and inquisition. It was absolutely necessary, especially now that things were set in motion. He flicked a glance at the papers scattered across the little fold-out writing desk. The stack of letters from the Japanese translator concerning the overseas sales of automata, and the single folded sheet from his son. From his own Arthur, in his neat hand.

"Mr. Hutchcraft?" The servant poked his head into the room again.

"I'll be along." Dane rose, looking from the prostrate visitor to the door and back again. He'd been standing guard all this time with nothing, and now that he was awake . . .

He hesitated. Leaned close to the man. "Don't move. I'll know."

chapter
THIRTY-THREE

Flying, it would seem, dearest Sophie, is not a matter of lifting oneself off the ground, but of merely not falling once you've sprung off the cliff. Even I can do that.

~*Emmett's letters to Sophie*

The realization hit me all at once. I stared at the coast, counting the smaller lights. *One, two, three . . . and a wide break. Then four more on the other side.* The snare. The rocky coast where many a ship had wrecked and been plundered. I grabbed his arm. "André. André, listen to me. We have to go around to another dock. We cannot go ashore here."

He frowned, eyes glowing. "This is the inlet. It's where we're *supposed* to dock."

"It's a trap. There are wreckers here who loot ships—we'll run aground on the rocks and it'll cut your ship wide open. Please!"

"Where did you hear—"

"Sophie's husband—he was one of them. You must believe me!"

"Sydney." He looked pained. "Enough with this Sophie person."

"André, turn the boat!"

But he didn't.

I grabbed the wheel and spun. The craft bore sharply to the left, the rigged wheel spinning.

André tumbled across the deck, then scrambled up—shocked. He grabbed the wheel with both hands—human and automaton—and threw all his might into steadying it. Straight toward the inlet. His glance toward me was darkened with doubt.

"Listen to me, please! We'll crash!"

His expression was hard. Plain.

"You *don't* trust me, do you? Why, André? Why can't you trust what I say?"

"Because you *aren't* who you say."

"Of course I am!" I yelled it above the wind. "Have you gone mad?"

He kept that steely gaze on my face. "The man. The one who washed ashore. He is Sydney Forrester."

Shock. Cold and hard.

"So who are you?"

I let go of the wheel and stumbled back. Panic, then dread. I groaned. "He's the fraud, André. Not me. I'll prove it. But there's no time now." I grabbed the wheel again, veering to the left, and the ship groaned and turned hard, laid down almost on its side.

I screamed. Clung as waves slapped the deck and soaked my feet. More lights bobbed ahead, and shouts could be heard.

André braced himself and righted the vessel, then veered it around the coastline and away from the harbor. He threw several glances my way, but said nothing while he navigated the coastline.

When we'd bobbed around the inlet, figures were visible on the beach, running about. I tumbled, grabbing at a rope as it flopped nearby. He bounded across the deck, yanking a pulley that lowered the anchor with a clink of chains. Leaping to another lever, he pulled it and released a small boat into the water below. "Come along."

One look at those churning waves tossing the boat about, and I dug in. Shook my head.

He put his arm around me, took one bounding leap toward the side. I slipped from his hold and collapsed on the deck. I stumbled to the railing and peered down. My senses swirled at the sight of the thick gray water below.

He stood braced on the deck, one arm out to me. "Come, Sydney. Come with me!"

I'd braced myself to handle the calmer water, but this made my stomach rise to my throat. "I can't!" If I jumped, there were so many places I might land besides the boat. So many dark and murky places.

Calculations. I could figure this out.

Five yards out, with a velocity of—what was airborne velocity?—but mere inches in any wrong direction—

"Do it now!"

I bobbed and swayed with the ship, clinging to the mast, mind spinning with numbers. Approximations. Invisible angles and a plotted graph of where I'd land relative to my leap. The little fishing vessel slid farther and farther away from the side of the ship, continually altering my projections, and in that moment I deeply regretted coming. Regretted leaving shore. Prison, at least, was on dry land.

"Now!"

But then I spotted the lights. Bobbing ones, like lanterns, just off the shore. They were coming. The wreckers. I was aboard a pirate ship, and someone was coming to loot it.

How is this suddenly my life?

Desperate, trembling, I made a mad dash across the deck toward the hatch, but an arm clamped around my middle, drawing me back as I flailed and argued, my fists beating at him in vain.

"Enough with your *mild expostulations*, Miss Forrester." He hauled me to the railing and clambered up without slowing. I cried out, gulped back nausea, and buried my face in his chest. Again.

I counted my heartbeats. Focused on the flex of his body. He was strong. Quite strong, and that's all that mattered. He knew what he was doing. We'd come out all right. I'd survive. Probably.

Then he leaped the rail and we sailed suspended through the air, dying at least forty-seven separate times in ten seconds, stomach up in my throat as I waited endlessly to strike water. Or rocks.

Just get it over with.

I clung, my scuffed boots kicking at nothing, dress flapping around me like a wilted parachute. Then came the water. It slapped the backs of my legs, then I was yanked out. Tumbled over wood and human legs. And I was alive, panting unceremoniously between the pirate's boots.

And the look on his face should have been a painting—horror. Sheer horror. "You are well?"

We were in the boat. Safe.

A giddy laugh bubbled out of nowhere and I shook, with cold and terror and hilarity, all of it. I scrambled to sit up, gripping both sides of the boat. "Yes. I am well. And we are *never* doing this again."

His face crinkled into a relieved smile. "Come now, where is your sense of adventure?"

"Back home," I yelled over the waves. "On the bookshelf." I pulled off my boots and dumped the sea out of them. "I had no idea how I was going to manage to land in the boat."

"You didn't. You had help."

I gripped the side of the pitching craft. "I'm glad of it. Still never doing this again."

"Remember, when you're out on the water, it's not about how, but *who*. You can trust me."

I launched myself toward him and clung to him, teeth chattering, not caring a whit for social conventions. This was the worst. Simply the worst.

"They've turned back. Water's too choppy for them, or they're hoping we'll drift inland and crash." He grabbed the oars and attempted to row us toward the lights.

Then a jarring crash, and wood splintering. Water sprayed and André gathered me up in a flash, scrambling out of the little boat as it began to sink. "You were right about the rocks. They are treacherous out here."

"Everything is!" Anyone who thought this sort of pastime amusing must be mad.

The water reached his thighs as he waded through it, climbing onto a rocky beach and setting me down. Whipping off his tattered duster, he wrapped it around me and stood back, surveying the coast. "I cannot see them. They're likely chasing down the ship. Perhaps they'll leave us alone for the moment."

He wasn't bothered by danger to his ship, it seemed. I'd dragged him to another country, risked his boat for what he considered an unrealistic manhunt—and he wasn't angry. To him it was nothing more than a giant riddle. How to keep alive? How to get home again?

Perhaps we were alike after all.

Could a lady hate adventures while also deeply admiring an adventurer?

With his good arm around me, we scrambled up the rocky hill together, up toward the light. Then he stopped me. "Stay low. I will be back for you."

"You will *not* leave me alone out here."

He glanced to the beach. To me. "Very well. But stay beside me."

I kept up my labored climb, panting, lungs burning. I pulled up on long tufts of beach grass, thick and straw-like, cutting my hands.

Then, a most beautiful sight. Above us, just below the circulating light, was the lighthouse. Sophie's lighthouse. Answers were near, good or bad. They were near.

We approached in the dark, wind whipping the grass around us. "This is it. André, it's her lighthouse." The chipping white paint, the squatty lighthouse with a purple door. It was the one from the pictures.

He banged on the door with his fist and it burst open.

"Hello?" I ran in and shut the door behind us, peering around in the darkness. A single kerosene lamp on a far table dimly illuminated what appeared to be a jungle of dishes, towels, and large, muddy boots. "Sophie? Sophie Holland?"

It was surreal. Another dimension. At any second, I'd see the woman I'd read about in all those letters. The one so adored from afar.

Wind howled outside, rattling shutters. Inside sounded like a narrow tunnel, protected from the breeze lashing the windows. I stepped over piles of belongings, blinking as my eyes adjusted to the dimness, and picked through discarded tunics, stockings, and hats.

All from men.

"She's hiding. She's here somewhere, and we need to rescue her."

With a grim look, André stalked through the mess, pulling open cabinets and pantry doors. Larder, wardrobe, tiny bedroom—no one was here.

I sorted through the mess on the table, at coffee-stained papers and bits of food not swept away. He poked with the toe of his boot through the mess in the bedroom, then returned to tell me the news I expected, yet couldn't wrap my mind around. "She isn't here. And it doesn't look as though she's ever lived here. There's no trace of a woman about."

Not a stitch of clothing, nor an inch of domestic cleanliness. Not a letter or a shoe or a hair comb to indicate anyone named Sophie Holland had lived here. Ever.

The truth choked me. My breath came in gasps. "She's real. I promise, Sophie is real, and she's here."

He frowned, but said nothing more.

"Unless we have the wrong coast." I ran to the window and squinted over the dim landscape, craggy and wild and wet. The beam of yellow light rotated above, highlighting choppy waves and grassy hills, but no person. No Sophie. "But . . . the purple door." I slipped off the heavy duster and handed it back to him.

"The men are returning," he said, shrugging his coat back on. "We must leave."

"Right. We can tuck ourselves away in—"

"Leave the island. Back to the ship, back to Farneham Heald."

"But we've just arrived! And we haven't even searched for her yet!"

You'll know where to find me. Past the lighthouse, tucked in the most perfect circle that ever was. Desperately, I ran outside and scanned the area. Circle . . . circle . . . *Past* the lighthouse.

"I didn't expect to sail into this sort of mess when we set out."

Icy winds whipped through and I huddled into a tree. There was a crash and a roaring on the beach.

He cast me a grim look. "We're in over our heads, Miss Forrester. That house—they have weapons. Many of them. These men are thieves, but not London fingersmiths. They've stolen large amounts of cargo. Killed people."

"How do you know?"

His gaze hardened over the sea below. "We haven't time to argue. Now, come!" Wind whipped his heavy duster as he grabbed my hand and pulled me along the sloping hill. We careened toward a little fishing dinghy leaning against an outbuilding. "This'll have to do."

I stopped. "Surely you don't mean for us to float back to England in that . . . *thing*."

And without Sophie. *Without Sophie.* Had it even been worth the effort?

"Just to the ship. If the men haven't ruined it yet."

"But what about—" I peered down the hill at the coastline, where we'd left our lifeboat. It lay splintered and broken, an unrecognizable mess among the rocks.

"This might do." He hoisted the bow of the borrowed boat, inspecting its integrity.

Behind me, a woman's low, moaning voice swept through the rocky shoreline, muffled and songlike, catching me off guard.

No . . . wind. It was the wind. And I was going mad. It was the riddle that was doing it, bouncing about in my brain. *Past the lighthouse, tucked in the most perfect circle that ever was.*

Perfect circle. *What* perfect circle?

Once we returned to the ship it would come to me, wouldn't it? That was the way of things. But I'd have already left Sophie here. My first adventure, a failure. My heart was like lead within. I shivered and spun back to the dinghy.

But that's precisely when the revolving light illuminated something surprising in the distance. The first traces of dawn settled over a garden edged with stone and hedges, set down in a deep valley below the lighthouse. It was frozen over, but the precision of its design was evident from this height. More than that—a small wooden bridge curved over the muddy lowland, with flowers that had frozen in bloom, caught by an early spring freeze and flattened to the earth around it.

I knew that garden.

I grabbed André's arm, tugging him closer. "André, look!"

He paused, casting a glance down into that valley that looked remarkably like the gardens at Blakely House, but he turned back to the dinghy.

"Look, it's hers!" I tugged harder. "It's Sophie's garden!"

Shouts came from the beach. The men weren't looting the ship—they were looking for us. André pulled his arm away and threw himself into his work on the dinghy, kicking and yanking the rough boards into place where they'd been damaged. "Take hold of the other side. Can you lift it?"

"André!"

The *ting* of metal on rock sounded. More shouts.

André paled. "Lift, *now*!"

The men were scaling the rocky incline with fierce yells. I grabbed the edge of the boat. Lifted. Fumbled it, and lifted again. Then André dropped it as the men charged up the hill.

A shove from behind. I tumbled to the grass and the boat was lifted up. I was rolled underneath it and the thing dropped over me. The world was dark and muffled, with ocean waves sounding like the inside of a conch shell from the beach as my pulse thrummed.

Voices. Men arguing. Then, laughter. The shattering of glass.

My heart beat against the ground. My breath warmed my face. What were they saying?

Then, with a few shouts and grunts, the men tromped off. Their voices grew distant. Then the hillside was silent, save for the distant sweep of sea on rock. With quick, shallow breaths, I pushed my back against the little boat—more of a canoe than anything—and released myself into the fresh night air and utter silence. They had gone. And once again, the pirate had saved me.

I stood on that hillside overlooking the sea, then turned to the lighthouse. The dark, haunted-looking lighthouse with the purple door where Sophie had once stood. Then down to the beach.

There. They were there. I squinted, trying to see André. To see if he was safe. Grabbing the tall grasses like handles, I made my way down the steep side of the hill, uncertain about what I'd do when I reached them.

I began praying. Short, desperate pleas sent up like pitiful arrows, and when I paused, looking up at the starry sky, the same awe came over me and I felt the hugeness—the magnificence—of the God who had created all this. Big as the sea was, big as the sky, he was bigger yet. *Please help me*, I begged.

Halfway down the hill, with the wet air upon my face, I saw it. In a frozen moment of time, I stared into the valley. Heard the song of the wind. And my gaze rested on that perfectly arched bridge . . . and the way it met its reflection in the water below.

A perfect circle.

A shiver coursed through me as my very soul felt beckoned into that valley, away from winds and wreckers where peace prevailed . . . and Sophie waited.

chapter THIRTY-FOUR

No, no. Flight, dearest Emmett, is a matter of constant opposition with your environment. You only lift as you push against it.

~Sophie's letters to Emmett

I hurtled myself down the steep incline toward the beach and my pirate, grasping at thick grasses and rocks. I paused to spit out sand and squint down at my destination. The others had fled into the shadows, and André lay sprawled on the beach, all in black, duster blown to one side as he lay perfectly still. What I'd do when I reached him, I had no idea, but I turned and climbed down, forcing myself not to look out at the water, praying I didn't strike rock.

I reached the beach, jumping down the last rocky outcropping, and looked about. The place was deserted. Gulls cried, the revolving light circulated overhead. I puffed out several breaths, shivering, and then stilled in the echoing emptiness. He was gone. André was gone.

No.

No, no, no!

I spun in the wet sand, forcing myself to face the sea. The waves. Then as tightness cinched around my ribs, I sprinted back to the rocks and climbed.

A voice behind me. "You would leave me out here, then?"

I looked back. And there he was, tall and dashing, boots planted on the rocky ground, standing just outside a cave. With a cry, I flew across the expanse and into his arms. "You're here! But I saw you and—you hid, didn't you? I thought you were dead."

"Fortunately, so did they."

I flung myself into his arms again. Then shoved him away. "You scared the life out of me. How could you?"

"Would you rather I stay lying on the wet sand?"

"I'd rather you not play tricks on me."

"I did nothing of the kind." He straightened his duster, testing out the automaton arm. "At least, not intentionally." The sparkle came back to his eyes.

I pulled back. "The boat. Where's the boat?"

"On the hill where we left it."

"No, your ship."

"We anchored it just around the bend in these rocks. It'll be a miracle if these wreckers haven't been out to it yet. I was so certain they'd spotted it." He squinted out over the sea, where the sun was barely beginning to break the horizon. "It is rather foggy, which may help. And they seem focused on finding us just now."

We turned, but then the moan of the wind called to me again. I stilled. Turned in the direction of that valley, which was now barely visible between two rocky outcroppings.

"We can't leave yet." Those purple flowers had frozen to the ground, waiting for the sun's rescue. "Sophie is here. I've found the perfect circle—it's her. It's *her*."

He stared at me. "We're leaving." He stalked down the beach.

But this was why I'd come. And I wasn't leaving without trying. "I'll catch up!" I yelled up over my shoulder as I darted toward the rocks.

André lunged for my arm. I bolted over the rocks and threw myself into climbing, tripping and skidding, sending small rocks skittering down. *I'm coming. Sophie, I'm coming.*

"Sydney!" The wind carried his voice across the beach.

I was halfway up the rocks, hands scraped and sandy, when the footsteps sounded behind me. A grunt. I climbed faster until I reached the crevice, then I lunged forward and forced myself deeper into the crack. Scraping my skin with grit and rock.

Then I clambered over and I was in the valley, and everything stilled. Just as with my first visit to Farneham Heald, reality was muffled in this chilly space, a sense of sacred grounds hidden away from the rest of the world.

A scrambling behind me. He was closer. With a cry, I hurtled the rest of the way down into the valley, breathless, praying my feet didn't snag a rock. Toward the bottom, my ankle turned, and I rolled, resting on a thick bed of wet, half-frozen leaves. I sprang up and winced, then stilled, listening to my breath in the dense quiet. I was quite certain my voice would echo if I spoke. I clambered around, searching over and around the bridge, that perfect ring.

Sophie, where are you?

The clouds rolled and a weak shaft of light fell upon the

bridge, lighting the crumbling structure in a gentle glow. And there, just beside the bridge, was a doorway built into the side of the hill, nearly covered with fallen leaves and climbing ivy.

My heart exploded. It had never pumped so hard. Even in the most daring novel scenes, my heart pounded within my chest. Now it threatened to leap out. For as low as those moments of danger had taken me, the seasickness and the chill, the sudden heights of wonder equaled it.

"This is madness, Sydney." André slid the rest of the way down, his boots sending a spray of dead leaves as he reached me . . . and he froze.

I glanced at André, his chest heaving, eyes wild. And I saw in his face what I held inside like a great ball of warmth. We'd found her. We'd done it. We'd *done it*.

It was a sacred moment, the lull in the midst of danger. The stone bridge beside us meeting its reflection in a quiet pool of water to form a perfect ring. I stepped closer and stood before the door I'd read about—*Sophie's* door—and this harrowing journey, the highs and lows of it, all funneled into this moment and what we'd find on the other side.

I approached the little hideaway as my senses spiraled, and I knocked.

chapter
THIRTY-FIVE

Do not try to dissuade me of what I must do—when something incredibly precious is lost in the bushes, one will hardly feel the thorns he must climb through to reach it.

~*Emmett's letters to Sophie*

The door creaked open and jammed against the clumps of leaves. No one appeared, so André edged it farther open, ushering us into the dark hovel beyond.

"Hello?" My voice thudded against what must be dirt walls and darkness. The only sound was our muffled breaths, but someone was there. I groped around the tiny space as a *thwick* behind me brought a meager light. André had lit a match, then held it to the wick of a whale oil lamp, bringing a soft glow to the little hideaway. It was larger than one might first expect, with a bed, fireplace, and cauldron on the fringes of the arched room. The wind howled above us while nothing in this place moved.

Yet the awareness of another person in the little space prickled my skin.

I glanced at André, who said nothing.

Then a little skitter like a mouse, and a figure scrambled from beneath the bed and collided into André, cowering against him as his arms naturally came around the slender figure. The small girl tucked her head against André, who looked down upon her with a sense of brokenness and wonder all in one.

At last she shifted her head up to look at him. Lovely, dark brown eyes set in a pale face were all I could make out—and that she was a child. A very dirty, starving child of no more than seven or eight, and *not* the lovely woman in the pictures. "Are you Emmett? Have you come for me?"

My chest tightened. André's look was slightly panicked behind a grim set to his mouth.

Yells sounded outside, and André stiffened. Stood.

"Take me," she begged. "Take me with you. Please."

"We cannot—"

"*Please.*" Sheer terror paled her face.

I looked at André with wide eyes, clinging to the back of the little chair before me. What should we do? What *could* we do?

She burrowed deeper into André, clutching his shirt and trembling.

I put a hand on her shoulder. "Sophie. Do you know Sophie Holland?"

She whimpered.

A bang sounded outside. I rose. "We can't stay here."

The girl flung herself against my legs with such force that I stumbled back, catching myself on a rickety chair. I put my hand on the back of her head. "We won't leave you alone—where are your parents?"

Her jaw trembled. She stared with large eyes, then whispered, "Dead."

And that was enough for the pirate. Without another word, André swept her up, jerked his head toward the door, and blew out the lamp. What *would* we do with her?

Precisely what Emmett Sinclair would have done. Like so many other outcasts and shipwrecked thieves, weary wanderers and drifting pirates, the girl would find her way to Blakely House . . . and be safe.

That is, if we made it back.

With the child in his arms, her bare feet swinging, André bounded through the valley, the solid wall of his back just ahead of me. We scaled the incline toward the water, but we bypassed the steep path that led up toward the lighthouse and the little boat. We picked our way over the rocks toward the west side of the coast, where André's ship bobbed in the gray-black water.

I looked over my shoulder—a bit like Lot's wife—and my heart seized at the sight of torches bouncing toward us from the inlet, swarming down the sides of the hill toward the beach. The search was intensifying.

André hoisted the child toward me. My arms instantly went out to accept her weight, cradling her close as André pounded off down the rocky decline, leaping from rock to rock in a display of agility and strength that always stunned me.

Steadying the girl on her feet beside me, I helped her climb down after André. When we reached the shoreline, André was bent over piles of logs, his duster whipping over his back, beating his shoulders like wings. With great, powerful jerks, he lashed the logs together with some sort of weathered rope discarded on the beach along with so much other debris, grunting with each yank. Gratefulness surged through me that I was not alone, that I had a partner who knew how to adventure . . . and how to survive it.

Then, with a glance back at the approaching lights, he shoved all his weight against the makeshift raft, barreling into the water until each wave swelled up around his thighs. One powerful leap and he was aboard, the craft rocking beneath his weight. He stood and waved to us, beckoning us on board.

It was the only way out. I knew that. Our rescue. Our only hope.

Yet my feet, firmly planted on the rock, would not move. The girl clung to my damp skirts. With each tip and pitch of the raft, which had moments ago been a haphazard pile of logs, my stomach did likewise. Then the tingles started—those pins and needles poking at my fingers and arms, then up my neck and overtaking my head. My senses. My breath came in quick, panicked gasps. My vision blurred at the edges.

I couldn't. *Couldn't.* I'd faint. I could barely see. I'd lose the girl clinging to me—kill us both.

"Come on!"

It was all too familiar, this panic. My chest squeezed. I couldn't catch my breath. This was it. No more. I was done. My heart would explode and I would die out here without ever seeing home again, or finding out what had become of Sophie or Emmett.

I anchored the girl against my side. I held her to me like a . . . what, a flotation device? A raft?

What was I thinking?

What was *he* thinking?

I couldn't move. My head swam, full of air like a balloon rising off my shoulders.

"You can do it, Sydney. For her. She needs you!"

Then a wave swept the little raft farther. My heart pounded a rhythm over my scalp and the child clung to me harder. The shouts grew nearer—the lights were rounding the rocks toward us. They'd spotted us.

"The rocks! Walk on the rocks, Sydney!"

I scrambled up onto the first one, pulling my charge up with me. Rocks were solid. I liked rocks.

"Keep walking. Come toward me!"

Slippery, slimy, completely waterlogged . . .

I tightened my hold on the girl clinging like a wet leaf and together we stepped farther out.

But the waves. The waves. Dark and thick and rough, crashing over my legs and tugging at me. Pulling me in.

"Don't look at the water, look at me. At *me*."

Time stopped, images flicked by at warp speed—I took in the whole of it. The sea, the giant ship, the vastness of the wind and rain and foamy water, and me huddled in the center of the chaos. Then the still sky above, a great, silky expanse of dark and light.

Something spread wide open in my chest, broad and full of wonder as the awe once again overtook me. And truth came back to me. Words long committed to memory with Aunt Lottie nudged to the surface by the magnitude of creation before me. A novel whose words flat on the page had suddenly plumped into reality—living, breathing experiences that I was seeing for the first time. I felt them—*lived* them.

For, lo, he that formeth the mountains, and createth the wind, and declareth unto man what is his thought, that maketh the morning darkness, and treadeth upon the high places of the earth, The Lord, The God of hosts, is his name.

I kept my eyes on the sky, hand on the girl's back.

"Sydney!"

My gaze snapped to André's. Then down at the impossibly small child wrapped around my leg. So trusting—clinging. Then clinging harder as I shifted. Oh, to trust that way.

It's not about how . . . but who.

I can't, God. I can't. A reckless panic spiraled through me. I looked down at the gray-black waves, the mossy rocks, and was nearly sick. I tested the rock with one foot and my boot slid. How? How could I do this?

"And Peter answered him and said, Lord, if it be thou, bid me come unto thee on the water."

I braced myself on those rocks, a sapling against the wind, holding us both upright. Then a low rumbling started in the distance and rolled closer, deeper, vibrating through my chest, drowning out even the roar of waves. Like a clock finally wound and stirring to life, every bit of Scripture my father and Aunt Lottie had me memorize in childhood stirred to life.

"The voice of the Lord is upon the waters: the God of glory thundereth: the Lord is upon many waters."

My eyes flew open and André stood rooted on a rock as waves swished around his legs. Our eyes met, and he held out his hand.

Come.

The men yelled from the beach behind me. Their bodies splashed into the water as they surged after us. But they were background noise. Eyes on André, heart abundantly aware of the Creator of storms, of his vibrant presence pulsing through the air, I stepped onto a rock. Onto another. I felt about and moved again and again, toward the waiting pirate.

I was doing it. I had climbed out of the boat and I was

walking on the water. How much farther? A cold wave struck my thigh and I braced myself. Held the little girl upright, and looked at the water swirling around us. Back at the beach, which was much too far for comfort. Out at the ship that seemed miles away.

"But when he saw the wind boisterous, he was afraid; and beginning to sink, he cried, saying, Lord, save me."

I looked ahead. Once again, André had vanished. He was gone, gone. Swallowed by darkness. My knees shook. Buckled. I stumbled forward, slid on a mossy surface. I scrambled for purchase, but my flesh met only moss. And slipped. I cried out, screaming above the roar of waves.

We splashed into the water and gurgled underneath. I fought for the surface.

Peter, flailing as the waves consumed him. Jesus, reaching out a hand. Grab on. Just grab on.

The girl was pulled from my grasp, and as I frantically slapped the water and called for her, I felt myself lifted with a great *whoosh* of seawater and thrown over a rock. No . . . a shoulder. "When will you learn to trust?" His voice rumbled through my midsection, which leaned on his shoulder. He had pulled me out of trouble, and it wasn't the first time. I should have known. Should have known. He had always been safe. Every time. This time too.

It isn't *how* but *who.*

"I will lift up mine eyes unto the hills, from whence cometh my help. My help cometh from the Lord, *which made heaven and earth."*

I looked back up to the starry expanse of sky above. Let my chest swell again with the largeness of it. And the pirate, my pirate, became the extension of a mighty rescuing God in whom I had scarcely begun to believe.

chapter
THIRTY-SIX

Some of my favorite moments, such as our fortuitous
first meeting, Sophie dearest, came about entirely because of a mistake—which leads me to disbelieve in the
concept of mistakes entirely.

~*Emmett's letters to Sophie*

BLAKELY HOUSE

Angel Holligan grabbed the edge of the table with shaking
hands and read over André's note a third time. Impossible. This was *impossible*! This man they'd rescued, he
had written, claimed to be Sydney Forrester.

But *how*?

André Montagne must have written this before he'd vanished, but he had put it in her *Thursday* apron, and he'd departed on *Monday*. She'd been wearing her *Monday* apron that
day. So it had taken four days to get to her *Thursday* apron
. . . and his note.

She read it again and jammed the paper back into her pocket. *Try to find out what you can*, he'd said in closing, and she meant to do exactly that.

Up in the abandoned owl suite, she stood and glanced about.

Mess. A royal mess.

Heart pounding, she bustled about sweeping up night-clothes, pens, papers, and a tipped sandbox for the cat. "Can't have this. No, can't have this." She hummed, worked, then bumped the little desk with her hip, accidentally unsettling the papers on it. *Quite* accidentally. "Oh! Oh, there, there." She shuffled the papers back together with brisk efficiency, moving them this way and that. And glancing them over.

Was she truly doing this?

How dare she. What a perfect invasion of—

Oh! A letter.

No. She mustn't read.

She poked her finger into the pile of tiny trinkets, swirling them around to see if a familiar key was hiding beneath them. This was wrong. Terribly wrong. A betrayal at least. But the mess! It simply could not be left this—Oh! A quick turn, and a little jewelry case was swept to the floor. "Oh dear. Oh me." She tidied it and replaced the box. No key.

Angel stood in the center of the now-tidy room, hands on hips. Sydney would want her to do this. She would. Holding her breath, Angel opened a drawer and plunged her hand in, feeling about the clothing. She whimpered, digging further, looking over her shoulder as she did. It was all for the cause of truth and integrity, and—

A voice.

She spun.

Cat. It was a cat.

Rawr.

But those marble-green eyes watched her with all the condescension of a high court justice.

"I'm trying to help her, I am. Honestly!" A huff. "You'd do the same."

But she couldn't do it any longer. Couldn't snoop.

A pile of books stacked on the bedside table caught her eye, and she wandered past them. "Pillows need to be fluffed, and oh!" An exaggerated fluffing, coming terribly close to those books. "My, my, heaven sakes." A swipe. A satisfying *clunk* sounded and she returned the pillow, glancing down at the floor. "Oh ho, now what might that be?" Angel snatched up the large metal key. "Well, look at this! Can't leave this lying about now, can we?" she said to the cat.

The animal blinked down in judgment from his perch.

"Well, then," she huffed. She swept out of the room as if she'd never nosed about.

Such a funny creature, that cat. As if he knew everything about everything. He wouldn't be above a little snooping, if it would help his mistress—or himself. She was quite certain of that.

Downstairs, she kept her head lowered and moved through the quiet corridors. A noise sounded farther down the paneled corridor.

Dane was coming. He was staring straight down. She moved this way and that to dodge him, but he barreled into her, his hard, narrow body colliding with hers.

"Oh! Begging your pardon, sir."

A scowl flashed, but then a benign smile washed over his face. "Think nothing of it. Oh, Mrs. Holligan, we'll be taking dinner late tonight." Then with a lift of his arm, he sailed off down the hall that he would *never* own, though he acted as if he did already.

Slipping into the study, she closed the door behind her and glanced about at the familiar clocks ticking, pendulums swinging, and the lump of blankets visible over the back of the sofa. She went and stood before him, staring down at his ruffled hair, the narrow, unremarkable face. No cuff links, stockings frayed a bit at the heel, and a pile of clothing on the floor beside him that had been mended quite a few times. He hadn't much money, which meant he could be who André claimed he was . . . or he could be a fortune hunter.

"Hello."

She jerked. He'd opened his eyes while she'd been staring at his stockinged feet, pondering his lack of fortune. Her eyelid twitched as heat climbed into her face. Brushing it off, she perched on the chair nearest the sofa. "Sydney?"

He blinked, then struggled to sit up.

"Sydney Forrester?"

"I'm afraid you're mistaken. Sydney is some woman they're—"

"Am I? Mistaken, that is." She fixed her gaze on him—the kind that had bored through the façade of six husbands to stir up the truth underneath. She added a smile. "Or are you the Sydney Forrester named in Mr. Sinclair's will? You might as well tell me. I'm rather mulish when I wish to know a thing."

He shifted to sit up against the pillows. "Who are you?"

"I believe I asked you first." A prim smile and a lift of her penciled eyebrows.

Pendulums clunked in the background. Somewhere, a cuckoo. Then the man sighed, looking away. "Very well. Yes, I'm Sydney Forrester."

"The heir." She looked him up and down, trying to wrap that identity over the plain, knobby, rather unpleasant-looking middle-aged person before her. Nothing of the spirit or pluck of the other Sydney. "The one named in the will to inherit everything. Your parents are . . ."

"Gabe and Genevieve Forrester."

She sucked in a breath. Genevieve! The sister who had married a swindler and died giving birth to their only child. A son—which would be *this* Sydney Forrester. This very man. She should have put the pieces together before, but there had been a great deal she hadn't known about Mr. Sinclair's sisters, and she'd simply assumed Sydney Forrester was descended from one of them.

But she wasn't. This wastrel was.

Please. Please don't let it be true. She drew out the key Emmett had given her for safekeeping and held it up. Tried to stop her hand from shaking. "I suppose you'll know what to do with this, then. He said you would." How well she remembered his careful instructions when he'd left it with her, folding her hand around it and waving away her questions about what it unlocked. "My heir will know. Keep it safe for Sydney Forrester."

And she had. Unfortunately. She held it out to him.

He brightened and took it, turning it over in his hand. "Perhaps you wouldn't mind fetching something for me. They won't let me out of this wretched room." He told her of a hidden compartment in the gallery, behind the framed portrait of the master's family.

She went and fetched, with shaking hands, a rather cobwebbed, dust-covered box with birds etched into the wood. She studied it as she brought it to the man, running her hands over the familiar etchings, then laid it on his lap.

He inserted the key and turned it, popping open the lid. "There! At last, I have it all. He wrote me all about this box years ago when he made me heir, but I never thought I'd see the day."

Angel peered in, and there lay the thickest stack of patents she'd ever seen—all with Emmett Sinclair's name inscribed at the top. She shot up, suddenly dizzy. Disoriented.

It couldn't be!

Then he snapped the lid shut and slipped the key into some hidden place on his person and gave her the contented grin of a conman who'd executed yet another con. "I'm deeply grateful to you, Miss . . ."

"*Mrs.* Holligan. And those are—" She sprang forward, but her chest met with the solid heel of his hand. *Oof.* He whipped his blankets over her head. She beat her way out of them, tangling herself in her panic, but when she'd gotten free, the man had disappeared.

She grabbed the sofa. Breathed harder and harder. The name . . . the name in the personals. It had been the *exact name*! Sydney Forrester, bold and black. Angel hardly ever took the papers, but something had compelled her to begin reading them for news of the master after he had disappeared. She'd felt so certain his story had the wrong ending, and that news of him would surface. But then . . . there it had been. Grainy in dark ink.

Daughter seeks mother.
Sydney Forrester, formerly of Drury
Hamlet, seeks missing mother,
known as Lady Gwendolyn Forrester of Manchester.
Reply to PO #14 in Grafton, County Shropshire . . .

It had been providence. No . . . *God.*

Hadn't it?

She clutched her hands to her chest, staring at the door where the man had fled. No, she had made a mistake. A terrible, terrible mistake.

She ran from the room with a cry but stopped short. Yelling. Angry voices. It was Dane Hutchcraft and several servants, pinning that wretched thief to the wall. He was weak from his ordeal, and they held him with little effort.

"You ungrateful *coward*, stealing from the house what rescued you." Jinedath had the man by the throat.

She hovered around the corner, ready to leap into the open and declare his true identity. Make certain they knew who they were dealing with.

But with a desperate wheeze, the man did it himself. "I'm Mr. Sinclair's nephew, and it is *me* you're stealing from. I'm Sydney Forrester! I tell you, I'm Sydney Forrester, heir of Blakely House!"

Thunk. The men dropped him. He sprang up, but Jinedath cornered him, his neck corded and red. "What exactly are you trying to pull?"

"My rightful weight." He crossed his arms. "I came to collect certain documents, in case I needed a bit of collateral to keep the upper hand, but as it turns out, I don't need it. The housekeeper has just informed me, quite by accident, that the latest known will clearly still names me as heir of Blakely House."

Angel groaned.

"So. You are the *true* Sydney Forrester, are you?" Dane stepped back, arms folded as he assumed a casual stance. "As it turns out, there's a warrant issued for Sydney Forrester on the grounds of probable murder of our uncle. We had the wrong Sydney Forrester as heir presumptive . . . and for the murder charges as well, perhaps."

Angel's fingers fluttered about her mouth. She could hardly stand this.

"You're suggesting I've murdered him?"

"Just how did you learn of his death, pray?"

"I read the newspaper, don't I?" He snarled the words. "I haven't killed anyone. You'll have a terrible time proving I did."

"We don't need proof from you, Mr. Forrester." She could hear Dane's smile. "We've already invented all we need."

"So who was the girl?" asked Tom Jolly. "Did *she* kill Emmett? Or did he?"

"I haven't sorted that out just yet, but I do know one thing." Dane held up the box the servants had extracted from the would-be heir's grasp. "James, call the constable. Tell him we've caught a thief. And with any luck, when he arrives, the other Sydney Forrester will have turned up as well. She'll never see *this* coming."

It was a mere hour before the police arrived, and the handcuffs seemed almost pointless, weak as he was yet. That blackguard—and she'd helped nurse him back to health, right in their midst!

"He won't bother you again," promised the constable sometime later as he set the patent box on a table.

The nephews stalled. They drew out the particulars with the police and did everything they could manage to keep them there. In the end, the officers left with the newly discovered Sinclair cousin before the tides turned . . . and without the other Sydney Forrester.

chapter
THIRTY-SEVEN

Strangers see your clocks that don't keep time, not having any idea they're all ingeniously modified—put together differently for a unique purpose. I would say the same about their creator.

~*Sophie's letters to Emmett*

THE NORTH SEA

I lay sprawled across the deck, coughing and gasping for breath. A drumbeat pounded in my ears as salt water poured from every crevice of my body. "The girl. Where is the girl?"

"She's here."

A small body was rolled against me. I grabbed for her. Shivered. Convulsed with cold and coughed again as I tugged her close, smoothing her chaotic dark curls down her back. Salt burned my nose and my throat.

I shoved up onto my hands and blinked seawater from my

eyes until André knelt before me, touching my cheek. "You are well?"

And though I was considerably worse off than any other time he'd asked, I said, "Yes. Well."

The men yelled, oars slapping water. Growing louder. Closer. Lanterns bobbed in what looked to be half a dozen little boats. Where had those boats been? Why hadn't we taken one of those?

The little girl shivered and clung to me, but then she was singing. A folk ballad in another language, strong and clear. I clutched her tighter.

André sprinted toward the mast and tugged the pulleys as if he'd been doing it for years, and the great sail flipped open, billowing in the wind. "The wind's in the wrong direction. We'll have to use the smaller propeller."

"Let's take the ship away from here first—then worry about direction," I shouted back.

A great wind swelled the sails and the ship heaved forward, away from the island. From the men.

A shot rang out. Wood splintered on the ship's side. The little girl whimpered, her wet hair cold against my shirtwaist. Then she lifted her voice again and sang out, even louder. Several more shots cracked against the side of the ship, and I threw myself over her and rolled us toward the far edge. Shoving the girl toward the hatch, I commanded her to stay put below and bounded back across the deck, toward the rigging.

Pulleys and levers. Gears and great, shining steel rods stretching over the masts.

Speed. We needed speed. Yet it would never be enough. I glanced through the foggy sea air at the men crowded onto lantern-lit boats that sliced through the waves with each powerful stroke of the oars. The velocity of our ship would never outpace their lightweight ones.

Desperately, I grabbed the lever of the giant propeller and yanked it down.

Wait, the button.

Button? Where had that come from?

I smashed it with my fist, then worked the lever up and back down and felt blessed resistance. Heard gears activate. A groaning giant rose behind the ship, unfurling himself into a massive beast, then whirred into motion, blades flailing wildly. Slapping water. Shoving us in all directions. It was broken—but it was moving. Trying. Groans and creaks of protest echoed across the water. Blades jerked erratically, spraying water. Beating waves uselessly.

Come on, come on! Work! I banged the mechanism. Jerked the levers up and down. But the great beast jolted in fits and starts.

The ship lurched and I tumbled across the deck, banging my shins, scrambling to stand—and gaped at what I saw. They were fleeing. Those big, burly wreckers were yelling and plunging oars into the waves, desperate to be away from the great metal sea monster attacking our ship. A few plunged into the water, screaming in the chilly sea air. They were terrified.

I cried out with joy. Relief. Laughter bubbled in my throat. "André! Look!"

He was sprinting to the wildly spinning wheel. He grabbed hold, trying to steady it as the ship pitched and tossed. It was too much for his one real hand. The large propeller, although defective, had heft and power, shoving us about.

I hurtled toward him and grabbed the wheel with force I never knew I possessed. Rain and sweat poured down André's face. My muscles burned. I cried out, willing the wheel to hold steady as the ship lurched about with each cresting wave. Swell and fall, swell and fall—then a metallic *clunk*. The tension on the wheel instantly broke. The blades of the large propeller trailed uselessly behind us, broken off.

But they had rescued us. "We did it! They're gone!" I grabbed fistfuls of his shirt and kissed him. Hard. Then shoved him away before either of us could react.

His grip on the wheel loosened and it whirled, throwing us both backward. André hit the deck with a grunt and I fell onto him, tangled in wet skirts and frayed nerves. The rain chilled my suddenly warm skin. I buried my face in his chest and laughed out all the intensity of that night. I laughed and shook and told myself I *hadn't* just kissed the pirate.

But reality still burned against my lips.

He shifted, leaning his automaton hand against the deck to sit up. "You are well?"

"You broke my fall." Wet skirts chilled my legs. I was shaking.

He helped me up and there we sat facing one another, breathless and soaked and shivering, alight with victory. Then like a music box that had been tightly wound and slowly released, the moment settled upon us. Each powerful exhale from him like a stallion's warm breath against my cheeks. And his face—oh, his face. This time I couldn't look away. His gaze wouldn't let me. There was something deep and honest about his countenance—something passionate. He felt everything. *Everything.*

His gaze roved over my face, as if he were memorizing it, trying to figure it out. Then he lowered his lips to mine and gently woke the most exquisite delight a kiss could ever bring.

Warm and velvety like a rose petal, but rich. Thick. Consuming and thrilling. His fingertips tickled my scalp as he drew me closer. Kissed me more. I melted onto him, coming alive.

Then he let me go, his nose brushing my cheek. His breath warm on my face. "Try writing about that in your books."

I laughed. Covered my warm face with my hands. I would never forget this night. Not ever. As heat swelled within, he helped me rise, then followed me toward the hatch, and together we climbed belowdeck.

The girl watched us with wide eyes as we descended, huddled beneath piles of canvas. Her singing had ceased and fear made her large eyes even wider.

I sat beside her while André flung open the stove and threw fuel onto the remaining embers, blowing on the tiny flames that leaped up. With a grunt, he spun the wheel that ignited the small propeller and the ship gave a small surge forward. Toward England or some other place, I didn't know.

The rescued girl continued whimpering, burrowing into my arms. I pulled her close, rocking her as the stove roared to life, and spoke over her the same words given to me on the most terrible day of my life. "I've got you. It'll come out all right. I've got you now and you're safe."

Those words unleashed a dam—the girl buried her face in my lap, clinging to my wet clothing, and wept. Endlessly wept, coming up for gasping breaths, then plunging back into sobs. André paced from us to the stove, shoving his hair back over and over. I smiled up at him that all was well, and it was. This is how it happens. Once a body is safe . . . that's when it all breaks free.

I rocked her on the floor, smoothing my hand over her damp, knotted hair, letting her feel everything that needed feeling. Making circles on her back. Her body released the tension and melted into safety.

When she had wilted onto my lap, I rolled her beside me and stood, trembling and chilled to the bone, and rummaged about for something dry to wear. Nothing but blankets and linens to be found. How foolish I'd been, thinking this to be a quick jaunt across the water. No more than an hour or so—no need for fresh clothing.

Flipping out a tarp and a tattered quilt, I began gathering what we had. I knelt before the girl and showed her a soft flannel lap blanket. "Shall we trade your wet things for this?"

She blinked up at me. When she didn't refuse, I led her behind a strung-up curtain and helped her out of the wet things, wrapping her in the oversized flannel. She hugged it to her, but made a mad grab for her wet things too. I let her have them while she looked at me with suspicion. Her eyes, puffy and red, were wide as a trapped animal's.

I offered a smile, then peeled off my own garments, down to my chemise and stays, and wrapped myself in another flannel. When I turned my back, she was humming. Almost as a way to stitch together her fraying nerves. To center her scattered mind.

Shivering, I carried the wet garments toward the stove while clutching the flannel around me. I spread our things out on the floor, then let the warmth soak into my skin. How lovely a bar of soap and a clean flannel bathing cloth would feel!

"They've gone," he whispered. "We've gone far enough that they won't come after us now."

I let out a long breath. When I returned behind the makeshift curtain, the girl had fallen asleep, completely spent, her narrow face resting on one pale arm, mouth slightly open.

Wordlessly I dug through the little larder with one hand as André shoveled more fuel into the stove and wrung out the wet garments. Tiredness pulled at me, weighing upon my body like a powerful invitation toward that bedroll.

Yet in true Sydney fashion, my mind had not yet disengaged.

After several hours of tossing about, I turned, remembering the girl, and saw her standing just outside the curtain. She clutched the flannel around her and stared at the glowing stove with red-rimmed eyes.

I went to her. "There, now. Do you feel better? What's your name?"

She shrank into the blanket. Went stiff. I put a hand on her shoulder, but she yanked away and stared down at her bare toes.

"We'd like to help you. Won't you tell us who you are?"

Silence. She was all eyes and long, tangled hair, both as dark as chocolate against pale, freckled skin. How lovely she was. And when she sang, she had a voice to match.

The stove roared and the small propeller made a great chugging, churning sound that echoed in the hold. But the girl said nothing.

The pull of riddles and unquenched curiosity was strong. I looked to André for help, who observed from his place beside the stove. He turned back to his work for several moments, then he spoke. "I could use a hand with the coal, if you wouldn't mind. A child with small hands would do best."

He continued picking about through the piles of coal, his back to us.

I handed her an oversized garment, which she donned then wrapped herself again. Then, like a butterfly, the girl slowly emerged from her cocoon of blankets, inching toward the stove.

"Ah! You shall do nicely." He knelt and handed her a small lump of coal. "I need you to find more dry bricks like this one, yes? Too many have become wet. I suppose it's the way we tromped about down here, dripping and flinging water all about the place." He offered a smile.

She stared down at the coal in her hand, then with suspicion at the monsterlike stove, glowing orange through the cracks.

"Would you like to know how it works?"

"Yes, sir."

I startled at the sound of her voice. It was the first she'd spoken since being rescued.

She lowered herself beside the coal and picked through the lumps, setting aside the dry ones as she watched André.

"These coals are what the fire burns. What it eats. Just like when you eat food, you have energy. When this fire makes heat, a great deal of it, it makes energy to accomplish something big. In this case, it moves a propeller. Have you seen a waterwheel before?"

She nodded. "A very big one."

The little rest seemed to reset something in her mechanism.

"Very good. So you will understand how this works. When it goes around, it pushes against the water and moves the boat. Not very fast, but enough to keep us going forward, yes?"

She smiled just a little. Then after a moment, "What if the fire goes out?"

"Well, the amount of force depends on how much heat the fire puts out. The more heat, the more power it gives. If the fire was not as hot, the propeller would slow and eventually stop moving."

"I've never cared for fire. Must it always run?"

"On the ship, yes. But when we reach Blakely House, everything is run by water pressure. Hydraulics, it's called."

"I do like water. Is it very wet there?"

"Inside the pipes, I suppose."

"And there is power? Like the lighthouse?"

"And mechanics and gears and fascinating machines . . . just you wait. It's like nothing you've ever seen before."

"What sort of machines?"

I sank onto the floor, encased in my blanket, and listened to them—him patiently explaining with his lilting French accent, her quickly opening like a flower, peppering him with questions.

"Why don't you change your clothes too?" she asked.

"The wetness does not bother me so much."

She frowned. "Do you like being wet?"

"I don't mind it. Now stand back so I can open the door."

"Must I?"

"Unless you want to be burned."

"How will it burn me? I won't touch the fire."

"The steam. It is quite powerful."

"What if I'm wet?"

Her mind worked like a windup toy with a tightly wound spring. For every answer he gave, she had another question—and half of them were simply, *why*? She was rather clever, actually—polished or especially intelligent, though I couldn't say exactly what made me say so. The way she rounded her vowels. The clear and succinct way she had of expressing each word.

As the sun rose overhead, then began to descend again, she voiced many years' worth of bottled-up questions. So long as the topic was not about her, she seemed eager to talk. Which meant that eventually she'd begin talking about herself too.

And I'd be ready for that conversation.

We took turns sleeping for a few hours at a time. Our little stowaway slept for eight and a half of those before stumbling abovedeck, still wrapped in the flannel, dark hair askew. A calm, starry night had settled over the North Sea, and the sails whipped overhead. She stood and stared at me, blinking, and it jarred me.

What had we done? What in heaven's name had we been thinking, taking this unknown child home with us? All I'd wanted was to steal her away from that dirty hovel, from the darkness and from those men. But what if she had someone else there? A sister out looking for her? I'd become so swept up in the moment, of feeling like Emmett Sinclair the rescuer, that I had allowed my whimsical nature to overtake my good sense.

She padded over to me, surprisingly at home on the sea.

I forced a smile. "Good morning, my lady. Might I offer you a little midnight luncheon?"

I held out the dried meats and watched her, expecting that freckled, dirty nose to wrinkle, but she came right over and plucked a strip from my hands.

"Have you lived at the lighthouse all your life?"

She turned and fell quiet for so long, I didn't think she was going to answer. But then, she did. "Too long, I think." She wandered over to the railing of the ship and stared out at the North Sea.

I joined her, sitting on a crate that was not too near the ship's edge, but didn't dare say anything more. Praying she'd open up a little and give us a glimpse into the mechanism inside.

"What is that out there?"

I forced myself to look out over the water. "They're ice chunks. Most likely broken off a large iceberg somewhere up north, where it's even colder."

Her shoulders trembled. "They float. But aren't they heavy?"

I explained how water expands, taking up a greater volume than the water around it. But even as I said it, the explanation didn't make sense. For everything in nature, when it froze, contracted. Why, then, did water expand?

"It's a good job it does, I suppose," she said. "Else the bottom of the ocean floor would be full of ice every winter and there'd be no fish to catch come spring."

My heart pittered. "Indeed." I couldn't unsee it now—the patterns and intention everywhere. It was no accident, was it? Creation was a delicate balance. A magnificent machine created just so. The continuance of life itself was a miracle that depended upon a most complexly ordered world. One whose rules were occasionally broken in order to sustain life. I stared at those floating bits of ice, the way I'd stared at the intricate clock when it had come into my shop weeks ago.

A lifetime ago.

"Tell me more about Blakely House," she said wistfully. "Is it magical?"

"Oh yes, I'd say so. Everything there moves on its own. A machine to wash dishes, a lift that carries tea above stairs, a clock that sings the hour . . ."

"I should like that very much. I love to sing. Are there still flowers?" The hope in her face melted my heart. "At least a few?"

"Do you like them?"

"To distraction. I cannot ever seem to own enough of them."

I smiled. "There are lots and lots of flowers. Whole hillsides of them."

She sighed, and for the first time, her little body relaxed. "Flowers. Yes, there are flowers. I shall take such good care of them for her."

Curiosity billowed, but something bobbed in the distance—land?

It was then, with the delicate weight of the small child for whom I was now responsible, that I felt the first churnings of dread at the thought of approaching Blakely House.

"Another few hours and we'll be back," said André.

She shot up and clapped. "Oh, I cannot wait!"

I offered a wobbly smile to hide the growing panic.

chapter
THIRTY-EIGHT

BLAKELY HOUSE

Dane held to the shadows as a figure hurried by. It was that woman—the cook. What was her name?

She was visibly upset. Hands over her face as she hurried away. With internal alarms blaring, Dane followed her toward the kitchen, and then the service door opened and shut. How curious—she'd gone outside. He strode to the window. She'd gathered her apron to make a sack, then nearly sprinted down the path.

She was bringing food to that woman. That Sydney Forrester. She was hiding her on the beach—he was certain of it.

Down the path he followed, until the cook reached the beach and seemed to melt into the rocks. He paused, then rounded the cliffs, and great caves yawned open before him. Men, women, and children languished there, reclining on rocks. Talking. Moving about.

One pointed at him, and the cook turned, crying out and dropping her apron of food. Bread rolled to the sand, hunks of cheese and dried meats. All from Blakely House's larders. "What is this? Are you *stealing* from Blakely House?"

"They need to eat. They all need to eat."

He stalked over to her and stared at the people making their home in the cave. "What is this? Who are these people?"

"They're from the shipwreck, sir." She stiffened. "They'd have been tossed in the gutter if you sent them ashore, and you know it. Penniless and half dead—nobody'd have helped them to so much as a meal, let alone a surgeon. Most of them would have died."

"And they have a *surgeon* here?" Heat rose up in him. Red-hot anger at being defied. Lied to. "They're no concern of—"

"It's a good job we're someone's concern," said a voice. A jarringly familiar voice, causing memories to wash over him. Good ones. Painful ones. A slender man in spectacles and a white tunic limped out of the cave and stood tall before him. "They saved our lives."

Dane clutched his chest. Stumbled backward in the sand as if struck. "Arthur."

The man smiled, shoving his spectacles up the bridge of his nose. "But if we truly aren't any of your concern . . ."

Shaking, trembling like jelly, he walked to his son, studying his precious face, that little-boy smile that hadn't changed. Then he threw his arms about his boy and held him close to his chest, where he'd held him as an infant. Rocked him as scrawny arms had wrapped around his neck. Now they were big, strong man-arms. "Arthur. Arthur, Arthur, you've come. You're here." Then he wept, releasing a vat of tears upon his boy's shoulder.

"Hello, Papa."

A flood of beauty and hope. He wept and clung, his mind on repeat: *he is here. Arthur has come!* Dane grabbed him by the shoulders, pushing him away to look at him. "You're so tall. Strong. And—"

"Married." He held up his left hand which bore a plain gold band.

Dane's insides quaked. "Married. You're married. Why that's . . . congratulations, my boy." More tears leaked. "How wonderful."

"We have a baby. A son. His name is Edward."

"Edward." He tried the name on his lips, fully aware that he sounded like a babbling idiot, repeating everything he said. "Edward—is he here? No, of course not. You'd not have made this trip with a baby."

"I wanted to see you alone."

Dane exhaled, and placed both hands on his boy's cheeks. "However you've come, with or without anything, I'm glad of it." Tears streaked down his weathered cheeks. "More than you know." He'd never actually believed his letters would work. They hadn't, for so many years. But in his heart of hearts, even with the draw of the automaton, he'd never actually believed he'd entice his boy to his side again.

A faint smile. "Thank you, Papa."

"Come, come. Up to the house. You shall have clean clothes and all the food you can eat." Arm around his back, Dane led Arthur up the path while a stunned cook looked on.

Let her stare. Let them all stare. Arthur was here. And Dane would do anything necessary to mend bridges—permanently.

"So this is Blakely House." Arthur glanced up at the massive house looking down upon the pair from its place nestled in the hill. "I suppose you enjoy living here?"

"There's plenty of room. Bring your entire family and stay here. Indefinitely, if you like, while we work on the automaton."

"So you've made progress with it?"

"Only a little. It needs your touch. Your clever intuition."

"This is only a visit, Papa."

His heart thrilled at the word. *Papa*. He'd said it a few times now, and quite naturally. "I know, I know. But at least test it out. See what you can do with it." And perhaps become caught up in the mystery of it and stay.

Even if it was a few days' time, they would talk, they would work, and Dane would serve him. He'd give Arthur everything he could ever want and show him how much he'd changed. How good it could be working together again.

He smiled at Arthur, and the boy gave him a distant smile back. Arthur glanced at the house, then back at the shore. "How often do trains depart from Northumberland?"

Pain squeezed his chest. "Let's see to luncheon first, shall we?"

chapter
THIRTY-NINE

Most think me merely a legend, Sophie dearest, since none have seen me. But I suppose they believe my intricate machines, which they themselves use, just accidentally fell into place and began to function!

~*Emmett's letters to Sophie*

THE NORTH SEA

The little girl sat before the stove, knees to her chest as I brushed her freshly rinsed hair. "Where we're going now . . . it's where Mr. Emmett lives?"

"Well." I paused and stared with her at the glowing orange flames. "He did, but I'm afraid he doesn't anymore. You see, he—"

"Doesn't exist. It's all right, you can tell me."

I heard it in her voice, that hopelessness. The dull awareness that no rescue was coming.

"Grandmamma told me stories of Andromeda and Hercules

. . . and Emmett Sinclair on his island. But they're all tales, I suppose."

I finger-picked my way through her tangles. "I can promise you, he is—*was*—quite real."

"You've met him?"

"I didn't have the chance. You see, he's died, I'm afraid. Before I reached the island."

She absorbed the news as if she'd done so many times before, still and grave and very grown-up. The gears of her mind turned, processing, recalibrating.

When we emerged again, the air had warmed enough to be tolerable, and the waves had calmed. I held out the sack of dried meat, and she tucked into it without hesitating, gnawing on one stick after another.

"At least someone will make use of all that dried meat." André, one hand on the wheel, glanced our way. "We'll be home soon now. Are you ready to see Blakely House?"

She nodded.

A wave of dread pulled at my heart, especially as I looked down upon the girl. She hadn't any idea what sort of mess she'd wandered into, or who her rescuers even were. I couldn't even see her settled. I could never, I realized with a twist of pain, go back to Blakely House again. I'd have to slip away into Northumberland before we reached the island, or I'd be arrested.

I moved close to André's ear and told him as much.

He gave a nod. "We'll dock at the island during low tide, and you will cross the causeway on foot. Tie your boots around your neck and hold your skirt hem aloft. Will that be acceptable?"

I nodded, then moved back toward the girl. The one and only spoil from my great adventure. She was quite lovely, her skin a little more ruddy now that it had been scrubbed clean. Her long hair hung down over her shoulders, curling at the bottom.

How badly I wished I knew her name, or how she connected into the puzzle. "You can trust me, you know." I reached out to brush hair off her face, but stopped myself. I understood, in a flash, the protectiveness Aunt Lottie had felt for me, ragged castoff that I was. "You can tell me anything." And I dearly wished she would. For her sake and mine.

She fingered the dried meat and stared up at the mainsail billowing overhead.

I held my breath.

André waved us over. "Look." He pointed out across the horizon, where the morning light was spilling over the clouds, highlighting their edges and gold-tipping each wave.

A gasp came from beside me. It was the girl, her wide eyes reflecting the immensity of what she saw. I lay down on the deck, spreading a woolen blanket, and patted the space beside me. "It's better watching it this way."

She climbed beside me and lay down, face tipped up with the same awe I'd felt at the northern lights. The awe I felt even yet as the great expanse above radiated beauty.

There was no sign of fear, no desperate look in her eyes. "How does it do that?"

"It's a refraction of light. The sunlight is made up of all the colors. They shine out from the sun and strike the clouds. Some of the colors are absorbed, but others are reflected and that's what we see."

"Like a watercolor painting."

Indeed. Something created by the obvious hand of an artist for the purpose of beauty, and nothing more. Then a sweet and soulful voice lifted to the heavens.

> "The day is thine, the night also is thine!
> Thou hast prepared the light and the sun,
> Thou hast set all the borders of the earth!
> The day is thine, the night also is thine!"

The Psalms. She was singing the Psalms, and it dislodged dusty old memories. Then out of the misty morning came a large white bird, flapping his wings at languid intervals as he floated above the ship. I squinted at him, at the way his wings were perfectly structured to suspend him in the air. To hold up his little body, with landing gear tucked firmly beneath his belly, ready for use.

He *was* something of a machine, with gears and mechanisms finely tuned. It was a work of brilliance and creativity and—looking at the bright orange, hooked beak—pure enjoyment.

> "Praise ye the LORD!
> Praise him in the heights.
> Praise ye him, sun and moon,
> praise him, all ye stars of light.
> Praise him, ye heavens of heavens,
> ye waters that be above the heavens.
> Let them praise the name of the LORD!"

The dulcet voice stirred me, as if her reverential song was accompanied by something else—something unseen that I could feel about us, thick in the air.

I drank in the view again, the magnificence of it. The sea and sky held apart by the air, the waves formed in perfect patterns, the ice that floated to the top to allow for the seas to continue teeming with life under the surface. And at every angle, the maker's mark that creation bore—*abundance*.

"I do believe you'll see for yourself about Emmett Sinclair," I told the girl, "from the first second inside Blakely House. You'll know soon enough how real he was—and what sort of man." I stared up at that vast sky, at the glorious array of light streaked across a great canvas. A gust of warm air swept over my skin like breath, and I closed my eyes, feeling a presence. An embrace. The big, bold rumble of thunder in the distance, and another sweep of warmth.

"For the invisible things of him from the creation of the world are clearly seen, being understood by the things that are made, even his eternal power and Godhead."

The girl's wide-eyed face reflected the awe that was awakening in me. Or rather, reawakening, like a long-ago dream before reality had jarred me out of it. Maybe it wasn't blind trust I'd lost, or a childish naivety, but wonder. I used to see holiness in the everyday happenings, spilled like a gift. Snowflakes etched artfully on windows. The magnificent power of a horse. A tiny kitten who appeared, needing me as much as I needed him. I could no more deny the existence of God the Creator than I could the man who had left behind a house full of his ingenious gadgetry.

"Tell me more about him," she said, still staring at the sky.

"It's hard to wrap him in mere words." I told her everything I could recall about the reclusive industrialist, everything true I'd learned of him from his creations and his home and those who truly knew him, leaving out the legends and folklore.

"He could fix nearly anything. Any machine, any gadget.

Any problem a person had, but he wasn't good with people and small talk. He was rather imbalanced, but in a good way." I smiled, recalling the conversations with Angel Holligan. "Just as he loved meat more than any other food. He'd fill his plate almost entirely with dried pheasant and pork rind, leaving off—"

"The sort that's on this boat. Dried pork rind, that is."

"Exactly." I frowned, turning this over in my mind. "Yes, exactly."

"That must be why there's so much of it."

Something seized inside me. I jerked my head her direction. "Indeed. Because . . . because it was for him." I sprang up, scanning for André. "And do you know, several bags of it had been emptied already."

The girl rose. "You needn't be cross with him. It wasn't all *that* tasty."

I grabbed her shoulders. "Do you know, I think you'll meet Emmett Sinclair in person after all."

She chewed her lip with a doubtful frown.

"André." I sprinted across the deck, scrambling to catch the rigging as the boat tipped. "André!"

He scaled down the main mast and sprang down, landing in a crouch and jogging to me. "What is it? What's happened?"

"Emmett's favorite cured meat is aboard the ship."

He blinked. "And this is . . . bad?"

"Empty bags. Some full, but several empty."

His brow creased. "What are you saying?"

"There's a compass belowdeck, tied together with twine. Obviously repaired in haste. In transit, perhaps. A temporary fix until he was back with his tools."

"You cannot possibly be suggesting—"

"Unless *you* did that. As well as eating his favorite hardtack."

He was silent for a moment. "So. It seems he was aboard this ship."

"*And* he took it somewhere."

His jaw firmed. "We cannot know that."

"He took it out. He rigged things . . . ate his meat . . . And the ship wasn't left floating out at sea, André." I grabbed his arm. "It was anchored at the rear of the island, out of sight. You'd never have known if it was gone for a few days, but the truth is this. It was at Blakely House *after* Emmett's death. Which means, *so was he.*"

Thoughts flashed over his features, then settled into grim lines. "I suppose this means you *won't* be sneaking across the strait."

"Oh, no." I gripped the railing hard. "Get us back to Blakely House just as soon as you can." I looked back at the little girl clinging to the rail. "We have to find Emmett."

We approached the island on the far side again, all of us looking up the hill at the massive towers of Blakely House. I stared at it, willing us closer. Faster.

The girl's rich voice lifted in one last burst of melody as she clutched the rail. It was a gift, this worship that spilled from her soul.

> "My help cometh from the LORD,
> which made heaven and earth!"

I glanced at André and smiled. Only two words swirled about in my head—*Worth. It.* André worked the levers of the main sail, angling it expertly to catch the gentlest of winds. He'd grown subdued as we came in sight of the place, but my heart continued to lighten. Books brought a thrill—as big as I'd ever experienced.

Until now.

If André asked me this moment if I'd changed my mind about adventures, I wouldn't know how to answer. But I knew one thing—I had done more than glimpse God out here. I had experienced him. Been driven to the edge until I tasted and felt him. And it left me utterly starving for more.

I turned and clung to the mast, glancing up to Blakely House looking down at us. Holding all its secrets close. Follow the path of power. Find the source. Someone had been operating those doors at night, the lights that turned on and off. It wasn't Angel. It had been, I realized, the inventor himself, drawing me into certain rooms. Inviting me to know him.

But how was that possible? How could he be alive if everyone thought him dead?

I'd have to slip in a service door. A window, perhaps. I must locate Uncle Emmett before they saw me. But once they saw André and the girl, they'd know I had returned as well. The hunt would be on.

Who would be swifter, me or them?

I felt a tug on my arm.

"What now?" Her voice wavered just a bit, and I heard the real question beneath it—*what will become of me?*

I didn't have an answer. This deflated my anticipation. Brought the hot-air balloon of my daydreams back to earth. "Well, I don't know yet." It all depended on whether or not I was right. And whether or not I could locate him.

André crouched beside her, long duster jacket brushing

the boards of the deck. "Do you know, Blakely House is not just any estate. The name of the island is Farneham Heald. It means a home for the weary traveler."

She glanced up at him.

"That's you, isn't it? A weary traveler?"

She nodded. "I'm nine years already, and I've traveled quite a lot."

That was it—that quality in her voice. She wasn't highly educated in the way of books and university, but she was cultured. Experienced. Polished by constant friction and movement.

"You'll fit nicely there, I believe." He smiled. "That is, if you can work."

"My papa taught me how to work." She squared her shoulders. "I can do most anything you can do. And I could stay in the island's monk caverns. I wouldn't be any trouble—truly."

André gave a nod, expertly concealing the smile that must have wanted to surface at her embellished imaginings of what she'd find at Farneham Heald. How had such a fanciful notion come to her?

He then loaded the anchor onto a thick piece of timber curved in the shape of a small canoe with one end missing and motioned for me to help. I grabbed one end and the girl rushed over to grab another. Together we hoisted the thing overboard and watched it float toward the shoreline. When it had nearly reached the pier, André gave a quick jerk to the rope attached to it, and the timber moved away, releasing the anchor to float to the bottom of the ocean.

"That's quite brilliant," the girl said. "Then how do we get the rest of the ship in?"

"Like this." André jumped to grab the anchor's chain as high up as he could and threw his whole weight into pulling it down, straining with his good arm while the mechanical one clenched in reflection at his side.

The chain clinked over the three wheels I'd set up, and once it began moving, the momentum pulled it even faster. Soon our great ship was moving closer to the dock, pulled by the anchor, groaning against the slap of waves. The sails billowed and released in the gentle breeze, and soon the side of the boat struck the pier.

My heart pounded. I could scarcely catch a breath.

"There!" She screamed over the crash of waves on shore. "There it is!" She did a wild little dance, hopping about the deck and pointing so hard I thought she'd fall overboard. "Look!"

We did, and there, draped in hanging branches and leafless vines, was a pair of small cottages built into the far side of the rocky hill, just a little ways up from the beach. No one would ever see them if they approached the island from another angle, for they were hidden in the rock outcroppings, rooves covered with grass, and doors that looked part of the very nature surrounding them.

"The monk caverns," I whispered. "They really are here."

"Of course they are. Didn't I tell you?"

I turned to the girl, staring at the smudged white face. The mass of tangled dark hair. The flashing eyes that held both innocence and wisdom. "Yes, but how did you know—"

"Grandmamma told me stories. All the time, stories about Emmett Sinclair and his island."

"Your . . ." André's hand on my shoulder stopped me. But the pieces melded together quickly. Beautifully. The girl was Sophie's granddaughter, and now they were back together. How well orchestrated this entire Blakely House adventure had been, with everything falling sensibly into place now. Making an entire picture. A great, big riddle far beyond the scope of anything an author could contrive to put in a novel.

Then she sprang up. "Ah! I know what comes next. Let me help!" She ran across the boat and gathered the coiled rope, but only managed a few coils. Now removed from the evil of those other shores, confidence brimmed. Energy and passion in full measure.

André helped her and together they lifted it toward the edge. André whipped the end toward the dock and it wrapped neatly around the post. They did it again with the other side, fully anchoring vessel to pier. She proved quite capable. With several strong tugs, his body leaning back, André pulled us into position and wrapped the rope around the post.

The girl took my hand, standing beside me as André secured the ship. Her arm shook and I squeezed her hand. "I did this once, you know. Coming to a new place after my father had died, depending on strangers. I was about your age." I took a breath. "I was terrified, and I wanted my mother. I remember it so clearly. I even asked God to—" I sucked in my breath, putting the brakes on my tongue.

"And did she come?" That clever gaze shot right to me. "Did he answer you?"

A lump rose in my throat, blocking the single word that was true then, and true now. That remarkable peace, the wonder that had filled me on the ship, began to ebb away again. The memory had punctured something, releasing a slow leak. I turned back to the sea, its choppy surface glinting with sunlight, but a familiar dull ache had closed over the awe.

"By the way," she said quietly. "My name is Hedda. My mum died when I was a babe, and my father died a fortnight ago."

I squeezed her hand. "I'm honored, Hedda. Thank you for letting me know you."

André threw down another coil of rope and looked up at the house, shielding his face from the sun. "Someone is here."

Glancing in the direction of the distant causeway, I saw several small boats secured at the beach where I'd originally landed. "Police?"

He shrugged, his look grim. "That aunt of yours, for one." He pointed at the wayward hat with flowers and pink tulle fluttering in the breeze that could belong to no one else.

Aunt Lottie. My stomach clenched—Aunt Lottie had sold the shop and come to live at Blakely House.

chapter
FORTY

At times it seems that humans are nothing but inferior machines, breaking down more often than they function as designed.

~Emmett's letters to Sophie

W e took Hedda into the old stables where she clung to André's arm, her eyes wide.

He set her on a crate. "We brought you here to keep you safe, and just now these stables are the safest place for you."

The constriction of my chest tightened as I realized what he was protecting her from—witnessing whatever might happen to me. "Stay here with her, Mr. Montagne," I whispered near his ear. "You'll be of more use here than in the house."

"You'll need me to—"

"She should not be left alone."

He touched my arm. "But neither should you." He tucked

my hand into the crook of his arm and turned us toward the door. I couldn't deny the thrill. The momentary sense of being part of a pair as I walked into battle.

We emerged and walked the path to the house, but Hedda came sailing out of the stables, her bare feet beating the ground. She threw herself at my legs and clung. I knelt and put my arms about her. At that moment, a familiar voice trilled out of the open kitchen window. "Shoo! Oh, shoo you rotten creature! *Oh!*"

Hearing Angel's voice gave me a brilliant idea. "We shall bring you to the cook. Her name is Angel and she'll take such good care of you."

Hedda's brow knit immediately. "Don't make me stay with that loud woman."

"I promise she's wonderful."

She fell silent and tightened her hold on me, her riotous curls silky against my hand. "She never did come back, did she? Your mother."

I sighed, lifting my gaze over her head. "Stay, Mr. Montagne. Please." I let my gaze linger, willing him to understand. *She cannot be alone anymore.*

He gave a single nod. Something relaxed around her mouth, and she buried her face in his arm. He scooped her up and carried her toward the side entrance into the servant's hall. "If you should need anything—even a little—ring the bell. You'll find the cord in every room of the main floor. It'll summon me, and I'll come."

I forced myself to turn and walk away, tension pulling my shoulders taut. I had work to do. Follow the path of power. I could find him. Focus. Then I glanced back at them and was seized by the look of a lost girl clinging to a stranger. I felt that look to my bones. Felt it, even after all these years.

I tried to pray for her. To summon the wonder and awe I'd felt on the ship, but I only felt a dull ache.

"I even asked God to bring her back."

"And did she come?"

I turned, that dull ache swelling to something bigger. Something hard and tight. Up the rocky path, through the pine trees into the shadow of that towering house I climbed, my pulse erratic.

No, she had not come. Not then, and not ever. That prayer from my most vulnerable moment still echoed against an empty nothingness above. I couldn't ever understand why God left so many things unfinished. Broken. Incomplete and abandoned.

In the great open entryway, laced with gold clocks and lamps and moving pieces from floor to ceiling, the largeness, the intricacies that made it Blakely House, pulled me back in as if embracing and welcoming me home. Coaxing me deeper inside.

I stood alone in the shadows, feet planted on tile, and listened to the voices of men not far in the distance. Several of them. They were discussing me, and whether I should be held at Hexam Old Gaol to await my inquisition or removed immediately to London.

The evidence was alarming. Written admissions from my own hand, as well as the missing pieces removed from Emmett Sinclair's downed flying machine tucked among my things . . . a bottle of strychnine.

Missing pieces? Strychnine? When had I ever possessed strychnine?

The conversation continued. Had I made any progress on the automaton?

Some, it is believed. Not much.

My skin chilled. Who were these men? The investors, perhaps? Police? I recognized Dane Hutchcraft's voice sliding up and down the familiar pitches, explaining and wheedling. There was no one on my side in there. Not one.

I was twelve again, standing before an unfamiliar door with a man who wanted to be rid of me, begging God for her mum and hearing nothing. *Why is it so, God? If you are great enough to create the seas, to control the storms, to bring about any circumstance with the flick of a finger, why do you leave small girls alone?*

I inhaled a shaky breath . . . then a warm hand slid into mine. I jerked away and turned. "Oh!"

Aunt Lottie's dimpled smile shone in the dim hall. "I promised I'd be back, didn't I?"

I flung myself into her arms, holding her tight. Probably all but suffocating her.

Then I pushed back and shook my head, my stomach sinking. She'd sold everything. She was dependent on me. "I'm afraid I've ruined everything." How did one apologize for ruining a person's life?

She touched my cheek. "Seems like I couldn't have come at a better time, then."

I slipped into her embrace again, leaning on her familiar frame. She held me close as she'd done when I was small, rubbing small circles on my back as she whispered. "It'll come out all right. It will. Tell me what needs to be done."

I pushed back, holding her at arm's length, keeping my voice low. "I believe Emmett Sinclair is alive. He's on the island."

"And that changes everything!" Aunt Lottie's eyes shone. "Right behind you, Syd. Let's find him."

A smile, a nod, then I bolted toward the narrow passageway

that led to the servants' quarters. The kitchen, the servants' hall—all dark. The path of power . . . follow the path of power.

As if on cue, the great beast of power driving Blakely House growled to life, groaning and thrumming as water surged somewhere deep within the walls.

From where, though? "Come. It's over this way." It came again, that beastly groaning. "The kitchen. It must be somewhere in the kitchen." There, among the gleaming metal and pulleys and electric levers, was a panel in the wall—not hidden, but certainly not as obvious as an ordinary door.

I knelt and pried at it with my fingers.

"Here," said Lottie. "Try this." She held out a butter knife. The knife fit smoothly, and with a puff of plaster dust, the panel came out. Behind it lay a metal box brimming with wires and levers. I ran my hand over the complexity, the masterful design, then grabbed hold of the box and yanked. It gave just a little. Planting my feet on the wall on either side, I hugged that panel and pulled with every inch of strength in me.

Finally it gave with a pop, a spark of pain on my chest, and I landed on my back, then sudden darkness. The groan of a dying creature as all fell silent. Once again, I had cast the sleeping spell upon Blakely House.

But this time, daylight brimmed through the high windows. With a quick glance about, I lit an old oil lamp and plunged into the cavity in the wall. Inside, I gazed upon the inner workings of brilliance. If Blakely House was Emmett Sinclair, his workshop the heart of him, his art studio the soul, then I had just wandered into his mind. His fascinating, complexly layered, cleverly arranged mind. And it was methodical and tidy. No matter how chaotic the rooms of his house, how scatterbrained people claimed he was, here behind the scenes

I found only order and sense. Purposeful design and neat, parallel lines with clear direction.

Which made it infinitely easier to trace. Then jerking my head toward Aunt Lottie, I took hold of the wires and followed them, tangling my fingers in cottony cobwebs.

"Oh, Syd. You'd better be right."

"It'll all be worth it, Aunt Lottie. It will."

My heart hammered as I felt my way through a labyrinth of cords and levers, copper pipes and cogs. Then my opposite hand brushed something smooth. I paused, holding up the light. It was glass, like a large, single-paned window. The light reflected off it, blinding me. Arm across my eyes, I lowered the lamp until its glow lit up the space without bouncing off the glass.

I blinked, and a figure materialized on the other side of the glass. A man, broad shoulders under a well-made suit jacket. Curled tufts of red hair. Tom Jolly. His head whipped about and he froze, staring at me through the glass.

Drawing room. The fireplace, angel statues, blue vase with flowers . . . he was in the drawing room. And I . . . I was behind the mirror.

"Quick, the light!" Aunt Lottie grabbed the lamp and blew it out, leaving us in utter darkness.

Jolly rushed upon the mirror, shoving his face up to it. Peering. Scowling. Then he lit a lamp and held it up to the mirror, peering in at us.

But not seeing. Not anymore.

I could see him clearly, though. The murderous scowl on his face, the tension behind his mask, the details of the room beyond. Beside the mirror was a switch. No, a series of them. Switches and levers in neat rows. I flipped one, but the connection was loose. I had blown the power by breaking into the wall, but when it was restored, these switches would most certainly control things in the room. The lights, the doors, the gadgets mounted on walls. A stroke of magic. An illusion.

My angry cousin took two steps back, glowering at the mirror. I shrank back against the wall behind me, pipes biting into my back. With a growl, he hurled the lamp. I screamed. Glass shattered, but it wasn't the mirror. He'd thrown the lamp against the wall.

Then, with two more backward steps, he yelled for Dane and bolted from the room.

"How clever is that man?" Aunt Lottie whispered behind me.

"Clever enough to see a hole in the wall. Not clever enough to set foot in the kitchen, though."

"But someone will. And soon."

"Let's use the time we have, then." Taking her hand, I pulled her through the darkness, feeling my way along the wall, keeping the cords always against my shoulder to follow their path.

"I've always wondered what it would be like to walk through one of our clocks," she said. "And now I think I know." She paused, struck a match, and again we had light.

I followed that path around corners, down long, narrow stretches, watching all the wires from every room meet and follow the path to somewhere beyond. When the wall ended, the wires continued up to the next floor. I handed my lamp to Aunt Lottie and grabbed hold of the copper pipes overhead. "Hold it up as high as you can."

"Where are you going? Syd! You will *not* leave me alone with the rats!"

"You'll be safe. They're not after you." I pulled up and kept climbing, praying those pipes would hold. I climbed until the light below me seemed like the lighthouse on a distant shore. Breathless, coughing out dust, I saw a sliver of light above me. I climbed toward it—another panel. This one, a little door. Crawling up and anchoring myself on a lever wheel and a cast-iron water pipe, I kicked, punched, and threw myself into that door.

It burst open and I tumbled into a stone room, lying on the rough wood floor, panting and staring up at the peaked ceiling. It was a tower. A massive stone tower with narrow arched windows and lit candles perched on jutted stone shelves all the way around. A large wooden door with an inviting brass ring handle was the only other way out.

"Sydney!" Aunt Lottie's voice rang out like a distant gong. "*Syd!*"

One I would heed later.

On the floor, a puddle of blankets spoke of an occupant. Books lay stacked around the walls. And mounted in several places were tall, complex control panels. Everything—*everything* in Blakely House could be controlled from this tower. And those goings-on hadn't been a fluke. None of them.

"Syyyyydneyyyy!" Aunt Lottie's voice plucked the strings of my mind, vibrating it most irritatingly. But my mind skittered here and there, puzzling over the room.

Emmett. Dear Emmett, who cared for everyone and asked nothing in return. And often received just that.

But that would change. Today.

Then a *thump* behind me, and a *swish* of footsteps. I turned. Tom Jolly's face appeared in the little panel.

"Syd!" came Aunt Lottie's voice again. A warning—one I now understood as Jolly crawled out of the opening from which I'd come, kicking the panel back into place so there was no going out or coming in from that doorway without great effort.

He towered over me, the jumping shadows casting a sinister glow over his face. "This won't end well for you, Sydney Forrester."

"He's alive," I blurted. "Uncle Emmett's alive, and I can prove it. I told you, I didn't kill him." I held out my palms as if to block him. "Let me find him. Please, it'll change everything."

"What do you honestly believe will come of this? You cannot possibly hope to evade the inquisition simply because a ghost lingers about. Every eerie old house has two or three."

I steadied my voice. "He's still alive, Cousin Tom. He is." I backed toward the door, feeling for the iron handle behind my back. Did the door open in or out?

"I cannot decide what is true about you—or even who you really are."

My mind spun.

"The real Sydney Forrester. He showed up, you know. Nearly drowned getting to the island—maybe you're responsible for that too. Can't have anyone threaten your little game now, can we?"

I blinked, my hand fluttering around for a grip on the iron ring. "What makes you certain *he's* not the fraud?"

"You look nervous, Miss Forrester." His smile was wicked. "We've verified his story—we couldn't figure out how a female Sydney Forrester fit into the family tree, but that's only because there isn't one." He approached, arms folded over his chest, his face passive. Controlled. "Sydney Forrester is a man. And he's here, in Northumberland. It'll be rather hard to argue with that."

I breathed as the pieces sunk into place. It was a mistake.

I wasn't supposed to be here. Wasn't even related. No matter what happened, I would never inherit Blakely House.

His eyes were snapping. "So who are you really?"

I opened my mouth, but something shattered within as I tried to pry myself loose from the pages of Blakely House's story. From the ingenious innovator and puzzler. The "broken" clock that was uniquely crafted. Like me.

"Very well, then. It doesn't matter anymore, does it? As long as your lies stop here." Then with a *whoosh* he shoved me and slipped out the heavy door, banging it shut and locking it behind him.

I sat breathing hard. I pushed up, scrambling to the panel and pulling at the crack. It did not budge. I shoved my fingertips into the crack, but the pieces fit too neatly together. Short, quick gasps of breath. "Aunt! Aunt Lottie!"

A distant echo. And silence.

"Climb the ladder! Take the light and climb!" But my voice thudded around the stone walls . . . and did not go beyond. She was down there, somewhere. Did she have the lamp?

And Emmett. Somewhere in this house, Emmett languished, with one bitter nephew sniffing him out like a bloodhound.

And I was trapped.

With a primal cry, I pawed at the panel. Scratched and clawed. Threw myself at it. Then slid down the solid stones and lay on the floor, shaking.

God . . . God . . . was all my mind could manage.

A moment passed, then a *rawr* came from nearby. I looked up and Micah—dear, bitter little Micah—squeezed through the narrow bars of the door's tiny window and leaped down to my lap, purring and nosing my hand. I curled around my kitty and cried.

The sun was going down. Orange light streaked through the high, narrow windows.

They were for guns, I thought idly. Guns pointed out at invading enemies while the estate owners remained protected inside.

What happened when the enemy was already inside?

I stood on tiptoe clutching Micah, then climbed onto a ledge, to peer out the lowest gun hole slit at the island below as helplessness settled over me. The orange sunlight that had streaked into the tower painted the air outside, with trees casting long shadows over waving grass, low stone garden walls. The hills sloped down onto a lake far below, a shimmering plate of glass, with caverns opposite it. That's where they'd fallen in love, wasn't it? Out in the beauty and splendor of natural creation. No wonder he—

A thump. A scraping. I spun and tumbled down off the ledge. Pounded on the panel in the wall. "Aunt Lottie! I'm here!"

But it was coming from the opposite wall. A metallic click, and a matching panel opened like a half door, throwing a new shadow in the old tower room. I stared with bated breath as a tall, cloaked figure I'd not seen before crouched through the opening with practiced ease.

chapter
FORTY-ONE

One day perhaps you'll realize how flimsy it is to have a million people read your words rather than one who has them memorized.

~Emmett's letters to Sophie

The being rose, taller and taller, until it towered over me and the hood fell back. A cloud of dark, silvery curls cascaded down around a familiar face, and two snapping eyes pierced me with their gaze. A more handsome woman I had never seen . . . except in her pictures. I could barely breathe. Though she had aged, she could be no one else.

"Sophie," I whispered.

Emmett's lost love was here, before me. Alive.

Her smile spread like poured honey over her lovely face, aged but not faded. "There, now. I could not simply leave you locked in here." Her low voice was a gentle croon that matched her elegant face. "I am impressed," she said slowly, "that you found this tower. I thought I might hide away in these inner tunnels for the rest of my days, stealing food from the larder and watching snippets of goings-on from behind the mirrors."

"Why hide away? What on earth have you been doing in this drafty old tower all this time?"

"Healing." She spoke the single word quietly. "People are capable of doing terrible things to one another. There was no one I wanted to see just yet."

"In the meantime, your silence has allowed Emmett Sinclair's nephews to nearly take over and ruin Blakely House. Have you not heard all that has happened?"

Her smile was calm and self-assured. "No one can simply *take over* a house like Blakely House. No, I haven't watched them, I'm afraid. I've been too busy studying you."

"Why *did* you watch me?"

"Because I'm hopeful about you, Sydney Forrester. Hopeful about what you might mean for Blakely House." She shifted her weight. "With all the evil people in this broken world, I despaired of ever finding anyone who was different. Who was . . . like Emmett."

I blinked away moisture. "I cannot believe you're here. So Uncle Emmett . . . *is* he alive?" I held my breath.

A single shake of her head, and a fresh wave of grief rose and crashed.

"So you were the one operating the house? I wasn't imagining it. The doors, the lights . . ." And Emmett Sinclair truly was dead.

"Ah, it was my Emmett who set it all up. I was merely pulling the levers and pushing the buttons he put in place. Did you like the books?"

"Books?" I trembled, blinking back moisture. Wrapping my head around the truth.

"The room of novels, on your first night at Blakely House. I hoped to make you feel at home. You didn't seem to care for the other books."

I smiled, remembering the little lights like fairies that had led me to the cozy room lined with stories. "I believe that is what settled me in."

She straightened her leg with a wince.

I glanced down—a metal brace. Jointed and complex, as was anything by Emmett Sinclair. "Your leg. What's happened to it?"

She sighed. "My husband's men. The cliffs . . ." She waved away the rest. "A story for another day. Were it not for Emmett, I should not be moving at all." Her smile increased again, a mix of fondness and supreme grief. "I returned to Blakely House years ago to visit after my accident, and he fashioned this for me, bless him."

I opened my mouth to ask her the question that had haunted me since coming to the island, but a lock clicked and the door crashed open. Men poured into the tower room with lamps and lanterns, clogging the doorway and talking over one another. Men in suits. Men in uniform. Familiar faces and strangers. I scanned the crowd for Aunt Lottie, but she wasn't among them.

"There." Jolly pointed at me. "I've caught her—" His eyes locked with the languid, unshakable gaze of Sophie Holland. He blinked.

Sophie stepped forward and extended her hand as if she were a countess welcoming a guest to her home. "Mr. Tom Jolly, in person."

He frowned at her hand, his face menacing in the jumping shadows. "Who is she? How did she get in here?"

I stood beside her. She smelled of violets and honey. "This woman belongs here even more than you do. Tom Jolly, this is Sophie Holland. The woman Emmett Sinclair loved."

His eyes widened, mouth pinching tight. "The gardener?"

"Uncle Emmett went to rescue her." I turned to Sophie. "He did, didn't he? That's why he left the island—and now you are the only one who can tell us what's truly become of him."

Jolly punched the door. "We *know* what's become of him—he's dead and buried. But what's important is *how* he died." He eyed me.

Sophie stepped forward, back rigid. "I can answer both of those. Yes, he is dead. He was killed by my late husband's men, a band of marauders on the coast. The moment I wrote and asked him to fetch me, he came with a small passel of sailors, rescuing me and sending me off on his ship without him." Tears coursed down her porcelain face. "Sacrificing himself so I might live out my days in peace."

The men watching exchanged looks. Tom Jolly frowned from the shadows.

I exhaled, long and low. Of *course* it would be this way. For the man who'd devoted himself entirely to easing the burdens of those around him, he'd been driven to leave his cherished island, his paradise and his safety, to meet with his heir—but even more than that, to rescue the one he loved, the very moment she'd been ready for it, and in the only way he could. By positioning himself between her and her enemies.

"I'd like to set the record straight on Emmett's death, if I may, but I will only say it once."

The constable stepped forward, his raincoat hanging on his frame. "In that case, let's have a talk downstairs, Miss . . ."

"Holland. Sophie Holland." Leaning on the arm of a servant, she made her way out of the tower and down toward the main rooms where more police officers milled about in the drawing room, lighting lamps and speaking in hushed tones.

She glided into the midst of them and raised her head. All eyes were on her. Talking ceased. "I am here," she said with quiet command, "to testify to the sacrificial love of Emmett Sinclair. He came to rescue me from a dangerous situation of my own making, and he was killed by the men who held me in their grasp. After my husband died, they wouldn't let me leave, so he . . . he came for me and they killed him. My husband's men killed him." Her arm trembled.

I grabbed her hand. I couldn't help myself.

She squeezed it. "I sailed back to Farnham Healde with Emmett's men, as he'd requested, and we laid anchor on the far side of the island, and they were off to their next journey. And I . . . I stayed safely tucked in the only home I've ever loved. Because of my Emmett."

Jolly scowled from the shadows. "Ha! Desert his mansion in the clouds to rescue some woman? A laughable story. He hardly knows you."

Sophie straightened, pressing her shoulders back and speaking deliberately. "He knew me," she said quietly. Decades of letters and unspoken affection brimmed up in those few words, spilling down her cheeks in glittering tears. Though separated by oceans, Sophie Holland had been as close to Emmett Sinclair as any human ever had.

"It was you, I'm afraid, who did not know him. You, and you, and you," she said, nodding to each of the groups present. "To you who lived in Northumberland," she said to the police officers and other local men. "To you who benefited from his innovations, he was a genie in a bottle. He gives you the miracle of light, and you were demanding. Fix it, make it better, give us more—*this minute.*

"And you." She faced the cluster of pirates-turned-staff huddled together on the fringes. "To you, he was little more than a disinterested master. You obeyed his orders so that you might *earn* your place in his home. His protection. Even though he freely offered it to you. And *you*." She stared directly at the two nephews, the would-be heirs, her words suddenly sharp. "What was he to you, a nuisance? An obligation?"

Dane Hutchcraft went stiff. "How dare you suggest you know *anything* about our family."

She observed him with regal silence, holding something back. Something important. "You settled for secondhand knowledge of him. Of knowing him only through the lens of very broken people who had their own prejudices. You never found out anything for yourself, did you?"

"You can hardly blame us, with the way he was toward us. All our lives!"

"He made himself known to all of you. In his subtle way. And he knew you—very well. Yet he would not force a connection, even with his relations. He always hoped for it. Patiently invited it. Starting with gifts."

"What gifts?" Jolly snapped.

She turned to him. "To what do you attribute your success in business, Mr. Tom Jolly? A coincidence, perhaps? Good fortune? The boy from the rookery who could now purchase ten of them, and who just *happened* to climb astronomical heights on his own?"

Tom went red at the neck, then he paled.

"And me? I earned every pound note myself," said Dane

357

Hutchcraft, stepping from the cluster of watchers. "He never gave me *money*."

"Because money isn't what you wanted most, Dane Hutchcraft," she said quietly.

His eyes narrowed. "Then what *did* he give me, pray?"

"I can answer that." The crowd parted to release a slender man, to much murmuring.

"Arthur." Dane went white. "He . . ."

"Came to see me a few months back. After I'd torn up every last one of your wheedling letters. You didn't honestly think those would compel me to come, did you?"

"He visited you too?" I asked. What an adventure it must have been, this great journey after never once leaving the island. A grand finale to his remarkable life. He'd gone to set so many things right and leave the world the way he thought it should be—*better* for him having lived in it.

"He came on a boat with propellers powering it and convinced me . . . well, convinced me that I only had one father." He bowed his head. "And that I alone was responsible for my part in that relationship, no matter what my father had done."

Dane sat down hard, face pale, but he didn't speak.

Sophie continued. "He invited all of you to know him, to learn from his genius, even after he was gone. Not one of you took him up on it. Except . . . well, almost no one." She turned to me, her expression softening.

My face warmed. "I think I would have loved him very much."

Her smile sparkled, as if to say, *I know.*

"Which is why I would be foolish not to consider you, wouldn't I?" Sophie continued.

"Consider her for *what*, exactly?" snapped Jolly.

"For the role of Mr. Sinclair's successor. I must decide on one of you."

"And what, pray, gives you the right to determine such a thing?"

But even as Jolly spit out the words, I somehow knew what she'd say.

"This does." She extracted a worn envelope from the folds of her cloak—the last will and testament of one of modern England's greatest industrialists. "Dated, signed, and witnessed just after meeting his supposed heir, naming and supersed-ing all previous wills. He had it drawn up after meeting his supposed heir in London and he secreted it away on his ship when he came for me, making me promise to carry it out for him. My Emmett wished for me to select the heir to his legacy myself, and he sent me back with a mission to do just that. You were not terribly wrong, Mr. Hutchcraft, when you told Miss Forrester this was a contest. It is, in a way, but there is only one question that will tell us who will carry on Blakely House as he did: *Who knew him?*"

I sucked in a breath.

A *thunk* sounded as the power was restored and the house awoke. Lights glowed, machines came to life. The company was silent for several moments as we drank in the sounds of Blakely House, and the presence of its late master. The gushing water, the subtle buzzing of power. The motion and warmth and life that he had left behind.

Emmett, dear Emmett. He'd been there all along, subtly obvious to anyone who had eyes to see, ears to hear. And he had ordered things for those he loved with the same precision with which he built his automaton and his flying machine. The same polish and sturdiness that was his trademark.

I should have known.

And I never should have worried.

It's not about how, but who.

"In fact, I've seldom considered anyone else, save one other. The butler. Which one is he?"

"The one repairing the power," said one of the liveried staff. "I'll fetch him."

Soon the crowds parted and André stepped forward and bowed, his hair once again secured at his neck.

"Ah, there you are. Always in the service of the estate, no?" She smiled. "He spoke highly of you, Mr. Montagne. Thought of you as one of his own. His right-hand man."

I caught his eye, and mouthed, *Where is Hedda?*

He smiled and gave me a wink.

Jolly's mouth went slack. "You can't mean to tell me you'd consider this little chit and his *butler*, of all people, above his blood relations?"

Her smile was slow and contented. "Yes, I would."

"But she—" He stabbed a finger at me. "She isn't even related. She didn't even know him!"

"And did you, Mr. Jolly? I do have one little secret to share." She approached him, lowered her voice to a near whisper. "You buried the wrong man."

Silence echoed through the tower room. The visitors exchanged looks. Dane stared, mouth slightly open.

"How could I *possibly*—"

"My Emmett was buried outside my lighthouse on the coast of Norway where he came to fetch me. We hid and fought off my late husband's men for days, but eventually he was killed there, and he never left. I buried him myself—with some help from his sailors—before I fled in his ship."

"Then who did I bury in the family crypt?" Dane said, voice shaking.

"I'm sure I don't know."

"They pulled him from that infernal flying machine, and there was no mistaking that contraption."

"Which was sold some months ago. There's a bill of sale somewhere, I believe. He'd meant to rescue me in it when he had it working, but when it was perfected, he sold it to some man who was desperate to have it, he said. Poor fool must have crashed the thing, whoever he was. That's what comes from not bothering with the inventor's instructions."

"It was compromised, I believe," one of the men said from the back.

"All I know is, it wasn't Emmett Sinclair in that flying machine."

Tom punched the air. "How in heaven's name could you have buried the wrong man, Dane? Didn't you notice when he didn't look like Uncle Emmett?"

Silence fell upon them all, as realization settled over the crowd that Dane Hutchcraft had never met the uncle whose legacy he was trying to own.

Sophie turned to him. "I am not without mercy, Mr. Hutchcraft, for Emmett wouldn't wish me to be. You will each inherit what you wanted most. He has left Blakely House to me as my safe haven, but I may dispose of his belongings—his genius and all of his treasures—as I see fit. Mr. Jolly, you shall have the Sinclair family jewels—especially your mother's. That should provide you ample capital.

"Mr. Montagne, you shall have every last one of your beloved master's unfinished inventions to complete as you wish. No one gave more care and assistance in that matter than yourself."

"And me?" said Dane petulantly.

"You may have the automaton, Mr. Hutchcraft. As you so desperately wanted. Although what good it'll be to you without the blueprints and instructions, I haven't any idea."

I gasped. "There are instructions?"

"Very detailed ones, actually. The automaton was created to perform hundreds of functions, and yes—he *does* function. Or rather, he will quite shortly. Emmet would have done it himself if his hands hadn't given him such trouble at the end. But it's all there in the notes."

"And who shall have those?" Dane asked.

She pivoted slowly toward me. "To Sydney Forrester who wanted, more than anything, the inventor himself, I give the very essence of Emmett Sinclair. All that is left of him. His legal documents, notes, and personal belongings—including all patents on every project, and his coveted blueprints, which no one else has ever laid eyes on. It shall be your own personal peek inside his brilliant mind, which I believe you shall appreciate more than anyone."

"*Her?*"

She smiled at Dane. "You may have the golden egg, Mr. Hutchcraft, but Sydney possesses the goose."

Silence swept through the room.

Dane's irritation leaked into his clipped words. "Might I remind everyone once again that this woman is in no way related? Her being here is a mistake. She's a stranger!"

"Relation or not, I find Sydney Forrester the perfect fit to continue Emmett's legacy, as if she had been uniquely created for the role."

Specially put together. A perfect fit.

"And perhaps, one day when I am gone, Blakely House itself shall be hers as well. In part, at least."

I could hardly speak. My legs trembled. I glanced around, and my gaze was caught and held by the probing look of a landed pirate—an adventurer who had found his chest of treasure, for his eyes sparkled. That look held as the tension eased and the onlookers began to dissipate and move away.

I worked my way toward him and spoke with a low voice. "I suppose we must find a way to manage together, Mr. Montagne. Even during the day. Now we share a cat . . . and more. Do you suppose—"

A cry speared the moment. A woman's voice calling out for someone to stop. "For the love of all that's *holy!*"

Feet pounding on wood. Then a ragged figure burst into the room, oversized cloak askew as she stood frozen in the middle of us, her gaze darting about, chest heaving in and out. Aunt Lottie stumbled in after her, cheeks flushed.

The girl's wild eyes found mine. Then Hedda's mouth fell open as she took in the great wonders of Blakely House. Her face glowed with dawning awareness.

The room held its breath as Hedda's gaze spanned the room, then landed on Sophie. A whimper, then she launched herself across the room, stumbling and tripping on the too-long cloak, and flung her tiny body toward Sophie.

"Hedda. My Hedda!" Sophie collapsed onto her knees, regal frame folding about the small child and pulling her close. She smoothed hair off the girl's face and dropped kisses all over her smudged cheeks, whispering words of relief and surprise and gladness.

When she leaned back, fingers tracing the girl's features,

their similarities were evident. Long, dark hair that had silvered on Sophie, slender frame, and wide, lovely eyes set in alabaster skin. "Where is your father, love?"

She dropped her head and whispered, "He got the fever." Tears leaked out, and she didn't need to explain the ending.

Sophie pulled her into her lap and rocked her. "I'm so sorry, dearest. I meant to leave you safely with your father, where you were—far away from danger. You should have written when he fell ill. I would have found a way! I never meant you should look for me, that you should—"

"You shan't go away again, will you, Grandmamma?" Her face nestled into Sophie's neck.

"Not without you, love. Never without you." Her slender shoulders shook as she cradled her granddaughter, pouring her calm into the child. "You belong with me, wherever I am."

My eyes leaked warm tears. The empty place my mother had left began to swell with beauty, for this scene was also a familiar one. *You belong here, Sydney Forrester.* Aunt Lottie had spoken those impassioned words so very long ago. *I shall be your home.*

"It's so fitting, seeing you here at last." I touched Sophie's shoulder. "He has prepared for your stay all these years."

She lifted her teary face to look at me.

"Come." I held out my hand to her. "I've something to show you. He is gone from Blakely House, but not quite."

She rose and I eyed André and jerked my head for him to come.

He gave a small smile—he knew.

FORTY-TWO

ndré Montagne turned both knobs and opened the double doors, revealing the ballroom, the great and colorful garden that had sprung up indoors, under Emmett's careful hand. The little girl clung to her grandmother, but once inside, she left her side to trace the painted flowers on the wall.

Sophie Holland stepped inside and gasped, hand to her throat, as she took it in for several moments. Tears poured down the woman's cheeks. She spun slowly, arms going out, taking in the immense beauty of it—the hours upon hours of work and intention, the fine details of each flower carefully rendered . . . for her. When she took in the sparkling imitation pond laid at her feet by Emmett, laid her palm on the millions of careful brushstrokes on the wall, she drew in a breath and André saw it anew.

Some are not satisfied, he'd told Sydney that night, *with less than what is real.*

Yet it shimmered with something quite real.

Clearing his throat, André approached, boots clicking on tile, and bowed. "Might I have this dance, Miss Holland?"

She turned to him, eyes glittering, but her face fell as she shifted the tip of the leg brace beneath her hem, out of view.

He tugged the glove off his automaton hand and flexed the fingers. "Please?"

She looked him up and down, tears trailing from soulful brown eyes, and placed one hand in his mechanical one. Laying his other hand at her waist, he gently spun her, boot heels and metal brace echoing on the tiles as he lifted her, helping her whirl and almost fly about the ballroom where she had always been meant to dance.

The other guests had fallen away, so now it was only Hedda, Sydney, and her aunt Lottie who witnessed their dance. Dear Sydney, her eyes brimming with all the romance she'd seen in Emmett all along. "You were wrong about me, I think," he said to Sophie. "I did not know him so very well."

"Yes, but you wished to. Tried to. You cared for him a great deal."

He gave a nod. "That I did."

"And you care for someone else, I'd wager." She glanced at Sydney. "I don't suppose you've told her yet, have you? That sweet tension of unspoken love . . . it is palpable."

A maelstrom of emotion rose up in his chest. A deep and gnawing hunger . . . and a piercing fear.

"I've read about pirates, Mr. Montagne. They don't do forever."

Sophie's watchful eyes did not leave his face. "You and I are made for exploration and discovery, Mr. Montagne. For chasing down every beautiful thing. Nothing draws us like the promise of a magnificent adventure."

"You read my mind, perhaps, madame."

"No, only Emmett's letters. He's told me everything about you." She smiled up at him. "I always liked you, Mr. Montagne. I feel as though we're cut from the same fabric, you and I. So it is with great humility that I tell you my one regret. For all I have seen and done and accomplished with my life, I do believe I overlooked what was most magnificent." They slowed and she brushed the painted walls tenderly, fingertips lingering on the artwork of the man who had loved her for decades.

She gave a faint smile. "There is something sacred and rather delicate, I think, in a deep, authentic connection. Something irreplaceable."

His gaze shot to Sydney, the slender package of constant surprises and curiosity. Of wonder and utter uniqueness that continually caught him just a little off guard.

"I've done and seen so many things. I've gone to university. Studied horticulture. Designed royal gardens and seen nearly every coast. I married a man of boldness and adventure, believing it would make my days thrilling. Then I bit down on the metal of my life to find it was brass, after all. The gold . . . the part most real . . ."

"You are telling me not to make the same mistake."

A flash of a smile. She withdrew a worn paper from her sleeve and handed it to him. "His final letter to me."

The note merely said, *I'M COMING FOR YOU.*

"I'm passing my love story on to you. It has concluded, but André . . . I wish for you to do as Emmett always did—keep the good parts but rewrite the ending. Take it from here, but make it *better*." Tears glistened.

He stole a glance at Sydney Forrester, her face dewy with emotion, her thoughts supple and fresh at the surface as she spoke with Hedda but stole little glances their way, watching the tragic love story reach a bittersweet ending. André would always come for Sydney. He would. No adventure was worth more.

Sophie offered him a wry smile through her tears. "Forgive me for doing a bit of the rewriting myself ahead of time."

"What do you mean?"

"Blakely House was left to me, Mr. Montagne. And I've decided to leave it to you when I am gone—*and* her."

He was stunned. Dumbfounded, really.

She winked.

Then his partner was leading, gently guiding him in large, looping circles until they'd reached the doorway. She released herself from his grasp and slipped something small and slender into his pocket. Placing Sydney's hand in André's, she clutched the joined hands and stepped back, urging another pair to finish the dance she'd begun so many years ago with Emmett Sinclair.

André took Sydney in his arms, and she tensed, blushed, then settled into the crook of his broken arm, leaning gently as he spun her around the marble floor. He reached into his pocket with his good hand and felt—of all things—a pen. One of Emmett's fountain pens that Sydney had once sprayed upon the page. *Rewrite the ending.* He took a breath and looked her in the face, enticing her to meet his gaze. "I'm not a pirate, you know. Not truly."

"Oh?" Her face was flushed, eyes sparkling. She ducked her head but stole glances up at him. Even still, after all they'd been through, he made her nervous. Which made him want to kiss her heartily.

He smiled. "A chartered vessel. That's what I captained—a chartered vessel, transporting the belongings of wealthy families, exclusive cargo, anything that was required to any place it needed to go."

"Well, that's far less exciting."

"So you see, Miss Forrester." He swallowed the lump in his throat. Swallowed again. "I'm not a pirate. Which means I *can* do forever."

Her eyes flew wide. Then her foot crunched onto his. "Oh! Oh, I'm so sorry."

He stumbled but gently spun her back into the waltz, a smile of amusement fighting its way to the surface. "You don't give a man much hope, Miss Forrester."

She lifted her flushed face. "How would we manage? I like my roots and my comfy chair and . . . and my books."

"You'd have to do with some unknowns. Some risk. Could you stand it? I cannot promise where we'd live or what we'd have. What we will do with our lives. What will become of us, because I haven't any idea." For years, he'd secretly longed to pick up the threads of Emmett Sinclair's legacy himself, to continue what the great man had begun. He was even more determined now, but not with the man's inventions. Just one very important aspect of his life. He dipped a glance at Sophie Holland, then back to Sydney. "But I *can* promise to love you well."

She stared, and he thought he'd go mad waiting for her response.

"So then you *are* giving up your adventures."

A crooked smile. "Not necessarily. Life is an adventure, Sydney Forrester. It's unexpected and beautiful and . . . and risky. I want the adventures, whatever they are—and I want you to adventure along with me."

She gave him a smile to rival the sun and nestled against

his chest, the shape of her perfectly filling the void there. She leaned into him as their waltz slowed, and he kissed the top of her head, paused to linger in the moment. The sacredness of it. This meant yes, didn't it? His heart pounded where her temple lay against it.

He held her away from him to look into her face. "I'm afraid I haven't much to offer you, Miss Forrester."

"Forever is quite enough for me." She reached up to touch his cheek and drew him down for a lingering kiss, then nestled her warm face into his neck. "And André," she whispered against him, "it's nearly dark out. Call me Sydney."

chapter
FORTY-THREE

Gravitational force lessens as you go higher. Therefore, the closer we are to the heavens, the easier it becomes to fly.

~Emmett's letters to Sophie

BLAKELY HOUSE, 1910

I stood on the cliffs of Blakely House for the first time in nearly ten years, my face lifted to the wet sea air, and I felt it. Felt that bold tingle emanating from my chest, spreading into my fingers. Fear, yes, but a different sort.

"Lift up your eyes on high, and behold who hath created these things, that bringeth out their host by number: he calleth them all by names by the greatness of his might, for that he is strong in power."

God had invited me into this adventure so long ago, into Blakely House, not because I was the right Sydney Forrester. The right heir. I wasn't, actually. He did it because he knew he couldn't reach me at home. Comfort and security had muffled his voice, and I'd lost sight of the miraculous in the daily grind. It had taken a harsh removal of my safety to realize where I was really safe. A removal of what I thought was the point . . . to find the actual point.

"Sydney Forrester." A lovely, joyful voice sounded behind me, and I turned to face the most striking young woman with long hair in dark, silky ringlets. Her bright, confident smile brought back a flood of memories. "You came."

I opened my arms to her. "It cannot be—little Hedda! How did you even know who I was?"

Her smile widened and she embraced me, kissing my cheek. "One never forgets the face of her rescuing angel."

"I'm no such—"

She took my hands. "I shall never forget you, Sydney. Nor the moment you broke into my little hovel. I've thought of you often—we both have. Grandmamma and I."

I looked past her up the hill to a regal figure in a lilac gown, long hair tossed by the wind as she stood among the wildflowers she had planted decades ago. "She looks at home," I said.

A nod of assent, and a smile. "She's content."

Yet she wore a deflated air. "She still misses him," I murmured.

"Like a sail without wind."

I waved at Sophie. But then a familiar squeal had me spinning around, and a pirate—*my pirate*—bounced a tiny darkhaired version of himself on his shoulder, propping him with his good arm. My heart raced as André neared and his face gentled into that familiar smile, the one meant for me alone. I nestled my face into my husband, hand resting on our baby son's chunky leg.

Sophie Holland was panting as she reached us, but she gave me a tranquil smile. "You have returned to us, Sydney. André. Welcome home. And your little one! How Emmett would have loved to see this day." Tiny flowers, exotic ones from Emmett's hothouse, graced her long, silver hair. The leg brace peeked out from under her skirt hem, and she had some mechanical contraption like opera glasses hanging from her neck.

I took a deep breath. "I feel him here yet."

Tears leaked from her eyes as she clutched the gadget in her hand. Though he was gone from this place, his presence permeated the atmosphere. The net he'd woven beneath my feet—beneath Sophie's and even Hedda's—held us up even in his absence so that we would never fall.

"Who is this bundle of sweetness?" Sophie whispered, hands open.

"His name is Julien." I held out my small boy, and he reached for her. I marveled at how easily he went to a stranger, but he was always that way. He'd have more friends by two than I'd had in my entire life.

I smiled and looked out over the sea that used to terrify me. It still did, but looking out at it also reminded me of when I had walked on it. It was so like its Creator, that sea—equal parts beautiful and terrifying, a little dangerous, and far too vast to see it in its entirety.

Lift up your eyes on high, and behold who hath created these things, that bringeth out their host by number.

I kissed my little boy's pudgy foot as it kicked me, and tickled his toes. A baby laugh erupted, and my heart nearly exploded.

"You make such a good mum, Miss Sydney." Hedda smiled. "Did you ever get your wish? Your own mother?"

"No," I said quickly, but then . . . "Yes, actually. Yes, I did."
I cast a glance toward Aunt Lottie, who smiled back at me.
She'd been visiting and traveling with us on occasion since little
Julien's birth, and her fierce love for me spread out to him in
even greater measure. I *had* gotten a mother—a better one than
the one for which I'd prayed. God had a rather unexpected
way of saying "yes" to little-girl prayers, slipping his answer
into the fabric of everyday life.

And when he wrote the romantic chapter of my story, he
sketched out not an average, suitable man, but a striking pirate to rival my adventure novels. A bighearted, strong-willed,
passionate man who still made my face grow warm—a man
with a heart that embraced my every quirk as if it was the cog
to his wheel.

That was not to say God had given me my every request—
for in the years since I'd married my pirate, many pleas ended
in heartache, and a gentle no, including several wee babies.
But I stood as witness that when the God who created planets
and sunrises and great, wild seas said yes to something, it was
never a halfway answer. It was always . . . *YES*.

One day I asked for a child with blue eyes. Here before
me was a boy with the largest, most sparkling blue eyes I had
ever seen. I asked for a shop for Aunt Lottie to replace the one
she'd loved so, and she had *three*. And then, when I asked for
a workshop of my own, and a few projects to complete, he
made certain I'd have a whole house full of them. For Sophie
had recently announced she was gifting us Emmett's great
Blakely House so that we might continue to make of it what
he had begun there.

I didn't know what would become of us, my pirate and I,
but after those God encounters, I could not hide myself away

on the island as I'd once planned to do. No amount of safety was worth it. Blakely House would be a beautiful stopping point for us between adventures, perhaps sometimes for years at a time, but never a place to simply hole up and avoid all danger. We'd go where we were sent and hold loosely to our sense of safety.

It is said that the monks who once inhabited this island used it not as an escape from an evil world, but as a filling point, topping off the oil in their lamps before taking them into the darkness. I had begun doing the same with our little flat in town, going out into the world wherever and whenever he beckoned, dragging my fear along with me at times. We'd do the same now with Blakely House, going or staying as God saw fit. For it wasn't about *how*, and it never had been. It was always *who*.

Hedda lifted her face to the heavens, one hand extended to the sky, and began to sing with the same richness she had on the ship.

> "Bless the LORD, O my soul.
> Who stretchest out the heavens like a curtain.
> Who maketh the clouds his chariot.
> Who walketh upon the wings of the wind!
> O LORD, our Lord,
> how excellent is thy name in all the earth!
> Who hast set thy glory above the heavens."

Her face was like Moses's after he'd been up the mountain, in the presence of the Lord. What a gift, this girl's worship— a crack in the shell between humanity and heaven, where a small glimpse of the Creator's glory shone through. The song filled the air, and then, so did he. Richness welled up in me as the words sank deeply, and my heart echoed them. And it grounded me.

I'd begun to trace the path of power, and in the sacred moments such as this, I at last found myself in the presence of its source. And though fear shadowed me, I'd keep looking, keep stepping out of the boat, letting him catch me again and again just so I knew what his arms felt like.

I had missed the point once.

I wasn't doing it again.

AUTHOR'S NOTE

Irst of all, the historical pieces. The setting is fictional but is based in fact. The Farne Islands off the coast of Northumberland, some of which actually can be reached by a low-tide causeway, inspired the island.

Blakely House was based on Cragside, the first hydroelectric-powered manor home, which was owned and modified by industrialist Baron William Armstrong. Although there was not a contest of heirs that I'm aware of, much of the gadgetry, power source, and even Blakely House's layout are based on Cragside.

Automatons were very popular among the wealthy in Asia, and a few brilliant clockmakers actually created them. Some exist to this day.

The spiritual arc of this book is different from my others because it's not really mentioned in the first part of the book. That wasn't my intention, but it was God's, apparently. I was surprised as I moved through the draft how little of him there was, but in the rewrites, traces of God came out between the lines, until he was just everywhere—but subtly. So treasure hunt as you read, dear readers, and take from it what you will.

But I will say this. As I wrote this book, I actually developed quite a bit of neck pain. "Poor posture," the professionals called it, but I like to think of it as poor focus. I have spent the last several years very focused—in a good way—on the precious gifts God has brought me. First, my babies. I am often looking down as they sleep on me, or while nursing them as newborns. I also tilt my head down to write—living out that lifelong dream of publishing books. That's my posture for reading, for preparing homeschool, most of my favorite things. The sweetest blessings I have encountered in my four-ish decades of life.

Yet they aren't the point. I was *missing* the point. I was focused on the creation, and not the Creator. Looking down when I should be looking up.

I often struggle to complete a novel. I couldn't write anything worth publishing on my own, and truly, I often don't see how my work in progress will ever be fit for human eyes. But that's only because I become too reliant on my abilities, I fall into productivity mode, and I lose sight of the larger spiritual undercurrent of life. Again, I'm looking down instead of up.

It's never about *how* it will get done, but *who* is working with me.

Eight books in, and I'm starting to rest in the fact that my abilities come to a real quick end—and that God's never do. I'm realizing that he doesn't actually care (as much) about the finished product. He just wants me looking up at him. And I'm also growing used to the fact that, no matter how close to deadline I run (it's now two hours until deadline), *God makes it happen*. And worrying about it is pointless. Worrying about whether or not it'll be done, if it'll be any good. Because the end product is not the reason I started writing.

Sometimes he likes to push me to the edge of the cliff so I have to leap . . . and trust him to catch me. Which he always does. Every book, every deadline, every day. I'm forgetful apparently, because I keep falling back into this downward-facing posture—focused on what he's given me, on what I have to do that day. Focusing on the waves like Peter, rather than on Jesus.

Then my neck is sore from looking down too much and I need to look up a lot more. Lift my gaze off the beauty of the created world, the precious fuzzy-headed bundle in my arms, to the magnificent God who made them for me, because they're wonderful, but they're not the point.

He is a wonder. A breathtaking, enormous presence like no other.

And HE is the point.

FOR MORE FROM JOANNA
DAVIDSON POLITANO,
READ ON FOR AN EXCERPT FROM

THE
ELUSIVE
TRUTH
OF
LILY
TEMPLE

AVAILABLE NOW
WHEREVER BOOKS ARE SOLD.

chapter
ONE

Life itself is the most wonderful fairy tale.

~Hans Christian Andersen

WHITESTONE MANOR, HOVE SEASIDE, 1903

I hadn't decided if I'd tell the whole truth or not, when the men arrived. Peter would have, because he's *Peter*. I, however, never let facts hinder the power of a good story. Like water, innocuous and common, a good tale rushes forward, carving its own path through rock and hill and sod, sculpting the earth into a bold new landscape before anyone knows what is happening. Where Peter used silence, patience, and unending *goodness*, the best weapon in my quiver was the pointed truth, driven home by the arrow of a well-told tale.

Truth has many facets, anyway.

Such as this place, for example. I sat back against the French provincial sofa, sipping orange blossom tea and appreciating the details of the well-appointed withdrawing room. It did not brag outright but held a subtle air of opulence, lace dripping like icicles off every surface, crystal accents hanging here and there from lamps and curtains. Solid mahogany furniture from the earlier years of Queen Victoria presented a shabby yet comfortable air. A steady Mozart tempo crackled over the gramophone, and a thick blanket spread over my lap kept me quite warm, along with the fire popping in the hearth.

Yet what an unmitigated disaster the place was from the outside. The half-abandoned, old country estate rambled more than Aunt Agatha on a winter's eve, with crooked turrets hanging off jettisoned walls, crumbling facades, and a pile of bricks that had once served as steps. Whole sections of roof were missing in the closed-off wings.

Ah, the deception of it all. That was life, though—the stories you tell yourself, and the stories you present to onlookers. Rarely did the two match. We're all of us a combination of romance novels, humorous tales, and tragedies, depending on what angle we show the world.

Me, I preferred adventure stories. Tolerated a romance now and again.

Another sip, citrus flooding the senses, and the front door clattered open—the men were back. I clutched the cup handle.

It was time.

My scattered brain thought of Peter again, his steady, watchful look that penetrated the fluff and pomp of my stories, my silly misdirections, seeing the truth immediately. I shivered in my damp clothing. In a way, it was to his benefit that he was locked up just now, and he could not interrupt my story or correct it.

It was all for him, anyway. For wretched, foolish, overly principled, utterly irreplaceable Peter Driscoll. Not that he completely deserved it, mind you—this rescue attempt. The man might be guilty of a great many things—petty annoyances and rude infractions and the like. Killing me, however, was not one of them.

The shucking of rain gear sounded, and the growl and tromp of a man in the corridor. I sipped. Waited. The parlor door banged open, and there stood the muddiest uniform I'd ever seen, worn by a giant of a man who looked mad as hops. "What . . . what . . . who *are* you?"

I dropped another sugar into my tea and gave it a good stir. "I'm Lily Temple, Mr. Mutton, and I'm here to help you."

He stood like a wide-eyed fool, dripping mud and rain upon the worn rug. "But you're in *my house!*"

"The most logical place to find you, sir."

In another twist still, the grand old conflicted mansion was, in fact, a prison. A temporary holding place for criminals of the Brighton and Hove areas while they awaited transportation to their own personal miscarriage of justice at London's Old Bailey.

My Peter being one of them.

"I'm not one for trekking over field and farrow to chase a man down, especially in a storm." I straightened on the horsehair sofa, shoving aside the lap blanket and tucking my booted feet beneath the sofa. Anchoring myself. "I've come to speak with you about a prisoner, if you could spare a moment. Maybe two or three, since the weather will keep you inside anyway. Come and sit, I've made a fire."

Still, he stood and dripped. "How in blazes did you get in here?"

"The door." I paused for a sip, and it warmed my insides. "I'd have to break a window otherwise, and I didn't cotton to the idea of shredding a new shirtwaist on the shards."

His gaze swiveled to the window as if to assure himself that rain did indeed patter on the thick glass panes, then back to me. "That door was locked."

"Indeed it was. Oh, how uncouth of me—there now, let me fetch you some too. Have you another cup?" I sprang up and walked to the cabinet where I'd found mine. "Do you take sugar?"

He took four steps in my direction, wood squeaking under his heavy boots, eyes narrowing in a rocky old face as his gravelly voice rumbled in my ear. "Get out, ye fool woman. *Now.*"

My hands closed around a cup, and I paused, breathing deeply of stale air. "After you've heard me out."

He wouldn't agree to it, though. I could tell by the look on his face.

He'd live to regret it. Lily Temple did have a few more aces up her sleeve.

The man yanked the empty cup from my hand and hurled it to the floor, stalking away. "Who the dickens do you think you are?"

"I told you. I'm Lily Temple, and it's in your best interest to hear me out."

His eyes went wide at the name that was only now registering. "You're . . . you're . . ."

"Stubborn?" I strode right up to him, the clicks of my boots resounding through the emptiness. "One hundred percent. And there's something you must know about Peter Driscoll. He isn't guilty and it's terribly vile, you holding him here this way."

He stared, pale and wide-eyed, then snapped back to composure. "I'll not be convinced of *nothing*, ye hear? They pay me too well to keep them locked up, and I won't ruin that to release 'em. Not even one. They're a dangerous lot, these prisoners."

I laughed. I couldn't help myself. Perhaps it was everything at stake, my taut nerves . . . or the idea of Peter Driscoll being called *dangerous*. "They pay you in what, lodging?" I glanced about the dusty old manor house–turned-prison.

He scowled over his shoulder. "Driscoll killed a woman—did you know that?"

"Did he, though?"

He looked down, then back up at me, quite obviously confused. Scrambling to understand. Or deciding whether or not to believe the name I'd given him. "Exactly sixteen different witnesses say he did. And he stole a priceless gem from her. The Briarwood Teardrop, no less. No magistrate in London will let him off. Not unless he dies before he reaches the gallows, God guard 'is poor soul. Mark my words, the man'll swing for it."

I dropped my teacup, which shattered on the floor.

Boots pounded by the front door. "What was that?" Then yells, echoing through the empty halls. "Here. It was in here."

Oh good, an audience.

Mutton thrust me toward the door. "Out, out, *out*! I'll not be caught with some little chit on my hands, all kinds of trouble to pay. Go on, out with you."

"But my story. You haven't heard it yet." My voice echoed in the narrow hall. "It's rather a good one."

He lunged with a growl, grabbing for me. He struck a three-foot vase instead.

Crashhhhh.

I froze. He froze. Wings flapped somewhere above in the roofless towers. Water trickled in distant places.

Voices . . . then stomping. Six or seven men poured through the doorway, including a red-faced Constable Willis, trench coat flapping. "What's this about, Mutton?" The towering bearded giant looked me up and down. "The deal was, *no women*. You're on your last warning, man."

And wait—who was that behind him? A rather dukeish-looking gent, with a very familiar golden crest upon the breast of his overcoat. It must be one of the infamous Marlborough House set, the fast-living social circle of no less than King Edward himself. The *king*. I tingled to my fingertips.

Audience, indeed. This would be *perfect*.

Poor Mutton still blubbered behind me. "She ain't—she's . . . she's leaving." He shoved me down the hall, palms rough against my shoulder blades, and I dug in my heels, stumbling as he pushed.

As if sheer force ever derailed the locomotive that was my plans. I ducked and twisted toward the men. "Check his pockets."

He shoved harder. "Out, you fool—"

"Wait a moment. What was that, miss?" The constable stepped toward me, shoving his open palm toward poor Mutton to silence him.

"I said . . . check his pockets." I stood arrow-straight, arms folded.

The guard's face was darker than the storm outside. With a low growl that made my hair stand on end, he kept his eyes on me and reached into his right trouser pocket, then his left. Pulled out the fabric lining of both.

"The other pocket, luv." I pointed at his chest.

He jammed a hand into his frayed waistcoat and lifted a long, dangling necklace by its chain. Upon sight, he flung that thing like a hot coal and stumbled back, colliding with the other men.

There it lay, the setting of that legendary Briarwood Teardrop on the worn carpet, six men hulking in a stunned half circle around the ancient gold piece, the swirls and leaves that were so recognizable now. Only, the large blue stone was prominently missing.

"But . . . where's the sapphire?"

They looked from the delicate gold piece to the man who'd dropped it, and back again as the thing wove its spell in the air. Distant thunder rumbled across the sky and rain torrented against the old walls. The clock ticked forward the awkward silence. Who would make the first move?

After thirteen ticks, I decided it must be me.

Always a woman who did the doing, wasn't it?

"I suppose you'd like to hear about this, since you are about to transport the man who supposedly murdered me and stole it."

"You?" Constable Willis blurted out the word, then slowed his stride toward me, looking me up and down. "You. You are . . ."

I stepped closer, feeling the power shift directly onto me. I quieted my voice, for it did not need to be loud now. I would be heard. "The roads are nigh on impassible just now, especially for a prison wagon. I'm surprised your horses have gotten you here. I should think a good story might pass the time. If Mr. Mutton can spare a few moments to hear it now."

Silence. Then the constable invited me back to the sitting room with a single jerk of his head.

I swept past the men and collected cups from the corner cupboard, kicked aside the broken shards, and poured plenty of tea.

The men filtered in, new arrivals silently boxing in the resident guard who was now tangled up in the gem mess.

Poor man glared. Snarled. "I know what you're about, and I'll not be manipulated. I don't believe you're Lily Temple, and the prisoner will *not* be released." He shifted, leather holster creaking. "There were witnesses. Plenty of witnesses. He had a gun. And a motive. He had a way in, and he knew how to get it. And you don't look a thing like Lily Temple."

"Every story has its layers. You'd do well to remember that. Sugar?" I dropped in two cubes before he could answer and handed it over.

He took it and I settled myself on the edge of a springy old chair, gripping the arms for all I was worth. I was an actress, a professional storyteller, here at the holding cell of a condemned man, armed with naught but a story. And hopefully the wits to use it well.

The dukeish-looking gent downed his drink as one who knew how to do it, then leaned across the table, elbows planted in the middle. "So, Miss . . ."

"Temple."

"Miss Temple. Right, then." He scanned my face as if to confirm or deny my identity. His narrowed eyes indicated he'd aired on the side of doubt. Surely I didn't look that different, did I, without the grease paint and costumes?

Yet he made no move to release Peter of the murder charges. Or even pose a few questions to his supposed victim.

"I'm interested in hearing what you have to say about the sapphire everyone in the world would like to lay hands on. The one that belongs with that necklace." He jerked his head toward the other room. "Where is it now?"

"Well, now. That would be giving away the end of the story." I poured him more tea and moved the sugar toward him. "Shall we have a listen?"

Mutton collapsed back onto an ancient chair. "You'll not listen to a fool *woman*, will you? With no less than sixteen witnesses—"

"And this?" I lifted a large blue stone from my purse, and the room hushed at the sight of it. Again I felt the power of that sapphire.

"Is it—?" the magistrate began, but I let the wondering hang in the air.

They looked back and forth at one another, as if debating whether or not I was actually parading a priceless gem before them. The stone flashed and sparkled with brilliant reflections of light, a deep azure color that looked like it had indeed been ripped from the sky, as the legends claimed.

I smiled at the blustery fellow. "He who has all the answers will never ask questions." I held it up between two fingers. "And he who doesn't ask the questions forfeits a wealth of knowledge." I covered the stone with my other hand, and with a flick of the wrist it was gone. I held out both empty palms. "Because even your eyes deceive you, and the truth is rarely obvious. But stories . . ." With a smile, I leaned forward and plucked the stone from Mutton's collar, holding it out to the watchers. "They tell us the truth our eyes miss."

"You put on a fine show, Miss Temple," said the crested, duke-like man calmly as he accepted the blue stone, inspecting it critically. "But you'll need more proof."

"You keep it." I jerked my head toward the blue stone. "A fine imitation, don't you think? Enough to catch a man's attention for a moment. Worth about two quid. I'll take my prisoner, though, seeing as I'm not dead."

"That isn't possible, Miss Temple. We simply haven't the proper authority to invalidate an arrest once it's made. You'll have to bring your proof to the authorities and let justice take its course."

"But I'm—"

"Nothing you could say will convince us to break the law and release him this moment, to risk our positions and reputations, so you'd best not waste your time."

"Don't be so certain. You haven't heard my story yet." I settled back in the chair, looking over their dubious expressions. "Now, then. The mud will keep us here awhile more, I'm afraid, and you are all curious, even if you're not admitting it. I trust I may proceed."

I took their silence as consent and drew in a breath, settled in, and peeled open the memories. "It began in the spring, when George Smith was setting off hot-air balloons and musical nights at St. Anne's Well Gardens, and Peter Driscoll happened upon me by accident. Or, so I thought."

It was easy to slip back into the story of him—the story of us. In some ways, my life hinged on that moment, and everything that had happened since. Even if I never again saw Peter Driscoll's face, if he was never released and—God forbid, perished in Newgate—I'd never in a million moons be the same woman I had been that night in the well gardens.

ACKNOWLEDGMENTS

I love the way God comes alongside me in every book. Inevitably I start thinking like Sydney, that it's all up to me, but then when I reach the end of my abilities and God steps in, I realize how he was probably waiting all along for the opportunity. So thank you to my Father for walking through this book with me, for unfurling truth, and especially for showing up in unexpected places on the page and showing me more thoroughly who he is.

I'm eternally grateful to my supportive friends who brainstorm and cheerlead through these stories. Especially Susan, Jennifer, Rachel, Angie, Kim, and my very writerly dad. I'm so blessed to have kindred spirits in you all.

The rock star of this novel was my husband. My very opposite, engineering-minded husband who walked me through an incredible amount of innovation and technology that I simply didn't understand. You've shown me, through your explanations of mechanics and gadgetry, how precisely and elegantly the world is put together as one great invention by a sovereign God. I had the pleasure of asking you questions and connecting with you in a new way as you opened up this wealth of knowledge and shared it with me. I knew you had this, of course, but it was incredible to hear all this brilliance spilling so easily out of your mouth.

At one point, he purchased a hydraulic Lego kit and sat down with me to show me how hydraulics worked. I honestly couldn't wrap my head around some of these machines until your explanations made me feel ten times smarter than I actually am. Thank you, thank you, for diving into my world of storytelling, and for bringing pieces of your world into it for me. Your help was invaluable to me. And wading through an unpolished manuscript to check for technical errors was a feat of true love. I'm grateful for you, my love.

Joanna Davidson Politano is the award-winning author of eight novels including *Lady Jayne Disappears, A Rumored Fortune, A Midnight Dance, The Lost Melody,* and *The Elusive Truth of Lily Temple.* She loves tales that capture the colorful, exquisite details in ordinary lives and is eager to hear anyone's story. She lives with her husband and their children in a house in the woods near Lake Michigan. You can find her online at www.JDPStories.com.

—MEET—
JOANNA

JDPStories.com

Be the first to hear about new books from Revell!

Stay up to date with our authors and
books by signing up for our newsletters at

RevellBooks.com/SignUp

FOLLOW US ON SOCIAL MEDIA

   @RevellFiction